Get Out, You Ghosts
Stories from the Workshops
Volume II

Short Works

Michael-Patrick Harrington

Also by Michael-Patrick Harrington:

Deep Autumn

I See No Angels

Saving Magdalene

Sweater Girl and Other Tales of Mondauk County

The Distant Sound of Boiling Tea

Everything's Ephemeral:
Stories from the Workshops Volume I

www.michaelpatrickharrington.com

Published by Silk Raven Press
a division of Mondauk Enterprises Inc.
PO Box 31, Ambler, PA 19002

SILK
RAVEN
PRESS

(SRP-007)

"Mount Rock" made the Honorable Mention list for *Glimmer Train's* Short Story Award for New Writers, 2018.

Photo by Sam Pineda

Design by Pepper Lillie
www.pepperlillie.com

<u>A Note to my Readers:</u>

This book contains many stories of which I am very proud to have been the transcriber (for who really knows where ideas and stories originate?). In this book and its accompanying volume, *Everything's Ephemeral*, you'll find the leaps and the stumbles, the tales that wouldn't let me go, and the made-up worlds I never wanted to leave, as I tried to capture the ever elusive *story*. Most of the pieces in these volumes originated in one of the five writing workshops I participated in at Arcadia University.

So step inside. Make yourself comfortable. Want to hear a story?

<u>This is Important:</u>

There are stories in this collection that deal with teen suicide. Although the situations and conceits are fantastical, it is possible that some readers could infer that the topic of teen suicide is taken lightly and believe that the characters' struggles and that of the bereaved are handled with discourtesy and disrespect. If I treated suicide in a frivolous or flippant manner, it was in service of the stories, which were excursions into the absurd. It was not my intention to offend or trigger anyone, and I encourage those in need to reach out and let themselves be heard.

The National Suicide Prevention Hotline is available twenty-four hours a day, seven days a week: 1-800-273-8255.

Michael-Patrick Harrington

TABLE OF CONTENTS:

Our death, the tree of knowledge, grew fast by;
Knowledge of good bought dear by knowing ill.
— John Milton

I did not die—I was not living either!
Try to imagine, if you can imagine,
me there, deprived of life and death at once.
— Dante Alighieri

…a fancy, a Chimera in my brain, troubles me in prayer.
—John Donne, from a sermon
preached 12 December, 1626

Here's a little ghost for the offering.
— R.E.M.

Get Out, You Ghosts
Stories from the Workshops
Volume II

Charnel House

He could strangle her to death.

Neal Roget pulled his ten-year-old Chevy into the driveway and through the front window of their split-level watched his wife and his daughter, sweet, troubled Emily, set the dining room table for dinner. Might as well have been sweeping the canvas of a boxing ring for a match between people who were deaf to the bell; rounds could go on and on. How much more he could take, he didn't know. He'd taken it for at least half the age of his car, maybe longer. How much longer could Emily take it? That was the question—or one of them. (He watched his daughter run upstairs as soon as she placed the last piece of cutlery.) Annette hadn't always been the necromancer she'd morphed into. Oh, but now she was a true raiser of the dead: every long buried argument, every seemingly ignored insult, even endless discourses on what her late father would do in this situation or that. (*He could strangle her to death.* How many times had he had that thought, and what had it taken for him to go from *could* to *would* to…well, to actually: to now?) *Double, double toil and trouble; / Fire burn and caldron bubble.* How he had come to love her, even want her, was impossible for Neal to see. Her once-shapely legs were now bowlegged and pocked with cellulite. The dainty makeup had given way to great swashes of plaster of Paris, so that even the obligatory good-night kiss at the rare social function was the equivalent of brushing too close to a wall of stucco. The last time he'd seen Annette naked (and it had been quite some time), her bush was unruly and her breasts sagged, not helped aesthetically by the fact that her nipples were now huge like saucers. (Had they always been that way?) Maybe the sagging breasts were unavoidable—she was no young chippy; Annette was older than he was and having a kid couldn't have helped—but the bush? Back when they first met, some twenty-four years ago, the amount of hair between her legs steadily decreased as the amount of sex they had increased. Now she was Sheena, Queen of the Jungle.

Not that he was a prize, a paragon of physical perfection. He had more hair coming out of his ears that he did on his head. Despite a daily regimen of sit-ups and push-ups plus the odd run around the common, his stomach still jiggled when he got up from the couch to move to another room whenever Annette deigned to sit near him, usually to complain about…him. Or their daughter.

He thought he suffered from hypermnesia, for while he couldn't remember *why* Annette (as opposed to anyone else) or *how* he'd fallen for her (and she for him), his memories of the romance were so vivid, it was like he could reach out and run his finger through the still-wet watercolors. (*He could strangle her.*) He could recall every word of every conversation they'd had, it seemed (at least those before they said "I do"), and with little effort he could bring to the forefront of his consciousness, to the point where he could just about feel them, every kiss, stolen or otherwise, and his nose twitched even just reminiscing about all of the secret scents that emanated from his once-glowing Annette, always a secret, always there, always his forever and ever. (*He was going to strangle her.*) He even remembered every Crackerjack prize—it was how they used to cap the night, sharing a box of molasses-flavored, slightly stale caramel-coated popcorn and peanuts before he followed her into the bed that was now a swamp of smells, his and hers, that were unfamiliar and never carried the too-sweet scent of Crackerjacks. He could describe the design of the cigar box in which they used to house all their prizes—the tattoos being the best, they'd decided—and how could he forget the look on her face, a somewhat terrifying mixture of choler and glee, as she fed the cigar box into the fireplace the minute he walked into the house one night from work. (He'd left the shed door open, and it swung, banging, back and forth in the day's gusty winds.) Now he tried to forget the myriad lines on her face and his own age-furrowed brow.

Neal closed the car door so that it wouldn't slam—a slammed car door could set Annette off, and then there would be no dinner at all. His fingers were stained with ink. Annette hated that too. In fact, Annette hated everything about Neal's job; she thought comic books were for little kids—little *retarded* kids, she'd said. (Annette had no time for political correctness, especially if her language could be used to offend *him*.) She hated the ink stains that sometimes appeared on his cuffs and pant legs and fingers and arms. She hated telling other people her husband made a living inking comic books, not even drawing them, but most of all she hated that he made more money than her. That last one really ticked her off. Annette taught English composition at the local high

school, and her job was *real* work. She wasn't just *tracing* all freakin'
day. (Inkers were so misunderstood.) Money was important to
Annette. She'd even left him once before Emily was born when
they going to be late on a mortgage payment. Her father had told
her money was everything (he hadn't had any), and whatever that
cruel, manipulative old geezer had told her was treated as holy writ.
Of course, Neal should have seen all these things during the four
years before he married her, but love and pussy has a way of
clouding the mind. Yes, he had been in love. (The words sounded
so absurd to him.) It was the last thing he was now. Most days,
before he left the offices of Empire World Comics, he dipped his
fingers into the ink for effect. The only problem with his little joke,
he'd always thought, was that if he *did* strangle her, he'd leave his
fingerprints for sure, inky ones. But this morning he'd grabbed his
winter gloves (it was only October) and shoved them in the pockets
of his windbreaker. Never could be too careful, he'd thought when
he left the office; opportunity could present itself without
warning—or, like tonight (yes, tonight!), it could just strike him as
time. So long as Emily was out of sight—with her gay aunts
perhaps, who only lived a few blocks away. Emily loved it there;
they were so carefree and craft-oriented, and they wore all black,
painters and poets both. Annette would no longer even step foot in
their house once they'd come out to their families. (What, he'd
asked her, you thought they were *roommates?*) Neal cherished the
times when Annette had to pick up Emily from Aunt Collette and
Aunt Jean's. (Emily walked to very places it seemed.) That really got
him going—the Christian values speech from someone who never
went to church. *He* took Emily to church (even if all Neal did was
peel ink from his fingers during the service). Of course, Emily,
who'd been grounded recently but was a free girl now, was of the
age (fourteen) where she often ate dinner at a friend's house rather
than at the gay aunts' (or at home), but she would still need a ride.
However, her return would rely less on the Roget taxi service than
on the friend's parental units, who were often pressed into
service—which meant there was at least a possibility, however
remote, of her coming home unexpectedly early, so he'd have to act
quickly, even though he still hadn't been able to get out the car. (All
of this might be moot given the introduction of Mr. X into the mix,
but he had to play out each scenario methodically.) If he hadn't
already pulled into the driveway, he could wait down the street and

see if Emily was true to form: escaping, now that she could; if given the chance, it seemed, Emily would eat her meals or hang out *anywhere* but home (where she usually barricaded herself in her room). In his supposed absence, Annette would be forced to take her wherever, then once Emily had been delivered his wife would come back to a seemingly empty dark house. Annette hated surprises, and for what little time she would have to comprehend it, she was *really* going this one.

Wait—he might have to drive her himself if he sat here much longer.

There was no backing out to park elsewhere; she'd hear, he decided. Annette had probably seen him pull in, and besides, what was a car motor to one whose ears could pick up the scratch of his pen writing a check from another room, even another floor. She'd hear… Maybe he wouldn't even be able to sneak up on her or jump out of the shadows. Maybe he'd have to take a much more direct approach.

Either way worked, he decided, and was worth the risk. Being parked in the driveway announced his presence (to his wife at least), but Annette, despite her well-tuned antennae, would never guess, that this evening, sooner rather than later, she would be drawing her final acrid breaths.

Still, he knew better than to think it was going to be that easy. Oh, Emily wouldn't be around for dinner, but she would most likely not be far (and wouldn't need to ask for a ride even if she needed one—and just because she wouldn't want her parents to know where she was going). Mr. X—that was what he and the Mrs. called him; his appellation the only thing they agreed upon these days. The boy was his daughter's…what?…crush?…suitor, if such a word was appropriate for kids their age? (He assumed Mr. X was an underclassman too, just from Emily's teacher's description, which was pretty much the only info they had.) Annette, who'd come to see all men as dangerous as well as worthless, questioned Emily for hours, in between lectures on teen pregnancies, HPV, and the inherent lecherousness of the male population, which could be interpreted as: Annette didn't want to look bad in front of the other mothers. Neal didn't take part in the grilling. (About the only piece of intel Emily let drop was that her mystery man lived nearby, which is why Neal knew she wouldn't need a lift if she was going to meet him tonight; he also knew if there was any chance in hell that she'd tell her parents where she was going and with whom, after the interrogation, it was gone and so was she. Her not needing a ride was the only clue, and he doubted Annette would pick up on it. Neal figured the boy, Mr. X, probably wasn't old enough to drive either. Maybe he'd even come to Emily rather than vice versa, though Neal didn't expect a knock on the door.) Truth was, he couldn't be happier for his daughter. She was kind of a loner and in a losing battle with acne, so it was nice to see that someone else recognized what he did: that Emily had much to offer behind her scowls and studied frowns. As long as she wasn't offering more than that, he was all for whatever made her smile a little. So while it was a safe bet that Emily would be out of the house, she would perhaps be closer than he would like. But even if Emily and Mr. X hung out on the front porch, he hoped she'd be too distracted to take note of a stray scream—the TV, she'd think if she thought anything at all (it was still iffy if she was close)—and his neighbors wouldn't make much of a brief noise: too many younger kids squealing as they played games on their front lawns or tried to catch lightning bugs. He would know if Emily's plans involved Mr. X or not as soon as he heard her music—which he did before he even got out of the car.

In the end it didn't matter—the gay aunts or Mr. X, once Emily was out of the house, Neal could dispatch Annette, dispose of her body or make it look like a break-in, and go to the movies. (It was better to remove her remains, he decided in the driveway, in case Emily came home early; he could report his wife missing this time tomorrow, although the evidence, particularly the note he'd find, would point to her leaving him and their child despite the fuss he'd make defending their marriage and her dedication to motherhood—a role he born to play.) He'd made a habit of catching a film after dinner. (Annette hated going to the movies.) Young Jimmy from the office would usually meet Neal at the Ambler Theater in the borough of Mondauk Proper; Neal had wanted to establish a pattern to bolster his alibi, and Jimmy was witness to the pattern. He would do whatever Neal asked him to do, including lie for him if necessary. Bit of hero worship there, but Neal had begun to think that Jimmy was *too* malleable. Better if he sat this night out. (He originally hoped Jimmy would help him remove and dispose of the body.) No need to make the kid culpable in any way; he'd have a role to perform later, and Neal thought it would be easier to play with his head than fill it up.

Something—a shadow maybe—shifted unnaturally among the trees near the top of the drive. He felt a shiver travel up his spine, and he squinted into the copse. Nothing—it was nothing. Just the last of his nerves acting up is all.

Little retarded kids. We'll see who has the last gasp, Neal thought. He'd had about all he could take and he could take quite a lot it turned out. Depriving Emily of her mother was an unconscionable sin but for the better good. Maybe they could even move. Annette had a life insurance policy, so there'd be some extra money. It would get Emily out of this neighborhood, the neighborhood he and Annette had fallen in love with as a young couple, befriending neighbors and kids and dogs but which lately (according to the news and the gossip) had become an umbra of secrecy and malefaction, with villains and adulterers lurking behind every berry bush and sycamore tree. That would take the cake, wouldn't it? If Annette was loaning out that hairy bush to another man? But no. Her hirsute hygiene told him as much. Who else could stand the shrill demands, the shouted expletives, the repeated put-downs? Over and over she'd told him he added up to nothing and that she always knew he would, but that wasn't true, was it? At first, she shared his dreams and encouraged him and told him just how great his talent really was. *Little retarded kids.* As he throttled the steering wheel, Neal knew that if he pulled this off, this which he had imagined and sketched so often in his downtime, it would be the greatest caper he'd ever been involved in—and he'd had the privilege of inking the now-classic battles between Amazing Boy and Maniacal. But Annette didn't need or want or even believe in heroes—their significance was lost on his wife: how they mirrored the better nature of ourselves, as clichéd as that sounded, and sometimes even the darker urges we tried so hard to suppress. He saw himself in every one of the cape-and-mask set, even the bad guys: Amazing Boy; Kid Lightning; Wanda the Willow Girl; the vigilante Penumbra; the Black Spot, an antihero; supervillains Maniacal and Lord Dramatica— it was through them and his contribution to their exploits that he would live forever. (One of his co-workers called him the Strangler because of a villain Neal had co-created years before; this was bad, with the thirteen or so unsolved strangulations this past year; he'd have to talk to ol' Paul Nelson, set him straight down that narrow road.) Yes, if he pulled this off, it would be the greatest erase-and-start-over of his career. The Annette of old would have been so proud.

+

She could poison the soup; that wouldn't be too hard.

Annette Roget watched her husband pull into the driveway and sit in his car, mulling over his characters or perhaps perusing the ol' spank bank, working up to a quick jerk in the shower after supper (and *could* became *would*). There wasn't any telling what Neal was up to these days. At one point, he was spending hundreds a month on vinyl bootlegs—surreptitiously recorded live musical performances, he called them. A few were crystal clear, but most sounded like they were recorded in a tin can that was eight hundred miles away from the stage. Another time it was baseball cards. Boxes and boxes of them. Now it was action figures that he never took out of the packaging. As if their family was made of money. As if her husband's career wasn't a glorified hobby. No advertising job for Neal, no, that would have pleased her too much, made her too happy. Inking comic books, for Christ's sake, not even drawing them. He traced for a living. And how could she explain that to Suzanne and the other members of the Book Clutch Club? She did as best she could, fibbing when necessary. He thought he was such a big deal. Neal the Deal, she used to call him in the early days but not because of his rapid rise in the comic book world (if one could call it that; Annette didn't think he'd left too many bodies in his wake as went from intern to inker); in truth the nickname was more of a (very) private joke that stemmed from her mother calling him a bargain basement find—a good deal, in other words, not exactly top shelf. (The woman had been a riot and nasty as all get out.) Then again her mother didn't put much value in her offspring; for all Annette knew, her mother might have meant that her daughter was marrying up.

Lighting the burner beneath the tea kettle, she thought, how did wanting to be a good mother and a good wife become a bad thing? In a marriage, especially after children, of which they'd had only one (Annette had started to grow unsure of Neal even as Emily was shitting in her diapers), one was supposed to quash any feelings of independent movement and separatist notions. All for one and one for all. As a teacher, she tried to imbue this notion to her students. She explained it like this: baseball was a sport where individuals could shine at bat, but where they worked together as a team was at defense. It did not excuse Stanley Driver from doing his homework nor did it excuse him from participating in her class, raising his freckled hand, giving forth answers as well as opinions. Of course, Stanley Driver had a pass; he knew it and so did she. As long as Stanley made a minimal effort, just for show, she marked his participation and homework grades as high as she could without rousing suspicion. Nothing good could come from Assistant Headmaster Bogle knowing that she was falling in love (in lust) with a fourteen-year-old in her daughter's grade (but, thankfully, not in her class).

Stanley Driver was Irish, despite the last name, right off the boat as a baby, and he had five brothers, three of whom had passed through her classroom on their way to sheetrock jobs or vocational school. Stanley looked like them: Black Irish, with freckles and a stare that shot across rooms on laser beams of anger or something else she wasn't quite able to put her finger on; he also had their faint Irish accent: musical, yes, but moderately insolent. Being one of seven (there was a sister too), Stanley's inventory of toys, games, and recreational devices did not include a PlayStation or even an iPad. He wasn't poor; he just wasn't rich, and Stanley wanted to be rich, at least rich enough to own a PlayStation and an iPad. Nothing untoward had happened between teacher and student. The farthest it had gone was Stanley trying to look up her skirt and her spreading her legs and letting him—but it was a mutual show-and-tell. She wasn't sure she wanted to sleep with Stanley, but he wouldn't leave her head, and that was how she knew she was falling for a teenager. Poisoning Neal wasn't the only problem she'd encounter if this went any further. There'd be a scandal and she'd lose her job. The Driver family would surely either ban their son from seeing her or maybe even attack her physically. That was what she would do if some adult teacher tried to approach Emily improperly. She'd told Emily about bad touch a dozen times if she'd told her once, and Emily just responded anymore with a practiced sigh: *yeah, mom, I've heard this speech before.* It was just that Stanley touched Annette (her soul, that is) in a way that teaching and marriage to Neal did not. Her life before Stanley Driver was filled with preparing dinners and packing lunches and ordering sweaters from L.L.Bean catalogs, calling their operators to check on a color or correct them on a catalog entry. She did crosswords but only halfheartedly. Words didn't have the hold on her they once did—books either. She was as bored as her students as they went over their summer reading list or her latest syllabus. But her recent assignment, *Romeo and Juliet*, had made her wet, and that was a first in many different ways. She hadn't been wet since she didn't know when. She hadn't even been wet the few times she'd had sex with Neal the last few months. (Hell, the last few years, if she was going to be telling tales out of school.) K-Y had been the order of the day, and she'd slopped it on like she was slopping the pigs back home in Kansas. Stanley Driver took her away from all that. She'd let him look up her skirt, and he'd shown her his sleek boner. Hell of a detention period. Where it was to go next, she didn't know. She was as confused as she'd ever been. (Stanley, she assumed, was the *opposite* of confused; Annette was pretty sure he knew *exactly* what he wanted.) At least if Stanley was confusing thoughts of sex with love, it was better than confusing love with sex and sharing a bed and raising a baby. Standing in her way, besides the Mondauk police, the penal system, the school board, and her own, long buried Lutheran upbringing, was Neal. Bland, white-bread Neal. But a drip of this here, a drop of that there, and, *voila!*, no more Neal the Deal. (She knew her daughter wasn't eating with the family—she'd set herself a place at the table for show—so there was no worrying about her reaction or accidentally poisoning her.) Then Annette could do whatever she wanted, dangle her feet over the fires of purgatory, damn any legal ramifications. Other than her daughter, who else would care that Neal was no more? And with Emily caught up with her mysterious Mr. X, Irish Stanley and his smooth, alabaster penis was there for the plucking. Annette placed her hands over her ears. It was all nonsense, all pipe dreams. As Emily stomped up the stairs, Annette turned to the front windows again and watched Neal bypass the front door and head towards the side yard (wait—where the hell was his car?), then stop to talk to someone—the paperboy collecting?; it was only Tuesday— before she realized she was beginning to scream and so was the tea kettle.

+

She could kill her parents.

Emily sprawled on her bed with her cell phone within reach, waiting for Mr. X's signal, her music blasting so her movements—when it came time to make any—wouldn't be heard. She rarely cranked her music. Despite what her mother called her "prickly demeanor," her musical tastes had been generally on the softer side: Sarah McLachlan and Alicia Keyes were favorites. But Mr. X had turned her onto bands that mirrored the cauldron of rage inside her that was always threatening to bubble over, and their music was meant to be played loud: Soundgarden, Savages, early Afghan Whigs, Metallica even. The table was set and her mother was doing God knows what. It wasn't like they weren't young— once. She knew they didn't have sex anymore—or at least not as much as they used to. The bedsprings didn't creak much these days. Emily thought it was her mother's fault. Her mother was frigid; she could tell just by the way she constantly crossed her arms, almost wrapped them around her body, as if she was always cold. Then again, her father was no prize turkey. A nerd still, from inking comic books (kind of cool, but it wasn't like he was drawing them) to his Star Wars collection and all his books. Who'd want to fuck that, if *that* could even fuck? Emily figured her father was a prime Viagra candidate. As Mr. X liked to joke: *If you have an erection lasting for more than four hours, call your baby momma!*

Yesterday had been the last day of her second grounding in as many weeks, and unlike the first one, where she was guilt-free, more guilty by association (the Salem Lights really *were* Maureen Finnegan's), this time one of the nosy nuns had seen her making out with Mr. X under the bleachers during a basketball game. Her mother's blood vessels had pulsed at her temples, but at least she didn't know his name. (He'd taken off as soon as they saw the nuns approaching; she didn't blame him.) Her father was calmer, trying to be Cool Dad, asking what grade Mr. X was in, did he play sports, how did they meet? She'd wanted to throw up and said little. The only crumb that escaped her chapped lips was that he lived nearby—she may have even said that he lived in the neighborhood (which he did), but she hoped not. (It was her mother who'd dismissively called him Mr. X; the supposed sin and its optics were more important than the identity of her partner in crime.) Her parents kept their distance for the most part. Her father was always home late from work, then he huddled alone in his little portion of their finished basement, working on yet another Millennium Falcon model or fiddling with Boba Fett's jet pack, probably high from the airplane glue. And her mother? Oh boy—prim and proper teacher by day, not-so-happy homemaker by night; Emily was pretty sure her mother mixed her first cocktail as soon as she got home from work. On the weekends, in the past, family time had usually been spent traveling to Gettysburg or into the city to visit Independence Hall or Edgar Allen Poe's house. Emily thought, somewhat wistfully, though she was too ashamed at her own emotions to admit it, that she *sometimes* missed those tiny trips. Boring as they seemed then, they were the last times she ever felt part of a family, even if it became fractured at the end. Family time eventually trickled away to nothing, and the trips came to a rather abrupt end, which was fine, she lied to herself; she was fourteen: the Franklin Institute and the Philadelphia Zoo had lost their appeal, along with the Mummers and the Phillie Phanatic. She was old enough to go to view the grotesqueries exhibited in the Mütter Museum, but not old enough to go to Hershey Park with Maureen and ride the Storm Runner roller coaster; it was like she was being punished for the disintegration of the parental unit. Weekends now were spent biding her time until she could leave quietly, unobtrusively, without her mother clinging to her like a leech, a viscid reaction that always felt more like a reflex rather than anything born of real emotion. Many weekends, her mother was in her cups by noon, and her father would be playing with his models in the basement or sitting at his drafting board in his second floor study, staring out the window, his eyes lost in the dense woods behind the house. No more was she his "little *luciérnaga.*" Those days were gone. She just wanted to grow up, graduate or not, maybe get a job with some advertising agency. She could draw like nobody's business. But mostly she wanted to get out of the house tonight, meet Mr. X, and enter the woods. He'd promised tonight things would change. She hoped he didn't think he was taking her virginity tonight; the time for that would come soon enough; still, tonight she was prepared to cede more ground than she ever had before.

It was true: Mr. X was older than she was. But it wasn't like he was forty. She knew right away, even before she recognized him, that he was broken. And maybe because her parents were so damaged, something inside her made her want to fix Billy Ray Parker. There—she said his name aloud. "Billy Ray Parker." And

Billy Ray was broken, broken in ways that Emily could only guess about. Was he born broken or was he made this way, she didn't know. In the end it was all the same, right? You were where you were, Billy Ray said, and he was so right like he was on so many things. He could draw too. Draw better than her, in fact. Mostly comic book junk, superheroes in tights, bad guys with elaborate inventions of destruction. At first they made her sick to her stomach, reminded her of her father's drafting board, the diligence with which her father labored over a panel, but Billy Ray *drew* his superheroes; her father just inked them. (His biggest claim to fame was co-creating a supervillain, the Strangling Shadow, who Amazing Boy defeated every time.) Eventually her nausea passed— it was her father who made her nauseous, not the superheroes she had liked since she was a little girl—and soon she was able to enjoy Billy Ray's lines and blocking, even his conceits. The only habit of Billy Ray's that was annoying was his asking about her dad—as if Neal Roget counted for one iota in her life! Billy Ray said he'd take her away, that where they'd begin from wasn't very far, but in the end, with his guidance, she'd find herself nowhere near here, and she'd be different, she'd be changed. He said her father used to call him Bucky, the name of Captain America's old sidekick, a piece of trivia that bored Emily. (Besides, didn't Bucky become the Winter Soldier, a brainwashed assassin? She'd been raised on superheroes.) She wanted to hear more about the woods, about going away forever, about beginning again in a new skin. Billy Ray said the time was coming soon, sooner than she expected, so she should start getting ready (though he never told her how). Other than kissing her, he never touched her, not a boob pass, nothing. Just talk of escape, transformation, egg, larva, pupa, butterfly. No longer the firefly. *Can't believe these things are happening,* she wrote in her diary last night. She wanted to be touched, she wanted to be dirty. Her mother's neat, white living room made her see red. She wanted to menstruate all over the white chairs and sofa. But Billy Ray told her that was just her changing, getting ready to make that last jump from pubescent pupa to full-blown butterfly. It was exciting. He told her she would become the most beautiful butterfly ever to be seen, he just knew it. He said he'd stand over her while it happened and would make sure the change was complete. Billy Ray said he wouldn't let her *not* transform. It was her time, just like it was his to help her. When he told her maybe tonight, just maybe, she had peed a little in her underwear. The grounding was over. Now it was her time. Now she'd show them. The hell with dinner. Annette and Neal, get ready. Your baby's leaving home.

+

He had two confirmed kills in Iraq before they sent him home.

Counting those two, he now had nineteen confirmed kills. Seventeen since he'd been back. But only girls. He'd tried a boy, a teen, convinced he'd like it, but when he grew hard after capturing him, he let him go. He'd had his black Lone Ranger mask on, a domino mask, which hid the area around his eyes and between them, so there was no way he could be identified. (Still, he hoped his eyes still blazed red when he swooped upon his prey.) People can't place noses and mouths when they can't see eyes clearly (or if the eyes were fiery and hypnotic). He still thought about boys occasionally—or young men, rather—occasionally, but he knew he could *change* girls; that was his special gift, his mission, chief among his powers, and he shouldn't stray far from the path. So other than a vengeance disappearance (he just beat a former altar boy within inches of his life and left him two states away, naked and bleeding, probably brain damaged), he stuck to the fairer sex.

The Army should never have sent him home. He didn't care about politics; he just cared about killing him some raghead motherfuckers. And he did, twice, but they said he was no longer fit for combat; he taken off active duty and was shipped home quicker than you can say Jack Rabbit Slim's, where he was sent to a special hospital and dishonorably discharged upon release. He'd done nothing out of the ordinary, at least nothing he could remember. He'd cut the last dead Iraqi's head off, and he thought he heard cheering. Even today, there's was always a distant cheering, an acclamation, when he strangled someone to their next stage, when he helped someone change. That he'd done this seventeen times without the police knocking on his poor mother's door just further verified that he was *supposed* to do this. The cops had yet to come up with a cool nickname for him, like his hero the Red Ribbon Killer. (Mondauk County was a hotbed for unsolved murders and cults.) They could call him the Mondauk Strangler (as the *Philadelphia Inquirer* did) or even better, Mister Metamorphosis, a name he'd come up with. Mister Metamorphosis sounded like a superhero name rather than a serial killer name (which was good since the United States had eighty-five percent of the world's serial killers, and he didn't want to be lumped in with the rest, the Red Ribbon Killer aside). Mister Metamorphosis described perfectly what he was doing: helping the uninitiated discover their true selves probably a wee bit earlier than expected. Egg to larva to pupa to butterfly, yes—but where Mister Metamorphosis was ultimately taking them was the end of it all. From there, his "victims" could start a new cycle of change, he believed, even come back, reborn and given a second chance in a new body with a new face. Yes, with some of the same heartaches and regrets, but now with a chance to make them right. He was, in the end, a genuine superhero. (When he changed the girls, he felt his soul ascend or descend with theirs, as he accompanied them to their astral field of transformation, a modern day Charon or Azrael.) And who would know better, if a shred of doubt existed inside Billy Ray's illuminated skull, who better to recognize his exalted state, the way he had recognized him when he was little, who better than superhero maven Neal Roget?

Oh, cue the violins, but it was true: Daddy had left when the boy was but three, leaving a trail of empty bottles, condom wrappers, and unpaid bills. Mommy had tried but she was angry, angry at everything, even angry at her former little pumpkin. Mommy would hit and smack with whatever was at hand: frying pan, yard stick, once a Tiffany lamp that had belonged to Grandma. But there were always comic books. Marvel or DC? Didn't matter. Green Lantern was his favorite for a while, especially the ones where he shared panel space with Green Arrow. Next came Thor, which led to a fall obsession with Norse mythology. Loki was a particularly terrifying arch-villain. Batman followed along with his nemesis the Joker. Spider-Man briefly—he wasn't dark enough for Billy Ray. He tried them all: *The Incredible Hulk*, Captain America and Falcon, Nova, the Legion of Super-Heroes (which he fell in love with but which weren't dark in the least), the old *Star Wars* comics, the Sub-Mariner, *Tomb of Dracula*, so many. And practically next door, two houses down, was a comic book guy, an inker, the person responsible for the shading and the nuance. The other kids on the block didn't bother with Billy Ray. There was a rumor he'd eaten dog shit. Billy Ray wasn't sure who started it, but he suspected God's little chosen one, altar boy Kevin Dove (recently vanished), who'd asked Billy Ray to watch him diddle himself in fifth grade (Kevin was an early riser); Billy Ray had assented, and this was what it had gotten him. The rumor spread like wildfire, as Mommy would say, and soon his pariah status was secure. If he walked into Mondauk Common, the boys jumped out of trees and scared him half to death. If he brought a basketball to the playground, the court would empty and he'd shoot baskets by himself to the hoots of his former friends and current classmates who watched him from behind the fence. Swimming: forget it— Billy Ray had given that up altogether. Too many turd-in-the-pool jokes at his expense, once resulting in everyone exiting the pool, leaving only Billy Ray dog-paddling alone in the middle.

But Mr. Roget was different. From their very first meeting, Mr. Roget had been kind where others were not. Sometimes he loaded Billy Ray up with so many comic books, he could barely carry them all home. Mr. Roget called him Bucky, not because Billy Ray had buck teeth (he did), but because Mr. Roget said he was perfect sidekick material. He said he'd use him one day, have him drawn into a comic book. Of course the name Bucky was already used by Marvel, so he'd have to come up with another one, but, by God, he'd do it. Billy Ray didn't want to be a nudge, so he was careful to only visit Mr. Roget once a week. He knew his young daughter, but only in passing, and his wife, glaring at them through the front windows terrified him. She could end this little relationship, her sour face said, at any second of her choosing. After awhile, Billy Ray stopped ringing the doorbell and only met Mr. Roget outside at the top of the driveway near a group of trees. He'd step out into the edge of the garage light only at the last second, but Mr. Roget was never scared or surprised; he was always glad to see Billy Ray. He'd even open his sketch pad on the hood of his car and show Billy Ray a few tricks of the trade, and he'd honestly evaluate Billy Ray's attempts at comic book art. If Mr. Roget knew what the other kids said or thought, if Emily ever told him, he never let on. He was a good egg, that Mr. Roget, and tonight Billy Ray, a.k.a. Mister Metamorphosis, would see if the egg had cracked, gone rotten or not, while he'd been away in Iraq and in the hospital. There'd been distressing signs before he left: there was never a sidekick with Billy Ray's likeness in the comics; there was never a new Bucky under another name. And Mr. Roget stopped having time for him when his marriage began to disintegrate (around the time Billy Ray enlisted)—that much Billy Ray pieced together from what poor, torn Emily (who wrote him his only letter while he was overseas), now his secret confidante, had told him, weeping into his shirt, sobbing like a damsel in distress. But tonight she would change; under his skilled (but maybe not so gentle) hands, she'd metamorphose. She'd *become*. And Mr. Roget would see just what kind of superhero he had so blithely ignored.

+

Neal Roget pulled on his gloves.

He didn't dip his fingers in ink today—he'd had a feeling early on that tonight might the night—but before leaving the office, he scrubbed his hands, but he could never get them a hundred percent ink free. Even if he had, he didn't know if he could still leave fingerprints on her neck (in the unlikely event that somehow the gloves came off during what he imagined would be a frenzied few minutes), but he didn't want to find out. He wondered if could get a peek at Annette's unruly mass of pubic hair before or after she died; he had to see it up close. He worried that Annette was teaching Emily similar "personal" grooming and hygiene habits, but he knew better. Annette only worried about surface things when it came to Emily: what she wore, what cosmetics she used and their application, what her hair looked like. Neal bet that Annette didn't even know the name of one of Emily's friends. She only glanced at her grades so she wouldn't be embarrassed at the next parents' tea-and-greet.

Neal pinched himself and held back from slapping his own flushed cheek. Things were getting confused at the head office. What was the plan, Stan? What was the agreed upon…approach? If he was the Mondauk Strangler (and he wasn't; at least not that one), or even the Strangling Shadow—he was a different, necessary kind of evil— then the sound of music from Emily's room that relentlessly made its way down to the drive told him that quite possibly his time was now—his daughter wouldn't hear anything. (He owned a gun but if he shot Annette, it would be easily traced to him; still, he couldn't count the number of nights he'd lain next to her in bed, fantasizing about blowing a hole in her wrinkled forehead that not even her Botox treatments could fix. It didn't matter though; he didn't have his gun on him, a mistake maybe.) Still, there was a chance Emily would see the immediate aftermath, which he didn't want to happen (so it was a good thing he wasn't armed—less messy). It would be best if stuck to his original plan and waited until Emily left the house—which he was quite sure was going to happen soon.

His daughter was blasting Nirvana, barricaded behind her bedroom door, most likely getting ready to sneak off to see her secret boyfriend, not visit her gay aunts, which meant she wouldn't need a ride. (Looking back at the dates he was pretty sure that Emily had spent time with the boy, Neal felt he'd already cracked the code: the louder and angrier the music, the more testosterone was involved in the evening's activities; he was pretty sure she wasn't having sex, so if she wanted to spend time holding hands or possibly participating in some hasty smooching—as she did under the bleachers apparently—he was all for it; this was normal teenage stuff, plus anything that kept her away from Annette's needy grip was fine by him.) Once Emily was gone, he could strangle Annette, check her pubes, and drag her off into the woods behind their house, all the way to the swift-flowing Pennypack Creek where he would dump her body. He'd ditch the gloves, maybe burn them in the laundry sink. In his pocket was the note she'd mailed—*mailed*—to him when she'd left before. It was generic enough, nebulous even; her main complaint was money problems, but he'd thought of that too and had just bounced two checks (recently enough that Annette hadn't been alerted by mail, and the contact number was his cell phone). He just had to pack a few bags for his wife after the deed was done. He'd take her car and drive into Philadelphia and leave it in one the worst neighborhoods. (He'd remove the license plate, which he thought would make the car look more inviting.) He'd ditch the contents of the bags (and the bags themselves) in various dumpsters, take a cab, several of them, back (returning, he hoped, before Emily did or things might go to hell in a handbasket, for he was sure signs of a struggle would be apparent)—then, after picking up the place, grabbing a quick shower, for the smell of deeds most foul would most likely ooze from his pores. Once he was squeaky clean, he'd go about his evening as if nothing was wrong. No sense finding the note until Emily was back; not that she needed the drama, but when he decided that Jimmy was too good a witness to help with anything, big or small, Emily was the only choice left really to be his audience when he "discovered" the farewell note, finally breaking down (being careful not to overdo it) when he noticed Annette's wedding band had been placed on top of the bureau. Emily, he was sure, remembered her mother's last abrupt departure, even though she'd been a grade-schooler when it had happened. (Though he'd done his best back then to make it seem like nothing—Mom was just going to visit Grandma in upstate New York—he was certain his daughter had seen right through his lies and playacting.) Nowadays it seemed like his daughter might be too jaded to let a few tears drop when she realizes her mother is gone, but he felt sure she'd call the gay aunts, who'd come flying over in their art house black like a murder of crows. All would look on the up and up. Annette's disdain for motherhood was well-documented. He even planned to remove the SIM card from his wife's cell phone and ditch them in separate places (in pieces).

In his pocket were stubs from two movie tickets for tonight's show that he'd purchased (and torn) during his lunchtime. He'd made sure Jimmy was so loaded up with work that he'd have to stay late, but the young letterer never acknowledged that tonight was supposed to their movie night—exactly as Neal had hoped. In preparation, he'd been varying the nights of their weekly cinematic sojourn. He didn't want Jimmy to connect the dots, for it was best for Neal to rely on their now well-established pattern of behavior as his alibi. The ticket stubs were his backup. Jimmy made a habit of pinning his stubs to the bulletin board in his cubicle at EWC. Neal had bought tickets for a movie they'd already seen, so it was simply a matter of removing the old stub and adding the new one. (They weren't pinned in any order.) While it seemed as if he was betting his future freedom on a flighty kid he didn't actually know that well, Jimmy *was* easily turned around and often confused, to the point of showing up at EWC on a Saturday, believing it to be a Friday.

The best plan for the aftermath was to act as normal as possible, considering the situation. After the scene in the bedroom with Annette's wedding band, he'd try to hold it together (in a most obvious way) in front of Emily. Save the emotional reserves for the phone call he'd make a day or two later to report her missing when she didn't turn up at her mom's, as indicated in the note, and (if it came to it) when they found her body—and there was a decent chance they would. His visit to the banks of the Pennypack the evening before didn't make him feel any better. Recent storms had left the large creek foaming and swirling, thick with flotsam, often trapped by felled trees. He knew it would most likely be a matter of time. (He'd hoped the creek would carry her to the river.) Although Annette resurfacing wasn't part of the plan, he felt he was ready for either outcome. Acting the part of the thrown over husband (for her note hinted at a secret love) or the distraught parent might take at least some of the heat off him. (No dramatics. Not yet.) But he decided early on that he couldn't make the house look like a crime scene, for that would surely lead to a county-wide search. He hadn't counted on the storms, but he had no other plan (and he'd had it up to here). It was more than a flip of the coin; it was all about who noticed if the side that landed up had a (possibly inky) fingerprint smudge. He'd have to identify her body, of course, the fish already at her face, her skin having taken on that comic book drowned dead guy look: bloated with blotches and discolorations. *Then* he could sob uncontrollably, beat his chest, vomit, question aloud to God. But not a minute before or they'd know.

Of course, Emily could tell them, innocently or not, of her father's outbursts; Annette could occasionally make him lose his shit. Then there'd be hell to pay—especially if they tried to pin the other strangulations on him as well. (Amazing Boy wasn't the only one haunted by the Strangling Shadow; his archvillain could easily further his descent.) That would be the worst possible outcome. He knew cops always looked at the husband or boyfriend first, and Emily could bury him. He was betting his life on a pair of ticket stubs, a swollen creek, and the idea that although his daughter didn't seem to like either of her parents very much anymore, it was doubtful she'd throw him to the dogs just to be free of them both. Child Welfare Services would come sniffing around unless Annette's equally annoying sister (the Dark Phoenix he called her—to himself) took her in, and Emily *despised* Aunt Dark Phoenix. The gay aunts could throw a monkey wrench in the works, but Aunt Collette, his step-sister—his father was fond of marrying, sowing his seed, and moving on—had a record, robbery, kid's stuff really, but she'd been eighteen when it went down and her cohorts had been minors. She was tagged as the ringleader and had to do a little time, after which she met Jean (now Aunt Jean), her parole officer. Neal was pretty sure that Jean's job wouldn't balance out a felony record, which would take them out of the running as far as legally taking Emily in. His daughter knew all this; he was sure that she'd work out that if she tried to bury her old man, she'd end up with Aunt Dark Phoenix or a foster family—and she didn't like the one she had; how would she react to having new rules set by strangers and most likely being sent to a new school? Emily, if she suspected him, would come through if only because—

The volume of her music jumped up, and he dropped his keys:

One baby to another says, I'm lucky to have met you.
I don't care what you think unless it is about me.
It is now my duty to completely drain you.
I travel through a tube and end up in your infection.

Neal shook his head. All *this* decided it. Annette was probably the only person (other than a nosy neighbor perhaps) who knew he'd pulled in the drive. The light had almost completely faded from the sky, and he had to feel for his keys. He'd pull out and park down the street. He just had to watch out for his daughter; just last week, a day or two before she was caught under the bleachers, she'd left her music blaring when she'd split for who-knows-where in order, he supposed, to throw her mother off, even though she probably knew her mom didn't give a good hoot unless her daughter's actions reflected poorly on her parental image.

With eyes so dilated, I've became your pupil.
You've taught me everything without a poison apple.

"Mr. Roget…"

Neal spun on his heels and hid his gloved hands behind his back, almost dropping his keys again, which he shoved in his back pocket.

"Yes, yes?"

"Mr. Roget," said the voice's owner, stepping out from the small gathering of trees next to the driveway, out into the light. "It's me."

"Me?" Neal asked tentatively.

(Mister Metamorphosis swallowed hard. It was getting to where he hated saying either of his old names.)

"It's Bucky, sir. Your old sidekick."

"It's Buck—it's Bucky? Bucky! What the hell are you doing here? I thought—"

"I was—away. But I'm out now. Out and better than ever."

Neal wiped flop sweat from his forehead. *Was Bucky wearing a bandit mask? A Lone Ranger mask?* He felt as if he'd been tuned to another frequency. He struggled until he realized (in the split of a second) that it was he who had turned the dial when this new element, this new wrinkle, was introduced. It reminded him of a song:

> *Switching it over to AM,*
> *Searching for a truer sound.*
> *Can't recall the call letters;*
> *Steel guitar and settle down.*

Survival of the adaptable, though he doubted he'd ever find a "truer sound"; even chameleons must forget their original colors.

"Ready to return to duty, sir." The young man saluted him and stood at attention. "Right by your side always."

Neal realized his neighbor was referring to sidekick duty and chose to ignore it; his racing thoughts didn't have time to incorporate whatever this was.

"Well, that's just fine, Bucky, just fine. Got yourself a job, do you? I bet. A girl too, hmm? Well, fine, fine. You deserve all the best. You had it rough, son. The neighborhood bullies didn't help much, I'm sure."

Bucky said not a word in response.

Neal stepped back and appraised his former protégé.

"Fine, fine. Looking good and don't you know it. Well, listen old pal, I've got to go into the den of inequity here, so don't be a stranger."

When he finally spoke, his voice was considerably deeper.

"I've got powers, Mr. Roget."

Neal scrunched his eyebrows in puzzlement, then dismissed the statement. "Powers. Yes, yes, fine, fine. Powers."

"I'm going to see Emily tonight, Mr. Roget, help her change."

"Oh, seeing Emily, are you?" he asked, distracted by a stray thought. "I'll...I'll send her right down. Yes, yes. Change, I see. Probably getting changed, you're right. Getting changed before her big—" No, can't be. *Stay focused.* "She never eats dinner—with us anyway. Well, I have to go in now, Bucky. You stay strong, my faithful comrade."

Mister Metamorphosis nodded his head and made a little bow, then stepped back into the shadows of the trees.

Neal stared for a minute and shook his head. When he reached the door, Emily burst out of it, kissed him on the cheek (now *that* was a surprise), and said she was going out with Debbie and Hannah. Neal nodded his head. Billy Ray and Emily just shattered his movie theater alibi and made moving his car pointless. The way it was always portrayed in the movies, the medical examiner would only have a rough time of death anyway, between such and such hours. It was going to come down to control. Maybe if he weighed her down... He'd just have to keep his cool. It was too late to lose heart now. He entered the house and crouched down, listening for sounds of his prey.

+

A half a cup of Drano in the soup—end of story.

The onions and the spices would mask the taste, she decided. It was going to be just the two of them for dinner (she knew Emily was going to get gone now that she was no longer grounded), and Annette never ate soup, hated it actually. She only ever made it because Neal liked it.

(Her daughter didn't even bug her for a ride. Well, at least she wouldn't be spending her first free night with the k d. lang fan club.)

She wanted one last cigarette before the show—Neal was probably still sitting in his car, daydreaming of capes or tights or tits—and when she opened the sliding glass door that led to the deck, Stanley Driver ejaculated into one of her potted plants.

"Stanley! What the hell are you—did you just...? You just came on my plant. Button up, young man. My husband's going to be in the house any second."

Stanley zipped up and wiped his hands on his hooded sweatshirt.

"I'm sorry, ma'am. I just watchin' ya through the glass there, makin' dinner, preparin' the family meal, and I got excited."

She squinted into the darkness as two shadows made their way towards the woods that bordered their larger than average-sized backyard.

Annette looked down at Stanley Driver and gave him a reassuring smile.

"My plant'll live, Stanley. No worries. Just learn to keep it in your pants until it's asked for." She returned her attention to the woods. If it weren't for the waning crescent moon…

"What are you lookin' at, ma'am?"

"Never mind that. What are you doing here, Stanley?"

The boy maintained eye contact and never even tilted his freckled face.

"*Dáiríre píre*, I only wanted to see you. I wanted to see you in…your natural habitat."

"With your trousers down around your…what the hell is that?" she asked, pointing.

On the edge of the woods, taller figure knelt over a smaller one who was thrashing in the leaves. Their figures were silhouettes, and Annette thought she heard a familiar squeak escape from the party on the bottom, the sound carried on the evening breeze.

"Jesus Christ—is that Emily? Is that my Emily?"

"Ma'am, never fear. Underdog is here."

The boy pulled the hood over his head and with one hand flipped over the railing, dropped to the grass below, and picked up a shovel.

"You're me mot, Mrs. Roget!" Stanley shouted.

She watched her student sprint towards the woods, a silent bullet, as if his sneakered feet knew instinctively to avoid twigs and noisy piles of dead leaves. Stanley Driver tackled the taller figure and, after a brief tumble (during which time, the smaller silhouette huddled against a tree), Stanley emerged victorious. The taller shadow skulked away, a little sob in his hitch perhaps. She had no idea why the boy let him go. Stanley raised the shovel in salute towards his teacher, and Annette raised one arm back semi-self-consciously—just as Neal came out onto the deck.

"What's going on here?"

Stanley thrust the shovel into the ground and reached for Emily, who allowed herself to be swept up into his arms.

"Nothing—I'll explain later. Why are you wearing gloves?"

"I had to look under the hood real quick. Didn't want to get my hands dirty."

"Did you move your car?"

"Didn't want the fluids to leak in the driveway."

"Hmmm. Did you try the soup?"

"No, I—"

"Don't."

Neal stood next to his wife and peeled his gloves off. Annette inched away.

"Is that...is that Emily? Who's that carrying Emily?"

It was Stanley Driver, hero of the desperate, thought Annette. Don't you see his hood? It's a cowl. His sweatshirt is a cape.

"We're having company for dinner."

Neal placed a hand over Annette's.

"It's gonna be different from now on, I promise."

He was lying, trying to get her to lower her defenses; she knew all his moves by now. Annette let her hand stay for a few seconds, then pulled it away so quick, her ring cut Neal's hand.

"Just for tonight, Neal, we'll play house—but not the whole night."

As Neal walked away looking for a Band-Aid, Annette watched her hero approach the deck with her shivering daughter.

Because after tonight, Neal, she thought, everything is going to be oh-so different, but not in any way that you expect. Shame about the soup though. It had been her preferred method of elimination, though she had to admit she hadn't thought the aftermath through. (Surely the Drano would be detected if there was an autopsy.) Before tonight, she'd flirted with the idea of using Stanley to rid herself of her husband—the poisoned soup had been a kneejerk reaction to Neal leaving his whiskers in the sink this morning—but she decided the boy got a pass for saving Emily and for putting on his onanistic show with the plant, which was somewhat flattering but not something she was prepared to explore, not while Neal snored next to her every night. She thought about goading her husband into a rage, but she'd have to bruise herself (he'd never hit her), and it took long enough to put her face on every morning.

No, she thought sighing, she knew what she had to do.

Before Stanley and Emily climbed the stairs to the deck, Annette adjusted Neal's gun in the back of her jeans. The games were almost over. They would be alone, if not tonight, then soon, and gun accidents happened all the time, even suicides, his inky fingerprints sad reminders that only superheroes were immortal.

-end-

Gaper Delay

Up ahead, the lanes are beginning to become jammed. The trees along I-476 S drip with the previous night's rain, and it's easy to imagine that each leaf reflects a shimmering image of our car. We've been in the Impala for over two hours and neither of us has said a word since we pulled out of the driveway. We'd been staying (in separate beds) with relatives in Owego, a small town in upstate New York. There was always at least one reporter staking out our home in Mondauk County, Pennsylvania, and the curious showed up at all hours. Shannon and I needed to hide out for a while. This trip back to the Keystone State (and it is only a trip) is something we never agreed upon, but somehow I came out ahead and here we are. Traffic begins to crawl, and I instruct the GPS to find an alternate route and take the next off-ramp. Soon we're rushing through the woods, mud splashing up on our sides and radio reception going in and out. I don't mind; the last few miles have been nothing but preachers and religious music on both bands. Some scary preachers too. " 'And when I saw him, I fell at his feet as dead. And he laid his right hand upon me, saying unto me, Fear not; I am the first and the last.' Are *you* ready to fall at His feet as one dead? Or are you preparing to simply fall and be in pain for all eternity? Take a stand, ye sinners! Take a stand against Lucifer by falling at the feet of the Saviour!"

I switch the radio off. We've been to too many religious ceremonies of late, heard too many priests and preachers spout the Word of God, as if it meant anything after what had happened and what is happening right now. They were empty words, I decided months ago, meant to bring succor, instill fear, inspire righteousness—I didn't know which—and I had grown tired of empty gestures. Hence the trip (take a stand, ye sinners!) and the silence from the passenger seat. It wasn't that Shannon believed the words in the numerous services we've attended; it was just that she wanted to—she wanted to believe in *something*. I tried to tell her those days were long gone—we're in a no man's land with no easy way home—but Shannon clung to whatever kept her afloat, whatever she believed kept her out of the mud, including copious amounts   of   rum   and   cranberry   juice.

"Gonna have to give her a good cleaning when we get home," I say as we go down an even muddier byway because of a road closing, but Shannon's arms remain crossed. My voice is scratchy; I've only spoken to a sleepy convenience store clerk since we left Owego. "We lost some time, but we should be there in an hour, give or take."

Part of Shannon refuses to believe that any of this has happened or what the consequences are going to be. It is a natural reaction. I didn't want to believe it at first. But our Joey is a junkie (or a recovering one), plain and simple as your mother's ass pimple (to borrow one of my grandfather's favorite phrases). Probably an alcoholic at fifteen, by our son's seventeenth birthday we were finding bent spoons, discovering spray marks of blood on the bathroom walls and ceiling, and finding needles buried in the trash alongside little baggies with white residue. Still Shannon refused to see. She blocked all my attempts to rein in our son. She even bought the boy six-packs so he could go drinking with his friends in Pennypack Woods. Problem there, besides the obvious, was that soon Joey didn't have any friends—not after the stuff he pulled. He'd used them all up, a dollar or a theft at a time. Shannon would share a bottle with him on the back porch, ignore it if he nodded off, even helped him get a fake ID, so she could take him out to a bar once in a while for a good talk. "It's how we connect. The *only* way we connect," she slurred to me once when Joey took off in her car after she'd fallen asleep on the porch during one of their bonding sessions. (Shannon could put it away when we were younger—Third Leg Shannon, we called her—but she could also set it down and walk away. Temporarily at least. Nowadays—who knew?) I wasn't even the bad cop. I didn't count. No one listened to me. I was "negative"; I always saw the worst. Well, that was because I was seeing it right in front of me. Then Joey took it up a notch, and it became apparent I wasn't seeing enough. I was the definition of a bad parent. Shannon had always shied away from anything parental in nature. She raised our son to be her accomplice, her sidekick, and once he hit his teens (which he did resoundingly), her cohort and confidante. Their intimacy, I always thought bordered on the inappropriate—but I did nothing to course correct either of them. Turned out that was what I was good at parentally: nothing.

"Wonder if the roads are closed because of flooding. It didn't seem like it rained *that* hard last night—well, in Owego anyway."

Whenever we visit Joey, he's usually nearly catatonic, even though he'd recently gone through rehab (for a fourth time) and kicked heroin and whatever else (everything but cigarettes) so that he'll be lucid during the trial. Now he just sits in Norristown State Hospital and smokes and stares and smokes some more. Convicts and rehab patients smoke a lot, I noticed, but I have to remind myself that our son hasn't been convicted yet. (That charade—the verdict a foregone conclusion and rightly so—is still a few calendar pages away.) Sometimes he'll stare at us, which is worse than when he stares at the walls. It's almost like he's blaming us. His doctor can't say much—I don't know why; we're his parents—but a sympathetic aide told me (outside of the unit) that Joey's angry that he survived, that the final bullet meant for himself never made it out of the suddenly-jammed gun before the police tackled him. Joey's on a lot of psychotropic drugs and tranquilizers now, enough to calm him down, but occasionally, they tell us, he has to be put in restraints. But whenever we see him, he's as still a sleeping mouse.

Shannon was usually happy whenever we drove the roughly twenty-five miles from our home in the town of Rhawnhurst to see Joey at Norristown. (From Owego, it's about 187 miles, what should have been a roughly three hour trip.) Unlike today, Shannon would often be animated on the way and talk like Joey was in some prep school instead of a psych ward lockup awaiting trial. I usually played along; there wasn't a need to disturb the fantasy, not if Shannon was in a good mood for a change. On the way back, it would be different. On the way back, Shannon too would be catatonic and quiet as a sleeping mouse. She would remain that way for at least the rest of the day, maybe some of the next. Lately, it's been like pulling teeth—all of them—to get her to go. (The silence of this trip is my punishment for pulling again.) But time is ticking. By pretending every approaching day means nothing—she even took down the calendar in the kitchen and ignores attempts at anything other than the smallest of small talk—Shannon believes she is the croc who swallowed the clock (forgetting the literary reptile's true intentions). But Joey's final arraignment is around the corner; wishful thinking or intentional ignorance won't change that, and I suppose we'll have to relive what happened all over again as the justice system grinds inexorably ahead. I always wonder what the people at her job think, but then again, I can just imagine what the wags at *my* job think: there goes the father of the Roosevelt Mall Murderer.

Our car slips in the mud only once, and then we are out of the woods and back on the highway, now jammed with idling cars. A few muddy vehicles follow ours and wait for an opportunity to merge. We were lucky. But according to my watch and the car's digital clock, we're going to be late and it's not going to look good if we are. Shannon must know this because she twists around and almost faces me. Still, she says nothing.

"This is a gaper delay, I know it," I say, just to get a rise out of her. Back in our college days, Shannon created a game where, day or night, she'd give me a handjob or more during a good, long gaper delay (pronounced as one on KYW Newsradio). I had to try to hurry and finish before we broke through, and sometimes I came to scenes of the grotesque: twisted metal, floppy limbs, seemingly disembodied crimson hands, and trails of blood overseen by firemen with often grease- and dirt-streaked faces. But there will be no handjobs or blowjobs today—on this or any other day in the future, I suppose.

The only good thing about the Roosevelt Mall Massacre was that the mall is an outdoor mall. Among the parked cars, people had more places to hide; the open space gave them more of a chance to run from Joey. There was a rumor he had an accomplice, but it was determined later that he had acted alone, pulling hand guns and a sawed-off shotgun from his black trench coat in imitation of John-John Hagarty's similar assault on Hoskins High the year before. (An accomplice would have required at least an acquaintance and he had none nor any friends we knew of). Shannon and I didn't own guns, so where he got them remains a mystery, although one was traced to a company that advertised in the back of a gun magazine. The bigger mystery should have been where he got the money, being only seventeen and jobless, stealing from us and his grandparents and God knows who else for drug money. Shannon remained mum on the subject, and the cops, to my surprise, didn't push. They knew too.

"Turn the car around," Shannon says, her voice Brenda Vaccaro-hoarse from lack of use.

"I can't. Where am I going to turn? We're on a highway, and it's just about bumper to bumper."

"Back to the woods," she says, her voice trembling now. "Back to the woods."

"Can't do it, Shannon. We told these people we were coming. We asked their permission..."

"*You* asked their permission. I told you I didn't want to goddamn go. They're just going to fucking hate us. Hate us. Stare at us. As if our Joey could have...as if Joey did these things they allege—"

"Shannon," I say as gently as I can, as gently as a fucking mouse murmuring in its sleep, "you're delusional. Our son bought some guns with *mystery* money, walked to the mall, and shot up the place..." My voice is now a throttled shout. "Killed seventeen people, then tried to kill himself. He shot a toddler, for Christ's sakes."

"It was the drugs," she says.

"Oh, *now* you admit Joey was on drugs. That only took a year or so."

A motorcycle zooms past on the shoulder, and the girl on the back gives us the finger for no reason I can tell.

"Turn the car around, Daniel, or I'm just getting out."

I can see the curve a half a mile ahead; it's a smoke-belching snake composed entirely of motor vehicles. The snake's flickering tongue is made up of red swirling lights and scurrying uniformed (or at least identically attired, color coordinated) figures reporting data back to their Jacobson's organ radios.

"We're about forty-five miles from home," I say, but I know she's not going anywhere. Where would she go anyway? She's as marked as I am. Besides: the snake has swallowed us whole.

Shannon goes quiet again and refolds her arms, which had been gesticulating wildly. The Impala has barely moved two feet. The sirens seem a lifetime away. A fire truck honks its way down the shoulder. I hope its blaring startles the girl on the back of the motorcycle—not enough for her to fall, but enough for her to injure her middle finger.

Killed seventeen people, then tried to kill himself.

Sixteen people, including two security guards, one cop, and a woman in a wheelchair, died that day. The toddler he shot survived somehow. A graze, I think. I haven't read the latest round of legal papers to know for sure, and I stopped reading the *Mondauk Common* and the *Philadelphia Inquirer*. The seventeenth victim, a sixteen-year-old girl from South Carolina, hung on as long as she could, but finally died from her wounds earlier this week. She was the last of the massacre victims in intensive care—even the toddler has gone home. In the parking lot of the Roosevelt Mall, the sixteen-year-old's parents are holding a rally of some sort—Down with Guns, Our Baby's Gone Home to God, Fry the Fucking Monster—or maybe it's meant to be a memorial service. I don't know nor do I care. But I know that in order to be able to make the next move, any move out of this malaise, Shannon and I have to attend. More than that, we need to address the crowd. This, I know, will be my job. I'll be lucky to get Shannon out of the car.

"Here's the thing, Shannon: if you want me to turn the car around, I'll take the next exit. We'll go back to Owego and go on pretending that Joey's a normal kid just away at summer camp. That he doesn't have seventeen lives on his head. That if it weren't for the 2005 Supreme Court decision to no longer put minors to death, Joey (who I'm convinced planned this so it happened right before he turned eighteen) would be facing the death penalty for sure, with many of his victims' families hungry for blood justice, just waiting for the pellets to drop. Or we can go to this thing. Honor the girl. She had a name besides Number Seventeen, you know. Sabrina. Sabrina Estes. Joey's last victim. And the fingers are pointed at us. But we're as lost as they are."

I grip the steering wheel, and I stare at my skull-white knuckles and think of the bits of skull that must have flown around the Roosevelt Mall as Joey unleashed his barrage, crouching military style, it was reported.

"And we can tell them that, Shannon: that we're shattered and adrift too. I'll tell them. No big speech. I'll just talk a little. I'll tell them how sorry we are. I'll tell them we lost our child too, probably a long time ago. No, not in the permanent way they lost theirs, but Joey's gone, Shannon, just the same. He's gone." My voice breaks a bit. "And if parenting is to blame, bring it on, because it can't be any worse than the beatings we've inflicted on ourselves…and on each other."

Shannon hugs her chest, increasing her cleavage, and maybe for the first time, I don't want to jump her when she does that. I want her to wake up and smell the burnt coffee. I want her to wake up and smell all the blood. Because it's everywhere in our lives, and no amount of cleaning will remove the stains.

The traffic starts to move a little until finally we are crawling along at under ten miles an hour, but it's stop and start. Shannon has no reaction to my little speech about no big speech. I punch around the radio bands but give up quickly. Holy rollers it is. "And what did the Lord Jesus say to the Canaanite woman? He said, 'It is not right to take the children's bread and toss it to the dogs.'" What good would music—rock'n'roll music—do us now? Our days of dancing at the Empire to John Eddie and the Front Street Runners or seeing Southside Johnny and the Asbury Jukes down the Jersey shore are long behind us. Back then, just the sight of Shannon's heart-shaped bottom in a pair of tight jeans could make my teeth grind in anticipation of our end of the night festivities. I loved the way she smelled after a night out dancing to our favorite bands—not a drop of sweat on her brow, but somehow sweaty nonetheless, her dirty blonde hair darker at the edges, the scent of her perfume mixed with the smell of stale beer and cigarette smoke. We made love back then like we danced—desperate somehow, as if one of us might fall out of the bed, away and out of the survivor's life forever.

It is not good to take the children's bread and throw it to the dogs. *What the fuck does that even mean?* What are we in this (possible) metaphor? The children or the dogs? Joey is surely the taker.

It's a traffic teaser as we near fifteen miles an hour; it feels as if we'll hit twenty soon and be out of this mess. But as we approach the wreck—two cars so horrifically mangled, they barely resemble motor vehicles; one is almost upright—we slow way the hell down: this is the inner sanctum of the gaper's delay, the alpha and omega. No bloody hand sticking out this time, but a bloody head, its hair dangling and what might have been a face staring back at me, surrounded by exasperated and feverish paramedics and firemen, the latter attempting to cut the victim out of a car shaped like an accordion. The police begin setting up a screen to shield the rescue workers' efforts. They are a little late with that, I think; some cars screech to a dead stop when they see the head. I notice Shannon attentively watching the goings-on too. I wonder if this is what the mall looked like (minus the mashed cars) when our son was finished exercising his second amendment right. God bless the late Charlton Heston. I don't think even he could have parted Joey's red sea.

"We go, I say a few words, we shake a few hands, shake off a few looks, share a hug or two, maybe even deal with our fair share of foul words, but at least—"

Shannon is out of the car before I can react. Her seat belt slithers back into place, all tight and snug and ready for when she comes back. But I know Shannon's not coming back, not today, at least not willingly. First she runs towards the bloody head but is rebuffed by an alert state trooper. She turns and runs back up the highway, passes our car, and I watch her go over the guardrail and enter the woods from the rearview mirror.

"You okay, mister?" a cop asks, leaning towards my window.

"Yes, I'm fine, officer," I lie, gesturing with my thumb to the path Shannon took. "A little postpartum depression, I'm afraid." A thousand years ago, the condition was briefly the center of our universe; she was terrified to pick up the baby; now she was unafraid of our terrifying son.

The cop smells like Trident spearmint gum and gasoline.

"You have to keep moving."

Moving? "She'll be back. Probably peeing."

The cop frowns but backs away from the car and waves me on. I'm surprised when I notice that I've inched past the accident.

Someone honks and I touch the gas. I have no choice but to move. Traffic speeds up now. Twenty, thirty, forty miles per hour, faster. Fifty. Sixty-five plus. I am heading towards a public lynching perhaps, but maybe one I deserve. After all, I helped to create him, even if very little of myself rubbed off on Joey. And I'm not even sure why I'm going to Sabrina's parents' event. It's certainly not for me, or Shannon, or even Joey. It's not even really for Sabrina. Maybe it's just because in my old life, none of this has happened yet; the children eat their bread while the heels are thrown to the dogs (who swallow them whole), and everybody laughs and dances until their sweat is redolent with stale Michelob and cheap tequila

" 'For ye are yet carnal…' " a different radio preacher says.

I near an exit. Get off, turn around, and try to find Shannon or continue on to Sabrina's rally/memorial?

" '...for whereas there is among you envying, and strife, and divisions...' "

I'm heading south to Sabrina's family because it's the only way I can think of to escape the present, even if it means confronting the past—again.

" ...'are ye not carnal, and walk as men?' "

I punch the radio until it breaks and my knuckles are bloody, and I pass the exit, continuing along the only way home that I know.

-end-

Dilaudid Dreams

"Va-gi-na. Say it."

"Get off it, Sam. We didn't score. It's all fucked up. She's dead. I'm outta here."

"Right through the name tag. Dead as a doornail. You are some cowboy. And now you can't even look at my ginny, let alone say it."

"I'm not kidding. I'm leaving, Samantha. Dilaudid, Oxy they had. And we got shit. Who would have known—?"

"You prefer cock, that's it?"

"Yeah, Sam, I blow dudes in between knocking off drugstores."

"Say it with me, Stewart. 'I love cock.' Say it."

"You're twisted. A clerk—some girl, some innocent girl—is dead and you're—"

"Stewart—even your name is gay."

"My mother named me Stewart."

"Your *mother*. Not your father or your parents. Your *mother*. Definitely gay."

"I didn't see her. I just heard someone coming out of the little bathroom in the back. Neil said he checked the bathroom, but he was so fucking lit, he couldn't find his dick with both hands and a flashlight. I panicked. That was it—a moment of panic."

"Don't forget to pack your dildo."

"It's Neil's fault. He never checked the little bathroom. Too busy rifling the comic book rack or droolin' over the spank mags."

"And now Stewie can't get it up. Little Stewie's as balls-out scared as Big Stewie."

"Sam, she's dead. It's not robbery 1 here or even assault and battery."

"I know, dear. Right through her fucking name tag. *That* was impressive."

"Cheryl. Her name tag read 'Cheryl.' Or it did."

"Cornbread, corn-fed. Girl was backwoods. This is Amish land even if she wasn't."

"You're cold. She was a pretty young thing. Golden hair, cute face—"

"Big tits. Or should I say *tit*, since you kinda, sorta blew one away."

"You're distracting my packing. You should leave too. Get yourself straight."

"With you? On some methadone program in the city? Living off food stamps and each other's love? No thank you, sir. I already have a pussy. Don't need two."

"Suit yourself, Sam."

"In about a minute or so, I'm gonna suit myself just fine, don't you worry, mister. Dip into my stash, tie one off, and rub one out. You'll just be a pink fuzzy memory."

"So then you still have some of that Rex's Pharmacy stash left?"

"More than some, honey bun. My cut, anyway. Why? You want some, Big Stewie? You want mommy to get you off? Gotta needle here with your name on it."

"I'd take…I'd take a hit. If that's cool. I can always pack later."

"Come to mommy, then. Rest your head right here on my thighs. No, it's okay if you cry. She had golden hair and big tits and a name tag that read 'Cheryl.' A lot to cry about."

"Yes, it is."

"Make a fist."

-end-

Get Out, You Ghosts

Darren's body had been in the water for a little more than two hours, and the Puddle had yet to regurgitate their best friend. The sun had been a squint when they'd started, and now it was pitch dark.

"I can't see my hand in front of my face."

Jimmy lay on the dock, his arms crossed over his eyes.

"Yeah?" he replied.

"I can't even see the blood."

Jimmy watched her through the cross of his arms.

Miranda danced in front of him, her shadows large and mutated against the tree line, the music she danced to her own.

"You look like a ghost."

"*That* kind of night."

Miranda's shoulder-length red hair caught the light of the stars off Pennypack Creek, what everyone called the Puddle. Her shoulders were bare, and he could just discern the outline of her pert breasts. But it was her shoulders he stared at, her creamy white shoulders reflecting the moon back to itself.

For Miranda, the music came from deep inside. They were free of the threat of Darren and danger by association. So she danced. Darren would have told. She knew that. What they did was both necessary and right. Poor little Jimmy Ferdinand, all wracked with guilt. There was only one way to erase that kind of guilt, Miranda knew. Besides, she thought, it would sort of be nice to fuck Jimmy one last time before she dumped him.

"You look nice," he croaked.

She didn't answer, just kept dancing. Her arms still had blood on them. She'd washed her hands, but she'd forgotten to wash her arms.

"Miranda…I don't know if what we did…I don't know."

"What don't you know?"

She lowered herself over his body, squatting on his crotch. She pulled his arms down and pinned them easily on either side of his head. The whirring of the cicadas and the hooting of the owls overtook the music inside her brain.

"What are ya gonna do now, Big Jimmy Jim? Pinned to the mat."

Jimmy turned his head away.

"Awww, now you've gone and done it, Ferdinand."

She dangled a strand of drool above his chin, then sucked it back up.

Jimmy could feel her breasts on his chest as she leaned in, and he thought of all the nights (and mornings) they'd spent together before getting involved with Frannie Tidwell. Getting high was just part of the ritual: a little dope, a whole lot of sex, and no one got hurt, no one got drowned. If Darren wanted to score with them, then fine. More than enough to go around. Darren could be a weasel, always deeply in debt but ostentatious. Darren's family lived in the Paradise Lakes Trailer Park going on three generations. This deal had been Darren's way out—assuming he didn't turn around and blow it all on dope again. Or get himself killed.

Miranda pulled her blouse over her head. She hadn't worn a bra in about a year. Better to give her B-cups some breathing room. Jimmy was somewhere other than here. She'd grab his focus now. Her breasts stood up at attention and said hello. Her areolas were pinker than most. Jimmy had said they tasted like cotton candy. Now her nipples were harder than Jimmy was, but that was about to change.

"Put them in your mouth," she said.

And he did, a good boy, always following instructions, even when word came down from Mr. Foster through Frannie that Darren was a liability. Talking too much. Flashing too much shit. Attracting attention. Making demands on Frannie for more dope. Mr. Foster had said Darren had to be let go, and my God, didn't Jimmy's mouth feel so good right now. His whiskers scratching her breasts, his beer and whiskey breath heating up her chest. It had to be the two of them. Darren was too wily, too wiry. And the three of them had been like the Three Musketeers since grade school. Darren would trust them both.

"He trusted us, Miranda."

"Yes."

"He was our best friend. Now he's a ghost."

"Unfortunate."

"Our ghost," he added.

"He was going to squeal, Jimmy. Detective Finnerty already had him in for questioning—twice—and Finnerty works Homicide. They were just trying to scare him, and it was working, believe you me."

"Darren was our best friend."

"What you fail to understand," Miranda said as she took his cock out of his jeans—and oh boy he was hard as a rock now, "is that he was going to take you and me with him. Not just Frannie Five Fingers. *Fuck* Frannie. Us! The Dynamic Duo."

Jimmy was quiet, concentrating on Miranda's hand on his penis.

"I never want to grow up," he said finally. "I never want to leave Mondauk."

"Someone's getting euphoric all of a sudden. You pop something you didn't tell me about, Peter Pan? Well, let me tell *you* something: Never Never Land wasn't just Tinkerbell and the Lost Boys. There was Hook and Smee and some motherfuckin' crocodile."

"I never want to grow up," Jimmy repeated.

"Fine, never grow up then. Little boys don't come."

She removed her hand from his member. Jimmy looked like he was going to cry. She'd never get it done this way. She placed her palms on his chest. Jimmy's heart was beating a mile a minute.

"Jimmy, this isn't some coming of age novel. What did Mr. McNulty call it? A *bildungsroman*? Well, this ain't one of them. No one's coming of age in this story."

When it was all over, she'd go to work on Mr. Foster's train, and she knew what that meant but didn't care. From Mondauk County to Chinatown and other (unknown) points in Philly. Round trip. *Choo-choo!* She'd spread her legs before, and they liked 'em young. She would earn some money to go back and finish college. A couple of years in service and then out. It'd be like joining the Armed Forces, and she'd be under Mr. Foster's protection.

She was still straddling Jimmy when a bird flew overhead making a sound like a loon. Miranda instinctively hid her face in Jimmy's neck, which she lightly bit a few times. That had always worked before.

"I don't think I want to have sex," he said.

Miranda smiled into his neck. Too bad for him then. Just made her job that much harder though, the bastard. If she went for it while they were having sex, he would be like Silly Putty in her hands. Then again, he was pretty fucking high.

"Sexy-without-sex then," she suggested. "Like we used to do at your mom's, remember. Way back when. Cuddle close. Dry hump. Sexy-without-sex."

She stretched her body so that it covered his. They gently kissed.

"Sexy-without-sex," Jimmy said. "I almost forgot."

"Now's the time to remember everything."

"Do you think they'll find Darren's body?"

"Not for a few days. The Puddle's pretty swollen from all the rain we had. When they do, the fishies will have had their shot, and by the time they identify his body (and we both know his mother's too drunk to get off the couch for at least a week), his face will look like a BB target."

"He didn't see it coming."

"They never do."

She squeezed her body closer to his, a final burst of warmth. She did love him, or had once. Meth had made it harder to love, harder to say no to Mr. Foster.

"Sexy-without-sex," he said.

"Never coming of age," she replied.

Miranda grabbed his head by his ears and bashed it against the dock again and again until a pool of blood reflected the moon and made it appear like a halo around his head. It would have been nice to fuck him into submission, but he'd been too out of it to put up any kind of resistance, so it wouldn't have been much fun. With some effort, she dumped Jimmy's body into the Puddle. Miranda then took a pill and masturbated on the dock, careful to stay clear of the blood. Fuck Frannie Five Fingers. *Her* orders came directly from Mr. Foster. *Goddamn.* Her fingers moved slowly, as she listened to the cicadas and the owls and closed her eyes and dreamed of all the crystal and all the ex she would have. No boyfriends, no hangers-on, no goddamn police, and absolutely no ghosts.

"Get you, you ghosts," she whispered as she came. "Get out, you ghosts."

-end-

Twisted Jute

My father always locked their bedroom door even after we had gone through the mess of growing up and moving out. He would brush his teeth and floss methodically, rinse, and once finished with his nightly ablutions, put on his tattered robe over his night clothes, walk the few feet to my parents' bedroom, and lock the door behind him. He continued this practice long after the need for privacy had been removed. Mother had told me this one of the last times I saw her alive (and at least somewhat clearheaded), and the way she told me, it was as if she was conveying an important clue, a state secret. Of course, she was—I was too caught up in my own glamorous life to catch anything besides a cold.

My father had been an English professor. ("Earn every death," he would tell me repeatedly when going through my writings.) In a way, it made sense that in his twilight years, he became paranoid about what was out there in the dark. A lifetime of reading and writing and teaching literature had overstimulated his imagination. If he locked the bedroom door at night, he had his reasons, and who were we to question them? What he failed to understand was that whatever was in the dark, if anything, was inside the bedroom as well as out. Locking themselves in or preventing my mom from cracking the window for air were fruitless activities; the dark knew no boundaries and respected no impediments other than light, and the weak circles emanating from their reading lamps provided, I imagined, little safety in their glow. But Father would never replace the lamps; he told my mom years ago that any change could attract unwanted attention.

By this time, however, my father was a nattering shadow of his former self. The robe had become nearly a rag and rarely came off. He rubbed an antique Santa Claus ornament obsessively. "They don't seem to recognize jolly old Saint Nicholas right away," my dad explained, "but soon enough…" He was always using Mom's silver snuffer to extinguish the votive candles that lately she had me light and place around the house whenever the weather clouded over or when it started to get darker earlier. "I don't trust the dark," she told me. (Apparently it was a family thing.) "I don't trust what's in it," my father said of the darkness, "but I don't want this place to be a votive lighthouse. The candles aren't warding them off; they're advertising our fears. Not all light is good." So went what passed for conversation.

My mom was somehow less of a concern. Alzheimer's, for all its ugliness and despair, was at least a disease my siblings and I thought we understood because the neurologist had given it a name, one we were familiar with from the movies and such. When she was good, she was very good, if inelegant; when she was bad, she was a train wreck—shitty diapers, yellow drool, and stories of the living dead such as long gone Uncle Elmer and his predilection for cheating at cards or her recently departed sister's dalliance at a formal with a Puerto Rican boy when the girls had been in high school. In my mom's world, they (sometimes) were only a phone call away. For this and other reasons, we kept all phones out of her reach, even to the point of moving the kitchen phone, the one with the long tangled, squiggly cord, up a foot. (Mother was short and getting shorter.) Still, the envisioned risen were never far from her mind; even when she would, for a time, adapt the vocabulary of a developmentally challenged three-year-old, she would tell of how they scratched at her window at night, beckoning her to play.

This one afternoon, the afternoon she told me that my dad still locked their bedroom door at night, ritualistically blessing both sides of the knob with what she supposed was holy water, I was squeezing a lemon wedge into a cup of tea for her. (She had been trying to squeeze a cucumber slice.) "The last time that man was in church," my mother exclaimed, "Pikes Peak was a pimple!" While I waited for my own tea to cool, I straightened up some, a habit I carried over from my own house, as if my small efforts amounted to anything (here or at home). Two kids and a spouse deployed overseas led to too much housework and not enough free time; there was no such thing as catching up when I started out behind the eight ball, but I tried anyway. All this left very little time to write.

"He locks it every night," Mother said, already gulping her steaming hot tea. Despite the cucumber, this was a relatively good day. Her eyes were clear and her tongue was unmoored from its morass of monosyllabic hell.

I rescued a carpet base caster cup from the microwave and replaced it under the sofa leg.

"Like he's locking me in, Jules," Mother said, "or like he's locking something out."

I pulled an Ikea wrench out of the otherwise empty birdcage.

"What you need to worry about, Mom, is when he *stops* locking the door," I said, followed by, in my head: *because when he stops his silly, rigid, habits, Mom, that's when we'll know (or have a pretty good idea) that he's just like you, which might be less for us to worry about—at least we'll finally know what's wrong with him—but you'll find that you won't like the break in routine one damn bit.*

For lunch I made her a salad from the meager ingredients I found in their fridge and silently cursed Valerie. It was Val's job to do their food shopping. Such a simple job, but it was Frank or I who always ended up doing it. Val was too busy with Pilates, gallery openings, and "interesting men," as she put it. Without a steady job or a family of her own, Daddy's favorite would just smile and flounce her fake tits, tactics which worked pretty well in McCullough's tap room, I was sure, but which meant jack shit to me and, I was certain, our father. (That was Val's response to *anybody* concerning any and all iniquities, as well as requests that made her feel put-upon.) Regardless, Father's bank statement showed that he had been writing checks regularly to her for well over a year. Mother was devolving right before our eyes, but Val continued to play up her Daddy's girl role so her rent would be paid. She was forgiven as soon as she transgressed, her sins, like not buying the groceries, forgotten almost instantly by increasingly brittle brains. Evil didn't always come in the dark, I thought. (Was that a little harsh?) *There will come a reckoning, my sister, and a—*

Mother interrupted my revenge-on-Val fantasies by throwing a lima bean at me.

"I don't like lima beans, Suzy," she said, calling me by my dead sister's name, and as I was supposed to be Suzy's replacement (she died in her crib), it was understandable, considering the Alzheimer's, if not a little disturbing. "Blood, Suzy. Flesh of my flesh, blood's what I need to survive." Well, if that was her way of thanking her *flesh and blood* for taking care of her, I'd take it. Otherwise this statement didn't even merit a raised eyebrow.

She threw a lemon wedge at me. "He doesn't like it when I'm up and about during the daytime."

"Who?" I asked, playing along.

"*Him.* He Who Calls."

"Right. So not Dad," I said. "Aggressive telemarketer?"

"Your father is turning into a loon. Don't believe his voice."

"Right. Gotcha."

"Jolly old Saint Nicholas my ass." She stared at her tea as if wondering what happened to the lemon wedge; I didn't give it back to her.

After I had changed her diaper and dressed her in the lime green nightgown she liked, I put my mom back to bed and was busy cleaning the kitchen when my father's hand suddenly covered mine. I never even heard him shuffle in. He had the vegetable peeler in his other hand instead of Santa Claus. Probably found it in the tray of kitty litter Mother insisted on keeping in the basement, even though I hadn't seen Zaleska in months. I stifled a sigh.

"Can't ever leave this out," he said.

Not for the first time, I thought I should baby proof all the drawers except for the one with the basic utensils.

"She'll try to peel her fingers," he explained.

"For the blood," I responded.

My father's eyes sprang to life.

"Exactly. Exactly, Juliet," he said, and now I was really shocked. My father hadn't called me by my name in a number of years. (He never even called me Jules; he didn't call me anything.) It was as if he'd forgotten his baby girl, the one that survived, the one that wasn't Suzy. But here he was, eagerly agreeing with me, waving around a rusty peeler.

+

The next day the phone rang and it was my father. He had never called my house before. When I'd left home to marry Jim, my mother said I broke his heart, but I thought everything she said was suspect. When he retired, over my mom's objections, he had so many plans, he enthused, but what they were and what happened to them, I don't know. I'd see him shamble about their house, but that was it; he never even visited his grandchildren. (I used to bring them over but not anymore; too many questions and not many answers.) That my mother might be right about him being a loon bothered me more than my father not calling. In a lucid moment, was it possible she recognized her own neurodegenerative disease in my father? Ever since my mother started losing her marbles, that was the way I wanted her to stay; to see glimpses of the woman she'd been before was painful. Lucidity was ephemeral.

"Do you have any rope, Juliet?" my father asked, breathing heavily into the phone. "Some twine, something?"

There was a hint of desperation in his voice, enough of a hint to send me to the garage, where I found a roll of gardening twine, some twisted jute.

"Before the sun goes down, Juliet," my father whispered into the phone, and I made arrangements with the babysitter. When I pulled up outside of my parents' bungalow, there was still enough light in the sky to distinguish the shade of my green twine from the verdurous weeds alongside the walk that my brother Frank had never pulled.

My father yanked me into the house and shoved a roll of Scotch packing tape into my hand. I noticed that he had worn away Santa Claus' face.

"There isn't much time. We have to secure the room too—as well as your mother."

"Secure the room...? Secure *Mom*?"

"They've already gotten to her. I've been trying to lock them out for years, but your mother opened the bedroom window after I'd fallen asleep, and that was it. Tonight she will rise, and she'll be hungry. She'll want her blood."

"Dad...?"

But somehow the sorrow in his eyes, which were like pools of fetid water, reached me. Didn't Dr. Solomon say of Mother that sometimes we had to play along with the fantasies? That it was easier than trying to break her mind of something she was totally convinced was the Bible truth? (Or did I make that up in my head?) I figured the same went for my dad even if he didn't have Alzheimer's—yet. As long as it didn't go too far, I was in. My father didn't know or had never realized it, but I was the offspring who was always in.

"Okay, what first?"

He produced a tape measure from his threadbare robe.

"First we measure the bedroom door." Which I did. Mom was snoring gently in bed, the covers pulled right up to her chin. Father patted the door lightly. "For stakes, if we need them," he said as he left the room. That was when I noticed the little-used axe in the corner.

For stakes. Right.

My dad returned from the kitchen with a bunch of garlic braids. Using some twine and rusty nails, we hung the plants around the door frame.

"Bind your mother's hands. Use the twine. Only use the tape if you feel the twine's not strong enough. She won't wake until it's time."

Well, I wasn't going to use tape to bind my mother, that much I knew for sure. The twine would suffice. *She won't wake until it's time.* I had no idea what that meant, but with all the medications she took, I figured she slept the sleep of the dead anyway and probably wouldn't wake up as I bound her and she didn't.

"Her feet too," my father instructed, and I did as I was told, pulling down her blanket and sheet. I was even giggling a little, as if this was some schoolgirl prank. I didn't know what came next, but I expected holy water would be in order, some incantations in Latin perhaps, a crucifix to the forehead. Then Mother would be cured— or, more importantly, Father would be. Dr. Solomon would have to be told of all this, of course, and my dad's medications would need to be reevaluated. But if a little ceremony allayed whatever ailed Father's mind, so be it. The green twine matched nicely with the trim of Mom's nightgown.

The worn Saint Nick ornament was placed on her neck, which was when I first noticed that my mom had a hickey.

"It takes a little while for them to turn," my dad said.

I suppressed a smile. I wanted to tell him: *it would fade quicker if you put a spoon in the freezer for a bit, then place it on the love bite.* But I kept my high school remedies to myself.

When the sun went down, my father told me to move back, move away.

I giggled again despite the seriousness of his tone.

When Father took the ice pick out of his robe, its point was stuck in a wine cork. He pulled it off and handed the cork to me, as if I was at some fancy restaurant and he was the eccentric sommelier. I focused on the cork and forgot about the ice pick. I covered my mouth, trying to catch my mirth before it dispelled the solemnity. (I was only semi-successful.) I smelled the cork and declared it a vintage bottle of AB positive.

Then the ice pick flashed in the moonlight (I guffawed at the cliché, but that was how I saw it, I told them later), and Father plunged it into my mother's chest, where it vibrated slowly, the last traces of maybe my last genuine guffaw fading as the vibrations seemed to increase for a moment before dying away, then suddenly going still. Then it was just my dad and me and my mom and this ice pick stuck in the middle of her chest. After the rattle and the throes, she just died and didn't turn to dust when she did. (No, it was much worse.) My father—the former English professor not the geriatric Van Helsing—would have said that the whole incident, on paper, was tired and melodramatic and more than a tad macabre. And maybe it was. But it was real. The ice pick *had* flashed in the moonlight, just like in the goddamn movies. I saw the reflection of my little gold crucifix pendant in the ice pick before it entered my mother, but that was just a projection of my guilt, they explain. They say an ice pick is far too slim to be able to produce a reflection I would be able to see in detail, but I have a feeling that what was left of me at that moment would have fit. Figments of my overactive writer's imagination, a doctor told me at our last session, not for the first time. But were my mother's sibilant screams, brief gnashing, and conflagrant final convulsions simply projections? Figments? I think not. But they keep reminding me that an ice pick isn't a wooden stake. This is true, but still… We didn't set her on fire. They suggest that Father had knocked over a votive candle. Not likely—he usually kept the silver snuffer in one of the pockets of his robe—but I was starting to learn to keep things to myself. I know what I think I know, and I saw what I think I saw, but I have no doubt as to what I *believe*. I don't even want to think about where the flames came from—there isn't an answer that doesn't make me want to fall upon a bed of ice picks.

The police and the court and the jury saw the whole incident quite differently than I did. Even the psychiatrists were hard-pressed to explain what they couldn't possibly understand. My father and I were tried (separately) and convicted.

Dramatic density, my father once told me, occurs when a boatload of action is packed into a short period of time. And dramatic density was my only defense. It happened too, too fast: my transformation from harried housewife to fearless vampire killer transpired merely in the length of time it took for my father to say my name.

But I don't ever need to worry about locking my bedroom door; it is locked for me every night with a clang. And every night I imagine I am sleeping with my crucifix on the outside of my prison garb, because they are so everywhere, even if you can't see them, and there's never enough twisted jute.

-end-

The Werther Effect

At Father Hoskins High, the girls' uniforms were blue, and Fontaine Black drove a fire engine red sports car. I bring up these facts only to highlight the brilliance under which the circumstances of this story took place. Blue like the inside of a new bruise. Red like type O positive. And black like the Puddle at midnight—which is where and when Stacey Dorf, the last of the Idol Ideation Girls, bought it. I'm not sure whether the *Mondauk Common* or the *Philadelphia Inquirer* coined the name Idol Ideation Girls; regardless, it was used casually by both. Those witty writers, these jocular journalists, they should have known better. Ideation is defined as "the capacity for or the act of forming or entertaining an idea." Suicidal ideation is the psych term for thoughts about suicide. But none of the so-called Idol Ideation Girls achieved membership in that exclusive club because they just *thought* about suicide. They became members because they actually went through with it (although, despite their moniker, how much they actually thought of their idol during their last exit was debatable). All in all, seven girls from Father Hoskins High School in Mondauk County killed themselves over Fontaine Black, or claimed him as their sole motivation, but only two of them actually knew Fontaine, knew him in any real sense. (In a medium-sized high school in the suburbs, everybody sort of knows everybody.) The papers got it mostly wrong. Oh, I'm sure there'd been a lot of *thinking* on the first two girls' parts, the girls who'd actually known Fontaine, before they took their own lives, but for the others that followed, thinking had very little to do with it, I'm convinced. What the papers concentrated on were the colors of bruises and blood; the blue of our uniforms and the red of Fontaine's car were just lurid background. Black was usually how they painted Fontaine. However, if black is all the colors mixed together and white is the absence of all color, Fontaine fell somewhere in between (like most of us). But he never held the palette; he was painted with brushes not his own.

The reason Fontaine Black is dead is not because he loved the wrong girl (or girls) or didn't love the right one (from someone else's point of view). Fontaine isn't dead because he used girls either; Fontaine didn't belong to the Four F club (find 'em, feel 'em, fuck 'em, and forget 'em). No, Fontaine is buried beneath six feet of grave backfill and worms because he loved *all* girls—it is also safe to say all the girls at Hoskins High loved him right back. In fact, he had them falling at his feet. That's not to suggest that Fontaine made love to the suicidal seven (he only dated the first two and those only briefly); it just means that Fontaine was girl crazy, like the teenage boy he was and should have been. Girls thrilled him, maybe even scared him. He told me once he frequently popped wood in class if a girl's skirt moved and he saw a flash of thigh. But Fontaine was never fresh, never out of line. Not one person with whom I've ever spoken has disputed this. The papers created his Valmont image, but those who knew him know that he was as awkward around girls one-on-one as he was Joe Cool around everyone else.

Maybe around boys Fontaine spun tall tales. Maybe those tales were the ones that made it to the newspapers. But all I ever heard were rumors of rumors. No boy ever told me that Fontaine had done this with that girl or pulled that with this girl. 'Course it's quite possible no one told me these things because I'm a girl. It could have been out of some misplaced respect for my gender or because of my relationship with Fontaine (if the teller knew one existed), but more than likely it was because there was a tiny fear, planted, in part, by the papers, that in telling me, I could end up putting stones in my pockets and walking into Pennypack Creek, à la Adeline Woolf, or sticking my head in an oven, like our poetic Ariel, "Victoria Lucas." Fat chance. Fontaine only *really* dated one girl—"dated" as in going out, being pinned (as our parents would say), going steady, boyfriend-girlfriend: me.

Even in grade school, I wanted to become a writer, and Fontaine used to tell me that I should write his life story someday. He was cool as a cucumber even back then. So unlike Virginia or Sylvia, I stuck around, if for no other reason than to set the story straight. (Not to mention that I don't have a suicidal bone in my body—some people are just wired differently. Still, if anyone should commit suicide in the wake of all this, it should be me, but even just writing that makes me seem like the most important girl in Fontaine's life, and I don't want the onus. I have my own cross to bear.)

Fontaine cruised through life oblivious to issues of race, poverty, or to someone being too ugly or socially backwards to have a date on Saturday night. About the only difficulty I remember Fontaine ever having involved his name. (Okay, yes, Fontaine wasn't exactly an A student, and he needed my help with his algebra and science homework in high school, but somehow he always managed to slide through—*muddling* through wasn't Fontaine's style.) Fontaine's mother had died when he was very little (he barely remembered her), and his father had regressed into a party animal. Fontaine's father loved drugs and women and sometimes men; that he held onto a job was either a minor miracle or a testimony to the man's constitution. He bought Fontaine the fire engine sports car to help his son, he said, "get quality pussy." Mr. Black was diagnosed with AIDS some time after Fontaine's death, as if his son, so Fonzie cool, had been the anchor preventing him from slipping into a deeper dark.

Fontaine's mother had named her son (her only child) after the actress Joan Fontaine. His mother's favorite movie had been Hitchcock's *Rebecca*, his father told him. She was crazy about the movies. Joan Fontaine was her second favorite actress. Ingrid Bergman was her first, but she couldn't very well name her son Ingrid (or Bergman for that matter). So she named him Fontaine. His father told him if baby names had been discussed, he didn't remember, and to top it off, he went on a bender after the boy's birth that lasted long enough for him to miss the christening. How Fontaine's mother was able to have her son baptized in the Roman Catholic Church with a name like Fontaine remained a mystery. (This was before the change in Canon Law in the early '80s.) Maybe she lied or slipped the pastor an extra couple of twenties. From the photographs I've seen, she was quite beautiful (a female version of Fontaine); maybe she simply flirted her way to the font. It stands to reason that even priests can sometimes be bought by a pretty smile and a generous eyeful of décolletage. But in Catholic school, Fontaine's name became an issue, a big issue. We were supposed to be named after saints. ("Like a cult," my mother said. Her anti-Catholic bias was never explained to me nor was the reason why she continued to send me to Catholic school.) There were thousands of saints to choose from and even a book, *Lives of the Saints*, to page through and help speed along the new parents' decision. The nuns were livid over Fontaine's name. It happened in every grade and only subsided in high school where there were fewer nuns and more priests and lay teachers. Priests were busy saying Mass and administering the sacraments, in addition to teaching; they didn't have the time to worry if there was a Saint Fontaine or not, or maybe they just didn't care. And *lay* teachers, Fontaine and I used to joke, were busy getting *laid*. (Well, it was funny back in high school.)

One tough bird in Assumption of Our Lady Elementary School, one-eyed Sister Agatha (who wore glasses with no lens on the right side and a thick Coke bottle lens on the other), made Fontaine's name a topic of many religion classes. It was as if every time she heard his name, it was for the very first time, and as her patron saint had maintained her devotion to God despite having to endure the rack, repeated rapes, and having her breasts cut off with pincers by the Romans, Sister Agatha did not suffer fools gladly, and in Fontaine, she faced off against one whose very appellation defined foolishness.

Once, Sister Cyclops (as we all called her—behind her back, of course) asked Fontaine, "*What* is your middle name?" as her gnarled, old hands clutched a blue yardstick, her weapon of choice.

I cringed and covered my face with my hands.

Fontaine leaned back in his seat and stretched his legs, as if he was at home getting ready to watch some TV after dinner. "Archer."

"*Archer!*" Sister Agatha screeched, her face a disturbing shade of red. She swung the blue yardstick wildly (her vision being compromised), hitting Joey Haverty in the nose. (More red.) "Archer! Is there a Saint Robin Hood I'm not aware of?"

But the outlaw hero had not been Fontaine's mother's inspiration. His middle name came from Newland Archer, one of the central characters in Edith Wharton's *The Age of Innocence*, her favorite novel. "Have you ever read it?" I asked Fontaine years later when we were at Finch's Landing, dangling our feet into the Puddle (which is what everyone called Pennypack Creek, for it often smelled like a fetid puddle). He took off his shirt and used it as a pillow. (I avoided looking at his chest.) "Nope. You read it," he suggested. "Tell me if Newland's cool or if I have to go back to Sherwood Forest." He smiled. "Sister Cyclops would have been surprised that I knew Sherwood Forest."

"You watched the Disney movie."

He shrugged. "Walt knows all. Just because a singing cock told the story doesn't mean it's not true."

The narrator of the film was indeed a rooster. But back in grade school, information based on animated poultry would have meant little, for the whole name thing appeared to be have been stuck in Sister Agatha's craw, and she soon emerged with the information that there was indeed a saint with the name Fontaine— sort of. St. Marie Magdalen Fontaine, a martyr guillotined during the French Revolution. The nun spent the rest of the school year calling my best friend Marie, which didn't seem to rile Fontaine one iota. He would often correct the nun. "Marie *Magdalen*," he would say, "if you don't mind, Sister," which sent the yardstick swinging every time. Joey Haverty, who unfortunately sat near Fontaine, never quite learned to when to move out of the way and was thus often on the receiving end of the wooden yardstick. Joey's mother eventually complained, and he switched seats with Greg Myers, a soccer player with great reflexes, who managed to avoid any collateral damage by ducking or shuffling his desk back just far enough to only feel the parting of the air.

Fontaine Archer Black was what one would call a looker. He had jet black hair that he let grow long in the summer. His bangs sometimes fell into his eyes, which were large and so brown they were almost black. Fontaine smiled often; he was mirthful, but his smile also opened doors that others found locked; it could have opened legs too had he so chosen. And dimples! My Lord! When he smiled, they sprang up, an unexpected pleasure, even if you grew up with him like I did; his dimples were never less than a surprise. I once put a finger inside one, and his smooth skin seemed to undulate; his dimple tickled the tip of my finger.

"That's how much I love you," he said. "Even my dimples want to kiss every inch of you."

Fontaine and I went out; we were boyfriend and girlfriend for seven months, which is a long time in high school reckoning. We were only freshmen, so I shouldn't have expected it to last, and it didn't. But while it did, it was glorious. We'd always been friends. Our mothers had been classmates a long time ago, and my mom, starting when I was in second grade, made a point of escorting me across the street and down to the end of the block to the Black house, so I could ask Fontaine if he'd like to come swim in our aboveground pool or play checkers. My mother usually walked me all the way to his door. By third grade, she would take me as far as his front walk; she wanted me to knock on my own—I was extremely shy; even trick-or-treating was an exercise in surrender to my mother's social wishes. (Once, when I when I was older, I went over to Fontaine's house by myself, and Mr. Black answered the door in the buff; he led me in, and while I waited for Fontaine to come down, he sat in a chair opposite me, finished rolling a joint, and proceeded to smoke it, while absently fondling his balls.) My mother impressed upon me early on that Fontaine could have it rough growing up without a mom (and without, she would tell me when I was older, a *real* father, one not immersed in narcotics and sex). But after the initial awkwardness that kids feel when forced together by parental decree, Fontaine and I became fast friends, inseparable even, a difficult feat considering the quick lines of division drawn between boys and girls early on in grade school. But those lines meant nothing to Fontaine and me; we regularly crossed into enemy territory and continued to have sleepovers until late in elementary school. As we grew older, we'd have marathon Stratego sessions late into the night or throughout the afternoon, sometimes laying on our stomachs in the Christmas sweaters my mom had made or even in our pajamas; other times out on our deck, we'd play while roasting under the summer sun, he in his swim trunks and me in my one piece. The sleepovers ended one night when one of us, I forget who, suggested strip Stratego. Neither of us objected, as I remember, and I had just removed my pajama bottoms when my mom entered the room. Not only were sleepovers outlawed right then and there, we never took the game off the shelf again.

(My mother sat me down—my father had passed when I was in the second grade, so Fontaine and I were in the same camp to some extent—and explained what boners were after Fontaine showed me his when we were drying off on the deck after a swim. My mother had been within earshot; she'd even caught a glimpse of Fontaine's engorged member when she ran into the kitchen and stuck her head out the back door to ask if we wanted any iced tea to cool us off. My mother said two things that I remember. One was that boners were what happened when boys—men, usually— grew excited at the sight of a pretty girl and wanted to have sex with her, which seemed both absurd and somehow perfectly reasonable to me. The second thing she said was that most boners I would encounter later in life wouldn't be as big as Fontaine's and that I should just forget all about what I saw unless I wanted to live the rest of my life in disappointment. And it was true: Fontaine was extremely blessed in that area, even as a late grade-schooler. I still remember it as the biggest boner I ever saw.)

Fontaine and I walked home together from school. We accompanied each other to the eighth grade dance. We traded books and records. I helped him with his homework, and he helped me be cool just by being around me. With Fontaine's help, I transcended factions. The Bod Squad was the reigning chick clique in Assumption and later in Hoskins, but they gave me a wide berth. They were jealous of me. I did Fontaine's math homework, and he shielded me from class warfare. All the boys wanted to be him, insouciant and laid back; they'd even affect Fontaine's easy, first-thing-in-the-morning drawl. All the girls wanted to be in my place; they assumed, wrongly, that we were an item (pre-freshman year). I used to think: if they'd only seen his boner! All the Bod Squaders would either faint or run for cover!

Falling for each other as freshmen, in retrospect, only seemed natural: hormones in overdrive, our close proximity, the glimpses of thigh or chest that a year before had meant little or nothing, now, for some strange reason, meant everything and kept us up at night touching ourselves, we would later admit to each other, in ways we hadn't quite mastered until then. I wish I could write that our seven months together were less than incredible. I know that was what the local TV news wanted to hear when they sent that nosy female reporter, Cox McGowan—the one the boys all called Cock and Balls—to our school and then to my house over and over until my mother threw an egg at the newswoman's cameraman (or, rather, his camera), missed, the messy yolk landing *splat* in Cock and Balls' carefully coifed, dyed-blonde hair. Once they found out I was Fontaine's first (and truly *only*) girlfriend—although somehow that *only* part proved elusive to Ms. McGowan and the writers from the *Common* and the *Inquirer*—they all wanted to interview me, but they just wanted to hear was what a terrible time it was. And it wasn't terrible at all. It was, as we called it, friendship plus. We did the same things we had done the year before in the eighth grade, but now we kissed. We rolled around. We brushed by parts that only recently we had never actively thought about. (The boner incident aside.) The summer before high school began, Fontaine and I started a little dance that began in

June during our first swim of the year—somehow the sight of each other in our bathing suits aroused us in ways we had hardly imagined possible—and continued throughout July and August. We held hands while we watched the Fourth of July fireworks in the Common. While taking turns diving off the pier at Finch's Landing, we smooched, briefly, in the water, the muck of the Puddle cutting our kiss short as we each became acutely aware of how bad our upper lips smelled. When we started high school, hand holding became the norm, and our courtship ended and our romance began. Sleepovers were out (my mother's rule; Fontaine's father couldn't have cared less), but we spent many, many nights lying in my backyard, looking at the stars, making out, occasionally putting a hand under each other's clothes, but nothing of major interest ever happened. It was tentative exploration, that was it. Neither of us ever undressed. There was no oral contact, not even mouth on breast. There were no orgasms—at least not while we were together. We went to dances as a couple, and our friends all said we would marry someday and that Fontaine would have beautiful children (somehow forgetting that I would not only be a factor in their genetic makeup but would be the one pushing out the kids).

Why it ended, I still don't know, but the ending seemed natural and right at the time and still sort of does. Sort of. We had known each other almost all our lives; there was very little, except for sex, that was still a mystery between us. That was it, wasn't it: there wouldn't be enough mysteries left, for I like to think now that it was sex that broke us up; after ten months of making out and very minor petting sessions, the next logical step would have been to have sex, or at least for me to give him blowjobs and such. (The male orgasm taking precedent in such matters, or so I'd heard.) Somehow, I tend to think now, that idea repelled us as much as it attracted us. I think Fontaine was fixated on the sin aspect of making love to me. (Not that he was incredibly Catholic, but one cannot go through nine years of Catholic school without having some of their dogma rub off.) Plus I believe he thought that doing *anything* would mean reaching the end of our mysteries and that he would also be breaking a taboo established by our long friendship. Me, I was ready to be broken, but I too was concerned at that possible lack of mystery. When our romantic relationship ended, gently, like a passing thing, he said, "You know, I think we should date other people when we're sophomores, starting in the summer even." I passively agreed and reluctantly rehooked my bra. Yes, it's true: I would have continued going out with Fontaine if he had let me; I would have been his girlfriend until I was his fiancée then his wife. However, from what I gathered in my mother's magazines (my sole source for relationship advice), he would need time in between there somewhere to sow the oats each young man is damn near bursting to sow—and I wasn't the candle in the window type of girl, I told myself.

The next day, our first day no longer boyfriend and girlfriend, Fontaine showed up at my door with a bunch of flowers and his swim trunks in one hand, two Yoo-hoos in the other as if nothing had happened. The flowers were the only indication that we had broken up, a consolation prize; he had never bought me flowers before, and when my mother saw them she asked me immediately when we had split up. But I was no torch holder, I told (lied to) myself. I promptly went out and lost my virginity to Damian Tyler, who promptly went around and told the whole school what a lousy lay I was. (And I was; I cried the whole time— as much from the physical pain as from the fact that it wasn't Fontaine huffing and puffing away on top of me while my mother was at work.) Fontaine punched Damian in the mouth so hard that Fontaine had to go to the emergency room for stitches. Of course, that didn't help my dating situation: not only was I known as a lousy lay, but everyone thought that Fontaine still had a thing for me. Plus the situation marked me as easy, which, after it became clear that I was no longer Fontaine's girl, made getting dates a breeze, but then it was either put out or shove off. I hated high school.

Fontaine took out a few girls during our sophomore year. (He'd exited the summer at least two inches taller, and his arms and chest evidenced the positive results of a strict workout regimen, although I doubted he'd grown into his penis.) We even doubled once, but it was so awkward that we both decided to never try it again, although we would go to parties and dances together with dates but always as part of a group—Fontaine's group; I didn't have one myself in high school. But the first filly that was officially announced as a girlfriend (at least she announced her status as such, but she wasn't a *true* girlfriend like I'd been) was Joanna Kilpatrick. Joanna was a wispy thing, small, skinny, no breasts to speak of, flat hair, but a face that could even make girls take a second look.

Joanna had large green eyes and a very adult way of holding herself, as if her body and her current station (she was a freshman) were but placeholders while she awaited her coronation as an adult, destined, I'm sure she thought, for great things. But I always had the feeling that Joanna would skip college (or at least breeze right through it) and land on the back stoop, trading gossip over the fence with the other young mothers. It wasn't that Joanna looked like or acted like a girl who wanted to be kept, but her mannerisms and such were far closer to the parade of young mothers pushing strollers in the early afternoon than to anyone my age. (And, yes, I was becoming cynical about marriage and motherhood, twin cages that I thought would never hold me, which is funny in a sad kind of way since all I wanted was to be held.)

Joanna was always very nice to me. That I was Fontaine's best friend was an accepted fact, and she didn't see me as a threat. That was not to say she treated me like one of her girlfriends either, but just as a casual friend, or rather, a new acquaintance. I liked her despite not wanting to. (I never really knew her before her appearance at Fontaine's side, where she seemed to come up only to his rib cage.) Fontaine told me, after Joanna was dead, that they had had sex. It wasn't very good, Fontaine said, but my inner glee at his lack of satisfaction (I probably should have been mourning) was quickly dampened.

"She was so...*small*, you know," Fontaine said.

I nodded, knowing how the story was going to end.

"Tiny. And, I'm, well...so I hurt...it hurt her."

He looked distraught, which, I was sure, had as much to do with the painful sex as Joanna's early demise and his perceived role in her death.

"She didn't cry though. I mean, tears came out, but she didn't make a sound, just told me to keep going, that sometimes it hurts at first is all, she'd heard. So I did, and when it was over, she rolled up into a ball and held her middle. There was blood on the sheets."

I nodded. I was familiar with the blood on the sheets initiation, if not the extreme pain of Fontaine's member.

"I just hate to think...we only did it that one time...I had to break it off. I couldn't stand to think that all the rest of the times would be like that first one. I wasn't trying to be a member of the Four F club. I just didn't want to hurt her anymore."

Fontaine was quiet for a time, and I let him be.

"We just didn't fit," he whispered eventually.

Joanna Kilpatrick swallowed about fifty over-the-counter sleeping pills with half a bottle of vodka mixed with Fresca. Word was that when her parents found her the next morning—she hadn't gotten up for school, so her mom went to wake her—there was foam all around her mouth and on her pillow. Her suicide note, a flowery thing whose contents were passed around the school by a less-than-trustworthy friend of Joanna's (her parents had shared its sad poetry with the girl's inner circle), implicated Fontaine as the root of all her sadness.

> If tomorrow i lay myself down
> Upon my pillow of
> purple satin
> And give myself over to Beauty
> Will You still love
> me?

I shit you not. That was what she wrote, random capitalization and all. She went on, in her brief introduction of the poem and in her postscript, to name Fontaine as the murderer of love. The last words she wrote were, "You weren't too big, my love. I was too small."

Joanna's death sparked an assembly dedicated to teen suicide, as well as a Mass in her honor. I wondered how they could hold a Mass for her if suicide was a mortal sin, but Mary O'Connell told me that Father Dave said to Mrs. Kilpatrick that he was listing Joanna's death as an accident.

People looked at Fontaine a little differently after that—students *and* teachers—but like most everything else in high school, this too passed. (In high school, things either stuck forever, like the perception that I was an easy lay, or were sucked up by the undertow of more pressing concerns like dating, exams, after school jobs, and college applications.) But even when things were at their roughest for him, Fontaine found no paucity of female companionship. (Not counting me, of course—I'm referring to a different kind of female companionship.)

One afternoon Fontaine and I ditched our last classes, and we hung out in my house while my mom was at work, the shades pulled down and the curtains closed so that the living room was dark. We played my mom's old records—Simon and Garfunkel, the

Moody Blues, the Beatles' *White Album*—and sipped from the liquor bottles she kept in the side table cabinet. We tried peach schnapps and Old Grand-Dad and some kind of rye. It didn't take much to get us pleasantly lit. Forgetting about the clock, we fell into a lazy, hazy conversation about everything under the sun: the latest music videos, the meanest nuns, pimples, peeing in the shower. Finally, emboldened by the mixture of various kinds of alcohol (I had never drank before), I asked Fontaine if I could see it.

He giggled. "See what?" He mimicked blowing out smoke. He'd just told me he wanted to take up smoking to look cooler—as if that were possible.

> *Nights in white satin*
> *Never reaching the end*
> *Letters I've written*
> *Never meaning to send*

I leaned my head back in his lap and peered down his long legs.

"Your thing," I said.

"My *thing*?"

I rolled my head so it leaned against his crotch.

"Oh," he said, growing hard beneath my cheek, "*that* thing."

I sat up. "Show it to me."

> *Beauty I'd always missed*
> *With these eyes before*
> *Just what the truth is*
> *I can't say anymore*

He started to unzip, then stopped. "Is this a good idea? I mean…"

I pulled his zipper down the rest of the way and pulled at his pants. "I want to see the mean, not-so-lean, killing machine."

Fontaine's face turned as dark as his last name. "That's not funny."

My face was warm—and crimson, I was sure. "I'm sorry…I didn't…"

> *'Cause I love you*
> *Yes, I love you*
> *Oh, how I love you*
> *Oh, how I love you*

"Nights in White Satin" was playing so loud that my mother entering the house and closing the door behind her were noises we never heard, and we were so buzzed, we never noticed her standing ten feet away.

"Why are you home? Is that...? Hello Fontaine. Have you...have you been drinking? Is that...?"

During my mother's questioning and greeting, Fontaine and I jumped up, and, predictably, Fontaine's pants, already unzipped and pulled down a little, fell to ankles, taking his underwear with it. I didn't see his penis, but my mother got her second eyeful. It shook her so that she stopped asking questions and had me make her a stiff drink. Fontaine had yanked his pants up and skedaddled.

"It was like a baby's arm," was all my mother said. "He grew up."

At the time, I thought it was ironic that Joanna Kilpatrick committed suicide when Fontaine had broken up with her because his baby arm didn't fit into the very place from where a baby's arm (and the rest of a baby) was supposed to come out. Maybe I was just being mean. Joanna had wanted a baby (she'd told everyone this), maybe even Fontaine's, but she couldn't take his baby arm.

Kerry Meadows was next, and I knew Kerry would have no problem handling a baby's arm. My mother said she thought Kerry could handle a whole bar full of sailors' baby arms, but that was just a mother's first impression, and Kerry wasn't the best first impression visually, which was too bad because she was nice as pie, funny, excitable, with dimples that almost matched Fontaine's. Kerry was what my mother called a "big girl," but she wasn't fat. My late grandmother would have called her "big-boned," which might have been a more appropriate description. Kerry was tall and her hips were a tad wide, her ass too. I never saw her in a bathing suit (Kerry was a fall and wintertime "girlfriend"), but I imagined that she must have had very large thighs. Still, Kerry was extremely pretty, and after a series of semi-chaste dates, according to Fontaine, they decided they were ready for the real thing. We were juniors now, and Joanna Kilpatrick was an unfortunate incident in the past. (It had taken Fontaine some time to get firmly back in the saddle.) Even the yearbook memorial page was anemic. Mary O'Connell told me that Rena Jennings wanted to include a copy of Joanna's suicide note (Rena claimed to have a photocopy of the actual document), but Mrs. Anderson, the nervous yearbook moderator and English teacher, almost fainted at the suggestion and had to be helped into a chair by Jerry the germophobe and art editor, who scrubbed his hands raw afterwards (They'd been under Mrs. Anderson's armpits.) What memorial there was consisted of three pictures, one of which was so blurry and out of focus it could have been my right thumb, and a Biblical verse that seemed to have no connection to Joanna, her manner of death (which I guess was now officially *not* suicide), or her inability to be the right fit. But Kerry Meadows, Fontaine told me, was a *good* fit, if a bit roomy. I thought, for you? But what did I know about anyone else's anatomy? I knew very little about my own. My sexual knowledge wasn't deepened until the night of my junior prom when a nice boy with very bad breath showed me what my clitoris was capable of accomplishing. Although I loved the feeling when he touched it (how I wriggled!), I loved it more because I had only been vaguely aware what of it was for or what it could do. (I usually caught up on my non-scholastic reading—*A Confederacy of Dunces*, Robert A. Heinlein, Jack Kerouac—during Health class.)

Kerry Meadows lasted a little longer than three months. As lovely and effervescent as her personality could be, Kerry proved to be as clingy as a koala. Fontaine couldn't leave to take a pee without Kerry trying to follow him. At first it was cute (or at least Fontaine thought it was; it made me want to barf until all my insides were outside), but soon it became an embarrassment. A trip to the bathroom during a dance would prompt a litany of questions upon his return, a real third degree, as he dried his hands on his pants (an endearing habit that seemed to drive Kerry and the late Joanna to distraction). Who did he see on the way back and forth to the john? What *exactly* did he do in there? Who else was in the bathroom? Did he stop to talk to anyone—any *girls*, Kerry meant—during his journey? If so, who? And why? What did he or she say? How long did the conversation last? If it was a girl, did she touch him, even squeeze his arm? All this would inevitably lead to her drilling Fontaine on who did what to whom sexually in his relationship with Joanna Kilpatrick, an obsession of Kerry's, never mind that her perceived rival was six feet under and no longer sexually active.

Fontaine broke up with her shortly after the holidays, and Kerry's parents found her hanging from the ceiling fan the very next day, a note pinned to her shirt. ("That must have been one strong ceiling fan," my mother commented, eyeing our perpetually broken one.) Kerry was no poet (not that Joanna was, but Joanna wrote for the school literary magazine). Still, she gave it the ol' college try; Kerry was not one to be outdone by her predecessor.

When evening settles on the snow
And teardrops glisten in the moonlight
Near your eyes; The darkness comes
When love just can't be found
Like a blossom on the water
It will bring me down
Like a flawless blossom on the water
I'll begin to drown

I found myself singing the words to the melody of Simon and Garfunkel's "Bridge over Troubled Water." And the part about "a *flawless* blossom on the water," well, one gander at Kerry Meadows' wide spread should invalidate that line, I thought, somewhat unkindly. But dead was dead. Fontaine had managed it again: he'd picked another wackjob, another lithium lady. It wasn't funny; I knew that then and I know it now, but there was something insanely humorous or maybe just plain inane about Kerry's self-departure. It wasn't just the fuzzy focus poem. Kerry had hung herself using a rope made up of Fontaine's school ties that she'd nicked and knotted together with part of a ripped sheet to strengthen it—at least that was what I heard. (The other rumor was that the sheet had been the one upon which Fontaine and Kerry had first made love; according to a couple of Kerry's waggish friends, the poor girl had saved the sheet, unwashed, in a trash bag in her closet.) So maybe it wasn't humorous as much as it was pathetic. "Had to be some *strong* ties," my mother said as she mixed herself a drink. "Anything less and that cow would still be a-mooing."

However one looked at Kerry Meadows' demise, the effect on Fontaine was devastating. I swear his hair started to fall out. He lost easily ten pounds. His strut was replaced by an uneasy run-walk with frequent glances back. He looked no one in the eye. I struggled to help him at least pass so he could make it to his senior year. It was taking a toll on my grades, those crucial junior year grades that colleges scrutinize so closely. My mother gave me a pass. She knew what I was doing. She only mentioned it once. She patted my shoulders from behind and told me I was a good friend. My mother was a mensch.

But passing his junior year exams was not to be. Amanda Pickler, a week and a half before finals, sat in her parents' car in their closed garage with the motor running. Her note, gripped in her sallow hand, contained one word: Fontaine. It didn't matter that Fontaine did not know who Amanda was. (I only knew who she was because she was the girl who giggled every time menstruation was brought up in freshman year Health.) It mattered little that Fontaine never dated, slept with, or received a blowjob from Amanda Pickler. (The girl was a vestal virgin by all accounts.) All that mattered was that she had chosen the same excuse as Joanna and Kerry had instead of spelling out her own. Suicide was seen by some adults as the lazy way out. I don't believe that, but I do believe that not bothering to leave a note was the very definition of lazy. Hell, the least Amanda could have done was tell it like it was. As far as her high school existence went, well, let's just say it didn't sound like much of a picnic. Unrequited crushes were her specialty, according to her friends, although all of them said they never heard Amanda mention Fontaine Black, not once, and Amanda was the kind of girl who spoke incessantly about whomever her latest crush was, as if that unlucky person were actually involved.

Fontaine failed his junior year. He went into virtual hiding during the summer. Oh, I'd spy him sometimes sitting in a lawn chair in his backyard staring at nothing, or I'd see him at Sol's picking up a gallon of milk. He'd nod or mumble hi, but he never stopped long. Not for me, not for anyone. My mother said she was worried about Fontaine. I was too, but as a teenager I wasn't about to let my mother know she was right to worry. Fontaine *would* pull through, but he would never be the same. At the beginning of my senior year (and the start of his second junior year), gone was the easy grin, the confident walk, even the bounce in his hair, which he'd cut super short over the summer (not quite a crew cut but darn close), maybe in an attempt to go unrecognized, but he turned heads still wherever he went, even if it was for a totally different reason than before. The prevailing wisdom of the student body was that Fontaine was a ladykiller—literally. The belief that he was a solid gold member of the Four F club was not in dispute. What was debated—hotly—was whether Fontaine could be classified as a serial killer. Lost in the discourses was the fact that Fontaine didn't kill Joanna, Kerry, or Amanda, but even that truth was occasionally contested. My mother told me Fontaine had been picked up and interviewed by the police following Amanda's death but had been released without incident. Whether the student body was aware of this, I didn't know, but I figured I would have heard if it was. There were kids who I guessed didn't know Fontaine and I were close (or had been), and they went over their Son of Sam and Zodiac Killer theories right in front of me.

Many times during that first month of school I tried to reach out to Fontaine. I'd let him be over the summer; he made it pretty clear he wasn't interested in our friendship then. But I renewed my efforts in September to no avail. He would promise to meet me at Finch's Landing or come over for some burgers and dogs on the grill, but he would never show. Sometimes he would attend class; just as often he didn't. But he was almost always on campus, I discovered, when I saw him shuffling from the guidance counselor office's a couple of times when he was supposed to be in Brit Lit. I found out he was required to see Mrs. Vogel, more famous for her shapely legs than her advice, three times a week. I thought Fontaine was getting a raw deal, that he was having his nose rubbed in it. Supposedly, he was also receiving counseling from the parish pastor Father Middy, who always liked Fontaine (despite the boy not having a saint's name). It seemed like Fontaine was being punished for having his name appear on three suicide notes. "Appalling," my mother said as she enjoyed her late afternoon cocktail, "but that's the Catholics for you: hand out penance first, ask questions later."

Three notes became five in October. (Sort of.)

Samantha Richardson and Sofie Skylar were not known to have been close friends, although they were both Bob Squad members in good standing. Both dated players on the school's football team, the Knights. Both were part of the cheerleading squad. Both occasionally partied with the Lakes gang from Paradise Lakes Trailer Park, who supplied them with alcohol and drugs. Both ostensibly had boyfriends, but it was well known that neither Bob Squader was faithful. The girls, Samantha blonde and fair, Sofie a brunette with olive skin, both with killer, compact bodies, were too hot and too iconic for their respective boyfriends to make much of an impression. Sofie, in particular, was known to be somewhat loose but would usually drop her conquests (*her* conquests, despite what the boys felt) like hot potatoes. Students said it was because her mother was Armenian and extremely strict, but what ethnicity had to do with it, I didn't know, and how strict could she have been? Sofie never missed a party, dance, or beer blast. Of Samantha, I never learned much. Before her photograph was printed in the papers, I couldn't have picked her out of a lineup despite her beauty. She was just another in a series of blonde Bod Squaders, a caste I made a point to avoid. I only picked up one bit of juicy information, and the source, a chatterbox named Mags Gilley, was suspect. (Mags was the girl who told everyone that she had played the part of Maria in Assumption's production of *West Side Story*, forgetting, somehow, that almost everyone at Hoskins High went to elementary school at Assumption, and that Assumption, at least during our tenure, had never produced *West Side Story* or any musical other than an anemic version of *Grease*— too many Pink Ladies and not enough T-Birds, who, let's face it, were no Jets.) Mags said that during Miss Richardson's sophomore year, Samantha had become pregnant with Davey Nolan's baby, and that her parents had the situation "taken care of." It wasn't long before for Mags' presumably tall tale grew legs, and soon the baby was Fontaine's. (Davey Nolan, for all his macho posturing with the other jocks, was rumored to be gay. Soon after Samantha and Sofie's suicides, he was caught on his knees in the boys' shower servicing the Knights' backup quarterback and "transferred out" shortly afterwards—the backup quarterback was allowed to stay. "For the Catholics," my mother sniffed, " 'tis far better to receive than to give.") Thing was, and this was a stone fact, Fontaine never dated or diddled Samantha Richardson or Sofie Skylar. I would go as far as to say he didn't even know who they were. They were just two more hotties in a school chock full of them.

Samantha and Sofie went out together. A suicide pact. Reportedly there was an Ozzy Osbourne record on the turntable, but that sounded too good to be true, real PMRC nightmare stuff. (Such was the '80s.) The turntable had been dragged into the bathroom. The two girls undressed, drew a bath, and got in. (I won't even go into the lesbian scuttlebutt that rumbled through the school, affecting the boys more than the girls. According to other Bod Squaders, "Sam and Sofie liked dick too much to go muff diving," although Sofie once French kissed another girl in the Lakes on a dare, probably while under the influence of a strong pharmaceutical.) Once in the tub, the girls drew razor blades (that they'd broken out of disposable razors) down their arms in the correct manner and bled out into the tub. The school grapevine had Fontaine's name written in blood on the bathroom wall. I scoffed. My mother asked, "Who would believe such nonsense? Sixteen-year-old Catholic schoolgirls, that's who!" But the grapevine wasn't far off: it was leaked to the *Inquirer* that Fontaine's name was scrawled in red lipstick on the bathroom mirror. (Samantha's house, Sofie's lipstick.)

Not soon after that, Fontaine threw pebbles at my window late one night, and I went down to let him in. It was freezing outside, and Fontaine wore only a t-shirt and thin sweatpants, no socks, no shoes.

"Why is this happening to me?" he asked before falling to his knees in the kitchen.

My mother turned on the dining room light, but I shooed her away, and my mom, bless her heart, quietly went back up the stairs.

"It's just a copycat syndrome," I said. "A *Heathers* thing."

"But why me?" he sobbed.

I pulled him to his feet. "Because you're beautiful. Because you're popular. Joanna and Kerry…"

Fontaine winced as if I'd burned him.

"…were unstable emotionally. If it hadn't been you, they would've found another reason. And Kerry may have just been following Joanna's poor example. Who knows? The others were just—"

"But *why?*"

I pulled his face to mine, unconcerned about my sleep breath. "Because every girl wants you and few have the privilege. There's no girl in the world who loves you more than me, and I couldn't hold onto you. You're a shooting star, my friend. These girls, Samantha and Sofie, these copycats, they're not even luminescent, let alone original. Don't let them get what they want. They want to go out associated with you, but they're not even creative enough to write bad poetry or come up with their own reasons. Don't let them drag you down. 'Stay gold, Ponyboy.'"

And that was when we made love on the kitchen floor (though, for whatever reason, I never saw *it* or even touched it). My mother knew; she told me years later that she'd heard us but thought maybe it best to let it play out. I'd like to say that the sex was passionate, the best I ever had, that it blew my mind, multiple orgasms, the whole bit. But the truth was: it was quick, a tad loud, slightly painful (Fontaine *was* that big), and more than a bit animalistic. He was hungry for validation and human touch; I was eager to heal my best friend and (surprising to me at the time) eager to have Fontaine inside me, no matter what the circumstances. We didn't use protection and he didn't pull out and I didn't ask him to. Let the chips fall and all that. The time for rational thought was long past. Afterwards, we sat on the kitchen floor, leaning against the cabinets, and shared a bagel, giggling like we had in the days that weren't so far in the past. The dimples I hadn't seen in a dog's age returned, as did the crinkles around his eyes when he laughed. He stayed until it was light out. Then he gave me a long, deep kiss and told me it was the first of many. He said he was back, " 'harder than a heart attack,' " and he grinned before he slipped out of the door. I would never see him again—at least not alive.

The very next day Heather Handtrow (known as Heather Handjob), a minor Bod Squader with a reputation for giving it up on the first date ("the number of guys who've pulled out and come on her stomach," one knowledgeable Assumption Knight said, "well, shit, it looks like a twelve-year-old boy's bedsheet"), blew the back of her head off with her father's service revolver. (Heather's dad was a cop.) I had several classes with Heather and sat behind her in three of them, so it was difficult to imagine her without the back of her head; often I was pulling strands of her hair out of my mouth, so fond was Heather of flinging her long straight brown hair back every ten seconds or so. This time the suicide note bordered on the Cliffs Notes version: before she pulled the trigger, Heather Handjob carved the initials F. B. into her arm (supposedly with a paper clip); just so no one missed the point, she enclosed the initials in a heart.

The national press descended. They'd caught wind of the six girls and the boy they claimed as the reason behind their suicides. Not one newspaper or television reporter mentioned the Werther Effect (let alone *Heathers*). The *Mondauk Common* even ran a picture of Fontaine from his freshman year, grinning insouciantly, his jet black hair in his eyes. It was obscene and, according to Ms. Stowe, my journalism teacher, unethical (even though Fontaine was eighteen). She'd written a letter to the editor of the *Common*, but she doubted very much that it would be published, and she was right.

Fontaine stopped coming to school. I don't think he left the house again. His father never spoke to me about any of this. He acted as if he didn't know who I was at his son's funeral, but, as my mother pointed out, his eyes indicated that he was heavily medicated or just plain stoned, and he had to be assisted in and out of the viewing by his current boyfriend, but I think if he did talk to me, he would have confirmed what I suspected: Fontaine not only never left the house, he rarely left his bedroom—only to forage or go to the bathroom. In school, Fontaine's name was mud. It was as if he had murdered the six girls (the Idol Ideation Girls as they'd recently been dubbed by the media), as if his hand had held the broken Bic razors or Officer Handtrow's gun, as if he had gone to the drugstore for Joanna or had fashioned a rope out of his neckties and a torn bedsheet for Kerry. I imagined Fontaine curled up in a ball or mutely flipping baseball cards into a hat, his eyes blank, his skin white, his hair greasy—and I wasn't far off.

The pariah effect extended, in a small way, to me. Most people knew Fontaine and I were inseparable. To some, I must have been perceived as the silent accomplice. There was even a nasty rumor that I killed those girls because I was secretly in love with Fontaine and wanted him all for myself. That one stung a little, but not because of the perception that I was guilty of murder, but because the secretly in love part might have been true. Pishaw, I said publically. But what no one understood, and I would bet still don't understand, is that love requires one to do what before love would have been incomprehensible. I'm not talking about a mother lifting a car to save a pinned child or a father working three jobs to feed his family. I'm talking about a swirl of blue and red. I'm writing here about an ocean of blackness. Love, true love, requires more than a toe dip; true love requires—nay, *demands*—full immersion. Sink or swim, baby. It was not for the faint of heart, whereas suicide seemed to be for everyone.

Take Stacey Dorf.

Stacey Dorf was a marginal student. This is not a reference to her grades (although, according to the *Common*, they were pretty mediocre) but to her high school social status. Stacey didn't belong to the Bod Squad. She wasn't one of the Lakes girls. She wasn't a stoner or a geek. (Well, she was a bit of the latter, but she tried too hard; full-blooded geekness should be a natural thing.) Stacey had poor skin, the bumpy kind formed naturally by a Droopy Dog kind of face and permanent but shifting acne. As bodies went, Stacey's was fairly normal, although whenever she showed up to the public pool during the summer in her one-piece bathing suit, her breasts appeared to be wildly uneven, one perky, the other deflated, defeated even. (One boy described her as a two-bagger; another said her face looked a little like Winona Ryder's after enough brews but like a bus driver's ass when sober.) Her brother Tom, older by a year, was almost popular, had a decent number of dates, and not a spot of acne, which I imagine must have driven Stacey crazy, but if so, she never let it seep out; publically, she adored her brother. Stacey studied the likes and dislikes of her fellow students and bought the albums she'd heard being discussed in the lunchroom and rented the same movies they did (according to the few friends of hers that would talk). She went to every party, I was told, invited or not. I know she was at every one I ever attended. Sometimes, just at the edge of an event, I would see her eyes searching for an opportunity to insert herself. Sometimes she did. Stacey succeeded occasionally because she was willing to drink to distraction, and just at the point of the party where the proceedings were beginning to break up and those remaining were pairing off, Stacey was willing to hook up with anyone drunk enough to mistake her for Winona, which is, I imagine, how Stacey ended up making out with Fontaine on a basement couch at the end of a party thrown by some public school kid. This was before thing got out of hand, before Samantha and Sofie drew their final bath, before Heather Handjob pulled her last, and after he'd quit his initial sequestration and returned to school on a sporadic basis. (I'd exerted no small amount of effort to get Fontaine to attend. The fact that the party was being held by someone who didn't go to Hoskins High was my big selling point, and after I got him buzzed and the wheels were lubed, we rolled our way to the festivities, where, as I'd promised, his celebrity went unrecognized, or at least unacknowledged.)

I'd been looking for him upstairs; I was ready to go home after watching yet another keg stand (apparently a favorite activity of the public school set). But Fontaine found me first, a frightened, queasy look on his face. He told me he'd been in the basement.

"She threw up."

"Who threw up?"

"Dorfdog—Stacey. The lights were off," he said, already trying to make excuses.I squinted up at him, ignoring the use of one of her derogatory nicknames, which I thought was out of character. "You were just in the basement in the dark with Stacey Dorf?"

He nodded, a tad sheepishly. "She was already coming up the steps. I was calling down for you. She was pretty drunk. I guess I was a little drunk too. I'm not drunk anymore though. I think I got the drunk scared out of me." I crossed my arms and he went on. "So she led me over to the couch and laid down. It was so dark, I couldn't see my hand in front of my face." He paused and looked at his shoes then looked back up. "So I laid on top of her. And we were making out. I *knew* it was Dorf…I knew it was her. I *knew* her face looked like lumpy lava up close. But I was drunk! Then it hit me: vomit. The smell was so strong, I don't know how I missed it at first."

"Stacey…"

He nodded. "Not right then. But right before she ran into me, she said. She must have wandered into the basement and vomited on the couch."

"Then she led you to the same couch and laid herself in her own spew?"

He nodded again.

I looked him over. "I don't think you got any on you. Where's Stacey now?"

"Still in the puke, I think."

I poked my head down the basement stairs and flicked the light. The bulb must have blown. I could smell it right away.

"Stacey? Stacey?" I couldn't leave her passed out in her own vomit. If the other kids found her, she'd be in worse social shape than she already was. That was when I heard the singing. It was a Duran Duran song.

" '*And you wanted to dance, so I asked you to dance*
But fear is in your soul
Some people call it a one night stand
But we can call it paradise.' "

I closed the basement door.

So at least Stacey Dorf had a claim on Fontaine, albeit a small one. And when she jumped off Olde Bridge into the Puddle (shortly after Heather tried to swallow a bullet), in her pocket, safe inside a Ziploc sandwich bag, they found a picture of Fontaine torn from the yearbook. Word was that she had drawn hearts all around his head with their initials inside and had blacked out his eyes. It was also reported that it wasn't the fall that killed her. (Supposedly she'd climbed halfway to the top of the bridge.) Word was when she jumped, she landed on the bottom of the Puddle with such force that she half-buried herself and drowned, trapped in the mud. According to several dubious sources (the only kind available), Stacey's eyes had been eaten out by whatever fish survive in the filthy creek.

If the press had gone wild before, once word leaked out about the sandwich bag, they practically came on themselves. A local TV crew camped out in front of Fontaine's house for a week. (The footage of Mr. Black cursing them out while wearing a kimono and pink slippers was aired—bleeped, of course—ad infinitum.) I took to leaving early for school and going the long way, especially after the press caught wind that I was Fontaine's best friend (me—a girl). Cox McGowan was hot for an exclusive.

Seven Gone—Who's Next? was the headline in the Friday edition of the *Philadelphia Daily News*. Who indeed? It *was* catching. The popular did it, the not so popular too. Girls who'd been Fontaine's girlfriends, girls who barely knew him, and one girl who made out with him for thirty seconds on a soiled couch. Anyone could be next. A boy next time? Not inconceivable. Fontaine was that beautiful. A teacher? Certainly possible. Fontaine had flirted with a few of the female instructors often enough, and he'd spent a decent enough time in leggy Mrs. Vogel's office with the door closed. A nun? (Now there would be a coup!) Despite his efforts to extricate himself from the morass of tragedy, Fontaine had become a reason and an excuse (for the emotionally unstable), a rallying cry and a cause (for anxious parents). What concerned my mother, although she never came right out and said it, but I knew, was that I would be the next domino to fall. Truth was, the thought terrified me. I don't believe I was remotely suicidal, but in those murky days of my senior year, particularly towards the end of it, who really was to say? It did seem like all bets were off. The other, unspoken of apprehension was that Fontaine would get it into his muddled head to do himself in. He was already a shut-in, a ghost of Joe Cool, a faded Fonzie.

Now I already wrote earlier that Fontaine Black was dead because he loved *all* girls, which is partially true. But what's important here is that I've already told you that he's dead. So you probably think you know how this ends. The Werther Effect doubled back on itself. Go, go, Goethe! But…well, let's just go on, shall we?

Fontaine's father found his son's body after Fontaine hadn't come out of his room for two days. (They lived in a rancher, so it wasn't as if Mr. Black even had to climb the stairs to check on his son, but, for whatever reason, he didn't, not for two whole days.) Fontaine had swallowed a boatload of Valium and Ativan. Where he'd obtained the drugs was unknown; neither Mr. Black nor his current live-in lover, Mr. Viktor, had prescriptions. (Illegal drugs they had, yes—the stash flushed, I was sure, soon after Mr. Black dialed 911—psychotropics, no.) Fontaine certainly didn't have a prescription for either (though he should have, some said, then maybe he would have never reached a suicidal state in the first place). There was some confusion in the papers over whether Fontaine overdosed or choked on his own vomit. (Somewhere Stacey Dorf was smiling at that one.) There were even a couple of days where Fontaine's death was reported as a recreational drug overdose. That rumor was too much for my mother, who'd always loved Fontaine and enjoyed his flirting. She marched down the street to the reporters on the Blacks' front lawn and told them that Fontaine was a good boy who didn't know from drugs. It didn't matter; the press filed the stories they wanted to until the ME's office came back with the suicide verdict.

And that was the end of the rash of Fontaine-related suicides. The stories dried up right quick, and the press, local and otherwise, Cox McGowan and her stylist too, scurried away to exploit the next tragedy. School motored on in the normal fashion, and eventually Hoskins High became a bright, noisy, relatively pleasant place to earn a diploma. Though still mourning, I was grateful for the return to normalcy, but I was startled (and a bit appalled) that no one, not school officials, not the papers, not the police, investigated the root cause behind the wave of suicides; there wasn't a mention of personality disorders, and if a psychiatrist's insight was sought, it must have been kept quiet or disregarded. The press was content with designating Fontaine as ground zero for Mondauk County's teenage suicide epidemic. The school had held a memorial Mass for Stacey Dorf (as they had for all the Idol Ideation Girls), but there was never a service in memory of Fontaine Black, whose death, I guessed, was listed as a suicide by the Church. It was sickening but at the same time lulling. I didn't know whether to cry or to sleep. I ended up doing a lot of both. My mother let me be. She only asked once if I wanted to talk to someone, but when I asked who, she backed off, for who would I talk to about the horrors that had occurred, who could really help? A love-yourself-and-the-world-will-love-you shrink or some drug pushing doctor? A priest? No drugs, no talk therapy, no act of contrition would absolve me—especially when I wasn't wrong.

So here's the skinny, here's the dope. Hold onto your hats. Here it is: I wish I could write that Fontaine killed himself; it would give the story a kind of closure, a measure of poetic justice, however tragic. But, but, but. Remember earlier when I wrote that I never saw Fontaine alive again after we finally had sex? I lied. (I am the consummate unreliable narrator. *Just what the truth is / I can't say anymore.*) That was what I told the police when they asked (and they only asked once). I told them we made love on my mother's kitchen floor. I told them what I knew of Fontaine's relationships with Joanna and Kerry and his minor hookup with Stacey. I was clear that he barely knew the other girls, if at all. I told them that I was Fontaine's best friend (which should count for something, I thought), but that maybe I held a tiny torch for him. This was a truth I'd never told anyone before or since—not even you (until now); hell, not even me—although I think my mother had an inkling. But what I didn't tell them (or my mother) was that I saw Fontaine again one last time. I've never told anyone that before and I never will again. But now you know...somehow I don't think you'll be telling anyone though.

My mother never asked what happened to her missing Valium or why half of her Ativan was gone. Whether she connected the dots, I'll never know, not unless she suddenly blurts out, "You killed Fontaine!" one day while she's in her cups, a not infrequent state for her these days, as she raves against the Roman Catholic Church and the Republican party from the safety of her Barcalounger. But they had to end, the suicides, and it didn't look like they were going to. And maybe, just maybe, I would be caught up in its snare. I could just imagine our commencement ceremony, half of the female graduates absent by their own hands and all of the missing with Fontaine-flavored notes, photographs of him, or maybe even tattoos declaring their love: Fontaine fever—as if these girls held a more important place in Fontaine's heart than I did.

(One Jersey paper called Joanna, Kerry, Amanda, Samantha, Sofie, Heather, and Stacey the Suicide Seven—the Idol Ideation Girls moniker having been deemed too passé for the Garden State, I suppose; I wondered what they would come up with if there was ever an eighth. The Exsanguination Eight? Not technically accurate, but it has that ring.) The source had to be destroyed, and I had to be the one to do it, because I was the only person who understood that while Fontaine had zip to do with the girls' deaths, he had become the invisible leader for the psychologically unbalanced, the figurehead for self-slaughter.

I stole the pills after my mother passed out on the sofa and headed towards the Black house in my bare feet with an old canteen filled with water over my shoulder. I hopped a few fences and ran through a few backyards to avoid being seen by our now hyper-inquisitive neighbors, but it was pretty dark. When I reached Fontaine's window, I tapped on the pane. Nothing. I tapped again. No response. Finally I slid the window up and climbed in. Fontaine was curled up in a ball, as I'd imagined, wearing only pajama bottoms. His hair was greasy and long. His skin was greasy too. The boy's eyes were open but he seemed asleep.

"Fontaine," I whispered, shaking him. He just stared at a point on the wall and drooled a bit.

"Fontaine!" I said a little louder. I pinched his leg. Not even a blink.

"Marie Magdalen," I said into his ear.

He sat up so quickly that we conked heads. "Sister!"

"No, Fontaine," I said, unwrapping the baggie full of pills. I knew I had to act quickly. "It's me."

"Is it time?" he asked, looking at his alarm clock.

Time for school? "Yes, it is," I said gently. "But take your medicine first." I placed a bunch of pills in his hand, and once he had them in his mouth, I lifted the canteen to his lips, wiping away the excess. "That's a good boy, just a few more now. Soon all this will be over. It'll be just a very bad dream."

"A bad dream with a body count," he said, and that was the only indication I got that he was lucid. After that, he returned to his stupor and swallowed every last pill. There were a lot of them.

I kissed him on his lips, which were badly chapped and dotted with puss. He smiled and I put a finger inside one of his dimples. He couldn't go gentle into that ambiguous night without a note, and I placed a pen in his fingers and guided his hand. "Me," his note read.

Me, indeed.

That was the last time I saw the only boy I ever loved. Fontaine Black. The suicide king of Father Hoskins High. But not a night goes by when I don't wonder: did I think at the time it was him or me? Or was I really trying to save the school, a school I didn't care a whit about? Or, like how the seven girls had a predisposition, a predilection even, for killing themselves, did I have a predilection for just plain killing? I'm a nurse in a hospital now. (I never made it as a writer; "too grisly," the rejection letters read.) There haven't been any suicides on my watch, but if my transfer to the ICU comes through—well, who knows? Love has a funny way of expressing itself sometimes. Valentines are red. Ghosts are sometimes blue. But my love will always be black.

-end-

Robin Violeta Chastain

Birth

Robin Violeta Chastain was born in 1967 to John and Summer in the backseat of John's '64 Plymouth Fury. (It had been snowing heavily, and John had gotten lost on the way to the hospital.) In later years, Robin attributed her rampant promiscuity to this makeshift manger (where she'd also been conceived).

Childhood

Robin had a fairly uneventful childhood: Catholic elementary school, deformed nuns armed with yardsticks, and a short stint as a Brownie. (She quit after a month because she didn't like being a member of a group named after a food.) The biggest excitement came when she swallowed a whole piece of chalk in the second grade to impress Joseph Delvecchio (who, she would find out as a teenager, was, like most boys, not that hard to impress). As she grew up, her face was often described as being exquisite, but she felt unfinished.

Adolescence

Robin first had sex when she was fifteen and liked it so much, she did it as often as she could with as many of her classmates as possible (including, once, with Cynthia Leach). But more importantly, in the eighth grade, when Robin was about to turn thirteen, she found rock'n'roll. She devoured her parents' record collection and spent her allowance on buying more. Her first love was John Lennon, but she always secretly hoped Mick Jagger would take her virginity. (That honor, unfortunately, went to Joseph Delvecchio and his baby-sized penis behind the McDonald's on Castor Avenue.) Robin covered her walls with rock'n'roll posters and her copybooks with Led Zeppelin symbols. In December of that year, John Lennon was murdered on a New York City street by a disturbed man-boy with a J. D. Salinger book on his person when he was arrested. Robin swore she'd never read Salinger and she didn't (almost flunking freshman English because of her refusal). When she seventeen, Robin started using angel dust and eventually became hooked on meth, her well-off existence and normal childhood having battered her with guilt.

Late Adolescence/Young Adulthood

When Robin was nineteen, a friend took her to Forest Green Temple, and there she met the person she claimed was the love of her life: the Venerable Reverend Elijah Green, who promised to teach her the secrets of immortality. Within two weeks, she quit college, moved out of her parents' house, and left behind her posters and records and drugs. She proselytized on her assigned street corner in Philadelphia wearing a thin dirty white robe over a pale blue prairie dress. She cut off all ties with her family and agreed to become one of Reverend Green's brides (even though she was a tad old for his tastes), and her name was entered into the Book of the Eternal. Her face was diagonally slashed on either side, deep enough to scar her. Now no one else would want her but the Master, she was told, which kept the temptation of apostasy away; they were constant reminders of her devotion to the Reverend's divine afflatus, but more importantly, her scars marked her so that she would be recognizable in whatever vessel her everlasting celestial soul chose after departing her current one, the wounds transcending mere flesh. She was no longer exquisite-looking, but was often described as beatific (if hesitatingly so).

Adulthood and Middle Age

Deprogramming hadn't worked (especially since she had to be kidnapped first), but an exit counselor later convinced her to admit herself into a anti-cult in-patient program in another state, and when Robin was twenty-eight, she left the Forest Green Temple, going so far as to file an affidavit as part of the DA's investigation into the church's recruitment of underage females. Without a college degree, Robin floated from menial job to menial job and oversaw the task of burying her parents. Feelings of guilt returned at their funerals: all the shame and stress she had put them through with her chemical addictions and then her immersion in Temple life overwhelmed her. Robin did not return to drugs, however, but retired from the workforce early with her meager savings and shut herself up in her apartment.

Old Age

At age sixty-seven, Robin has a chance encounter on a street corner with the friend who'd first brought her to the Forest Green Temple. Remorse arose: the friend still wore the traditional clothing and she looked happy even as she recounted the Master's final days in his temporal body. Her friend wore a silver wedding band on her finger, just like the one that Robin had long ago buried in the jewelry box her parents had given her when she was seven, the one with the oddly bent ballerina who no longer pirouetted to the faux classical melody that now played like a dirge. After retrieving her ring, Robin rejoined the Temple and, as a bride of the late Reverend Green (whom all believed had chosen a new vessel yet to be revealed), she quickly became a leader in the church, overseeing the recruitment and indoctrination of guilt-ridden, confused young girls for the high priests to wed. Robin herself no longer felt guilty, especially after one of the priestholders revealed himself to be the chosen vessel of the Master.

Death

When she was seventy-three, Robin Violeta Chastain was murdered on a Philadelphia street corner by a female ex-Temple acolyte with a fetish for J. D. Salinger. She was buried in a pauper's grave and was eventually disavowed by the church for not being immortal—a new vessel had not presented itself to the congregation. Robin's name was struck from the Book, and on what used to be her assigned corner, a young underage girl she'd recruited, attired in a dirty white robe over a pale blue prairie dress, proselytized to passers-by and felt the guilt wash off her in waves. On her ring finger was a silver band, and her blissful face was scarred diagonally on either side.

-end-

Mount Rock

Saturday, April 14–Saturday, May 12, 2007 (Days 1–29)

Andrew Albrecht arrived at the Green Rock Mountain Remnant Church in Anchor Hop at seven in the evening, a half an hour before the service was advertised to begin. A thin, white-haired man in an unironed shirt meticulously straightened rows of old red folding chairs. The church was little more than an overly large meeting room and not a very large one at that. There was no stage or chancel, just a little rise with a beat-to-hell wooden pulpit in the center. Before Andrew knew what was happening, the white-haired man he would come to know as Pastor Ezekiel (or the Apostle), embraced him and welcomed him home, and Andrew cried like a baby.

The next day, it was as if it had been a dream, except Cindy wanted to know where he'd been all evening. She'd given up on him and had gone to bed. The service had lasted over two hours, a little long for Andrew's tastes, but he'd never been hugged so much in his entire life, not even at his wedding, maybe not even by his wife, and he and Cindy were very much in love and fairly physical. He didn't know why he'd gone. He'd been raised Roman Catholic and had lately been attending Methodist services sporadically with his wife, but he'd never felt a yearning for spirituality; it was just something he was supposed to do, go to services on Sunday, so he tried to find the best fit and the denomination that would be least intrusive upon his easygoing, largely Norman Rockwell lifestyle.

But lately something was missing. He and Cindy had been spending a lot of time with another married couple, their neighbors, Walter and Bev Baxter, playing cards on the screened-in porch at night and drinking sweet drinks. Pleasantly lit, they got very chummy; he and Bev flirted, and Walter flirted with Cindy. (But Walter flirted with *everybody*.) Then one day Bev up and filed for divorce, leaving Walter to cry in his sweet drink. (Curiously, there were no tears.) Andrew got to thinking: if Bev could walk out on Walter without so much as a note, then Cindy was capable of the same behavior. It seemed it was all Andrew thought about, day and night. He became snippy with Cindy, even commenting on her leg dimples. To stop, he tried to lose himself in work—his crew was in the middle of a big construction job—but his boss, Big Rick Malone, who was older than he was, found him weeping behind a stack of lumber. Instead of calling him a pussy, he gave him the name of a church. Sure, Andrew had seen the large sign on the lawn outside the Remnant Church before. (It was on what appeared to be a small utility trailer, out of place in upscale Anchor Hop.) He'd read the sign's oft-changing messages while going to and from various job sites, messages such as THE RAPTURE: SEPARATION OF CHURCH AND STATE and AS SURE AS GOD PUTS HIS CHILDREN IN THE FURNACE, HE WILL BE IN THE FURNACE WITH THEM. He'd heard of the Remnants' shady past and of their standoff with authorities that led to a fire that almost took thirty children's lives in the borough of Mondauk Proper. "But that was almost forty years ago," Big Rick told him. "This is the *new* Remnant Church. Come see Pastor. Come listen to the Apostle."

So he went—and kept going. Cindy largely ignored it at first, treating it like he was going to a weekly poker game—four nights a week plus Saturday mornings. She had her shows to watch plus she spent a lot of time on the phone with her mother and on the screened-in porch drinking with Walter, consoling him. When Andrew finally submitted to baptism, he came home damp, feeling lighter than he ever had. Cindy didn't say a word as he peeled off his clothes and described being dunked in the above ground pool. In fact, she didn't say anything until Andrew told her that Pastor asked if she would come tomorrow night. Then she said, "No." He told her, "Pastor is the spark that lights the way. He knows our hearts, he's in touch with our immortal souls, he has the gift of prophecy, and when Jesus leaves the sanctuary on the last day, the Remnants will be carried into the clouds by angels."

"Poppycock," his wife said.

+

Tuesday, January 4, 2011 (Day 1,362)

It was his fault she was even here.

Cindy sounded desperate, but she was also glassy-eyed and her movements were somewhat robotic. Andrew hadn't been permitted to live at home or see his family for almost a month and a half (part of his punishment for asking bold questions of Pastor in front of the congregation), and he was shocked to see how pale his wife had become. She looked like she hadn't seen the light of day in a dog's age.

The only time she sounded anything like her old self (and this was when he thought he heard desperation in her voice) was when she said, "Seems to me it's really hard to get into heaven."

He was only allowed to speak to Cindy through the screen door of their house. Big Rick stood watch a few feet behind Andrew; the construction supervisor's large arms were crossed atop his standard sport coat and golf shirt combination. Big Rick was Pastor's pit bull. When Pastor barked, Big Rick bit, and the loyal attack dog looked ready to gnaw off one of Andrew's legs when the chastised congregant went to open the screen door he knew would be locked even before his wife shook her head. So he backed down the porch, careful to avoid the Pastor's muscle. He knew that what he wanted to do wasn't going to happen overnight. It might take weeks of planning, months even. And there was April Anne to consider. The little girl was almost all he ever thought about anymore. Cindy might be a lost cause (though he'd forgiven her even if he didn't understand the reasons behind her never discussed transgressions or her strict adherence to Remnant principles, the latter a way of punishing herself for the former perhaps), but April Anne was young enough to shake off the Remnant yoke like a cold—he hoped. Still, he knew the young often soaked in the sins of the old, and just as often those sins took root to blossom at a later date, or so Pastor had preached. Her mother's refusal to even look beyond what she was told could be catching.

His anger and frustration was such that Andrew paused his retreat, and as Big Rick took a big step forward, he watched the older man chew on an end of his mustache, never a good sign; it was the pit bull's tell. Andrew turned and headed back to his car. He wasn't ready to have his ass handed to him just yet. Calm, cool, and collected, he'd just drive back to the one room apartment they'd stuck him in. He wished he could have seen April Anne today, but he was more likely to get a knuckle sandwich than see his daughter. When he looked back, he caught Sister Deborah, Pastor's wife, peeking through the curtains. She was pulling Cindy's strings as well, Andrew knew. The white-haired witch with the German accent was probably holding April Anne too—and doing God knows what with her.

It was a conundrum. He couldn't allow April Anne to suffer Pastor's "thrashings of love" anymore. But if he left... He couldn't leave. He couldn't make Cindy leave either. The devil makes your bed, Pastor always said, but you choose to lie in it. Andrew felt like he was fluffing his own pillows.

+

Tuesday, May 29–Wednesday, June 13, 2007 (Days 46–61)

Cindy went reluctantly. She said she needed to be around for their new Chesapeake Bay retriever puppy, Stella (named after the beer, Stella Artois, they'd gotten drunk on when they decided to get a dog); she told her husband she needed to be around for Walter (whose drunken phone calls were almost a nightly event), but Andrew practically begged. Pastor was adamant: Andrew needed to bring his wife if he intended to stay. The Remnant Church was a family. The first evening, Cindy ran out in the middle of the service in tears. Pastor told Andrew to let her walk the over twenty miles home, and he did. (He found out later she'd called Walter for a ride.)

Cindy came back to church later the same week. Pastor was enthralling, charismatic, Andrew knew. When the Apostle spoke, it was like he was unraveling age-old mysteries, and he did so with the dramatic suspense of a skilled storyteller. Services lasted two to three hours. Sister Deborah sat next to the pockmarked pulpit, looking up at her husband, her facial expressions color commentary on the sermons and Bible readings. Big Rick, Andrew was surprised to learn, was Pastor's right hand man and not the real construction boss at all—the firm belonged to Pastor. The church, the parsonage, all the buildings in the small development behind the church, were all built by his company. Pastor owned it all.

On June 13, Big Rick escorted Andrew and Cindy into a little windowless room where Pastor was waiting for them. The Apostle proceeded to expound on the end days for two and a half hours. He told them how there would only be a hundred and forty-four thousand Remnants left behind to continue Christ's Church on Earth after the apocalypse. Pastor told the couple he wanted them to be two of a hundred and forty-four thousand. When Pastor finished, Cindy knelt before the preacher, and said, "But I am a sinner."

Out of nothing more than habit, she would continue to mortally sin for about a month, mostly with Walter, though Andrew wouldn't find this out for roughly twelve hundred and fifty more days.

But Pastor knew. He told her privately that he would not baptize her into the hundred and forty-four thousand until her actions matched her words. "Corinthians 6:18, child," Pastor said. "Close your legs,"

Big Rick whispered harshly, as he walked her back to her husband. "It's not that special."

+

Thursday, July 12–Friday, August 10, 2007 (Days 90–119)

Services were held on Saturdays, most of the day (Saturday being the Lord's Day, for the Remnants were a breakaway Seventh-day Adventist sect), and Monday, Tuesday, Thursday, and Friday evenings. On Thursday, July 12, after service, as many of the congregants walked to their nearby homes behind the church and parsonage, Andrew and Cindy headed to their car. (The houses in the Church's development were rented to the parishioners by Pastor's company; they were single homes, large, identical, and white with expansive backyards; many had large sheds and, as Andrew was soon to learn, bunkers.) The heat of the day was giving way to an insistent cool wind. Andrew was so high from speaking in tongues (it was only his second time) that when he tripped over his dog's decapitated body, he didn't realize it was Stella until Cindy started screaming. For a few seconds, Andrew thought she was screaming because he'd fallen and cut his chin, but when he opened his eyes, he was staring at Stella's head underneath their car.

That was the night Cindy poured out all the Stella Artois and other beers and liquors they had in the house. That was the night Cindy said she wanted to sell their home and move into a house behind the church. "I want to live in Mount Rock," she said. (Although it was called Green Rock Mountain Remnant Church, there was no green mountain or rock, just the church atop a small hill and the manicured lawns of the land behind it.) "We need a bunker—for the end days," Cindy said, "and we can't very well build one in our tiny backyard." Andrew, torn between happiness (Cindy was finally one of them), sorrow (who could have done that to little Stella?), and disbelief (sell the house they'd scrimped and saved for?). He asked, "But what about Walter?" Their neighbor, often in his cups, still seemed in need of Cindy's comforting (around Andrew, Walter kept a stiff upper lip) and appeared needier since Cindy started attending all of the week's services. (Walter had politely turned down Andrew's invitations to meet Pastor for some spiritual healing.) As an employee of Pastor's company, Andrew knew the houses they constructed were fairly sound, but the abodes at Mount Rock were built before his arrival and he didn't know if they came with bunkers or if they would have to build their own. And renting from Pastor instead of owning? But Cindy grabbed his cheeks with her beer-soaked hands. (Her arms were still stained with Stella's blood; she'd insisted on holding the dog's corpse while Andrew dug a hole in the yard.) She told her husband, "Forget about Walter, honey. Forget all about Walter. Forget his name."

The next day, Friday the 13th, they put their house up for sale (through Pastor's reality company) and began packing, for Pastor insisted they move right away.

That evening, Cindy was baptized in the church's cramped basement, surrounded by what appeared to be long abandoned cribs and broken toys. Kneeling, her head was dunked three times into a baby pool while Pastor Ezekiel read Matthew 3:13-17, detailing Jesus' own baptism. (No more full immersions; the above ground pool had been vandalized—the Remnants were seen as a pestilence by the largely Catholic population of Mondauk County.) After the ceremony, Pastor told Andrew he should be proud. Now husband and wife would survive the end days together when Christ would descend from the sanctuary to judge the living and the dead. Andrew smiled, but his stomach was uneasy when he saw how Cindy's eyes were somehow both fervent and blank. He wished he had a Stella Artois or two.

Later, at services, with Sister Deborah sitting by his side, a tight, knowing smile pinned on her face, Pastor unveiled to the small but growing congregations the Eight Precepts.

1. All Remnants must live at Mount Rock. {Andrew and Cindy had been the last holdouts among the recent recruits.}

2. All accidents and all excommunications {a couple from the Heights had left the group loudly during the middle of a service, but the wife had come crawling back and was made to divorce her husband} are the result of the devil's handiwork, and all good things occur because the angels are working in the Remnants' favor. {Stories circulated among the faithful of near-miraculous events; knowing the truth, Pastor said, has it dividends.}

3. The world is black and white, and one must strive to be virtuous. Guilt and shame are the Lord's ways of reminding us that we've lost the path and are no longer counted amongst the hundred and forty-four thousand. {A number with a constantly shifting membership.} Personal decisions should be left to the group and, ultimately, Pastor Ezekiel. Purity is the goal and can only be attained through the Remnant Church. Only Pastor and Sister Deborah are pure of heart.

4. Sins are to be confessed immediately—before the group. Self-degradation through confession is a pleasure granted to us by the Lord through Pastor. Remnants are to report those congregants walking around with unconfessed sins. Sins are Lucifer, the Morning Star's constructs, but they are also God's way of keeping the weaker amongst us in line

5. The Remnant Church offers security. Pastor Ezekiel is infallible in all ways. His teachings and the teachings of Sister Ellen G. White {an early leader of the Sabbatarian Adventist movement in the mid-nineteenth century, they'd learned} and the wisdom found in the Old and New Testaments constitute the Truth. If one word is false, then all of the teachings are false, and since our faith has taught us that every exegesis by the Pastor, every book by Sister White, every syllable of the Holy Scriptures came from God's lips, then every word is true. The logic is too sacred to call into question.

6. Proselytizing is mandatory, but Remnants are to learn a new language of watchwords designed to end coercing conversations, confrontational discussions, and insidious infiltrations by sabotage-minded intruders. ("Apostates," "the Truth," and "the hundred and forty-four thousand," for example, are words that carry judgment and negate ignorantly indignant outsiders unworthy of consideration by their own actions.) Study and the Word will reveal itself.

7. Doctrine is more important than any one person. Pastor is more important than any other Remnant. The Remnants are more precious in God's eyes than other human beings, for we alone worship His might and bow before His glory and His representative on earth, Pastor Ezekiel, and we alone shall live to witness the glory and awe of the apocalypse. Remnants should strive to be near the Truth. To tithe is to be closer to God.

8. Children are to be homeschooled to avoid having their souls tainted by the offspring of apostates and the godless. Unbelieving parents and grandparents, meddling siblings, dissenting adult children must be cut off completely. During the end days, the Seventh Angel of John's Revelation will not discern between blood relatives, only between the faithful Remnants and all others. Pastor decides who has the right to exist.

"Seems to me it's really hard to get into heaven," Cindy said after the service. He couldn't disagree with her.

Andrew tithed twenty percent of his salary from Pastor's company to the Church. (He also paid the exorbitant rent—higher than his mortgage payment had been—to live in Mount Rock.) Cindy tithed too. Soon Pastor told Cindy to quit her teaching job at the university so she could learn humility. (Sister Deborah called Andrew's wife opinionated, but it sounded to Andrew like she was calling Cindy a whore. She also referred to his wife's small home library as a collection of "fancy books.") So Cindy left the school without notice and found a job that very week working in a fast food restaurant and continued to tithe twenty percent. (Twenty percent of next to nothing.) Andrew often cruised by the drive-thru just to see that it was actually the woman who'd sweated her way to a PhD in American and British literature serving greasy hamburgers to obese housewives and their chunky children. Her degrees did not adorn the walls of their rented house the way they had in their home—the home that they'd been so happy to buy they moved in without any furniture, crashing out (and making love) in a single sleeping bag on the hardwood floor for nearly a week. After leaving the university, all the "fancy books" were packed away or donated to Goodwill. Andrew wondered if the degrees now hung in the fast food restaurant next to the sign declaring that all employees must wash their hands when they finished using the rest rooms.

When Cindy told Andrew she was pregnant, he thought they'd gone too far now to course correct. Cindy looked worried.

+

Monday, April 7–Tuesday, April 8, 2008 (Days 360–361)

April Anne was born on April 7, twelve days before the Seder meal. Natural childbirth at home; Pastor's orders. A midwife sympathetic to the Church (though not a Remnant) was given special dispensation to provide limited care for Cindy, as well as to attend to the delivery. Pastor clapped his hands when told of the birth and said, "So close to Passover, so I shall declare her passed over! She shall live!" Andrew accepted Pastor's rough hug and Sister's equally rough though teary one, but it was not without revulsion. Who was Pastor to declare April Anne "passed over," he asked himself. And the baby's name—Pastor's hand again. They wanted to name their child April after her birth month (and theirs), but Pastor insisted that all children born in Mount Rock bear their father's name—hence Anne for Andrew. (Pastor had a preference for one syllable names, so Andrea was out.) Cindy was too exhausted to care, but Andrew seethed. He'd already started to question everything about the Church—but not aloud; it wasn't a crisis of faith, he told himself, just some healthy doubting. Still, they bucked Pastor's wishes by calling her April Anne—in private.

Cindy started hemorrhaging after giving birth. It seemed like it would never stop, but the midwife was an old hand. No hospital though. (Against one of the Precepts somehow, though

Andrew couldn't figure out which one; they changed with *Animal Farm* frequency.) Cindy fought the abdominal and vaginal pain without drugs and was largely left alone by the Remnants once the bleeding stopped. (The midwife was dismissed once her patient was out of mortal danger.) Weak beyond measure, Cindy could only watch as they carried her baby away to be blessed by Pastor. The next day Andrew stayed with his ailing wife (the baby was still with the elder sisters) until Big Rick showed up at his door. "Pastor says today is a workday." So Andrew arranged for a Remnant woman (Minnie, one of the least scary ones) to keep an eye on Cindy. Pastor drove Andrew home at the end of the day, and when they entered the rented domicile, Cindy was curled up in a ball on the floor, and Minnie stood over her, reading the Bible aloud. "Get up, woman," Pastor said to Cindy, "for your man needs his dinner. He has worked and sweated the earth today and deserves to be greeted with a banquet." Pastor told Andrew, "Take a shower. When you are finished your ablutions, your wife will have dinner on the table." And she did.

Later that night as they climbed into bed, Cindy, with a weak smile, said, "Seems to me it's really hard to get into heaven."

+

Tuesday, October 26–Wednesday, October 27, 2010 (Days 1,292–1,293)

When he woke up, he didn't know who he was. He no longer recognized the face he shaved each morning, and he certainly didn't know his wife anymore. And how she allowed Pastor to…ahh, that was his own fault too, Andrew told himself. He'd been there. How many times had he watched Pastor and Sister and the priestholders with the children during what were called Faith Tests? He'd even provided the ecclesiastical leadership with something from the job site they could use as a weapon for just such occasions. (He could always be counted on to follow instructions.) And now April Anne…in the hospital…again… There would be no divine healing. He readied himself for work, as his wife prepared for the breakfast shift and an afternoon spent flipping burgers. What else could they do? Pastor had decreed that Andrew and Cindy could only visit April Anne in the hospital during the evening and only if accompanied by a priestholder. Their daughter's stay was short, thank God, but he had to speak to a social worker before she was released. (Cindy was working the drive-thru.) But the social worker was bored, and Andrew's tongue failed him, what with a priestholder standing in the doorway, and his daughter was discharged without incident.

At lunchtime, he took off before Big Rick could gather the employees for noon Bible study at the job site in New Hope and drove all the way across the county to Marlo's Bookstore in Rhawnhurst. (He wanted to cut down on the chances he'd be seen.) There he bought all the books he could find on cults. The Branch Davidians. The Manson Family. The Moonies. Books on the Mormons and the Adventists and the Christian Scientists too. *Dianetics* even. That night after Cindy went to bed (they only made love on those nights Pastor had marked on a calendar), he cruised web site after web site, searching for crumbs, clues, hints of an existence outside—*after*—the Remnant Church. His existence *before* he seemed to barely remember. As it was, he only glimpsed the outside world through the thick shimmer of Mount Rock's bubble (where even newspapers weren't allowed). Oh, he saw plenty on the Internet (the parental controls set by the priestholders were easy enough to get around)—pornography sites, gambling sites, even wife-swapping sites—but he didn't want to masturbate or gamble (both forbidden). He wanted to find other people who'd lived in a Pentecostal community—a fellowship not normally associated with a destructive cult environment—or had been part of an Adventist offshoot group with heavy millenarian beliefs. He wanted to know how those people lived with themselves. Andrew wanted to know if they recognized their own faces in the bathroom mirror or only saw what they'd been told to see.

The next day on the job site, Joe Kirnen, the supervisor of the plumbing and sewer crew (not part of Pastor's company), came over to Andrew and, without looking at him, said, " 'Suffer' in early seventeenth century English, when the King James Bible was published, meant 'permit' or 'allow,' not 'suffer' as we know it." Andrew stared straight ahead. Joe Kirnen was one of the few outsiders to be around Cindy and April Anne for any significant length of time. (Although it was like being around visitors from another planet, they'd been host to Joe and his wife a few times while the current job dragged on due to permit complications and other degradations perpetrated upon the Church's company by outsiders; Pastor allowed the Kirnens to be invited to various churchgoing employees' homes because he thought they were ripe for the picking, but Andrew didn't even try.) " 'Suffer little children.' Sounds creepy now no matter what you think 'suffer' means, right? But the full verse from Matthew is: 'Jesus said, Suffer little children, and forbid them not, to come unto me: for of such is the kingdom of heaven.' The context is clear." Andrew began walking away. "I've seen the bruises, Drew." Andrew stopped but pretended not to hear. "And I know the reason I haven't seen them lately is because the police and Child Welfare Services have been out to Mount Rock. And I know this because my wife and I called them. And I know you and Cindy didn't hurt April Anne; if anything, it appears that you're looking for ways to protect her. And I know that the reason your pastor and his wife aren't behind bars right now is because they were tipped off. I don't know by whom, but your pastor has more fingers in more pies in Mondauk County than he has actual digits—and pies equal friends. And, finally, Drew, I know that if Child Welfare Services came today and checked the tops of the children's heads or the bottom of their feet, they would find the bruises and burn marks that not so long ago were on their cheeks and foreheads and arms." *So he knew.* Joe Kirnen stuffed a card in Andrew's front pocket, right beneath his name patch. "You can at least get a recommendation." Andrew looked at the card later when he was alone in his car. It was for Steve Hassan, cult exit counselor and expert in the field of thought-reform—brainwashing—and coercive cults, at the Freedom of Mind Center in Massachusetts.

+

Thursday, January 7–Monday, October 25, 2010 (Days 1,000–1,291)

January 7 was the day they first heard of such things, and during the service the next evening, Pastor preached, "If you love the devil, even a little bit, even just enough to sin that one time since your baptism, then a true Apostle of Christ, such as I, can declare that your children be destroyed because they will have the devil in them too. But if they still have a *pinch* of love for our Lord and Saviour, I say unto you, perchance Lucifer can be beaten out of them. The thrashings of love. 'Suffer little children!' " That night, during the children's Bible study, Pastor knocked five-year-old Nicky Dettori from his blue chair and stepped on his stomach. In February, a piece of PVC pipe Andrew took from the job site and cut to his boss' specifications began to be used by Pastor and Sister (and sometimes Big Rick and the other priestholders) to regularly beat the children in order to ascertain, the preacher said, which of them were merely sinful (those that cried) and which were the devil's spawn (those that didn't). All cried—which increased the beatings; Pastor couldn't be wrong: if the Apostle said that Lucifer's offspring were among their own, then it must be so. In June, seven-year-old Stacy Miller was sent to the emergency room after being tied to a chair for three days by Sister Deborah and deprived of food. (She'd cried too quietly.) "I love her *so* much," Sister said as the ambulance pulled away. That anyone called 911 was a surprise, as the Remnants generally avoided doctors and hospitals and the police. Soon, Child Welfare Services started poking around, but Pastor ordered Big Rick to only beat the children on the bottom of their "cloven feet" or on the tops of their "horned heads," presumably to hide the bruises. The CWS investigation came to a quick and quiet conclusion. Andrew thought they either believed Stacy's parents when they said that their daughter had been so sick, she couldn't keep anything down, or Pastor had some pull with the local authorities. Child Welfare Services also stated that they saw no signs of abuse or neglect of the other Remnant children.

In October, in the parsonage, Pastor picked up April Anne and placed her left hand on a lit stove burner. She had giggled during the evening's service.

+

Tuesday, November 23, 2010 (Day 1,320)

April Anne was playing in the sandbox by herself, wearing an ill-fitting, ragged parka, when Andrew came home from work. An older girl, maybe eight years old, stood nearby poking a dead bird with a stick. "Where's Mommy?" he asked. His daughter could sometimes speak like a four- or five-year-old, a result of being exposed to endless Biblical readings and exegeses, he supposed. But she just as easily slipped back to the jabbering that seemed (to him anyway) somehow more appropriate to someone younger than thirty-one months.

"Wray for Dada Wata," was April's answer.

"I didn't quite—"

The older girl, without looking up from her bird, spoke up: "She said, 'Praying for Daddy Walter.' "

Daddy Walter?

Andrew shook his head as if to clear it. He checked the top of the child's head, which seemed to be healing nicely, and the bottom of her feet, which were black and blue and tender to the touch. Her left palm was tattooed with angry red scars, and she had a sandwich baggie over her hand; he assumed it was meant to keep the sand from irritating her burns.

"Tell him, Anne," the older girl said in a yawn. She'd skewered the bird with her stick and now swung it lazily through the air. "Tell him like they told you."

"Pastor got him, Daddy," April Anne said, pointing to her feet. "He caught the devil just in time." Then she tore the head off a Barbie and began ripping its hair out.

That evening at service, in front of the others, Andrew confronted Pastor and Sister. (Cindy weakly reached for his arm like a zombie on Valium but missed and spent the rest of his harangue staring at the wooden pulpit, drooling slightly.) He'd questioned the Church before but had never accused its leaders. "You hit our children. You beat them." He pointed at Sister Deborah who wore a disbelieving smirk on her wrinkled face. "You starve them." (Andrew hoped she wouldn't speak; he'd begun to fantasize that with her heavy German accent, she was actually a Nazi in hiding.) He could hear the division in the congregation behind him, but he didn't dare look back. Some yelled, "Apostate!" Others murmured the names of their children. "You burned April Anne's hand!" Andrew howled, looking at his own hands. To each accusation, Pastor leaned on the pulpit, casual as hell, as if he was just leaning on the counter at the Eagle Diner or the post office, shooting the bull, and said, "I don't recall that" or "I don't remember it that way." When Andrew had almost exhausted himself, saving his best punches for last—he'd followed up on the Kirnens' efforts and had gone to the police and filed a complaint; he too had called Child Welfare Services (who'd seemingly thrown up their hands, but it had been worth a shot) and he'd contacted a cult exit counselor (although he still wasn't sure the Mount Rock Remnants were a cult; they didn't seem at all like the People's

Temple or Heaven's Gate, but he didn't voice this doubt out loud)—Pastor unleashed a haymaker: "But you were there, Andrew. If you saw these things you say happened, if you saw children beaten with your PVC pipe, if you saw your devilish child burned, what did you do? You did nothing. If you bore witness, you lifted not a finger. You stood by. You were there. What kind of parent would stand by and watch this sort of thing, I ask you? Verily, I say unto thee, no parent at all, rather a vessel of the Morning Star." He paused. "You were there, Andrew. You were there when it happened."

Cindy fell to her knees but managed to deliver the knockout punch. "I sinned with Walter," she said in a soft, choking voice, not looking up at her husband. "April Anne is…"

Big Rick escorted Andrew out of the church and beat the living hell out of him behind a dumpster.

+

Tuesday, January 11, 2011 (Day 1,369)

He had tried to find out where they'd taken April Anne, but the most he could piece together had been that "Aunt" Minnie had taken his daughter to the group's new satellite church in upstate New York. Hardly anyone would speak to him. If they did, it wasn't for very long. They called him a heretic and a cuckold. He had been fired. Then on January 11, he was excommunicated and told to pack what he could from his one room apartment and vacate the premises immediately. (The building was also owned by Pastor's company.) Big Rick, chewing on the ends of his enormous mustache, watched as Andrew threw what little he had into a cardboard box. But amongst his meager belongings Andrew had his own piece of PVC pipe, and he applied it to Big Rick's head, putting Pastor's pit bull down long enough to run back to his former (rented) house. No one answered the door at first, but he knew his wife was in there. He could hear her praying with Sister Deborah and some other female Remnants. When Cindy finally came to the door, Mount Rock's Eva Braun stood behind her, glaring at Andrew, giving him a Remnant-flavored *malocchio*. Another woman whispered into a cell phone, "*Breach, breach!*"

"Wellspring Retreat and Resource Center in Albany, Ohio," he panted, pulling a much folded pamphlet from his pocket and pushing it through the mail slot. "They're not involved in deprogramming, the literature says, just reintegration into mainstream society. And they're Christians. I got the recommendation from…doesn't matter. Come with me. We'll find April Anne, and we'll—"

"No." Just like that. Sister Deborah nodded with satisfaction and bared her yellowed dentures. Cindy told him, "Pastor is the spark that lights the way. He knows our hearts, he's in touch with our immortal souls, he has the gift of prophecy, and when Jesus leaves the sanctuary on the last day, the Remnants will be carried into the clouds by angels."

"Poppycock," he said, and Cindy shrunk away from the screen door. He knew that the next time he heard from her would be through a lawyer when he was served with divorce papers.

He walked backwards down the walk, keeping in mind that a recovered Big Rick was more than likely coming his way. He just kept his eyes on Sister Deborah, who wore her trademark smirk and a beautiful diamond choker.

-end-

The Martyr School

————A Novella————

Quotes I Like

I expected to find that God had simply been a projection of human needs and desires…that "he" would mirror the fears and yearnings of society…. My predictions were not entirely unjustified…. [I]t is far more important for a particular idea of God to *work* than for it to be logically or scientifically sound.

Karen Armstrong

[R]omantic comedy is the genre most prone to distortions and deceptions…because it's all about identity, [and] the stories it tells are the ones that people tell themselves about themselves. Its revelations are the most troubling, and its clichés are the most comforting.

Richard Brody

+

So of course we were concerned when my sister Lori said she wanted to move to New Orleans. *Transferring* had become a mystical word for her. She said she was having a time of it at St. Hubert's High as a freshman, what with the school shootings, being dumped by Gerardo after only two months of bliss, having no one ask her to the freshman dance, and not passing Mr. Hugh's Shakespeare class, which was not, as she'd originally thought, a drama class but a literature one. The Martyr School was for her, she claimed.

When our mom expressed surprise, Lori said, "I thought you knew." Knew *what* was the mystery. "Why are you getting so upset?" Lori asked, feigning surprise of her own before she delivered the knockout punch: "Daddy would've let me go." He wouldn't have, I was sure, but Lori knew how to shut down an argument before it could take shape. She believed her redemption lay in Louisiana.

At first, I assumed Lori's wish to become a martyr was largely symbolic, for it belied her long-held belief in the redemptive nature (and epistemic curiosity) of romantic comedies. She watched the best (and sometimes the worst) of the genre ad nauseam and nourished herself in what she believed to be their auspicious glow. My sister even kept a list of the ones she'd seen in a spiral notebook, assigning each a number grade. Lori wrote their overfamiliar declarations, bon mots, and ripostes on her arms and her legs, but like a cutter, she always wore long sleeves, even in the summer, and never wore shorts. Mom and I only saw her quotable body art during unguarded moments that occurred naturally in a house of only women.

You complete me.

I'm also just a girl, standing in front of a boy, asking him to love her.

You will never age for me, nor fade, nor die.

Nobody puts Baby in a corner.

Even in cinematic moments that appeared hopeless, these words were imbued with hope. So why would a girl who cried every time Westley said, "As you wish," in *The Princess Bride* want to become a martyr for Christ? Mom and I could only think of one reason that made an ounce of sense: the Gerardo Incident, as we called it. When the essence of Meg Ryan movies had failed to translate into experience, Lori found a new altar—not one to kneel before but one upon which to sacrifice herself. She'd never had the best reactions to romantic failures.

Gerardo was of Italian descent, somewhat good-looking but vaguely defined (in that way where you could see his future possibilities: a growth spurt leading to locker room godliness or a developmental stagnation and a descent into full-blown geek). He was a freshman like us, but because he'd been held back a year or two somewhere along the way, he had his license and drove an '80s Camaro complete with a tape deck and a collection of his mom's disco cassettes. (The car had been hers during her salad days.) That was Gerardo's claim to coolness, I suppose, or at least Lori thought so, since she mentioned his car every third sentence. His less-than-cool aspect was apparent in the elastic band attached to his glasses and wrapped around his head. Gerardo told Lori his parents made him wear it because he'd been an overactive kid who was constantly breaking his glasses while, I don't know, running into the television during *Outer Limits* reruns or maybe hitting himself in the head with a fungo bat. The real reason, others in my class suspected, was that the jocks (and sometimes even members of their female auxiliary, the self-named Bod Squad) would smack Gerardo in the back of the head whenever they caught him in the hallway or at the urinals. (The latter strictly the boys' turf naturally.)

Lori and Gerardo would hang out in our basement, slow dancing to Styx's "Come Sail Away" or making out in the dark. Our dad kept opening the basement door, making a racket on the landing, and turning the lights on. He was only half-serious; he liked messing with Lori; Lori was easy to mess with. Shortly before Gerardo, without warning, dumped my sister, Dad's hand was caught in an old industrial ironing and folding machine at work. The machine lacked a properly installed safety guard and his co-workers had been unable to shut it off. As if our father's folding fatality wasn't shocking enough, Lori's announcement that she wanted to move to New Orleans to attend the Martyr School (and would run away if not allowed) rattled what remained of our family. We were adrift without Dad.

My sister and I were twins, the Duke twins, Lisa and Lori, but we didn't have what twins in the movies and on television shows had: we weren't telepathic and we didn't feel what the other felt. We were about as opposite as twins could get. We were fraternal, not identical, twins, but like many siblings, we had shared features; it was just that my sister's were scrambled. I was considered pretty, Lori possibly cute (except for her not-so-slight mustache). Only in very dim lighting did we resemble one another. But looks weren't the only department where Lori and I differed. I was a neat freak; Lori actually enjoyed making a mess. I liked to think of myself as demure; Lori lived to create drama (and I believe she measured her worth in the reactions to her histrionics). While I strived for honesty (or my version of it), Lori could be manipulative, sometimes in the subtlest of ways. (She hid her snicker beneath a veil of ingenuousness.) Lori hated her middle name (Mathilde) and would make up her own when it suited her; I loved my middle name (Alessandra) and would say it in conjunction with my first name just to get under my sister's skin. In grade school, I'd read the Hardy Boys because I thought boys had more fun; Lori read Nancy Drew, Mom said, because my sister wanted to be more like me: a little lady. Though I found the assertion dubious, I dropped the brothers Hardy like hot potatoes. While I envied Frank and Joe their intuitiveness and inherent tidiness, I did not wish to be a paragon of anything.

School eventually created chasms between my sister and me where there had only been cracks. It wasn't just that I excelled in my classes, while Lori merely sputtered along. Though not a member of the Bod Squad, I was popular with both boys and girls. (But I didn't date much yet; I wasn't boy-obsessed like my sister.) Lori was immensely unpopular except with her own kind: God's Rejects—that was what someone started calling them late in grade school. Weight, hygiene, social manners, alleged wealth—these were all factors in whether you sat at the cool kids' tables at lunch. Once someone was classified as a pariah, they were unable to ever claw past the cruel determinations of the pre-teen set. (Lori never got a pass because she was my sister, and she would have resented me if she did.) Rejected boys were routinely beaten up by the bullies (close associates of the jocks), but I thought the girls had it worse. Unless the boys were getting physically abused, they were generally ignored (cruel moniker aside), which was what I figured they preferred. The Bod Squad elevated ignoring the rejected girls into an art, their outcast status made clear not only in the schoolyard but also in those precious couple of minutes between the start and end of every class, when we lined up in the hall before entering the next room. This barely supervised time was a beehive of social activity where hands were held and Jolly Ranchers exchanged and paper fortune tellers, which revealed your favorite color or the name of the boy you liked, were passed on. During these times, the offscouring of scholastic society were constantly reminded that not only did they not belong with the beautiful people, they were not wanted—they would never be rescued from their plight. Ugly ducklings could never become swans because they were born repellent; such deliverance only occurred in romantic comedies.

But Lori wasn't hideous or disfigured, just socially feeble with looks that were somewhat askew. Thus among the big boned girls and the girls whose faces could stop a truck (to use a favorite phrase of Dad's), Lori was top of the heap. This, of course, meant nothing to the beautiful people—the heap was still an unsightly pile of Clearasil-deficient Dungeon Masters with *Star Trek* communicators in their pockets. With her own kind, Lori blended in; she was (somewhat) normal, invisible in a way that wasn't negative. I'd watched her go from oblivious to depressed to openly reveling in being reviled. Lori was not one to spend her time with her nose pressed up against the glass looking in. The only upside to being a nobody was that the dating pool was a captive audience. Only in the movies did the geek girl snare the hot guy; in real life rejected girls could have their pick of the runts.

Because of Lori's grade school propensity for public disasters, like being caught picking her nose during math class or leaving a wet spot on her seat, her social status followed her to high school, where my friends called my sister and her lunch table companions the Substrata. (Better than God's Rejects, I thought.) So I knew little about the Gerardo romance when it was happening and knew even less about its ending, except this: Gerardo had gotten laid during their time together and not by Lori. It was some heavyset public school chick from over in Mayfair, who had more of a mustache than Lori had. My twin was crushed, and per the pastor's instructions, we watched her carefully for signs of depression. But Lori had us beat. The pastor had shown us an article that claimed "the topmost layer of malaise is a blanket of depression about being depressed…" Lori, it turned out, had accepted her despair, and though I'd never known her to be particularly devout, she felt her melancholia was a calling; the absence of expectation gave her faith—in what, I didn't know.

+

From the *Martyr School Handbook*:

All students are expected to arrive with an appropriate amount of number two pencils and black ink pens, notebooks, appropriate clothing for when not in uniform (nothing tawdry or slatternly), toiletries, and straight razors. First aid (when appropriate) and educational tools, such as textbooks, rope, and practice weapons, will be provided by the school. There is a lab fee due in the freshman year, but it is a onetime fee.

+

Lori had applied to the Martyr School unbeknownst to us. Her essay must have been particularly convincing because they accepted her immediately, full scholarship. Mom didn't even have to submit financial information. My sister would begin her sophomore year in New Orleans if my mother permitted her to go, but it was usually difficult to stop Lori (and Mom had become something of a pushover since Dad died). "Fine, whatever," my twin would say when she was told no, sulking and generally making life miserable for all those around her, behavior which frequently made our parents cave. (Her antics had the side effect of turning things upside down a bit, making me, the good kid, inconspicuous at home, but I discovered I liked going somewhat unseen; if I'd desired doing so, I could have gotten away with everything Lori wanted to with very little effort.) But since Dad's death, Lori didn't always wait for her demeanor to turn our mother around. Mom was super Catholic (and attended as many funerals at our church as she could), but the Martyr School was beyond the pale. She had every intention of forbidding Lori to go to New Orleans, but if playing the Dad card didn't result in immediate capitulation, I knew Lori would just sneak out of a window, hitch her way south, and attend anyway. Lori's outsider status had made her stubborn.

Besides, Lori had a history of the sort of behavior advocated by the Martyr School, whose brochure heralded it as being a place for the "worthy and the shattered." It was behavior, our mother thought, that a good (legitimate) prep school could correct, but Lori had no intention of being fixed. She always allowed her worse tendencies to define her. In the eighth grade, she'd dated a boy named Donnie Benz for eight months. They'd even gone to second base she'd told me in one of her rare sharing moods. (I wasn't quite sure at the time what second base was, but it sounded far since I'd yet to be up at bat.) Then Donnie threw her over for a girl who looked like a damaged pop singer and was known to go to third base (which sounded *really* far). Lori didn't take being dumped well. She did, however, take what she called a *bunch* of over-the-counter sleeping pills. Lori told me that she had to have her stomach pumped, but Mom said that she found my sister with her finger down her throat in the bathroom, where she confessed to taking the medication. The ER doctor called it a suicidal gesture and told our parents that my sister probably only took three to four pills. Lori had to see a psychologist, who told Mom that what my sister needed was fresh air and recommended that she join the Girl Scouts. When Lori met Andre, an Austrian exchange student, a few weeks later, we were elated that she was moving on, but when he hooked up with her then-best friend Michelle before he flew back to Europe (doing the deed, word was), Lori walked around with a belt strapped to her throat for two days. This time our parents made Lori see a psychologist *and* a psychiatrist, but in a sudden rush of sisterly affection, she wouldn't see the former without me. The psychiatrist didn't last but a minute; Lori couldn't handle the psych drugs prescribed. She said he seemed more like a salesman than a doctor. The psychologist (not the Scout-espousing one) lasted a little longer only because of my presence. In the end, the man's habit of wearing black socks with corduroys combined with the creepy double set of doors in his office (designed to keep the sound of neuroses from escaping to the waiting room, which was filled with creased copies of *Highlights* magazines that were older than we were) led Lori to cut her therapy short. Like I said, it was impossible to stop my sister.

Like a little child peeking through her fingers, I wanted to believe that the Martyr School's perilous notoriety was due to its relative proximity to what was referred to as the badlands of the Lower Ninth Ward, where a couple of Mom's friends at church told us that the days were nearly as pernicious as the nights—and the nights were given over to pure savagery—and that was *before* Hurricane Katrina; none had dared gone back since the floodwalls and levees had been breached, as the city, they believed, was now a watery soup of lawlessness. But I could only peek for so long. We knew of two kids who'd attended the Martyr School in New Orleans: science geek Jenny Branch, who'd gotten pregnant during her sophomore year only to lose the baby dramatically during algebra, and Teresa Devalcante's cousin Margaret from Mondauk County, who was devoted to the Virgin Mary and paranoid to the point of pleading to her parents to put a lock on the refrigerator so that the terrorists wouldn't break in and poison the bologna. Both Jenny and Margaret had graduated with honors from the Martyr School. I remember hearing that after her miscarriage, Jenny tried to slit her wrists with a razor, but she only made minor, surface cuts that went the wrong way. Apparently her resolve and the direction of the blade were addressed during her time in New Orleans. I don't know where Teresa's cousin was interred, but Jenny was laid to rest in Crestview Cemetery, and every year her family went en masse and had a picnic at the gravesite. (Jenny loved picnics—the girl had a thing for ants.)

I thought Lori was on some Goth vision quest, a self-imposed rite of passage that required her to go to a school with a reputation for quiet extremism that came with a body count. How does one study to become a martyr anyway, I wondered. Wasn't that something one stumbled into? Wasn't doing it yourself cheating? If the school's handbook (translated from Latin it claimed) held any answers, Mom and I didn't know—when it arrived, Lori read it cover to cover and rarely let it out of her sight; she even put it under her pillow when she went to bed. I was only able to glance at the first couple of pages when she was in the shower. (It was the New Revised Edition, according to the title page; I wondered if the changes or additions were also translated from Latin.) When a second copy was delivered days later, my twin frowned, and I was sure my countenance was similar. Lori stomped up the stairs, and Mom just looked at me and mouthed, "Please."

So Lori boarded the bus to New Orleans and the Martyr School, and I went too with explicit instructions to not get swept along and kill myself while I went about persuading Lori to return home with me.

No pressure.

+

A week before we left for Louisiana, I walked to the delicatessen two blocks over for a final hoagie, something to cheer me up. I couldn't pretend that the small prep school for the soon-to-be-dead was anything other than what it was, but as far as specifics went, I chose to remain ignorant, never even opening my handbook, so I didn't know what to expect.

Mrs. Armstrong, who owned the deli, had a daughter who'd gone missing a few years ago. (The police believed she'd died in a crack house fire.) After Mrs. Armstrong rang me up, she placed a slick hand upon mine, gazing, as she had done most likely hundreds of times a week, at a wallet-sized photograph of her Sylvia taped to the side of the register and told me what she probably told every customer: "My Sylvia sent this to me. The police don't believe it's her." The girl in the picture wore the soon-to-be–familiar black jumper with the crimson and bone insignia, but at the time, it meant nothing to me. I didn't know Sylvia, but you could forgive the police their disbelief: the girl's face was covered in scars and did not at all resemble the little picture from the St. Hubert's yearbook that was taped to the side of the deli case. Mrs. Armstrong patted my hand. "There was no return address. That tells you something, don't it?" I nodded as if I understood, said thank you, and left, wondering when does someone let go of death (I was devastated that my dad was gone, but I didn't lose *me* when I lost *him*), when the question I should have been asking was: how does someone give up on life?

Well, let me count the ways.

+

Sister Ignatius, a hunched over nun whose face was covered with moles of various shapes and shades, measured and weighed and poked and prodded me while I stood before her in only in my underwear and bra. A line of similarly clad girls waited their turn in a dusty hallway behind me; the girl who was next had one foot nervously placed over the other with only the wall holding her up. We'd all deposited our cell phones into a garbage bag and fed the clothes we'd arrived in (except for our undergarments) into a furnace. There were two other nuns in the room, which was stuffy and smelled like I imagined a boy's dirty socks would smell. Sister Ignatius didn't smell much better; the edge of her coif was damp with sweat. I could see the hints of white bandages around her wrists, stark against the cuffs of her habit.

"No ligature marks, no telling scars," said Sister Ignatius. At a tiny desk, a tall nun with hair on the swell beneath her chin nodded her head violently and proceeded to scribble on a form with such fury that it seemed as if I could hear each letter being engraved on the white paper. When she absently hiked up her habit to scratch her hairy upper leg, I caught sight of a metal cilice—a spiked garter—wrapped around a thigh engulfed by inflamed purples and blacks. Were the Order of Martyrs ascetics or just poorly groomed masochists?

Sister Ignatius pulled at the band of my underwear and let it snap back. "Cotton blend," and the scribbling nun and the plump one who stood behind a wooden counter shook their heads. Without warning, Sister Ignatius shoved her hand down the front of my underwear, and her long fingers probed the inside of my vagina. I wanted to run, but my bare feet felt soldered to the floor. *Sharp pain.* "Intact," Sister Ignatius announced. Not anymore, I thought. As the nun at the desk dutifully recorded my virginity and Sister Ignatius washed her hand in a silver bowl of water, I wondered if a nun from the Order of Martyrs had just popped my cherry.

The plump nun behind the counter said, "So medieval," but her disapproving tone sounded practiced. She stood in a small room adorned with shelves, my next stop after being probed. When she turned her round full face towards me, I gasped (to myself): the left side, from her forehead to her multiple chins, was blistered and scabbed. She handed me a school uniform, a jet black jumper with a splash of crimson and bone over one breast: the school's insignia, an oval with the institution's name in Latin (*Schola Martyris*) running along the edge of the top half, beginning and ending with a small Cross of St. John (a downward dagger adorned with *fleurs-de-lys* at the top and on either end of the cross arm). In the center of the insignia was the Lamb of God, halo and all. Usually the Lamb was depicted holding a pole that bore a small banner (decorated with a cross) and topped with the Chi-Rho Christogram (☧). But this Lamb was not metaphorically sacrificial—it was blatantly martyred (with a disturbingly placid look on its face): livestock no more, its bent leg didn't hold a mere pole, but a spear that went through the bottom of the Lamb's neck and came out the other side, the point of the weapon aimed towards heaven. Below the pathetic beast was a chalice adorned with more Latin: *Felo de se Christus*—a felon of himself to Christ (according to Sister Ignatius).

"Someday you will offer your own full chalice to the Lord," said the recording nun in a pinched voice and with a wistful look.

"Uncross your eyebrows, child," the pudgy, scorched nun whispered to me, as her oversized thumb caressed the insignia on my carefully folded jumper. It was then I noticed the crimson droplets that fell from the underside of the Lamb into the chalice.

"What the…"

The nun who wore the cilice stopped scribbling.

"…duck?"

"A substitution for an expletive is still a sin, girl," said Sister Ignatius, "because you *thought* the word."

"Like witch for bitch?" I stage whispered. The pain between my legs had climbed into my stomach; every muscle movement threatened a hail of vomit.

All three nuns nodded. A few students near the doorway awaiting their turn snickered.

"This is how they begin, child, imbuing you with the language of the bully, the abuser," said Sister Ignatius. She appeared to be trying to tie the cloth measuring tape into a noose.

"Who did this to you, my dear?" asked the burnt nun. "Who taught you these words?"

I was dizzy. I wanted to tell them to listen closely to kids in the schoolyard. I wanted to name any number of R-rated movies I'd snuck into.

"That's the first step: know who your persecutors are," said the tall nun who probably wore a hair shirt beneath her habit in addition to the metal cilice. "What must be considered is whether their maltreatment is worth dying for."

Sister Ignatius pooh-poohed her. "Your presence at our school is evidence enough that you have unduly suffered. Stay on the path, child, and Monsignor Jaeger and the Elders will see your death recorded in the *Martyrologium Romanum* while your soul ascends to heaven."

The recording nun sniffed and said, "Not all are worthy."

"Is that why you're all still here?" I asked, as if joking around, but sarcasm, I should have remembered from eight years in a Catholic elementary school, more often than not went over like a lead balloon when it came to nuns.

The tall sister and the plump one stared at me, then started talking at once, as I resisted the urge to throw up.

"Shhh!" Sister Ignatius said to the other nuns, rubbing her temples, as if battling back their bad mojo, but she didn't sound authoritative, her exclamation the hiss of a leaky tire.

The burnt nun ignored her. "In our order, we almost die every night," she said, raising a hand to the damaged side of her face, never actually touching it, "and every morning we are still here.

"Try not to stain your uniform," she added as I left. "Blood is so hard to get out."

+

From the *Martyr School Handbook*:

There are many methods of self-deliverance, many roads a student can take. But all roads lead to God if a student's intentions are clear and honorable. If life has become unbearable, it is usually because events have conspired against any reasonable expectation of tolerance. Even Job, from the depths of his depression, cried, "Let the day perish wherein I was born," and only broke his lamentations when the Lord spoke to him from a whirlwind. But we are not all Job, and the noise of the day distracts us from recognizing the voice of God in even a zephyr let alone a thunderclap. "To each his own suffering," wrote the first patriarch of our order, "and to each his own death." We take leave of what is corporeal not because we are unwilling to struggle but rather because we are overrun and outmatched. But we are doughty warriors for Christ, and as such, we offer our misery and our torment to Him that sacrificed Himself upon the cross. When those who embrace the Cimmerian shade place knives at our throats, for Him we fall upon our swords. We may fashion our own nooses but only because ropes were placed around our necks by those still in darkness. "For God hath not given us the spirit of fear," the Apostle Paul wrote, and at the Martyr School you will learn to embrace your persecution and "be of good courage," for there will come a time when you have no cheeks left to turn. Your hand stayed, the only blood you have to spill is your own.

The authorities would have students believe suicide is murder, and they are correct. So to be murdered, as a Christian, by one's own hand, in the face of overwhelming situational persecution, is to die a martyr. "Ye have not yet resisted unto blood, striving against sin" (Hebrews 12:4), but soon that hour will be upon each and every student.

Please note: in the back of this book, pupils will find our school's regulations and rules of conduct, including the honor code. Study these well. Ignorance is not an acceptable excuse. Your comportment, adherence, and obedience are presumed. As a former headmaster wrote, "One cannot take the great leap if one's shoes aren't shined."

+

I didn't sleep the first night at the Martyr School. I just listened to Lori's easy breathing as she dreamed, and I wondered how she'd had the time to hang all those posters on her side of the dorm room. The second night, what sounded like a moan from the floor above sent me straight out of bed to call our mom on the phone in our room. I was breathless and making little sense. The truth had hit me like somebody else's cold, wet washcloth. What had been a cause for concern was now as real as the gallows on the far side of the soccer field. The enormity of it all came out as babble, but all Mom said was, "You have to go along to get along, dear." Pause. "Just don't *really* go along." I wanted to scream, but the way she sounded, like she was caught in a bear trap and trying not to alert the hunters, shut me down. I was here for a reason. I needed to assimilate in order to fan the flames of fear. Extraction was a last resort. I knew I couldn't convince Lori to leave until her dread overtook her programming, and I had to be there when it happened. The way I figured, Lori was here because she thought if she *believed*, she could become visible (to more than just her mother and her twin). To make Lori believe in me, I had to become the opposite of visible. I had to immerse myself—without forgetting to dog paddle.

So I went about getting along and for a little while, forgot about the washcloth.

+

When Lori and I had first arrived, I thought the kids here were a gloomy bunch, but once we were among them, what seemed unusual became commonplace and in no time, the student body was just another messy and messed up bunch of teenagers. (There weren't many of us, so almost every experience seemed intimate.) I found I was excited to be away from home, which I hadn't expected, so thrilled, in fact, that the other kids' preoccupations with the big sleep stopped being odd (and immersion no longer seemed an effort). Even the way some of them traded tales of their brushes with death and compared scars and other self-inflected wounds seemed almost normal once Lori and I were inside the womb of the school. Milieu control, I thought, remembering Ms. Shevchenko's lectures on thought reform—i.e., mind control, menticide, coercive persuasion—in our Social Justice class (back in our local Catholic high school), but this observation began to seem meaningless once stuck in the Martyr School's muck and mire, which forced students into each other's arms or, even better, into isolation. It was difficult to keep my head about me at first.

The main building resembled a crumbling castle that leaned in such a manner that it appeared to be shambling towards the western woods, where the detritus and duff quickly gave way to the swamplands and its bald cypress and tupelo-gum tree sentries. It also appeared as if the castle had spawned a few smaller, most likely equally unsound buildings, including a former seminary, part of which had been haphazardly turned into the boys' dormitory, haunted, the upperclassmen told us, by the diaconal ghosts of guilty masturbators past. (The school's grand ruin, one teacher told us, reflected the state of our souls after being persecuted by the bullies of the world: still whole but showing signs of stress and imminent deterioration.) On the northern side of the girls' residence hall there was a large section of an old iron red-rusted fence topped with spikes at regular intervals, which in the twilight looked like a row of blood-covered spears—and during the day, it always felt like twilight, the students crepuscular creatures scurrying from building to building, for the numerous southern live oaks, bearded with Spanish moss, shielded us from the sun and gave the school a vespertine atmosphere. Even the soccer field seemed to always be in the shade. I don't know if the original intent of the fence was to keep intruders out or intimidate those within, but no one dared touch what remained, for its surface moisture left your hand flaked in what looked like dried blood. Everything seemed to sweat: students, buildings, even rocks. The heat of the day crept out of the bayou that ran through the southern part of the campus, often becoming oppressive with seemingly impenetrable fatigue draping our heads like wet blankets; as time went on, it felt less like heavy bedding and more like hands determined to push us straight into a soggy hell. At night, we could hear the Mississippi tell its stories through the moist air, but no one believed it would ever tell ours.

The campus was surrounded by a ten-foot tall stone wall, decaying in places. From the outside, it would be hard to distinguish the Martyr School from an old prison, aside from the absence of barbed wire. (The top of our wall was decorated with large pieces of glass embedded into the rock; this was a common deterrent on many roofs and walls in certain parts of New Orleans, especially in the French Quarter.) There were even guard towers. What kind of religious order had what amounted to a not-so-secret police force, the Sanguine Knights of the Martyrs, the SKM? The students called them the Scum; the school quaintly referred to them as campus security guards. It became clear not soon after our arrival that the Scum weren't guarding the school from the outside—no, the Sanguine Knights of the Martyrs were there to make sure none of us left without permission during the school year. Passes to go off campus to the French Quarter or the Garden District were bestowed upon upperclassmen after approval from the vice provost's office. And even then...well, more than one student complained that they kept seeing a particular man during an evening out, only to notice him later in a Scum uniform on campus. We learned that if you had a pass to go outside the walls and explore the Quarter or the Marigny, there was a curfew, but it wasn't really enforced after your first couple of sojourns; the night and the early morning hours were yours, as long as you made it to your first class (which our Scum tails, we figured, would ensure). You didn't have to be bright-eyed and bushy-tailed, just awake enough to take at least semi-legible notes that you could decipher later.

The powers-that-be probably thought that the circus atmosphere of Bourbon, Royal, or Frenchmen Streets would help keep upperclassmen returning after Christmas or summer break. (The Scum, or so it seemed, couldn't do much outside of its sphere of influence.) The Order relied on the cloven-hoofed thump of the blues and the squeal of the damned that was jazz, to keep kids from running away, although the number of students of a particular class that tried to escape decreased by their third year, since those that made it that far in the Martyr School were pretty well indoctrinated by then. Ghost walking tours and po' boys, street musicians and Mardi Gras were simply used as tools of misdirection by the school, dazzling upperclassmen with passes: look at the wanton women showing their breasts, focus on their prized beads around their necks, glittering in the party lights, and pay no attention to your hand holding a gun to your head. If underclassmen could experience New Orleans like upperclassmen did, the number of freshman and sophomore runaways would dwindle; all you needed was a little cash from home or a job in the school kitchen after classes to have the night of your life if you paced yourself and didn't blow your wad in a fancy French restaurant or a seedy strip club that looked the other way when students entered—although the latter probably happened because of the presence of the Scum and not because of a lax age restriction policy. The Sanguine Knights were everywhere but home, the juniors and seniors told us, and the only reason they weren't there was because other states and territories, other cities and towns weren't willing to turn their heads the other way like Louisiana and New Orleans were, although, on occasion, a student who had to make an emergency trip home (family illness, what-have-you) was accompanied by at least one of the Scum (at the family's expense probably), but these were usually seniors prized either for their academic record or for the generosity of their families towards the institution. (Hard to believe, but there were wealthy families who would go on to support the school long after little Jimmy finished his hemlock infusion.) The Scum made sure the esteemed student made it back in time to die.

There were even rumors that the dorms were bugged, but if they were, not a word was said when Avery Pike and Delaney Kenis, before a small audience of girls trying their best not to laugh, simulated at top volume tribbing and cunnilingus, though we all thought Delaney would have preferred to be doing the real thing with Miss Pike. If the Scum were listening, school officials never called Avery and Delaney on the carpet, but probably only because debasement was encouraged. There was even a course dedicated to the practice of using degrading, demoralizing, and depraved behavior (including, but not limited to, homosexuality and promiscuity) to hit bottom and stay there. But breaking the rules was another story; infractions could land a student in more than hot water. There were no washouts at the Martyr School; no one tapped out here; the recalcitrant students that were sent to the disciplinarian's office emerged with a new vocabulary, a new sense of purpose, and lash marks across their backs and buttocks.

+

From the <u>*Martyr School Handbook*</u>:

Students planning to enter the accelerated program are expected to register with the front office before the end of the second week of a given semester. No diplomas will be issued to families of those students self-departing early without enrollment in the accelerated program or express consent from the headmaster.

+

On the northwestern side of the campus, in a cleared area of the woods, was a potter's field called God's Allotment. (All apologies to Thomas Hardy, I thought: "…in that shabby corner of God's allotment where He lets the nettles grow….") It was a skid of dirt and skeleton shrubs (with two old southern live oaks) where students whose deaths were not authorized and whose remains were not claimed by their families were buried, the latter happening more than half of the time, if the faculty were to be believed. But it was the unapproved suicides that landed the all-too-eager (dubbed the Fallen Failures) in coping graves with often three or four unclaimed and unembalmed bodies buried together about three feet underground in unfinished pine boxes. (At least that was what we were told.) Their final, crowded resting places were each surrounded by a retaining wall, no more than a couple of feet above the ground, designed to pack in the soil and protect it from rising water levels. This was a cheap way of burying the dead. Some of the older coping graves were covered in granite, but most were just topped with soil, many covered in moss. Upperclassmen told us to be careful not to step upon an earthen surface of a coping grave lest our weight be enough to break the lid of a coffin that had not yet succumbed to the climate-facilitated breakdown of body and box and had migrated near the surface.

Because of New Orleans' high water table, above-ground tombs crowded the city's cemeteries, and they were present in this part of the campus. To the east of God's Allotment was a parcel of consecrated ground surrounded by a short cast iron fence, rusted over, where the mausoleums that housed the deceased members of the Order of Martyrs could be found. But the clergy and the unordained religious, it seemed, fared little better than the Fallen

Failures: the mausoleums were far more decrepit and closer together than the ones tourists crowded to see in places such as Lafayette Cemetery in the Garden District or St. Louis Cemetery No. 1 in Tremé. The dead priests, nuns, and brothers were interred twenty to thirty to a mausoleum, their names affixed (barely) to the outside stone on worn copper plaques. A tiny cross following a name meant that the deceased had committed suicide, and there were very few little crosses on the tarnished plaques. *Do as I say, not as I do.* The burnt nun had implied that members of the Order were only allowed to bring themselves to the brink of death—after all, someone needed to see the teenagers off—so it was possible the few Order suicides were mistakes or perhaps they'd grown weary of the crimson circus—or maybe, just maybe, the weak-willed and those that dared to ask questions (or became infirm or demented) were dispatched by the Scum on orders of whomever wore the episcopal ring around these parts. (It was believed, for no discernible reason, that Monsignor Jaeger and the Elders didn't have the authority to knock off one of their own. But did no one think it odd that a school advocating martyrdom by suicide had enough senior clergy and laity of a certain age to make up a cabal called the Elders?) Of course, I never mentioned my theory on the Order's retirement plan aloud, and I never asked about the Elders' continued existence, but I didn't have to; rumors were a constant murmur at the Martyr School and impossible to avoid, and whatever I had thought had most likely been thought before—a sobering notion, but one that was not all that startling. No, what surprised me was that I wasn't disturbed by my grim speculation of ecclesiastical hits. Gloom was the norm here, but I was falling for the city (although I hadn't seen much outside of the campus yet). It was the little things like the intense scent from the Confederate jasmine that grew everywhere, covering even buildings and tombs, a bouquet that left me heady (but not enough to be compliant). If gloom was part and parcel of life at the Martyr School, so be it; I was determined to watch the train wreck from the safety of the platform; just how to get Lori on the right side of my metaphor, I didn't know, but in the meantime, we were eager to be initiated into the partying lifestyle of the self-declared doomed (or at least I was; Lori rarely missed a gathering, but she never seemed engaged and never missed an opportunity to vomit).

It turned out that the Order's graveyard (known as the East Lot) was a great place to get high or drink a few beers if you didn't want to bother with the wet shoes and mosquitoes (and who knows what else) that came with partying in the swamplands. It was in the East Lot that Lori and I listened to our classmates try to top each other's ghost stories, as we hid from the Scum between the mausoleums. But quite often the squeak of the gate or the screech of an owl could send us scrambling back to the dorms. In the East Lot and in God's Allotment, it was fairly easy to spook even the death-seeking students of what I was sure Ms. Shevchenko would term a destructive cult. Still, we frequented the Order's cemetery but never for large gatherings; it was a more intimate place. Suzette Downey from down the hall claimed Avery had told her she'd had sex standing up between two mausoleums, and that even though she couldn't help but imagine the smell of rotting priests, it was the best orgasm she'd ever had. (Suzette's tentative gestures towards her crotch suggested that all of her experiences with the opposite sex were secondhand.)

The only road to the cemeteries was one that was true to its name: Quartz Road—even if that was simply what the students called it. I don't know what it looked like during the day, but at night, when there was at least a quarter moon, the quartz sparkled from the rubble, evidence of an attempt to pave the road long ago. The older kids told us that Quartz Road ended (or began) at the school's morgue. Nervous laughter all around.

In an unfenced, poorly-tended area behind the East Lot, was a small cemetery (*le Cimetiére des les Abandonnés*) where the ashes of the students who'd had high GPAs and authorized exit methods but whose remains were unclaimed by their families were interred in brick columbaria that appeared hastily built. (I imagined broken urns and farraginous piles of ashes.) The people who tended the grounds never trimmed the trees there, but no one spent much time among *les abandonnés*. The reality of what could be the end result of my fellow students' choices stood in stone silence; the desolate land behind the East Lot gave them the shivers in a way that God's Allotment never could. (The pallet of bricks in one corner didn't help.) As Suzette (needlessly) explained to me in whispers that held the hint of a watermelon Jolly Rancher, *le Cimetiére des les Abandonnés* reminded students that they could succeed at the Martyr School and still end up in an urn encased in what appeared to be a shoddy brick dovecote whose pointed roof had been torn from the structure in a Biblical rage. Not that we ever partied there, and we certainly *never* raised a beer in God's Allotment. If for some reason we had to traipse through the potter field's spent soil, we did so carefully, not only to sidestep the coping graves, but to avoid knocking over the small wooden markers that crowded the head of each burial place. We didn't even like looking at the markers. As if to send the clearest message, not only weren't they in the shape of a cross, they didn't even bear the fallen students' names, just their school ID numbers burned into the wood. Even at our most fucked up, we never switched the markers, and we never spoke of which among us was most likely to end up in God's Allotment.

+

From the *Martyr School Handbook*:

The Meet-Cute

This handbook is not a guide on how to commit suicide—techniques and methods are subjects addressed in the curriculum. A student's guidance counselor and teachers, as well as the headmaster, will instruct pupils further on the theological nuances of martyrdom by suicide and will counsel them on deciding upon an academic track and method of exit. Parts of this handbook are given over to practical concerns, but various sections are dedicated to highlighting some of today's prevailing secular circumstances and what your expected behavior should be.

The meet-cute is an often comic situation where a man and a woman with seemingly opposite personalities, who would not have anything to do with each other normally, meet under circumstances unusual (e.g., mistaken identity) or exaggerated (e.g., a clash of beliefs), quickly establish a rapport, and fall in love. The meet-cute is one of the more popular devices used in romantic comedies, which are partially responsible for conditioning students to believe that hope can be found in chance. But *to hope* is not *to wish*, and wishing should never be confused with prayer, just as luck should never be thought of as predestination. It is important to understand that coming through the other end of a meet-cute together does not make the situation unique; at best, it is still a trope. (Couples who feel that they are two peas in a pod fail to understand the population of a seed-pod.) The difference between what is facile and what is sublime depends upon whether or not the unlikely romantic pair has left room between their bodies for the Holy Ghost.

+

Everyone called him Christy. He was a senior. His Christian name was Christopher, and his overwhelming life circumstances began with his parents not letting him stay out late at night with his friends and ended when he was locked in his room for three days with only his school books. They had confiscated his phone and removed his computer and anything fun. He was given one meal a day, and it always included lima beans, which he hated. On the morning of the third day, he jumped out of his second floor window, survived unharmed, and took a bus to New Orleans. (He was the recipient of a scholarship too, provided for by the families of alumni who wished to venerate their martyred son or daughter by aiding a promising applicant.)

I used to joke that windows were Christy's preferred portals of egress. We'd met late one night not soon after my sister and I had arrived. I was attempting to climb into a dorm room (not mine) through a window at the exact moment that Christy was preparing to exit from it, and it was in the window frame where we shared our first kiss. Maybe "shared" is the wrong word, for I'd been drinking with some upperclassmen (I made friends quickly), and I was three sheets to the wind and horny as a three-balled tomcat. I believe I would have kissed the first boy I came across—and one coming through a window in the moonlight, towheaded and pale, well, I couldn't ask for a more romantic situation, so I grabbed him and attached my booze-flavored lips to his. However, my kiss with the ghost boy ended abruptly when, startled, he pushed me and I fell backwards off the recycling bin I'd pushed over so I could reach the window. I landed on a weather-beaten stone gargoyle that had most likely been dragged here after it fell off the main school building by students who'd wanted to give their dorm room that extra touch of gloom. It had undoubtedly proved too big or too heavy to get through a window, and the stairs weren't an option, for the noise would have surely gained the RA's attention, so it had been left here for me to fall upon—or it could have been there the whole time; the campus was, in a word, shambolic, and I would not have looked twice at an out of place gargoyle. But regardless of how long it had reclined there, my back screamed even if I did not. (I tried my best not to attract too much scrutiny at the Martyr School, although being a twin came with its own spotlight.) Christy jumped down, coming to my rescue, and I told him that the fact that I hadn't spilled a drop from my go-cup was a sign—of what, I didn't know. He helped me into the window, pushing on my butt, and once we were both inside, I threw up on his penny loafers. I peed a little too, but when we heard someone stirring, I took his hand and we ran to the room I shared with Lori on the second floor, leaving behind plenty of forensic evidence. I wondered if I should brush my teeth before Christy and I started necking in my bed, but I didn't and after a rather intense hour, I reluctantly shooed him away. In the shower the next morning, I closed my eyes and remembered how tentative his tongue had been and how insistent his hardness was when he intermittently humped my leg as we rolled around in my bed, fully clothed, trying not to wake my sister. As I vigorously touched myself, I was thankful each room had its own bathroom, unusual for dorms, but a perfect spot for those wishing to end it all in private. Fifty percent of psychiatric hospital inpatient suicides occur in the facilities' bathrooms; I don't think it would be a stretch to equate the population of a psych hospital with that of our student body; the only difference I could see, as I rubbed my way to heaven, was that we were *all* to be taken out in body bags.

Lori never said anything. Still, I could tell she was unsettled that I'd found a boyfriend before she had. But the world was upside down here. Even Nestor, the mailman who pulled his truck up to the administration building Monday through Saturday, hit on me (and others) whenever we passed him, but not on my sister so much, which pissed her off more and more every time it happened (or, rather, didn't happen). That it occurred when I was alone probably got her blood up even more (I shouldn't have told her, sibling rivalry being a cliché and all), but I was only one of Nestor's targets, a fact Lori would have known if she wasn't so busy worrying about sisterly equity, even when it came to the potentially pedophiliac postman. Nestor was in his early fifties probably with short grey hair, and he always appeared to be between shaves (which just made his pockmarks stand out even more). He also smelled like he bathed in the cheapest cologne possible and had just smoked a cigarette in a small closet. No matter the weather, he wore regulation USPS shorts that were way too tight. I could practically count his penis wrinkles. He also had a bit of a beer belly; while not particularly large, it showed promise. At first I thought that Nestor just had a thing for young girls, but once I watched him try to chat up a nun—and not a young one. He may have been an equal opportunity poon hound, but there was no denying that young girls in black jumpers (and white knee socks in the winter) were what really scrambled his eggs. Whenever he espied one of his favorites among the student body (his "darlings," he called us), he would make a circle with his forefinger and thumb and stick his tongue through it. (This despite the admin building's many cameras.) Making matters worse, his tongue appeared to have a rough, white base, perhaps as a result of his smoking, which he never dared to do on campus, but that cigarette smell clung to his clothes and was especially rank when it was damp out; mixed with the strong smell of his sweat and fetid cologne, it was almost enough to make me switch teams. Why Lori would be jealous of me regarding the postman was baffling.

I ignored Nestor (and Lori) unless the school was getting me down (which was often); then I'd walk by his truck (alone), drop a pencil, and bend over to pick it up in what I imagined was slow motion, oddly enough enjoying the attention as the mailman stewed in his middle-aged horniness—until the time Nestor told me where he'd like to stick his tongue, a place that had never before occurred to me. Before then, Nestor just seemed to look through Lori, but after I started giving him a wide berth, he began giving her a lot of attention, and Lori encouraged him (in her own awkward way), maybe because she thought it would irk me or perhaps she was just lonely. But when I told her about his offer of anilingus, she freaked out, especially after the next time Nestor stuck his tongue between his circled fingers and wagged it in her direction. Envy cured.

From other girls I learned that Nestor was obsessed with the posterior orifice. "He's what you call 'anally fixated,'" explained Carmen, whose father said it was her mother's dying wish for their daughter, a perpetual honor roll student, to attend the Martyr

School, but Carmen swore her mother, demented and near consumed by fever, rasped, "Pass the butter," not "Mass for martyr." Before being sent here, Carmen wanted to be a psychologist. The profession was anathema to the Order of Martyrs, and Carmen was made to flog herself nightly for an entire semester for simply inquiring if the school offered any psych courses, but we respected her opinions. According to Carmen, Nestor didn't care if something was going in or coming out of a butt; anything to do with the anus seemed to make his penis strain against his shorts (or so I imagined; after my first glimpse, I never looked). From Nestor we actually learned new vocabulary words (creampie, gaping, prolapsed) and phrases (double penetration, mud on the helmet, reverse cowgirl). Carmen would provide the definition and context. For all of his staring at our rear ends, whether in our uniforms or in jeans on a Saturday, Carmen hypothesized that he wasn't drooling over the form and its variations; the cheeks were just a place for him to rest upon between immersions and explorations; he was fantasizing about what was buried between them.

Nestor was incorrigible. Once Lori began avoiding him ("I don't even want to touch the mail without gloves," she told me), he resumed harassing me. It came to a head one day when it was raining cats and dogs, and I had classes in different buildings. (Not all classes took place in the castle.) I had to pass the admin building and didn't think of the time of day or of Nestor. There were other, quicker routes, but I didn't feel like dealing with all the mud that would accumulate on my shoes if I cut through the trees. So there he was, grinning in the rain, his hand caressing the front of his shorts, and without so much as a hello, the mailman asked me to stick the handle of my umbrella up his ass. (It wasn't one of those curved one.) I backed up, and as he advanced, I looked down at my hand wrapped around the handle, imagined what it would look like in the aftermath, and dropped the umbrella before skedaddling out of there. I was done with our mailman. Whatever comic relief he provided had dissipated. His theater of operations was a sad circus; Nestor was a clown who desired the benefits of practicing proctology, but when his makeup was removed, I was sure that when he was alone, each midnight a slice of an unending dark night of the soul, he was revealed to be an escapee from a freak show not worth the price of admission. Suzette called him a little boy playing dress up. (She was probably right; I never actually saw a bulge in his too-tight shorts.) I put Nestor out of my mind; I had my own boy (who was actually a boy) to deal with and to kiss and to hug. Thing was, what nestled in Nestor's shorts also dangled between Christy's legs and would prove to be almost as irksome.

+

From the *Martyr School Handbook*:

Over the years, students and parents have asked for a class on marriage. We do not encourage our students to marry (when of age), and since we are a preparatory school for martyrs, there is no need for such a class. There is no future, we teach, except that which exists when in the bosom of the Father, drenched in the blood of the Son, and marked a martyr by that which emanates from the Holy Ghost. Our students expire in grace, not in union. However, we are not blind to the plight of teenagers and their hormones in a co-ed school. Our Spiritual Advisor is always available to assist students who find themselves one undone button away from sin. If our school did have a class on marriage, it would consist of one phrase: DO NOT TRY BEFORE YOU BUY. But as there is nothing to "buy" when working towards the holy bosom, the blood, and the light, we ask only that students think twice before undoing that last button—unless sexual debasement is part of their approved program.

Girls who become pregnant will be expelled. The unborn cannot be martyrs. Inseminators will be chemically castrated but may continue to work towards graduation.

+

The second month of my relationship with Christy started out as the least stressful one—for me anyway. He was always after me to have sex, and I had thus far rebuffed him, but in the third month, I broke down and gave him a blowjob, which he seemed to appreciate at the time (I would have appreciated a little warning before the big finale), but it turned out that it only made him more agitated.

One night Christy snuck into the dorm room I shared with my sister (through a window, of course); he was naked, his boner leading the way. (Lori was at her drama club meeting; she was the new recording secretary, the last one having checked out early by driving her Honda into the Mississippi.) I didn't wonder how my boyfriend had reached a second floor window, for he was always stealing one of the old ladders from the maintenance building for just such purposes. No, the first thought that went through my head was: *he went from the boys' dorms to the girls' residence hall starkers? Surely there must be a robe or at least a crumpled towel draped on the ladder or over the remainder of the spiked fence.* Even though I'd had it in my mouth once, it was only that night that I noticed just how purple his penis was and how, seeing him completely naked (which I never had before), how that purple stood out against his almost alabaster skin.

"Julie and Francis did it," was Christy's opening remark.

"Julie always does Francis' homework," I said. "She'll have to cut his wrists if he ever expects to graduate."

"You know damn well what I'm talking about."

Christy figured he had an out if he ever got in. He was on the normal track and wouldn't end it all until the final week of this, his senior year. Plenty of time to confess a mortal sin like sexual intercourse. That was his big thing: he didn't want to die a virgin. If he spent as much time studying as he did trying to get into my pants, he would have already known the prescribed path, as regards to sex, from the handbook—and the Bible. (Faking my religious fervor was exhausting in general—at best I was agnostic—but, really, I just wasn't ready for sex.) This wasn't the first time Christy and I were at odds. Our bickering was a constant source of amusement for our friends and even a few of our teachers.

"You two!" Mrs. Goldfarb, the biology teacher, had said more than once. "At it again!" Mrs. Goldfarb had what looked like ligature marks around the many folds of her neck. What did Bernard Shaw write? "He who can, does. He who cannot, teaches." (English was my favorite subject.) I wouldn't equate Mrs. Goldfarb's injuries with the seemingly perpetual wounds of the nuns until later.

"So you're not going to do it with me?" Christy asked. "Ever?"

I was feeling less than generous. I had geometry homework to finish, plus hanging over my head was a paper comparing and contrasting sticking one's head in the oven with sitting in a running car in a closed garage.

"Never." I returned to my textbook. "Besides, it looks like an agitated rhubarb stalk."

Angry, Christy sat down hard on my bed. His boner never abated. He tugged on it absently. "You don't love me."

I blushed. The initial I-love-yous had come a tad early, after the first month of dating, but I'd thought Christy was an integral part of Lori's crowd. (Turned out he wasn't; my tradecraft was wasted.) Still, I wasn't being completely insincere. It did seem like the Fates had it in for us. Our second meeting occurred when we literally crashed into each other in the western woods during the dusky aftermath of a freshman's early exit. (Christy wanted to see exactly how the girl had done it before the Burial Team arrived— Mr. Horner had gotten out his pointer, ready to instruct, time permitting; I was running the opposite way, fleeing the scene after a failed attempt to drag Lori with me.) Christy didn't seem like my type (a bookish chevalier), yet after a month of mostly playful squabbling, I had developed genuine feelings for the lad (even though our make out sessions somehow failed to match the intensity of our first one). But I could never lose sight of why I was at the Martyr School. Plus, I had no intention of losing my virginity to this skinny boy with a swollen petiole as long as his life goal (besides getting laid) was to hang himself from the bell tower for his senior capstone project.

Christy stood up and pressed his rhubarb stalk into the side of my face. "You did it with Finster, didn't you?"

Finster was a junior whose chosen method (or major) was ingestion: sleeping pills, narcotics, draining fluid. Finster had a Scottish accent and skin like a relief map of the Scottish Highlands. One of his ears constantly seeped. (The ear was believed by some to be the reason behind his attendance; rumor was his father had kicked his head as a baby, but many, including myself, thought the seeping might be related to his infrequent bathing habits.) I would no more sleep with Finster than I would with my (thankfully absent) sister. But Christy's penis against my face made me cross.

"If you must know, Finster's ear isn't the only part of him that seeps." I rapped Christy's boner—hard—with a pencil. "Heck of a lot bigger than some Irishmen I know."

If his Irish wasn't already up, I would use that cliché, but nonetheless Christy sputtered and spat. It wasn't so much that I admitted that I had slept with Finster (which I hadn't); it was that I said a Scot was bigger in the pants than a Paddy.

He stuttered, "I hope…I hope…"

I turned in my chair to face him and watched the rhubarb wilt. "Go on."

"I hope…I hope…I hope you live!"

With that Christy went out the window (another second story jump), but this time he wasn't so lucky. I don't believe he was trying to do anything other than make a dramatic gesture (or maybe he was just leaving via his preferred portal). But he was either so overcome with phallic anger that he forgot or was simply so dumb it never occurred to him that the windows in the dorm room I shared with Lori faced north; regardless, he was skewered in the groin on a metal fence spike. I shut my window and returned to my homework. The next day, people I didn't know clapped me on the back or just lightly touched me, murmuring, "Good transition," and "Way to go," congratulating me as if I were Christy. Even if early, unapproved exits were against school policy, the recently deceased received a locker room postmortem valediction, regardless of whether the school deemed the student a martyr for Christ or a nitwit damned for all time.

+

At commencement, the section that would have been normally populated by graduating seniors in other schools had been reduced at ours to rows of empty black folding chairs upon which sat red graduation caps, red being the color of martyrs according to tradition. An incoming senior was given the task of moving the tassels of the caps from the right to the left after the names of the newly consecrated martyrs were read. While not quite a Fallen Failure (from a certain point of view), Christy's name was not among them. The litany was accompanied by sobs and curses from the rows of parents who sat behind the empty chairs, most of whom had footed the bill for their son or daughter's martyrdom—

as to why they had, that was generally kept a family matter. Christy's parents were absent, of course, but a girl who looked just like him, but older, spent a large part of the reception afterwards staring at me. I wondered how she knew who I was until I noticed Lori staring at me too. I blushed. I probably shouldn't have brought a date—and for sure I shouldn't have been making out with him. But Jerome was so cute, and we couldn't bear to be apart, not during such an emotional time.

+

Lori told me that Gerardo wasn't the only reason she'd come to New Orleans. Like me, she'd always wanted to come to Crescent City, NOLA, and soak up the music, the art, the inherent craziness, and, of course, the Hurricanes (the drinks not the weather phenomena)—if she could get someone to buy them for her. (But getting served turned out to be not much of a problem.) New Orleans seemed the complete opposite of life back home in Philadelphia, where there was fierce neighborhood pride. Manayunk, Torresdale, Fishtown, Grays Ferry, Strawberry Mansion (for example)—these weren't just names; they were badges: what neighborhood you came from mattered as much as where you were, more if you'd moved out of the City of Brotherly Love. But while you were a denizen, you knew everyone who lived on your block; you knew the couple running the convenience store on the corner. I couldn't speak for the rest of New Orleans, but at least in the *Vieux Carré*, the French Quarter, we discovered that it seemed like no one knew each other, not for long, except maybe the shopkeepers and street musicians. (The Martyr School was just outside the Quarter in Faubourg Marigny.) The *Vieux Carré* was a good place to get lost for a spell. Mardi Gras or not, everyone looked dislocated (except for the natives); even the tourists filled with drink appeared more transported than transplanted—and everyone was a mark. Blending in, sticking out: these were relative terms. The difference between the lurkers and the topless was usually about two shots of well liquor. I thought that if the women flashing for beads along Bourbon Street really wanted to stand out, they should try showing off their assets in Salt Lake City, Utah, for in the Big Easy, tits were a dime a dozen. For Lori, New Orleans was more than a place to get lost: it was a good place to get lost for good; it was a good place to die.

Lori said that back home she was always taken for granted (ha!) and that decisions were usually made for her; she said she was often told to make a choice, knowing the whole time that the outcome had already been determined (ignoring her age and the efficacy of her stubbornness). "If Daddy hadn't worked in an industrial laundromat, if Daddy had lived," Lori contended, "Mommy wouldn't be so passive–aggressive." I didn't disagree; it wasn't worth the headache. I thought Lori was just throwing around jargon she'd learned from a magazine but didn't understand, because if anyone fit that label, it was my sister, whose two favorite words were "fine" and "whatever." But how much of Lori's life was predetermined and how much she was taken for granted were things I feared I would ponder the longer we were enrolled in the Martyr School, but for the moment, her buzzing was just so much background noise.

+

From the *Martyr School Handbook*:

Infatuation

Students should be wary of emotional hazards that can lead them to believe they are ready for transition before they truly are, for these are perils that can make them see with the eyes of the serpent, so that they confuse contemplative prayer for a highly mediated dialectic, use self-slaughter for manipulation, and repudiate the sacrificial blood upon the altar for the pheromonal heat of a lover's lap. One such peril is the state of infatuation, which should be avoided until a student's senior year when the anguishes and inherent rejections can be properly studied and assimilated into a pupil's particular course of suffering, as an infatuation is often a major impetus behind teen suicide—irrational belief in the improbable—and as such, should only be experienced with faculty supervision, lest a student's offering leads them to become merely a statistic.

Intense (and usually passing) crushes are a natural enough phenomena but are deceptive by nature; the severity of longing, the unrequited essence—are these not experienced in prayer and in the struggle to recognize the gift of faith and extend the grace of forgiveness to those whose barbs and fists and unchecked desires opened wounds upon wounds and ultimately led to the path of martyrdom? Thus do not those crush-induced passions demonstrate a lack of mindfulness? "Be still, and know that I am God" (Psalms 46:10).

Students would do best to remember that *infatuation* and *fatuousness* share the same Latin root, *fatuus*, meaning "foolish." The poet John Donne confessed to both states: "I am two fools, I know / For loving, and for saying so / In whining poetry." While debasement is encouraged at the Martyr School, students must first learn how to use abandonment and rejection against themselves properly, for wishing easily turns into pining, and compulsive masturbation can lead to penile chafing or vaginal dryness, all signs of *reacting*, not *enacting*. Students should never forget that they are not here to be oppressed, but to be their own oppressor. Yes, at times infatuations can lead to actual relationships, but more often than not they are simply a form of greed, turning the naïve one into a needy, covetous sycophant rather than a student of Christ and *suicidium*.

+

By the time our junior year started, the turbulence of the summer was over, the dust had settled, and so had Jerome and I. When we were sophomores, Jerome Cummings had asked Lori to the Kateri Tekakwitha Dance, held after fall midterms ended, but he'd left with me—by accident. This was two weeks after Christy exited from his final window. The dance was held outside, and when it started pouring and the wind responded in kind, a bunch of us girls, shivering in our sleeveless dresses, searched for our shoes in a pile of footwear. (Moments before we'd been gathered in a circle, swiveling in our pantyhose.) Jerome grabbed my hand thinking I was my sister (I'd never found my shoes) and took off for shelter in the gazebo where the DJ was still playing music. Twins and all was Jerome's excuse—Lori and I were the same height and our hair looked the same soaking wet, draping and partially hiding our faces. At least I believed he thought I was Lori, and I made no attempt to correct him. (Lori was wearing a pretty red dress; I was wearing a blue one that wasn't nearly as nice. But it *was* raining.) Later on he said he knew it was me and maybe he did. It would have been hard to miss the looks I had thrown across classrooms at him just as it had been hard for me to hide my disappointment and surprise when he'd asked Lori to the dance instead of me, especially since my sister said she'd never spoken to the boy before. Jerome was almost freakishly tall and hairy, and he was the kind of handsome that wasn't readily apparent, but I thought he was the bee's knees. Lori didn't even try to hide her feelings when Jerome and I were Frenching in the gazebo, a certain Styx song our soundtrack; she threw her shoes at us, hitting one of the chaperones, our astronomy teacher, Mr. Sackrider, instead, who then stalked amongst the wet and the drying, high heels in hand, confronting the shoeless. Right on cue, the power was cut. It was easy for Lori to dart in and out of the shadows, evading capture. On top of everything else, Lori blamed me for the loss of her favorite pair of shoes, but I could no more return those to her than I could give back Jerome.

> *A gathering of angels appeared above my head*
> *They sang to me this song of hope and this is what they said*
> *They said:*
> *'Come sail away,*
> *Come sail away*
> *Come sail away with me'*

The whole situation made for an awkward Christmas break. Lori and I only went home for three days. My sister sulked and disappeared for hours at a time, even once during a heavy snow. I was ascending to cloud nine (young love and all), so when Mom told me that she planned to have Lori abducted by two second cousins and taken to a cult recovery center in Paramus, New Jersey, I just laughed. (That the cousins were currently under indictment and out on bail—they were accused of stealing puppies from breeders and pet stores to start a puppy fight ring—meant little to Mom when it came to rescuing Lori.) Deflated, our mother tried to recreate the Christmases of the past, right down to leaving out cookies and carrots for Santa and Rudolph. Lori and I left the next day.

At the beginning of our sophomore spring term, I made the decision to lose my virginity, and soon an easy comfort existed between Jerome and me. So easy that I largely ignored Lori. So easy, in fact, that the lack of friction between my beau and me eventually became an annoyance, which, at first, I tried to keep to myself. Still, I often stayed in his room, which was strictly forbidden by school rules, but he didn't have a roommate and his RA had electrocuted himself in the shower and word was he wouldn't be replaced until towards the end of the semester, so who would know? (His RA had been a hard-ass when it came to sleepovers and six packs.) Our domestic bliss—Jerome's words—continued when I decided not to go home for the summer break before our junior year, much to Mom's consternation. (I still called weekly to file my progress reports, such as they were.) Even Lori made a surprise visit home; Mom staged a hastily arranged intervention, but the few people that came brought covered dishes, and my sister slipped out the back door and returned to New Orleans. Jerome's parents rented him a tiny place off campus for the summer in Tremé, near Louis Armstrong Park, just a couple of blocks from Rampart Street and the Quarter. (I guess they *really* didn't want him to return home for anything longer than Christmas break.) After I moved in with him for the season, I watched Lori ride her bike past our humble abode at roughly the same time just about every day she was in the Big Easy. (She lived in the mostly empty girls' residence hall.)

Things worsened. Lori stopped returning my calls and would ignore me when I shouted and waved as she passed. One night, Jerome and I woke to what sounded like birds committing suicide by flying full force into the front of our shotgun shack. We ran outside, and I ducked as something white flew over my head and splattered next to the outside light. Across the street was an old warehouse; it was difficult to make out the assailant hidden in the shadow of the building. I stopped Jerome before he charged into the gloom, turning him around to face me. "Good God!" he cried. "Look at the—" A gargling noise came from his throat. I kept staring into the shadow across the street, waiting for it to shift. I'd seen what now strangled Jerome's speech: egg whites and yolks were dripping all over the front of our little place; splattered egg shell stood out against our green door. I was unfazed. Jerome had never experienced Mischief Night, Halloween eve, where egg projectiles and toilet-papered houses was standard fair in the Great Northeast neighborhoods of Philadelphia. (Granted, this was summertime in Tremé.) When a figure finally emerged from the shadow of the warehouse and pedaled away, I waved and I thought I saw the rider give a little wave back.

The attacks decreased as the summer progressed (I still opened our mailbox with caution after twice reaching in and touching a dead bat), and Jerome and I got on with playing house. I knew exactly how he liked his oatmeal and toast (lumpy and burnt), and he knew to lay out the funny pages for me as soon as he brought in the paper. He made sure I was on time to my summer job, and most days, he walked home with me afterwards. (I worked at a store in the Quarter, Marie Laveau's Voodoo House and Magick Adult Emporium [Readings by Appointment] that had a huge, taxidermied armadillo in the window and sold, among other things, spell kits and ritual bags, voodoo dolls, and plastic mainstream glow-in-the-dark religious figurines, along with sexual devices that often shared the same iconography.) I made sure to assume the position Jerome liked best (doggy) as soon as the foreplay was over—which was quickly: I would put him in my mouth and fondle the balls; he would go down on me while he squeezed my boobs, and a couple of minutes later we were good to go, same thing every time in the same order. By the end of the summer, our lovemaking could be timed down to the second. I didn't even bother to fake orgasms anymore. (Poor Christy: he missed my sexual awakening, such as it was, by mere months.)

This was love and love was exactly like what Mom said it was: a well-worn blanket that you knew intimately and were always meaning to throw out and replace, but when you imagined it gone (sometimes for reasons that had nothing to do with your thoughts of replacement or mending), you shivered from phantom cold.

I'd never mentioned my somewhat rather perfunctory, by-the-numbers sex life to Miss Marguerite, the elderly woman with cobalt blue eyes and black fingernails, who owned Marie Laveau's and looked like every old gypsy in the movies, but one with a retinue of brawny men in black t-shirts, often with dreadlocks, to whom she generally only communicated in whispers. (I had no idea what kind of work they did for her, but I believed whatever they did was in the name of good—or at least her interpretation of good). One slow night, as she sat at the front counter dealing from a Tarot deck (she gave readings to tourists, both the giggling and the stricken), surrounded by spirit wangas, plastic Madonna and child figurines, and jars of incense, she suggested that I buy one of the various Mary Magdalene strap-on dildos she sold—to kick it up a notch in the bedroom, she explained in her thick Slavic accent, which was both intimidating and oddly maternal. Her ancient, corpulent cat, Jubes, a grey ball of fur and dust, nearly blind and almost perpetually asleep, dozed next to her; his lids never fully closed, and when she ran her hand through his tangles and knots, the cat emitted his approximation of a purr, sounding for all the world like a death rattle, and his blank eyes seemed to stare at me, as if he were taking part in the conversation. I told Miss Marguerite that a strap-on wasn't my speed, and I thought I was a pain in the ass all by myself. (I was pretty sure too that Jerome wasn't a bottom.) The dried roots hanging over head swayed gently, the only beneficiaries of the tiniest air conditioner I'd ever seen, and Jubes passed wind.

" 'The way you walk is thorny,' " Miss Marguerite said, slapping a Tarot card on the counter.

Good God, was she quoting from the old gypsy woman's speech in *The Wolf Man*? Appropriate for the overly-hairy Jerome, but still…

(While Lori had gorged herself on rom-coms, I'd been fascinated by Universal's classic horror pictures.)

Without looking up, Miss Marguerite said, "You should fuck him under before he fucks you over."

I had *no* idea what that meant.

I continued to dust the shelves and statuettes, as she shuffled the Tarot cards again and recited more of *The Wolf Man* speech, almost to herself: " 'But as the rain enters the soil, the river enters the sea, so tears run to a predestined end.' " I shuddered and before I could turn away, she cut one of her brown, wrinkled fingers on the edge of a card—on purpose or by accident, I couldn't tell. Regardless, Miss Marguerite ignored the blood that dripped down the card. The cut appeared to have opened up an older (but still recent) wound whose angry slashes outlined the latest one. (Was she cutting herself in the same place over and over? If it weren't for her disdain for the Martyr School, I would have wondered if she was an Elder.) I'd seen her going over the invoices while she kept on eye on the tourists, stapling her papers with significant force, as if to remind her would-be customers that she was watching. One crowded night, as she stared down two teenagers who looked ready to pocket a bottle of Father Zombie's strawberry-flavored Spanish fly, she somehow managed to pound a staple into one of her fingers; her expression didn't change as she pulled it out with her teeth. The boys left without their aphrodisiac.

Miss Marguerite showed me the Tarot card she'd picked up, which had been in the fourth position, the Advice position. It was the Ace of Staves (or Wands). Blood traversed its once slick surface, now as cracked and wrinkled as the brown fingers that held it.

"Hmm, a pivotal act, yes? A fateful stop perhaps—one that unleashes a chain of events. This is the suit for risk-taking, hmm-hmm." She closed her eyes for so long, I thought she'd fallen asleep. (It had happened before, mid-conversation, but never when there were people in the store.) When her eyes sprang to life, she shook the card, startling Jubes, who rolled off the counter. "You have to remember why you're here, but change will hinder you if you do not act like a cat who landed on a burner." I stared at Jubes, who slept where he'd fallen, splayed like road kill. Miss Marguerite stuck her bleeding finger in her mouth and sucked on it. "In other words, girl, you have to remember what you need to do, even if what you need to do changes, no?"

So she gave me a Mary Magdalene dildo with the double-leg strap harness—the seven-inch shaft was adorned with the saint's image—as well as a small bottle of Mother JuJu's Anytime Anal Lubricant.

"The cock glows in the dark," Miss Marguerite cackled, "so you can always find your way home."

+

From the *Martyr School Handbook*:

All students must strive to be pure of heart and say their prayers at night. All students must drape a scapular on their night post. All students will be provided with fresh wolf's bane or monkshood, which should be kept in glass vases on their desks at all times. All students must hang garlic over their dormitory windows and doorways.

At no time should a student engage in sexual activity unless it is first approved by the headmaster's office as part of their sinful path to redemption. Without signed permission slips and consent forms, there can be no sacramental absolution. All other mortal sins should be cleared first with the academic dean and should only be committed immediately prior to going to confession.

Please note: only seniors are allowed to keep vehicles on campus. Those vehicles must be registered with campus security and all keys must be surrendered when the vehicles are not in use.

+

The members of the Order of Martyrs were not Donatists or Circumcellions, early Christian sects who believed suicide was an acceptable path to martyrdom. (The Circumcellions took this idea to an extreme: they would attack passersby with clubs, shouting "Praise the Lord," in the hope that the victims would become enraged and kill them.) The Order of Martyrs believed that suicide was the *only* path to martyrdom—with the exceptions, rumor had it, of when the school had to put down an incorrigible student for appearances' sake or had to *handle* a senator's son, who was beginning to attract the spotlight once his father discovered what kind of school this was; Daddy never uttered another word though when, according to the wags, he received photographs of his twelve-year-old daughter touring the campus the same day he received word that his son had quit the school, whereabouts unknown. The longer we were there, the darker the rumors, the more they multiplied, and the closer fiction crept to fact until stories like that of the senator's son seemed less like exceptions and more like the norm. The Order was a secret society—an open secret, sort of like the polygamist sects in Utah. They avoided the spotlight without hiding, policed their own, and flourished in New Orleans alongside schools for vampyres and lycanthropes. Back east, the existence of these special schools was but a whisper, but one heard loud and clear by Lori in the wake of the Gerardo Incident.

Thing was, I never believed that Lori wanted to die; that wasn't why she enrolled. At first I thought she was merely looking for visibility: she wanted to be seen. But no, Lori wanted much more than that: she wanted to be special, the irony of which was that it led her, in a circular motion, back to why she'd come here in the first place. Yes, she'd bought into the oft-repeated phrase, "We didn't choose the school; the school chose us." But feeling unique and beloved, one of the called, appeared to have the opposite affect than the one intended and brought back, enhanced, the part of her that had been so consumed with romantic comedies and their emphasis on happy endings. Lori wasn't looking for death; she was looking for love. And where better to find love, she discovered, than among the damaged and the spiritually needy, a more well-stocked (albeit melancholy) dating pool, significantly more desirable than the Substrata's puddle of male offerings. Maybe it was just a case of extreme circumstances bringing out the extreme, for Lori's response to the Martyr School experience was a longing for romance that was significantly more intense than it had been back home, obsessive even. Of course, I had to figure this out on my own, and by the time I did, it was obvious and in my face. It shouldn't have been: each new boy was her saviour, and each first kiss came with a soundtrack of wedding bells. Even as we started our junior year, I just thought my sister had fallen into a cult because of a broken heart, a cult that had sold her on the notion that the little death she sought was her own. This cult didn't promise to heal her heart; it promised to help her stop it beating. Her heartbreak would make her a martyr. She hadn't suffered for God, it was true, but the school would make sure she was pure and right, so she could take her misery and misfortune and offer it to the Lord before offering herself—an Old Testament sacrifice except my sister was the sacrificial animal.

Lori was the kind of girl who wrote her initials and the initials of her current love in a heart. These hearts decorated her notebooks and binder and the inside of her gym locker. In our junior year, she returned to body art and took to drawing with a ballpoint pen on the inside of her arm and down her thigh like she used to do with movie quotes, only now it was initials: *L. D. loves J. C.* In between repeated viewings of *When Harry Met Sally* and *It Happened One Night*, my sister had apparently become very into Jesus, I thought, although I never heard her mention being saved and more than once I caught her dozing during morning chapel. At lunch one day, Suzette Downey asked me if J. C. weren't also my boyfriend's initials, and I smiled and nodded and inquired if she'd experienced a second coming. Having most likely never experienced a first, Suzette Downey blushed deeply and hightailed it out of the cafeteria.

The way I saw it, the return of the romantic comedies (which seemed to run in a loop in our dormitory) tempered the Jesus love graffiti, so while the latter disturbed me a little, it was only a very little. I believed I was right that Lori truly didn't want to die. Still, as my mom reminded me during every phone call, Lori had chosen to come to the Martyr School; she hadn't been recruited. While I didn't want Lori to transition early because of her newfound love for Jesus, she'd shown no interest in the accelerated track and had even passed on taking the self-immolation class (it was an elective), so I let our mother shoulder the lion's share of the worrying. My life with Jerome and my growing love of New Orleans took up most of my attention. I coasted by in my classes. (I barely passed Asphyxiation II and Pre-Calculus.) Lori and I eventually slid into mutual forgiveness, and I tried to make sure I spent as many nights with my sister in our dorm room as I did in Jerome's. She refused, however, to fess up to the summer egg assault.

Jerome and I took advantage of being upperclassmen, applied for passes (which we had to do each time), and spent most of our free moments during the school year in the French Quarter. After our first few visits, our curfew melted away. (But the Scum continued to stick to our shoes, as it were; after a while, they were easy to spot; there weren't many people talking into their sleeves or skulking about with clipboards.) Lori sometimes tagged along, as we soaked up the street music and the offbeat stores, maneuvered around the weaving tourists, and contrived elaborate ways to lose our Scum tails. It was my kind of town (or part of town). At first I had to fight the urge to just let loose like everyone else, but during the summer I'd learned that it was best not to bring *any* attention to myself in the Big Easy, though standing out in the sea of glittering debauchery was a feat in itself. (Beauty could hamper you, and I had nice legs if nothing else. The one time I wore a miniskirt to Marie Laveau's, I was followed after work by a beery, grizzled man who sang a sea shanty, as I led him away from our shack—*"Farewell and adieu you fair Spanish ladies. Farewell and adieu you ladies of Spain"*— and finally lost him when I slipped down Pirates Alley and ducked into Faulkner House Books, whose owner was kind enough to let me stay there and read—I was a frequent patron—as long as I vacuumed after they closed.) You wouldn't think staying out of the limelight would be a problem in the French Quarter where everyone was going out of their way to let it all hang out, but better safe than sorry, as our mother always said. Truth was, unless you were on fire—and this was a not a given—it was near impossible to truly stand out for very long; the image of the lady with sequined wings gave way half a block later to a stumbling middle-aged man in a rock'n'roll belly shirt bleeding profusely from his forehead, generally ignored, though cheered on briefly by inebriated frat boys. The *Martyr School Handbook* recommended that we dress somewhere between a tourist and a denizen, but we had no idea what that would look like. (Conventional wisdom for out-of-towners was to not sport Mardi Gras beads, unless it *was* Mardi Gras, and to never wear convention badges—or prep school gear.) When off campus, the handbook advised, it was better to be ignored than to be seen. The thing was that lying low could also be nothing more than a temporary state in the Quarter, since the focus of the intoxicated could land on you at any time.

We'd learned early (the hard way) to avoid the scamps who, without preamble, dropped to one knee in front of, say, Jerome, squirting water on his sneakers and gesturing for him to place one foot on the boy's knee, so the lad could "shine" it with a filthy rag while offering a wager. "I bet you twenty dollars that I can tell you where you got these sneaks," the boy would say, offering his hand to seal the deal. Shaking would place Jerome off-balance, increasing the discomfort that came with having a sneaker on someone's knee. "I always know where you got those sneaks, yes, sir, I do," the little hustler would tell my boyfriend, not looking up from his exertions until he brought it home: "You got 'em on your feet!" Jerome would hand over the green without hesitation—and he wasn't alone. Tourists more often than not took the wager and bit into their budget to pay. As students, pocket money was precious (parents tended to not send a lot of dough when your death was relatively imminent), but we were acutely aware of the number of local eyes we had on us—other boys, yes, for they never approached solo, but often an adult, a southern Fagin, would be watching from the corner or a window—and we were confident that the SKM would abandon us at the first hint of a kerfuffle. If not right away, the rule would become clear: make no eye contact with the scamps or their more nefarious adult minders, never engage verbally, and keep moving, back the way we came if necessary.

Of course, there was always the opposite route: let your freak flag fly and take what sin may come your way. You'd make a splash for a block maybe before you just became one of a number of flame-outs. In that way, the French Quarter wasn't much different than the Martyr School for a brave few. Jila Kim, who'd been sent kicking and screaming to our school, told me when we were sophomores, shortly before her unsanctioned, apparently self-orchestrated anal gangbang that ended with her bleeding out (she simply left an unoccupied boys' dorm room open and kept her bare ass, topped with a bow, raised for all who dared), that it was better to make some noise, stand out, and maybe the bloodlust that the Order cultivated would overtake a few fellow students and inspire them to murder you before you could be celebrated for murdering yourself, which Jila desperately wanted to avoid—the celebration more than the self-termination, for the latter was considered a mortal sin by the Orthodox Catholic Church she grew up in. (The rumors about the Scum dispatching the reluctant or the escape-minded had yet to make the rounds.)

Student-on-student homicides occurred about once a year, but there were never any official inquiries (by the school or the authorities), just automatic graduation for the victims. But, to add insult to injury, they graduated as *confessors*, who bore witness to the faith by their conduct, as opposed to *martyrs*, who died for it or because of it. Students who exited in the ordained manner were beatified during their commencement ceremonies, making them one step away from canonization, whereas confessors were honored as "heroic in virtue," a step below, which made the Kim family, already unsettled because the school only told them that Jila died during "private exertions," absolutely furious (according to Suzette, our eyes and ears). We wondered: what did that mean—dying during private exertions? We doubted that it was due to dorm room calisthenics, though Jila was known to work out to Beachbody videos. Death by masturbation? It didn't sound like a bad way to go, but it only took a couple of days before we learned the truth. (The Martyr School leaked like a sieve, and Suzette was always there to read the droplets like tea leaves.)

It was Suzette who told us that the Order already had a signed death certificate for Jila—prepared before she expired. For some reason that didn't seem surprising. Did they have them for all of us? Jerome wondered what they did to her body to ensure that her murder could never be traced back to any students, because surely that was what they did. The thought made me shiver, not because of how horrible it was but because of how logical. Later, we heard that the school had actually told Jila's family that the private exertions had led to a fire that had burnt her body to a crisp. (We imagined the scenario presented as being variations on a theme: a multitude of candles knocked over during an involuntary vaginal contraction, accidentally rolling around naked in lighter fluid near a cracked but lit lantern, humping a pillow that wasn't flame retardant while lighting a poorly rolled joint.) So it was surprising when the family attended the commencement ceremony, but apparently it was only so Jila's father could make a statement by ripping up her confessor certificate, as well as her diploma, shortly after accepting it from Headmaster McCaffrey, vowing to go the police, the FBI even, if necessary. He was escorted off the campus by the Scum, his feet never touching the ground. Before the brouhaha, a student (Suzette didn't know who) had given Jila's mother the bow her daughter had worn during her defiant (and public) last stand, a bow that had somehow survived the invented fire intact. Suzette heard that it was dropped in Mrs. Kim's lap with a whisper during commencement. Was the bow stained? And what about the whisper? Was it what sent Mr. Kim over the edge? In the end, what did our conjecture matter? Jila's father's body was discovered in the parking lot of the Superdome, his throat slashed, an old straight razor that his family swore they'd never seen before, in his hand. That was what we heard from Miss Suzette anyway. Regardless, it was clear to me that making some noise and standing out was probably *not* the best approach to the madness of the Martyr School (or even the Wild West of Crescent City or its French Quarter). True, it had served Jila's purpose, but I can't imagine she'd have allowed her ass to see the light of day if she knew that it meant her father's light was going to be switched off. Sometimes it's hard to see past yourself. (Then again, the Kims had insisted upon her attending, so maybe Jila had been more forward-thinking than many students gave her credit for; nothing says *I love you* like saying *fuck you* on the way out.)

Forgetting (ignoring) all about the wisdom and falsehoods regarding attempts to blend in, I uglied myself up whenever we journeyed into the Quarter, attempting to hide in plain sight. (My miniskirt had been retired.) If you were beautiful—which I wasn't;

my grandmother called me "poor-light pretty," but she had cataracts— then in the long New Orleans night, you could easily become the center of your own whirlpool (that is until a more attractive girl walked into view), a possibility that forced you to experience Bourbon Street with eyes in the back of your head and running shoes on your feet. I soon found it wasn't difficult to hide my long, straight brown hair in a baseball cap. I wore big clunky glasses (I normally wore contacts) and clothes that hid my minimal curves in the hopes that my efforts would keep me off the beer-breath college gorillas' radar in the event their attention strayed from the beads and boobs crowd. (Some teachers at the school, approvingly, said my natural thinness was the result of an eating disorder and encouraged me to join what students called the Skeletal Club, which met every Tuesday evening, not, I assumed, to trade confectionary recipes.) Lori was a paler creature with hollow eyes and cat-eye makeup, a look that somehow accentuated her long pointy nose and dimpled chin, both of which I have but not as pronounced or, as far as my chin went, as bristly—also I plucked my nasal hair. And then there was the faint mustache of hers. For reasons unknown, Lori had dyed her hair several shades darker, added teal streaks, and cut off the hair on one side of her head with an apparently dull pair of scissors. You would think these differences would make her stand out a bit (the French Quarter revels in differences, at least for a little while), but every fifth person there had a Goth look. (Lori's black wardrobe was the result of having an aversion to shopping—plus she was lazy with laundry; she believed black never looked dirty; as a result, she always smelled a bit funky.) Regardless, Lori's costume (I could describe it no other way) probably upped her chances of being plucked by the wasted and the malevolent and required Jerome to keep an eye on her and step in if she was about to become, momentarily, the center of attention.

But Jerome never complained of having to pull double-duty, and he was exceedingly polite to Lori, never considering her a third wheel. (I sometimes did.) Once he even bought her flowers from a street vendor, and Lori seemed to blush the rest of our day in the French Quarter whenever she looked at them or him.

+

The Pop Song Montage

There will be times when a student's experiences at the Martyr School will seem overwhelming. Maybe it will be the workload or homesickness or difficulty in choosing the proper exit method. It may even feel like a rushed, seemingly random series of events, clichés even. But remember: Jesus knows why each student is here, and the flickering images are just more of Lucifer's stumbling blocks. Students should pray hard to not let their lives become a series of scenes accompanied by a soundtrack of inanity. Dancing for the devil is no way to go out.

+

I'm walking on sunshine—whoa oh!
I'm walking on sunshine—whoa oh!
I'm walking on sunshine—whoa oh!—and don't it feel good!

Dad used to say that life is like a pop song: 3:30 and it's over, and someone is always trying to scratch the record or lift the needle, sometimes even the listener. The fact that I preferred Otis Redding and Aretha Franklin to Lori's '80s fixations ("Come Sail Away" notwithstanding) made zero difference and was beside the point, which took a few years to sink in. While there's no accounting for taste, there is an *accounting*, if not by God, then by those you inevitably leave behind.

I caught Jerome sitting under the huge willow next to the East Lot cemetery with, of all girls, Willow Christian, a surname that I supposed made up for her wanton reputation. (That she lounged beneath a *willow* was just tacky.) The girl was easy, or so the campus yentas said. Word was she was caught giving head to two boys from the soccer team in the girls' laundry room. While I found that story a little extreme, I knew Willow was a huge flirt, and to see her hand touching Jerome's leg as he turned the pages of a textbook made me nauseous. I spotted Lori hiding behind one of the mausoleums, and as she watched Jerome and Willow, my sister threw up. Jerome told me later, after the third degree (my annoyance unleashed), that he'd been tutoring Willow at the behest of Mr. Snell, the chemistry and poisons teacher, a claim Jerome knew I would never follow up. Mr. Snell reeked of formaldehyde (he also taught biology and embalming) and made me almost as nauseous as Willow Christian. But finally there was some friction between Jerome and me; it made our relationship less heady and more grounded—as grounded as it could be in a school with a class on ligature compression and carbon monoxide poisoning.

> *When tragedy befalls you*
> *Don't let them bring you down*
> *Love can cure your problem*
> *You're so lucky I'm around*
>> *Let my love open the door*
>> *Let my love open the door*
>> *Let my love open the door*
>> *To your heart*

One night in the winter of our junior year, Jerome and I finished making love in his room, and as he heaved himself off me, I saw his penis sticking through the top of his cherry red condom.

"It broke?" I asked stupidly. This wouldn't have been the first time; the boy was, in my limited experience, unnaturally large.

He grinned. "Yeah."

"And you knew? You knew it broke and you kept going?" He had been more considerate during previous incidents.

As if weighing his answer, Jerome removed what remained of the rubber and pulled on his boxers before responding. "I couldn't help it," he said, as he wiggled a finger at me through the ruptured prophylactic, his voice lowering an octave, "You just felt so good, baby."

Nobody puts Baby in a corner.

I snapped, and I punched and slapped him until he pinned me down, paying no attention to where the broken condom ended up, as one of my wild swings had taken out the lamp. In haste, he snatched another Trojan from the box in the nightstand, yanked his boxers off, and we had the best sex of our relationship, although I worried he would get in trouble for the hickeys. Afterwards, he swung the full (or more accurately, the bottom heavy) condom like a pendulum in front of my face. (At least I thought it was a full Trojan in the dark.) Then he left his bed, he said, to toss it in the toilet.

"Hurry, hurry!" I yelled after him. "I have to pee."

Jerome charged back into the room seconds later, and we made out some more. Finally, I shoved him off me and went into the bathroom. Jerome had left the light on (naturally), and as soon as I entered, I saw there wasn't a red condom floating in the toilet.

"Did you flush?" I called out, confused. Jerome never flushed the evidence away; he would just drop the exhausted latex into the bowl. In fact, Jerome hardly ever flushed unless he did more than urinate.

"Did you hear me flush, babe?"

Then it hit me. The second condom had broken too and he *had* flushed—there could be no other reason why it wasn't in the toilet. All the noisy face-sucking had distracted me (and I'd completely lost track of the first one). I pawed through the overflowing bathroom wastebasket just in case.

Jerome just stood in the doorway playing with his penis, looking amused. When I looked up, he just shrugged his shoulders.

"You bastard, you motherfucking bastard," was my battle cry, and this fight didn't end in sex but with the recently installed RA reporting us to the disciplinarian's office. Although it was common practice, girls and boys weren't allowed in each other's dorm rooms without special permission; some RAs were hard cases about this rule while others were slightly more lax, but this situation, accompanied by raised voices, was difficult to ignore, especially when the boy was clad only in boxers, which he'd pulled up just in time, and the girl was wrapped in a sheet.

It wasn't until I searched Lori's room as my time at the Martyr School was coming to an end that I found (what I assumed was) the first broken condom in her sock drawer. The semen that had not escaped through the tear was dried out, of course, and the Trojan's familiar red was covered in stray fuzz. Just how Lori came by the first broken condom would remain a mystery. I don't know what happened to it after Jerome had used it like a finger puppet. She had to have found it on the floor of his dorm room—and if so, what had she been doing there—or, *shudder*, did he give it to her? It had to be from that absurd night. Why else would Lori have placed it in a Ziploc bag (other than to prevent further fuzz accumulation)? On the bag she'd drawn a heart around Jerome's initials and mine (LAD) in magic marker, then slashed through it with a black ballpoint pen with such violence that she ripped the polypropylene in places. There were other used condoms in other

Ziploc bags that bore identical hearts (none of which were scratched or slashed out) but with slightly different initials (her much hated middle name the differentiating factor), all rendered ornately in a style I recognized from my sister's notebooks and body art. But I couldn't talk to anyone about what I'd found. As far as most people knew, Lori had remained a virgin. Who was I to muddy the myth?

> *Love's strange, so real in the dark*
> *Think of the tender things that we were working on*
> *Slow change may pull us apart*
> *When the light gets into your heart, baby*
>> *Don't you forget about me*
>> *Don't don't don't don't*
>> *Don't you forget about me*

However, even the collective memory could be selective, for there was a time when Lori decided she wanted to shed her virginity, and being true to her school (and using Jila's example as a template), her plan was to go about it in a most suicidal fashion: she invited three lacrosse players to visit her in our room. (I'd told her that I planned on sleeping in Jerome's bed that night, as long as we could avoid the RA.) When the boys entered, according to someone in the know, Lori was on the bed, naked, her legs spread apart; a candle lit by the bed. The lacrosse players pounced, but Lori suddenly decided she wasn't ready to be fucked to death (or screwed period). She screamed, and the RA was able to break it up before Lori's hymen was broken, her virginity an assumed thing. (There were whispers that she was tied to the bed when the players entered the room, which was balderdash, as it would have required assistance from someone else. But ashamed at her failure, Lori never addressed the rumors, which only made them grow into a possibly miraculous event, despite my twin's original intention and the eventual presence of the RA.)

Jerome went out the next day with two of his larger friends and beat the heaven out of two of the three offenders. The third checked out early with his father's .38. Lori called Jerome her hero and kept touching the edges of his shirt from her bed in the health center. It became so annoying, I pulled Jerome out of the room. When I came back later, Lori was asleep. I made sure no one was around, and I placed a lacrosse stick, nicked from the gym, on her bed.

+

From the *Martyr School Handbook*:

In the last semester of the senior year, the master of methods will assist those students ready to transition for Christ per their academic tracks. Final approval for capstone projects are based on a student's GPA. Those with a GPA of 3.5 or higher will be able to choose their own poisons, as it were, and scenarios. Weapons, tools, pills, and injectables will be blessed by the monsignor before being given to the students who require them by the master of methods.

Students with a GPA lower than 3.5 but at least 2.5 may expire per their course of study and thus graduate, but all particulars will be determined by a three person panel consisting of the academic dean, the master of methods, and the disciplinarian in his role as the master of the mediocre.

Note: students wishing to jump from a great height for their capstone project must clear the end spots with the master of grounds.

+

There was a bar on Bourbon Street, Blues End, whose house band, Captain and the Licks, was led by an elderly black man in a captain's hat, who wore a microphone headset and carried a guitar with active electronics. He wandered among the patrons (seated at really long picnic tables) and bumped and ground against any woman willing to stand up and shake a leg with him when he wasn't singing or playing a solo. The Captain had three shout-outs that resounded through his mic during his pelvic thrusts: "boys, we got a hot one *here*," "hot licks, hot chicks" (which I assumed wasn't a reference to his band's name), and "boys, I'm goin' home with this one!" A fourth, "little girl lost," was reserved for those reticent female patrons targeted by the Captain. (Most of the women jumped up, full of liquor and fun, to shake it with the old guitar player.) While the band played "Hoochie Coochie Man" or "Back Door Man" or an old Temptations number (sung, as most of their Motown repertoire was, by the bored looking trumpet player, as if he'd done this for time immemorial) or even Hall and Oates'

"Maneater," the Captain would molest the audience until he narrowed his focus and cajoled a bashful or inhibited woman he obviously found attractive. When his victim eventually stood up for a bump, the place would erupt in cheers. We were semi-regulars and usually drank undisturbed by any Licks or their Captain, but this one night the little girl lost was Lori.

The Blues End—like the Black Penny on North Rampart Street, Le Bibliotèque, a dive just outside the Quarter past Esplanade Avenue, or our favorite haunt, Pirates Cove—never carded us. It was a dark joint like the Old Absinthe House (whose barkeeps *always* carded us), but it was a hell of a lot noisier. The Blues End had no doors, just two large garage-like entranceways so that the Captain and the Licks could be heard loud and clear to the passersby on Bourbon Street, teeming as spring began its charge towards a close. The Captain even occasionally wandered outside to entice potential customers. (His spiel wasn't all that different from the pitch of the barkers working outside the strip joints.) The Licks were all male except for a very tall woman who played percussion and took the occasional lead vocal. (The ever-sensitive Jerome thought she was actually a he, just tucked in real well.) The band only played covers, and every song, whatever the tempo, had a bluesy feel. The keyboard player, who apparently fancied himself a dude (going by his mixed decade appearance, best described as Fonzie with a Members Only jacket and lots of mousse), would stop playing occasionally (there wasn't much musical difference when he did; the Blues End was loud) to stare at a woman dancing in front of the stage (where the brave and the drunk boogied), his chin cupped in one hand, elbow on the keyboard, drool practically sliding from his open mouth. One night in the Blues End, we watched two businessmen (two *large* businessmen; the smaller of the two must have weighed easily two hundred and fifty pounds) cavort with two busty, very young women. (Hookers, had to be, we said.) One of the girls (who looked barely older than us), wearing just about nothing (but with enough makeup for three women), repeatedly stuck her tongue in the largest guy's mouth and played with his man boobs. A swarthy-looking guy in a bright yellow sports coat, who'd been hanging outside the Blues End on the corner of Bourbon and St. Louis (we'd seen him from our bench), came in shortly after the illicit party of four took their seats. Money changed hands. There was little effort to be discreet. The man in yellow was a pimp, Jerome said. The mountain of muscle who stood behind the man in yellow kept reaching down to adjust what appeared to be a baby's arm between his legs, its outline clearly and disturbingly visible through his pants. It was obvious too that he had a gun stuck in the front of his waistband; the butt strained against the fabric of his tucked in, too-small *Welcome Back, Kotter* t-shirt. The Blues End was a fascinating place.

"*She'll only come out at night / The lean and hungry type*," the Captain sang (his vocal doubled by the sax player) as he tapped Lori on the shoulder. My sister shook her head. Go on, I told her. Take a spin.

"What we got here, Licks," the Captain said between verses, "is a failure to communicate!"

"*Oh oh, here she comes!*" the Licks sang.

"*Watch out boy, she'll chew you up!*" the Captain responded.

"*Oh oh, here she comes!*"

"*She's a maneater!*"

Jerome whispered something in her ear—I didn't asked him what, not then—and Lori finally stood up, blushing and fighting a smile. She managed a pale imitation of a hip shake then plopped down. The crowd booed. The Captain dismissed her with a dramatic wave of his hand. "Little girl *lost*," he concluded.

It was then I recalled what happened at the junior-senior prom the previous month. Lori had announced she wasn't going. She said she couldn't find a date. She said no one had asked her. Jerome offered to fix her up, but my sister declined. Too much studying. She had a big paper due on apocalypticism in the very Protestant *Foxe's Book of Martyrs*. (The Martyr School considered itself Catholic, even if they didn't exactly bow to the Pope. I think the fact that Popes weren't engineers of their own demise gave the very living Board of Trustees pause. Apparently, as a body, the Board was indifferent, immune even, to the pile of ironies their existence born.) I told Jerome to let it go; once Lori had her mind set on something, like coming to New Orleans post-Hurricane Katrina to become a suicidal martyr, no amount of outside effort would change it. (I once jokingly told Lori it was a good thing my beloved French Quarter was largely spared by Katrina or I would have had to kill her myself—the Quarter was the only good part of being at the Martyr School besides Jerome, who I hoped was so taken with me that he would drop this silly suicidal ideation. Lori didn't even blink when she responded: "It's too bad then, but good job so far.")

When Jerome and I walked into the room reserved for the prom at Latrobe's on Royal (held oddly during the third week of March), I was struck by how few of us juniors there were; there were even less seniors. The tables were spread far apart; the dance floor seemed immense. (The venue usually hosted wedding receptions, not dances for the soon-to-be-dead.) Those not seated were in knots around the boundaries of the dance floor, as if its center was a maw. Scum maintained key positions, and a few of our instructors acted as chaperones. The lay teachers were accompanied by their spouses, who seemed to look at us the way I imagine I would look at cows as they waited for their turn at the slaughterhouse. It was a total surprise to discover that the band on the small stage was led by my balding history teacher from eighth grade, Mr. Wattsman. (What was he doing playing a gig in New Orleans? Last I heard he was still teaching in Philly.) I was a tiny bit embarrassed, but he didn't seem to recognize me. Maybe it had been too long, or maybe, no longer in my elementary school uniform, in foreign surroundings (with boobs!), I didn't resemble my former self—but more likely he just didn't want to acknowledge that we were both at a Martyr School function. It was the first time I was acutely aware of how others saw me: a brainwashed teenage cultist. I was part of an underground society as heretical as the Donatists or the Circumcellions and with values as far from the norms of civilization as one could get; it was as if once enrolled, being in the tiny sphere of the school (with the otherworldly French Quarter as our backyard), martyrdom by self-slaughter seemed *almost* normal.

I couldn't stop touching the triquetra pendant Jerome had bought for me. Since he usually only bought gifts when he did something wrong, I'd been initially suspicious, but between the brightly colored lights and the thump of the bass, the pendant made me feel special and put me in a forgiving mood, though I didn't know yet what the crime was.

The band's first song? "Maneater." Watching my old history teacher sing (quite well) about being eaten by a woman was disquieting. (For the Captain, it was just part of his dirty old man shtick, not a statement of purpose; the Captain's bump and grind made clear that he was the devourer not the devoured.) It made me wonder what Mr. Wattsman was really thinking about he when spoke of Elizabeth I's and Joan of Arc's military victories. Mr. Wattsman also taught eighth grade gym where he made us do endless legs lifts. The girls had to wear shorts under their Catholic school skirts, but Mr. Wattsman must have gotten an eyeful of twelve- and thirteen-year-old female thighs, the memories of which, perhaps, ate him alive when he was alone with his thoughts. (Heather Lucas always claimed she wore absolutely nothing beneath her skirt, to which Mina Weber would always whisper to the rest of us: watch out for a sudden influx of crustaceans!)

"*The woman is wild, a she-cat tamed by the purr of a Jag-u-ar,*" Mr. Wattsman sang, his balding head bobbing along with the rhythm. He bit his upper lip between lines. "*Money's the matter; if you're in it for love, you ain't gonna get too far.*"

Jerome tugged on my sleeve, disrupting my psychological evaluation of my former history teacher. "Hey, isn't that Lori?" He pointed towards the stage.

I shielded my eyes from the party lights and followed the direction of his finger, and there, peeking from behind an edge of the drawn curtain: my sister's face, which appeared in the shifting shadows to be an unfinished version of my own. As I walked towards the stage, I could see she was watching with a rapacious aspect. But she wasn't watching me. I tried to follow her gaze through the festively decorated room. It wasn't directed at Mr. Wattsman or even Amy Butters, whose prom dress looked remarkably like something Madonna wore in 1984. No, Lori was staring at Jerome, taking him in, *soaking* in how sharp he looked in a tux with his hair slicked back and a fresh shave. I remembered what she'd said once about Gerardo: he looked good enough to eat. I turned to look at Jerome to see if he noticed (it always seemed to me that he'd forgotten he'd ever asked my twin sister out), but he was watching Amy Butters. (One of Amy's pendulous breasts had fallen out and it took her a few seconds to notice and tuck it back in.) When I turned back around, the drawn curtain rippled just the tiniest bit. Lori was gone.

It wasn't until the end of the prom that I realized only one girl (a transfer student from the Lycanthrope School) had asked after Lori. When I shrugged, the girl bowed her head and said, "She's doing God's work then."

When I got back to the dorms early the next morning, my shoes in my hand, my feet tired from dancing, my breath reeking of alcohol from an unapproved post-prom visit to Pirates Cove (we'd snuck out before the last song, and by the time the Scum found us, we were too tight to be concerned with their exasperation or any possible punishment), Lori was sitting up in bed reading *Pride and Prejudice.* Two other books lay open on the bed face down: Alice McDermott's *Charming Billy* and Joyce Carol Oates' *Monster.* (Lori had a thing for female writers; she also tended to read more than one book at a time, sometimes devouring a chapter of one then gulping down a chapter of another, back and forth.) She didn't look like a maneater to me anymore. She looked like my sister: a little lonely, a tad pathetic (sometimes a lot pathetic), and definitely lost. I wondered if the books she was reading were meant to be signals: Elizabeth Bennet's bumpy journey to love, an Irish-American family's struggle with the cost of secrets and regrets, and a serial murderer's attempts at creating a perfect companion through ice-pick lobotomies. If so, whatever they were meant to convey was lost on me. I pushed the books aside to sit on her bed for a sister-talk. Even though I was still in my fancy dress, Lori never asked how the prom was. As she briefly fingered my triquetra pendant, I started to tell her about Mr. Wattsman but stopped when I thought she might tell me she already knew, meaning she'd seen him from another angle, not just from the back. I didn't want to think of my sister spying from different positions, so I kissed her slick forehead and went to bed.

My junior prom reminiscence over, the Licks took a break soon after Lori had been cajoled to not-quite-dance to "Maneater," and the three of us left the Blues End. The next night, in his bed, I asked Jerome what he'd whispered in my sister's ear that had made her get up for a weak shimmy with the Captain.

"Not much," he answered.

It was dark in his room and I couldn't see his face, so felt it with my hand.

"But something," I said. "You said something to her."

I felt him smile.

"I told her I'd give her a shiny new penny."

I smacked the side of his head with my pillow.

"I gave it to her too," he said.

+

From the *Martyr School Handbook*:

The Contrived Mix-Up

From time to time, students may find themselves in situations where the onus of the behavior of others may be placed upon them. These types of situations are somewhat unavoidable in close quarters. A student may be blamed for another's slovenliness or lumped in with a group of ne'er-do-wells. He or she may be set up to receive the lion's share of the blame for a scam or a crime or even be named as a plagiarizer when an actual one is caught—the guilty love company. But students should clear their minds of impure thoughts of revenge. Yes, the truth will suffice when confronted by figures of authority, but certain circumstances require students to put into practice what they have learned here. They must be martyrs. God will sort it all out in the end. But often it need not go that far: if Christ could take the mantle of King of the Jews and be sacrificed, surely our students can handle mix-ups with a minimum of fuss and without the direct involvement of the Sanguine Knights or the disciplinarian.

+

I didn't speak to Jerome for a good while after I'd discovered them. He left flowers at the front desk of the girls' residence hall for me and even managed to slip a note into my gym locker. "It was your idea. I'm sorry," the note read. How true. It had been my idea, the date, but not what had followed. My communication with Lori was terse since I'd found them, but my sister made it easy for me: she kept out of my way, going so far as to stay in another dorm room—in whose, I didn't know; Lori didn't have many friends on campus, and the ones she had seemed interchangeable. What galled me though wasn't the mystery girl in the dorms who offered her shelter but the sudden changes in Lori's temperament and personality. I would watch her walk around campus as if she were floating above everyone else, no longer the cringing wallflower. Her reign as the passive-aggressive, virtuous queen of the campus (coronated by others, of course) would be short but a thorn in my side nonetheless.

Though I only admitted it to myself, what happened was partially my fault. I set it up and put it in motion. I thought Lori was lonely. She hadn't gone to our junior prom. (Not really.) Boys didn't ask her out. She'd begun to disregard her appearance. She had stopped washing her hair, even stopped bathing I thought. Students started calling her Lady Rancid (but otherwise still treating her with reverence). I thought she needed to get out and not necessarily as a third wheel. She needed a date. Jerome laughed and said she needed to get laid. I smacked him upside the head, but he did give me an idea—and he was part of the plan.

Jerome was to ask Lori if she wanted to go into the Quarter with him. Just the two of them. I guessed she would stutter and demur, and I was right, so I found her in the library later (where she was researching Great Britain's Official Table of Drops—hanging drops). I took her chin and turned her head towards mine and told her this was my gift to her. Take Jerome up on his offer. Go out on a date. Lori stared back at me and her eyes twinkled—from excitement maybe, though later it struck me that it was the same look she wore when she had a secret. (Lori always acted like having a secret made her special.) Regardless, Lori nodded her assent, and that night I helped my twin prepare for her date. I did her hair (though her extreme cut and fading dye job left me little to work with) and painted her nails something other than black. I helped her pick out her bra and underwear. (Although it wasn't going to be that kind of date, it would help her mentally, I thought.) I lent her a backless white skater dress that tied at the neck. I picked out some jewelry including a lovely pair of earrings (before I realized Lori's ears weren't pierced). She recoiled at first when I pulled out my coral lipstick, but once she saw the result, she kept pursing her lips into the mirror until I made her stop. Lori picked out shoes from her meager closet. They didn't really go with her outfit, but she seemed so pleased with her selection that I didn't mention it. I slipped her a twenty (feeling oddly maternal) and gave her a kiss. I couldn't be there when Jerome arrived. That would be too much.

I resisted the urge to follow them into the French Quarter. The streets were so thick with tourists, it would have been easy not to be seen, but it would defeat the purpose. After the Gerardo

Incident, Lori had been upset enough to apply to the Martyr School. It was my job, my mission, to bring her back home before our senior year began—at the *least* before graduation. My mother had expected this homecoming to happen almost immediately, and when our sophomore year and the ensuing summer had passed with Lori briefly returning home only twice since we left, our sole remaining parental unit was less than pleased. For most of our junior year, I fielded angry phone calls weekly and vituperative letters biweekly. I had no real excuse, although I presented many different ones. Really, I had barely tried. Thing was: I was enjoying my time in Crescent City. The school itself frightened and repulsed me, but I played along for Lori's sake (or so I told myself). I had zero intention of taking my own life, but despite how I embraced the city, death never seemed far away in New Orleans, with its above-ground cemeteries and jazz funerals and with our school being in rather close proximity to the Vampyre and Lycanthrope Schools. (The former being decidedly not Catholic; its student body was called Legion, and they could be a fun group when they weren't practicing being gloomy—although, like the Maneater, they only came out at night, lean and hungry types. Students from the latter school were a bit of a drag, guilt-ridden Catholics who howled at the moon and cried about it afterwards.) If I could give Lori a slice of my enjoyment, well, at least I would be doing *something* in the way of getting her head out of the noose. I knew she liked Jerome. She had accepted his invitation to the Kateri Tekakwitha Dance, and even though I ended up leaving with him (due to a supposed mix-up) and that was a terrible thing to do, especially to a sister, the fact remained that she had found Jerome attractive enough to say yes in the first place. Lori never found fault with me "taking" Jerome, or at least she never voiced it or acted upon it (aside from throwing her shoes); she never even mentioned the events of the Kateri Dance. True, I'd never asked her how she felt, and even though her spying spoke volumes (about what, I wasn't sure), I still comforted myself in her silence.

Jerome had a rather large do and don't list for this faux date. I gave him *very* specific, detailed instructions. He could, *if and only if* the opportunity presented itself (meaning that Lori gave him the appropriate signals), kiss her. If Lori went so far as to place her hands on his face or the back of his neck or his chest, he could use his tongue. Jerome was allowed, in the most extreme of circumstances, to squeeze Lori's boobs—an over-the-dress squeeze. If Lori (and I doubted this would happen) invited him to untie her dress (or she untied it herself), I couldn't fault him for touching her breasts—but no sucking of the nipples. That seemed too far, but I told myself if he admitted it to me that he had (and I expected a full blow-by-blow when all was said and done), I wouldn't throw a fit; it was easy to get carried away. He was forbidden to go under Lori's dress other than to rub her thighs (and even that move was suspect, but I would allow it). Any higher and he was a dead man. And if his penis came out, if it even peeked from his fly, I would personally see to his castration. Although I could never imagine it happening, I told Jerome to accept Lori's touch if she went for his nether region (outside his pants), but he was to make sure that would be as far as it went. Jerome getting hard for Lori might actually be a good thing for her, I thought. It would show her that she had something to offer a guy. (How I expected Jerome to be able to apply the brakes once he was hard, I didn't know—guys had a difficult time finding the off switch once the motor was running. I'd gone out on a couple of dates in the *very* short time between Christy and Jerome, and although I remained a virgin during the interim, I wasn't a prude; I knew firsthand that an erection obliterated rational thought in a boy, and all it took was a strong breeze to make a lad stiff and antsy.)

When the night came, I waited in our dorm room, trying to read *The Portrait of a Lady*, but finally I gave up and grabbed a *Vanity Fair* and stared at the photographs of movie stars. This date was more than just a gift to Lori. In a way it was one for Jerome as well. After the incident with the broken condoms, I withheld sex from him; it had been little more than a month, which was like a year in boy reckoning. Oh, I would still dispense the occasional handjob, usually in the shower, so he wouldn't become *too* backed up, and I blew him a couple of times when I was super horny. As far as the date was concerned, casting Jerome in a chivalrous role would be good for his ego. I always knew that I would give in to him eventually. (I missed the sex too—I was just freaked out by the ripped rubbers.) And tonight would be the night. I'd already gone out and bought a box of Trojans. When Jerome came back, possibly flushed from a make out session with my sister or maybe just bored out of his skull if nothing at all had happened, I would be ready, already naked, arms and legs open.

+

<u>From the journals of Lori Duke:</u>

A Quote I Like

When we invest in a story about two people in love, we are programmed to expect it to [end] with the two of them together, living their snuggly, wuggly best life. But if you've ever been in love...you know it doesn't work this way. Falling in love can be glorious, but navigating it is a challenge, and sometimes it all just ends, slowly or with the brutal sting of medical tape being torn off the skin.

Jen Chaney

+

After midnight, I began to worry. Even if they walked instead of taking a taxi, they should have been back by now. I'd told Jerome 11:30, no later; Lori wasn't a late night girl. I paced until the confines of our dormitory room seemed to close in on me. I couldn't risk pacing in the hall; there'd be too many questions, and I'd worked hard to keep the operation a secret, not easy in a school our size.

But by quarter to two, most of my fears had long since congealed then melted away. They were in the French Quarter. Jerome was showing my twin sister what a good time was all about—a good time with a boy who wasn't a complete jerk—and I knew how easy it was to lose track of time in the *Vieux Carré*, where many bars never closed and fewer carded. I decided to make a silly gesture to make up for my distrust and worry (not that Lori would know of either). Two days before, Jerome had given me half a dozen red roses he'd bought from a street vendor, and I was touched by the gesture. I had been working so hard coaching him, laying down the rules for the date, I'd grown exhausted and begun to even question our relationship. The next day he showed up with the roses. I was so thrilled, I ran to find Lori right away to show her. She merely blushed and said they were nice but avoided looking at them when she was back in our room. In fact, it seemed like she kept situating herself so the glass vase of roses wouldn't be in her line of sight. I understood then, at quarter to two, how awkward my relationship with Jerome had been for her. Not because he'd asked her to that silly dance and left with me—that was ancient history. But knowing that the nights Lori slept alone in our room were nights I spent making love and sleeping next to a boy who was head over heels in love with me had to be tough. (I'd never told Lori that Jerome and I were no longer doing the deed.) Back home, Lori had been the constant dater, always in love with love; she didn't like being alone. So I decided to leave one of the roses Jerome had given me on her pillow. In retrospect, maybe it was a passive-aggressive way of reminding her that I'd leant her my boyfriend, but I honestly didn't mean it that way. I just wanted Lori to know that I understood her and I loved her for understanding me (although I wasn't sure either statement was completely true).

I also decided to sneak into Jerome's room and leave a rose on his pillow too. I wasn't sure why—a thank you maybe. A six pack would have been more to his liking, but a rose would have to do—a rose and a strip of condoms. I knew his new roommate, Evan, was dating a girl from the Vampyre School, and so most likely he wouldn't be around at night. (He took major advantage of the lax curfew for upperclassmen; I imagined that he ran the Scum ragged.) The RA wasn't anywhere in sight, so I sprinted up the stairs of the boys' dormitory. I crept down the hallway of Jerome's floor until I reached his room. I knew his door wouldn't be locked. (It was a point of contention between us—I didn't much care for an audience during sex.) The lights were off, which was odd; Jerome never turned the lights off when he left. But rather than turn them on, I felt my way across the room.

As soon as I heard the noises—the sighs and grunts and bed squeaks—I started to beat a retreat. The last thing I wanted to see was Jerome's roommate getting it on with a vampyre girl. I assumed there would be lots of blood. I'd told Jerome to try and switch roommates in case Evan was bitten and turned. (I also wondered if the Martyr School would consider that a form of suicide or would Evan then require a stake.) When I heard Jerome say, "Baby," I felt for the light switch. If Jerome was back, where the hell was Lori? Before my fingers flicked the switch, Lori said my name, and under the bright room lights, there they were: my sister and my boyfriend in bed sans clothes. I bolted, not caring if the RA or even the Scum popped up and caught me. Somewhere outside, I dropped the rose, where it could wither and die alongside the condoms, all of which I freed from their wrappings, so they could be no more than symbols of a cautionary tale. Reverberating in my head was a line from Othello's soliloquy before he murders Desdemona: "When I have pluck'd the rose/I cannot give it vital growth again." Was this morbidity caused by the murder of love or by the deflowering of Lori? Did it matter? Betrayal by any other name...

Jerome caught up with me halfway back to the girls' residence hall. He was wearing only his boxers. I slapped his face.

"No," he said gently, "I thought she was you. We got really, really drunk. I dropped Lori off at your dorm, then went back to my room to crash. When she came in, the lights were off. I thought she was you. You're sisters, for God's sake! The Duke twins—no, no, right, not identical, but it was dark. I couldn't see the mustache, couldn't feel it. I don't even know that I got it up. I'm still pretty drunk."

And I believed him, probably because I wanted to. (I conveniently ignored the fact that his excuse was similar to the one he'd used in the aftermath of the Kateri Dance: confusing fraternal twins due to rain.) I still didn't speak to him for a spell, but I no longer considered the rose pluck'd, our love assassinated; what happened between my sister's legs was her sad business. Lori stayed away from me for about two weeks (which was also the length of time I kept Jerome on ice). I heard that she was staying with Amy Butters (the mystery girl!), which I thought was appropriate. Amy was widely considered to be the school slut; if she objected to her reputation, her affinity for accidentally walking into the boys' gym locker room didn't help her argument. When Lori finally moved back into our room (the same day I stopped ignoring Jerome), I was sitting up waiting for her (having been alerted in advance by Suzette). My twin climbed on my bed and hugged me, not saying a word. I told her Jerome had explained everything. I didn't ask her why she'd gone to my boyfriend's room. My sister was probably lonelier than I had imagined; inhibitions erased by spirits, she'd run straight to the bed of the man who had just given her probably the only decent date she'd ever had.

"There, there," I whispered as I held her, "your knight in shining armor will come one day, my princess. Just wait and see."

I moved back so I could see her face, oddly absent of tear tracks. I tweaked her nose and pinched her cheeks. "You never know, sister of mine, what you'll find right under your nose until you look."

+

From the *Martyr School Handbook*:

The Lottery of Future Saints occurs in the second semester on the first Friday of May, and is open only to seniors. Each academic year, the method of martyrdom changed. Participation in the Lottery of Future Saints is mandatory. Seniors are expected to always be ready to die for the Lord in any way that is available, even if it is not by their own hand, an exception made only for the drawing. The winner of the Lottery will automatically graduate and be beatified after being martyred. A diploma will be mailed home or can be picked up if the family wishes to attend commencement. Any student chosen whose GPA is lower than 3.25 will only be allowed to experience the method but not expire. Medical treatment will immediately be available, and another senior's name will be drawn in the Lottery.

A number of students have had our crimson and bone insignia tattooed upon their arms, legs, or back. Normally tattoos are considered a desecration of the body (like graffiti upon the temple) and are forbidden without permission from the headmaster's office. Consent for an insignia tattoo is only given to those whose grades indicate their devotion and dedication to divine self-destruction. However, students sometimes are tattooed without permission, an act that may come with repercussions. If a Lottery winner is a true scholar and ink free, they will be tattooed with the crimson and bone shortly after being chosen. But if a future saint has a GPA less than 3.25 and was already tattooed with our insignia, it will be scraped off prior to the ceremony. If the tattoo is of anything else, it will be burned off.

+

Burning, I'd heard, was rare, but whether it was inking or scraping, during the Lottery students crowded into the same room where I'd been digitally invaded by a nun to watch. I'd witnessed a scraping when I was a sophomore, having been caught up with the mob. One Scum handled the removal of the boy's skin, while another one made sure the student didn't pass out—and when he did, the Knight would use an electric cattle prod to bring him back.

+

Every year, the Martyr School chose a different classic martyrdom scenario for the Lottery winner: burning at the stake, decollation (beheading), the ol' upside-down crucifixion, and so on. For the Lottery of Future Saints, Headmaster McCaffrey spun the handle of a huge oblong cage, inside of which there was a tile with each senior's name written on it. If your name was picked, then you were dispatched by whatever that year's martyrdom scenario was: the Brazen Bull (being cooked alive while locked inside what looked like a large metal pregnant cow), immurement (being walled up, à la "The Cask of Amontillado"), pressing (being crushed by mounting weights), impalement by seven swords, flaying, evisceration even. (The last two were messy but crowd favorites, according to Suzette, who'd never witnessed either one.) The Order would probably feed a student to a lion, if they were allowed to keep one handy. The Lottery served another purpose too: it made all seniors want to keep their GPA up. Being chosen when your GPA was less than 3.25 meant that you were, for instance, only partially dipped into boiling oil; tortured, in other words, but not to death. We'd watched that happen during our sophomore year when a hapless senior with a low GPA—Russell Donoghue—had more than twenty arrows shot into his outstretched arms and legs (after his tattoo had been scraped off). He spent most of what remained of the school year in the infirmary convalescing. He did, however, bring up his GPA and exited in an approved manner before graduation.

(One of the more disturbing rumors that made the rounds concerned seniors whose GPAs were lower than 2.5, the minimum required to graduate. Although students didn't have access to others' transcripts and therefore didn't know for certain anyone's grade point average, seniors who claimed to be in trouble academically—and there were very few—tended to go missing. While it was possible one or two could have evaded the Scum and escaped, students believed that if a senior didn't have the required GPA, they were eventually taken out by the Order, sacrifices to their apparently very angry God, with their parents being told their son or daughter ran away. If this was true, were their bodies tossed in the coping graves in God's Allotment or just thrown in the incinerator? Students worried in whispers, but if anyone bothered to read the handbook beyond the few first few pages, they would have been clued-in early to the fate of the scholastically-challenged: "Per school policy, seniors carrying a cumulative GPA lower than 2.5 into their final semester will be transitioned with assistance but will not graduate—unless the students' instructors can show evidence that the pupils in question will rise to the occasion and end their final term with an acceptable grade point average." Not that it mattered—rumors were enough to keep most of the student body on its toes academically, reinforced by glimpses of the seldom-seen Elders in their robes and hoods, grandmasters all and us their chess pieces.)

The martyrdom method for the Lottery this year was lapidation, aka stoning. (Two years before it was fire ants, the seniors said.) We heard that there hadn't been a stoning at the Martyr School since before 9/11. Lori was beside herself. As juniors, we were not eligible for this year's Lottery, although we could participate as volunteers. (The Lottery of Future Saints coming around again reminded me that I had to turn Lori, extricate her even, within the next year. Neither of us planned on going home for the summer, except for a visit, so I figured I would use those three months, when I wasn't spending time with Jerome, to dissuade Lori from ending it all, to deprogram her and convince her to leave New Orleans before our final year began in September— waiting until before graduation was dicey. Still…. Missing the senior prom would be regrettable—I had my eye on a dress. Maybe it would be okay if I got her to leave before our senior finals, a time when bodies began dropping with some regularity. It was a risk, but the shoes I'd picked out for the prom were to die for, really.)

"It's not fair," my sister said. "I wanted to be stoned to death. It was my safety method."

At the start of the sophomore year, students were required to choose two methods of exit—how a student committed suicide had to be authorized by the school—and one safety in case the methods a student wanted weren't available. (The school only allowed so many of any one style of exit per year, whether it be overdosing, hanging, or the head in the plastic bag routine—and whatever method was chosen for the Lottery was limited that school year to just the winner.) Lori claimed her safety was stoning, and she sulked and acted as if the chosen's imminent bashing precluded her own, but she was missing a finer point (an obvious one that showed that the school paid scant attention to some of the paperwork required of martyrs-in-training).

"Honey," I said, stroking her hair, "stoning isn't a way of killing yourself. *Other people* have to stone you. I would think that stoning yourself would be quite difficult."

"Unless you're stoned," Jerome added, and Lori giggled.

"Besides," I said, ignoring their little moment to hammer home the obvious, "it's not your senior year."

(Stroking Lori's hair didn't feel all that different from stroking my own, and it was easy to see how, in the dark, Jerome had *almost* made a terrible mistake—until the fingers ran over the stubbly side of her head where the hair had been roughly hewn. Even in the dark, how had Jerome missed something so obvious? I knew that when he got all revved up, all the blood drained from his brain to his penis. Maybe that was it. It was starting to become a day for running smack into the obvious—and ignoring it.)

We were staring at the school's main bulletin board along with a bunch of other students. The stoning announcement had just been tacked up. Suicide by homicide was forbidden, I thought, but I suppose the Order's choice of stoning was meant to frighten. It seemed to me that fear was the whole point of the Lottery; it was meant to keep students from even thinking about leaving. (Another rumor was that Lottery winners were captured escapees.) When we'd first arrived, I thought it would have the opposite effect with students fleeing in all directions, but the Lottery was more than just a show of strength; it also displayed the school's affinity for violence and demonstrated their utter disregard for the student as an individual; it telegraphed that it didn't matter who you were (or who you thought you were), the Order saw the student body as a future pile of student bodies. The Lottery pretty much confirmed (for me at least) that the whispers were true: the Order would go to savage lengths to make sure we took our own lives, even if it meant taking them for us and claiming otherwise.

How far would the Order go? How about this? While school was in session, parents had to come visit underclassmen (if they so desired), but upperclassmen were allowed to visit home (with permission). However, a Sanguine Knight would call on the family first (earning plenty of frequent flyer miles), and before the student departed, they would be shown a photo of the meeting. Surveilling Jerome and I when we lived off campus for the summer was one thing, but this advance form of intimidation was a whole new level of crazy. (Lori never seemed bothered by the photos of Mom and the Scum, and I kept my mouth shut.)

In the pervading miasma of rumors, there was one I absolutely believed (considering the others involved the less than scholastically lauded, it seemed that the school would not be denied and therefore the details of this rumor made perfect sense, if I may use that word): that seniors with a solid GPA who chickened out during their final week were slaughtered by the Scum, and their remains thrown to the alligators in the swamp, not good enough even for the incinerator, I suppose—and students who'd come to their senses (regardless of grades) but were caught during their inevitable escape attempts during finals week were dispatched in such ways that allowed the Scum to stage their deaths as suicides. If all this was true, then the Order was knowingly beatifying students who hadn't self-terminated, which meant—*gasp*—this, the school, all of it, was so much horse hockey. I found this rumor to be much more frightening than the similar one involving students with low GPAs, mainly, I supposed, because having almost two years under my belt, I was becoming acutely aware of what those in charge were capable of doing—and inspiring. In fact, when I realized that my grades were good enough for me to be invited to join the honor society, Epsilon Delta Sigma (Excellence Dignity Sacrifice), the Eds, a group so fervent, they embraced exams and suicide with equal amounts of alacrity, I began to tank the occasional test or muff a paper here or there until the invite was rescinded.

As we huddled around the bulletin board, afraid to break ranks, I suppose, I kept staring at the announcement of the Lottery method, as if I expected it to change.

"I'm not watching this," I said in a loud voice, a little boastful. (As we crept closer to the end of our junior year, I often flaunted my contempt and even broke a few more rules than usual.)

"Lisa, you have to," Lori said, all saucer-eyed. "It's in the handbook."

"It's mandatory," said the Japanese-American student whom everybody, racist or not, thought would commit *hara-kiri* as her capstone project.

"I can't wait," said Jerome's roommate Evan, who had what looked like two small hickeys on his neck. "Bam!"

"I hope it's me!" cried a wisp of a girl everyone called Piper, gripping her school books to her flat chest. "I hope it's me!"

And it was.

The tile with Piper LaRue's name was the one drawn, and she had a 3.9 GPA. When the day came a week later, there was a Latin Mass first thing in the morning with readings from the *Acta Martyrum*, then blessings from a traveling bishop. (If there were other dioceses, I didn't know where they were.) The prelate—who was younger than the first bishop we'd met—had been sent by the Patriarch of the Order to oversee the Lottery and serve as postulator for beatification; after Piper's death, the bishop would investigate her life for proof of at least an attempt to live up to Christian ideals before bestowing upon the dead student the title of Blessed, which was one verified miracle away from being a saint. In other words, I told Lori, the bishop was here to verify that Piper had indeed martyred herself. (I wasn't sure a homicide detective would see the Order's distinction between the girl being martyred and being murdered, because regardless of how Piper had lived her life, her death had been overseen by a shadowy, crimson cult—but I knew better than to voice that thought, especially since the police and local government, up to the state level, appeared not to be bothered with the goings-on at the Martyr School.) Piper's father sat in the first pew and left as soon as the service was over, but word was that her mother had been against Piper going to our school and had refused to come. Piper had been given a farewell party in the lobby of the girls' residence hall, but it was sparsely attended. Piper hadn't made many friends at school. Though pretty in a washed out pixie sort of way, she dated little. (There were whispers of lesbianism.) She was standoffish, a little off-putting even. Out of all the kids I met at the Martyr School, Piper seemed the most vocally eager to die. A nun once told her to pipe down in class. (Hence the nickname.) "One is not to be *eager* to die," Sister Sebastian told her, "just ready to expire and willing to prove it."

Were there rumblings of students chosen in Lotteries past who found that they had no desire to die at that particular moment, arguing, among other things, that they were not spiritually prepared (playing to their audience)? Yes, Father Caleb told us in our Study of Human Nature class, but for every one there was an official refutation, followed by a justification for seeing it through, which "*always*," he emphasized, brought these students to their senses. Father Caleb explained that it boiled down to this: God in his omnipotence had chosen these students to die for their faith in the Lottery, yet imbued them with free will, as with all of our kind, but in His omniscience, He knows which of the possible choices would eventually be made: the one where death is accepted as a sacrifice, so that others might clearly see the path to the beatific vision awaiting at the other end of martyrdom. If free will seemed to be ignored when the winner of the Lottery sometimes had to be brought by the SKM to the killing floor (kicking and screaming holy hell before they were sedated—at least that was what we heard), we should take on faith that we do not understand what the concept of free will means to He who grants us such a gift. In the final breaths of the winner ("the chosen" was the preferred appellation), God's ears will hear the words He knew were coming: *O Lord, I offer my life to you.* Father Caleb told us that the student body was in a state of liminality, a transitional phase which lasted until the moment of our self-deliverance (or, you know, execution) during which we lacked social status and were expected to be humble and obedient acolytes, following "prescribed forms of conduct" to live up to our calling as martyrs, exceptionalism in the classroom rewarded only with leashed walks beyond the walls when school was in session, since our true recompense was on "the other end of the sword." What this gobbledygook meant was that we had to earn the right to be a martyr, despite having heeded the call; it also meant that since the Order had no intention in letting us leave the school alive—the escape success rate was poor, from all we'd heard—we might as well go along to get along, that way, when we reached heaven, bloody and bereft, we'd have a reserved table.

If nothing else, the Lottery of Future Saints was meant to convey that the Order, through their claim of divine authority, decided who died, or rather when—what Ms. Shevchenko would have undoubtedly called a key component of a thought reform environment. There was no running from a God such as this, the

Lottery implied; here was the New Testament God requiring Old Testament sacrifice. The Lottery was designed, it seemed, to keep the young would-be martyrs on their paths, for even the most frightened students would rather stay the course than find themselves a Lottery winner or worse. Each step away from the group made the act seem less urgent and more futile. Breach the walls and you will be breached, the disciplinarian told us, and Headmaster McCaffrey was clear: knowledge of dissent equals consent.

There was very little rebellious chatter, and what sedition existed was rarely expressed widely; cemetery or swamp parties or even excursions into the French Quarter came with the risk of too many ears; it was generally reserved for lavatory whispers amid constant flushing (in case the toilets were bugged or one of the Eds was nearby). But the truth was: I found very few students who felt they were there against their will, and even most of those were willing to go through with it, having been properly indoctrinated. Maybe that was why, according to those in the know, the most fractious or potentially dissident were never chosen in the Lottery. (Its randomness was the belief of the easily stupefied.) Would-be rebels were subjected to hours-long theological lectures during detention instead, while the weak skipped merrily to the guillotine. Perhaps the Order thought making a public example of a heretic might inflame others of their ilk, even awaken those lingering in the twilight, but more likely they didn't see the point of using the Lottery as punishment (the Scum were at the ready in any case) because it would take the focus away from the Lamb willingly walking into the slaughter—sedated perhaps but smiling.

So on the appointed day, the student body was herded onto the soccer field. A hole had been dug near one sideline, much to the soccer coach's consternation (the master of grounds pointedly ignored him), and a large pile of rocks had been dumped some feet from the hole. At the designated time, Piper was led out to the field to a big cheer. The school's insignia had been tattooed just above her right ankle. Her hands were bound with purple ribbon (and rope), but she was not blindfolded. Martyrs have to see it coming, Headmaster McCaffrey had said during the pre-bloodshed service the night before. During the liturgy, the volunteer stone throwers were absolved and told to be careful not to sin during the night, which many students took to mean: don't touch yourself inappropriately under the covers. Lori was one of the volunteers. It made me sick to my stomach, and on the eve of the Big Day, as Mr. Horner called it, I barely slept. I knew I couldn't talk Lori out of it. She'd already been blessed and forgiven in advance. It was out of my hands. But the blood would be on hers. Jerome treated it like a sporting event. I swear he would have snuck a beer onto the field if he could have gotten away with it. The event teetered between solemnity and a party atmosphere.

The headmaster, who was also a priest, said a few words, and Monsignor Jaeger sprinkled Piper with holy water. After a short hymn that we sang too fast, as if giving glory to the Lord was an impediment to the bloodletting, the monsignor smeared oil on her forehead (already oily with innumerable tiny pimples). "Go with God," Headmaster McCaffrey told her, and two deacons lowered her into the hole and began filling it in so that only her upper chest and head were visible. She wore no makeup, but she didn't need it: she looked beautiful actually, probably for the first (and definitely the last) time. Her hair was long and waved about her shoulders as the wind played with it.

The volunteers stepped forward and were told to each choose a rock. Some did with reluctance, their prior eagerness quite suddenly weighing heavy on their souls. But not Lori. She must have had her eye on a particular rock, because she went right to one and evaluated its heft in her hand. Pleased, she stared down her target. I wanted to look away, but I couldn't—not because I wanted to see Piper stoned to death, but because my sister would be one of the ones doing the stoning. I had no hope that she would change her mind (and I was pretty sure the punishment for doing so would be severe).

"Begin," Headmaster McCaffrey instructed, but the volunteers stood still and mute, looking at one another. When it came to it, no one wanted to cast the first stone, except for maybe Lori, who appeared to be aiming, but even she didn't throw her rock immediately; perhaps she was taking her time to ensure accuracy. Regardless, it had to be the volunteers who did Piper in. The other students hadn't been absolved, and the faculty wouldn't dare get their hands dirty for fear of a lawsuit (plus no teacher wanted to be accused of playing favorites). Several minutes passed by, the headmaster's face growing redder by the second. The prelate looked put out. Only Piper seemed to be enjoying the morning breeze, her face tilted up, her eyes taking it all in, a smile spreading across her face.

The first rock hit Piper in the middle of her forehead and split it open. No more pimples. Her smile disappeared, and her eyes suddenly seemed to be further apart. Blood was everywhere, and before the second rock hit her, it was fairly obvious Piper was dead or at least unconscious, maybe brain dead. The rocks came fast and furious after the first two until all that remained of what had been Piper's head was a vaguely round crimson mass. One of her eyes lay on the ground looking skywards. The headmaster blew a whistle, told everyone to lower their heads, and said a prayer. Then two teachers held up a wine-colored sheet to block us from witnessing the deacons digging out what remained of Piper.

Lori came running towards Jerome and me, her mouth open. I held out my arms, but she ran into Jerome's, who didn't look surprised. He shrugged at me.

Lori was shaking and crying and part of me was secretly happy: maybe this would mean we would be leaving the Martyr School sooner than expected.

"I did it," Lori said, snot running from her nose. "The first stone—that was mine. I did it. I sent her to heaven. I opened her skull and exposed her brain to Jesus."

"Well, shit," I said to no one. I massaged my temples and part of a line from Shakespeare's *Cymbeline* rattled around my skull: "…our very eyes / Are sometimes like our judgments, blind." Even though we'd been dissecting the play in my Jacobean literature class, I had no idea why this particular quote had surfaced from my aching brain. I even thought of what Shakespeare scholar R. A. Foakes wrote about this line, "Eyes and judgments are bound to deceive sometimes, in a world such as this," but its meaning was lost on me—even in a world such as this.

Lori continued sobbing into Jerome's chest, and Jerome seemed to forget I was there. He closed his eyes. He stroked her hair. He squeezed her tight.

Then he sang to her in a barely audible voice: "*The woman is wild, a she-cat tamed by the purr of a Jag-u-ar.*"

This seemed to calm Lori down a little, although she didn't let go of my boyfriend until I said, "Hey guys," in the friendliest voice I could muster. With what I thought was an obvious reluctance, my sister tore herself away and wiped her eyes with her sleeves. She looked dream-dazed, woozy. Jerome slunk away and joined a group of his buddies hooting and hollering as the hearse backed up to the soccer field and the coach moaned. Piper's body, except for a dangling leg, was covered by a black sheet emblazoned with the crimson and bone school insignia, matching the fresh tattoo on her right leg, which dangled from the stretcher. The calf tattoo was the only thing that made it obvious that the odd-shaped pile beneath the black sheet was Piper LaRue, and the surrounding hoopla made what was obvious that much harder to see.

I pulled Lori away from Jerome and held her chin until she looked me in the eye.

"Lori," I said, "when we were at Blues End, the three of us—what did Jerome whisper in your ear that made you get up and dance with the Captain?"

Still looking a bit disoriented but with a slight smile beginning to tickle her face, she took hold of my arm without looking at me.

"He told me I was his Maneater."

Nobody puts Baby in a corner.

I threw up on my shoes, but Lori didn't notice. She walked away—almost skipping actually. I turned to look for Jerome in the crowd, but he was gone.

+

From the journals of Lori Duke:

Quotes I Like

[I]f you have no past or future which, after all, is all that the present is made of, why then you may as well dispose of the empty shell of present....

Sylvia Plath

For a movie to be a romantic comedy...there has to be a scene where, after the two have realized they've fallen for each other, something happens that forces them apart.... And there has to be a scene where one of the people involved in the relationship makes some big gesture...hopefully in front of as many people as possible...

Amanda Dobbins & Shea Serrano

+

From the *Martyr School Handbook*:

The Angry Breakup

There comes a time in almost every student's life at the Martyr School where the pupil starts to question his or her choice of vocation. This is Lucifer, the Morning Star, whispering in the student's ear, seeking to incite enmity and apostasy and to precipitate a wrathful separation from the Lord. This is a test. The Morning Star's sibilant susurrations are just perversions of self-reflection. If a student begins to question martyrdom, it should be seen as a sign that martyrdom is the appropriate calling. One cannot breakup with Jesus. While some will walk gladly into the flames, many will struggle with, balk at, and attempt to resist the idea, none of which should be viewed as negative reactions, although those irresolute will require reeducation in order to graduate. But as it is written in the Epistle of James, "Resist the devil, and he will flee from you." Persevering will help the student reap the benefits of the afterlife as a martyr for Christ. The world has persecuted our students. More importantly, our students have persecuted themselves. As our first Headmaster, Rev. J. M. Born, wrote in his initial tract to the first senior class, "Hang around for the hanging, even if the noose is for you and tied by your own hand."

+

Being without Jerome for most of the merry month of May was complete hell. What had happened after Piper's head was turned into pulp, what played out in front of me while I tossed my cookies on my black Mary Janes, turned out to be, I believed, the dissolution of whatever I had with Jerome, and although the clues had been there, dangling as bright as party lights, I'd been too distracted by everything to notice. Call me clueless, obtuse even, but the last thing I'd expected after the public execution of Piper LaRue was the public demise of my romantic relationship—or, rather, the big reveal that my boyfriend had a twin on the side and it turned out to be me. Judging from the looks I received the rest of the day, this situation, this *arrangement* (for at least a few of them must surely have seen it that way) was not unknown to some of my fellow students, many of which, I was sure, believed that whatever passed for a relationship between Lori and Jerome was a chaste one.

But I wasn't one to hide my head beneath my pillow. I needed a breakup moment, something more *palpable*, without a crowd and most definitely without my sister. Jerome had been caught unawares. My breakup moment manifested itself as a brutal and furious mental onslaught—but first I bit my lip; though I needed to taste blood that night, I wanted to make sure that I didn't get caught up in the bloodlust currently coursing through the student body. But physical outrage, destruction—these felt like appropriate reactions, particularly after Piper's explosive end. The campus guards had to remove me from Jerome's room, which I'd trashed. (Jerome was alone; I'd waited until Lori left there for her study group. Evan, his roommate, had already flown the coop—literally; he'd somehow managed to end up at the Vampyre School.) Before the authorities arrived, I'd scratched Jerome's face and bit into his arm. I swear that if I could have reached his eyes, I would have clawed them out. I squeezed his nut sack until he screamed like a little girl. As the Scum lifted me up and carried me away, I managed one last kick that landed square on his nose, breaking it, I heard later.

It was hard enough to accept that my boyfriend was screwing someone else for God knows how long, but the fact that it was my sister—my very mixed-up sister—made it that much harder. But then again, how mixed-up was she? She'd been able to hug the shadows without being caught out of character. But my accidental interruption during the date night I'd arranged—and I was convinced of this—was nothing more than a contrived mix-up, a trope that had been spoon-fed to me.

I would like to be able to say that I didn't even consider suicide, but I would be lying. I didn't make solid plans like my classmates or sit in on any electrocution seminars. But the thought did cross my mind from time to time. I even found myself walking slowly past Nestor the horny mailman. I must have done this often enough that he felt safe squeezing my butt (through my uniform) before making his trademarked tongue-through-the-encircled-fingers greeting. He was right: I only lightly slapped his face; my inclination before my discovery of infidelity would have been to have Jerome break Nestor's arm in as many places as he could manage.

Lori didn't sleep in our room anymore. She could have been staying at Jerome's. I'd slept there often enough, but I never moved in; his old RA or the Scum would have surely ferreted me out. Certain RAs turned a blind eye as long as their feigned ignorance wasn't abused. This was not the case with Jerome's latest RA. Still, he wasn't the brightest bulb in the patch, so while it was risky, it was far from impossible to get around him. But I figured Lori wouldn't want to taint the vestal virgin image she'd cultivated after the lacrosse players incident. Truth was I didn't know where she laid her head. After Piper was killed and the Maneater truth revealed, I skipped classes and traipsed around the bayou, eventually planting myself against a southern live oak with lateral limbs that just about reached the ground. It was only beneath its green canopy, protected, it seemed, by its splayed branches that I allowed myself to cry—about all of this: about where we were and the stoning I'd just witnessed, about what was happening with my twin sister, and about the apparent demise of romantic love or at least my sliver of the pie. I cried until the mosquitoes began to get greedy.

When I returned, it was growing dark and all of Lori's stuff was gone from our room. I had to wait an excruciating two days before I could get someone to talk. (How did Lori ever earn this level of respect?) But I figured our resident gossip must have been near-bursting from holding in what she knew. Suzette, who planned on going out in a surprisingly quiet way by downing a shitload of pills and a chilled bottle of Stoli while listening to Pink Floyd's *The Wall* on vinyl, told me that Lori (Suzette said her name with reverence) had moved to the top floor. The Jumpers' Floor we called it. The hard cases who wanted to fall to their deaths often requested the top floor. (They also preferred the infinitive phrase *to jump* rather than *to fall.*) Sometimes they would climb to the roof, and if we were walking on the grassy common, we could see their heads peeking over the ledge, as if they were picking out their spots. The Jumpers' Floor, five flights up, was a mixture of seniors and some juniors. (Like the boys' dormitory, the girls' residence hall had plenty of vacancies and half-filled floors; the student population was relatively small and often shrinking. The boys' dormitory was wider but had only had four floors, and the girl jumpers lorded their building's additional height over their male compatriots.) Although I didn't know what exit path Lori had chosen (she'd never told me—I only knew her safety because she'd been so vocal about it prior to Piper's pummeling—and I'd never asked because I believed we'd be on a train or a Greyhound before graduation), I doubted it was jumping; she had a fear of heights. Lori just wanted to be far away from her sister and in a place severe enough to upset me. (Potential jumpers, for reasons I didn't understand, were treated like royalty on campus. Maybe it had something to do with the method's inherent theatricality.) Here was kicker: I actually believed that Lori's fear of heights would bring her back down; the stubbornness of my naiveté was nothing less than astounding.

I didn't tell our mother about all that had happened, and I guessed Lori didn't either, for when I placed my weekly phone call home (a ritual Lori had long ago abandoned, choosing a more sporadic approach), Mom didn't mention my breakup with Jerome, and Mom always brought up or asked about *everything*, from the mundane to the important (often with the same tone of voice). Although they'd never met, my mother was keen on Jerome, if a little frightened because of the time I'd told her of his exit path, but it wasn't his chosen method that scared my mom, no; it was that he had one. Still, Mom played along even though she knew (or at least hoped) I was playing along too—gamboling, to use her word. She understood that I was a teenager to a point. The school wanted me to be a martyr; our mother wanted me to be a saviour, and saviours don't canoodle with boys, even nice ones, not if doing so takes precedent over the mission. The main thrust of each conversation (if you could call them that) was to ascertain if I was any closer to bringing Lori home. Once that information was relayed and absorbed (and my tongue-lashing wrapped up), the meat of the call was pretty much covered. Oh, there would be the standard Jerome grilling, shorter and shorter each time, as if she was afraid I'd bring up his exit path again and that such talk would lead me to bring up Lori's, which she probably assumed I knew. All that remained would be neighborhood minutiae that made me both extremely glad I missed the events described *and* nostalgic for a life, though simple, that was generally free of the stench of death and flop sweat (though Mom still went to every funeral possible). *Did I know* (and I never asked how that would be possible) *what Mrs. Browne next door had done to her Pekingese?* (The woman had Alzheimer's and had kicked her dog like a football more than once, thinking it was an overly developed mouse; but her kicks were weak, the dog stalwart.) Or...*do you believe what Mr. David said to me at the Acme this past Monday?* (Mother thought Mr. David, who manned the deli counter, was always trying to hit on her by lifting his thumb from the scale and giving her extra bologna, which Mother secretly fed to Mrs. Browne's Pekingese to build up his strength.) Lori's move to the Jumpers' Floor remained my secret, as did her presumably ongoing affair with my ex-boyfriend.

I wondered if Jerome still planned on going out with a suicide bag—basically a plastic bag with a drawstring that he'd place over his head. In the bag was the end of a hose, the other end of which was attached to a helium or nitrogen tank. (Any inert gas would do.) Before securing the bag (and the nozzle), he'd turn on the tank. If done correctly, the gas would largely prevent the panic—and thus the struggle—that often accompanied (the sense of) suffocation, or so we learned. Loss of consciousness after maybe the second breath, dead in about ten minutes. I always told him he'd chicken out and rip the bag after the first breath. Jerome always did what was easiest.

With the room to myself and a decided disdain for the opposite sex, I took to masturbating with a vengeance. A hairbrush handle was a particular favorite, but I tried everything: letting the force of the water from the tub faucet splash my way to temporary oblivion, rubbing myself against a pillow, humping the corner of my mattress, whatever it took. Once in a while, I even rubbed one out in class just for the thrill of maybe getting caught (which didn't take very long). It wasn't sexual frustration that I was working out. (I was used to being frustrated; my sex life with Jerome, with a few notable exceptions, had become increasingly mechanical and predictable, like what I imagined happened to middle-aged married couples, except instead of doing it once every two weeks barely looking at one another, we pounded away on a dorm room bed almost every day when we were together, but with little to no variation. Before I knew my sister was Jerome's maneater, I wondered would he love me when were in our mid- to-late-forties, a small spare tire around my middle, otherwise thin, but with my 32Cs sagging big time? Would doggy style become the norm— better to look at my cottage cheese ass than to watch my breasts flop all over the damn place? This was what I was torturing myself about while he nailed my sister.) No, the excessive masturbation was role reversal, I thought. By having all these orgasms (at least three a day), I felt I was experiencing what Lori was (which was what I had experienced during the early days with Jerome when we'd screwed like Energizer bunnies that had lost their batteries and were experimenting with new power sources). While orgasms certainly weren't new to me, and maybe they weren't new to Lori (for all I knew, she'd masturbated constantly pre-Jerome like I was doing post-Jerome), her having them with someone else certainly was. Her expression when she answered "Maneater" made me sure Jerome was her first; maybe she'd been broken in the night I'd interrupted them with a rose. Having a partner administer the soft blows of love was a decidedly different feeling.

I believed, with no rationale, that masturbation was the only way I could force myself to forgive Lori. So I did it till my vagina was numb. I did it until I couldn't even feel my body shudder. I did it until I was caught with my fingers up my cooter in Advanced Biology (appropriate). The teacher, Mr. Caspar, was droning on (again) about the various ways one could stop their own heart (who would go through the trouble of shocking themselves with jumper cables, I didn't know), and I was absently rubbing and fingering myself. I was so bored and so intent on finishing the job, I failed to notice my jet black skirt was raised up to the tops of my thighs. But leave it to Angie Mascalone, who hated my guts because everyone called her Karl Malden. (We'd been friends since sophomore year, but Angie had taken up with a crowd of field hockey chicks who seemed intent on beating the living bejesus out of each other, even in the dorms, where once Angie's stick missed my head by inches and I punched her in her sizable nose, which swelled twice its size.) Angie turned in her seat and said in a voice loud enough for everyone to hear, including the monotonous instructor: "What's that *smell?*" The class turned, and there I was: three fingers, knuckles deep. I lowered my skirt and collected my books (Mr. Caspar turned and stared mutely at the blackboard), but before I left, I stuck my fingers beneath Angie's honker. In a school as small as ours, getting caught diddling in class would probably have been a life-altering scandal, but at the Martyr School, public self-abasement was encouraged. I walked calmly to the girls' lavatory where I completed the business at hand, and as soon as I came, I knew I was finished with masturbating—or at least I'd reached the end of my onanistic fever. I also knew I had finally forgiven Lori.

I approached my twin sister after last bell on the Friday that marked the third week since my little world had been split apart like Piper's forehead, and we spent the rest of the day together. But despite the détente that ensued, I avoided being around when she and Jerome were together (I think Lori was careful to make sure that didn't happen often), and Lori never moved back down to our room. Everything else returned to normal. We were friends again, and my mind was clear enough to focus on my real reason for being at the Martyr School, my sole objective: bringing Lori home in one piece—and not in a body bag. This wasn't the Vampyre School or the Lycanthrope School where the students either were truly vampyres or werewolves or incredibly delusional head cases. This was a school where a stoning was considered both a holy act and good entertainment and classes were taught on the best ways to shoot yourself. Philadelphia had race issues and entire sections of the city given over to drugs, plus a branch of the Mafia that couldn't shoot straight and corrupt politicians aplenty (one climbed up to the City Hall observation deck and had to be talked down— there was a pending indictment for trading favors to businessmen who paid his credit card debt), but what it didn't have was a school that taught you how to end your life. Lori needed to be home, and our junior year was nearing its end. We weren't returning to Philly for the season. (What was a trip to the Wildwood boardwalk compared to the French Quarter?) This summer, I told myself over and over; I can get her home this summer, Jerome be damned.

+

From the *Martyr School Handbook*:

The suicide note is the most important piece of writing for a student at the Martyr School. It is considered a student's thesis. In that light, all English classes, beginning in the sophomore year, will spend time on the suicide note, which will count as a quarter of your capstone grade in your senior year. All suicide notes require faculty approval. Seniors who self-terminate without an approved suicide note will receive an incomplete and will not graduate. One cannot become a martyr without discipline.

+

At the Martyr School, we learned the following important information:

1. How best to slit your wrists: not across but up or down. We memorized the location of the radial artery, ulnar artery, cephalic vein, and basilic vein. Key vocabulary words: exsanguination, hypovolemia.

2. A bullet through the mouth is twenty to thirty times more effective than one shot through the temple, where the bullet could rattle around your skull and leave you a vegetable. Mrs. Bottoms, an elderly, weathered schoolmarm with a sizable bald spot on the right side of her head and (as expected) a bottom as wide as Montana, said to us, "Vegetation, my poppets, leaves you drooling with a big fat F."

3. If you don't have a garage in which to run your car while you sit with the windows down sucking in the carbon monoxide, you can always a stick a gas-powered water pump in the backseat or burn charcoal in a sealed room. Either way, your skin will turn yellow.

4. Jumping in front of a train requires a witness in order to graduate, as there will often be little left of you to identify. However, suicide by train has an astounding 10 percent survival rate, though many are left with brain damage or physical disabilities. ("Vegetation, my poppets…") Also, this method may cause the driver of the train to go into shock or even cardiac arrest and possibly later suffer from post-traumatic stress disorder, particularly if one lies down on the tracks in broad daylight. (The driver is usually unable to brake in time.)

Causing complete strangers to suffer from unwittingly taking part in your self-termination could lower your final grade. However, if this information came to the Order *after* graduation, it will be noted but nothing more, as it is apparently unheard of to strip someone of the title Blessed once they have been beatified. Once you're in, baby, you're in.

5. Suicide by hanging is more prevalent in rural areas than in urban. Dying from autoerotic asphyxiation is no way to get into heaven.

6. Firearms account for 53.7 percent of all suicides in the US. "Originality counts, children," Headmaster McCaffrey told us repeatedly. Still, half of all graduating classes shoot themselves and are proclaimed martyrs. In our first year at the school, the valedictorian received special dispensation to deliver his address, which would have normally been read by the academic dean (as all seniors were expected to have punched the clock before commencement). Upon finishing his address, the valedictorian pulled two revolvers from beneath his gown and placed the barrels on his eyelids. The boy's cap was taken to his empty chair, as his corpse was whisked away.

7. The Thích Quảng Đức Method (self-immolation) requires two years of meditation classes. Even though the Buddhist monk set himself on fire as a means of protest, the lesson to be extracted is that his belief gave him the will. Eighty-five percent of students attempting to burn themselves up try it near a fountain or pool and quickly put themselves out. "Concentration is the key," Master Shimizu told us with a smile during our sophomore year, then demonstrated by pouring lighter fluid over one of his hands and igniting it. He was quickly put out with a fire extinguisher and taken to the infirmary, no longer smiling. Screaming, yes; smiling no. He never returned to the Martyr School. (Like Defence Against the Dark Arts teachers at Hogwarts School of

Witchcraft and Wizardry, instructors of Contemplative Prayer over Pain rarely lasted a full term.)

8. It is very, very difficult to import an asp. "Cleopatra had ready access, people," Mr. Thorndale told us. "Don't try for the impossible. To do so means you're not ready or your head's not in the right place." (Mr. Thorndale informed us, proudly, that he'd been arrested twice for violating customs laws.)

9. Apocarteresis (death by starvation) requires time. However, a *hunger strike* is not considered a proper suicide method, as it is, by definition, an act of protest. Dying by starvation can take up to forty-six days, but there is a documented case of it taking eighty-three days. The body uses up its glucose in the first seventy-two hours, then the liver starts processing body fat. After about three weeks, the body starts in on the muscles and vital organs, looking for something, anything, to survive on. Commission of death by starvation requires approval from the Order. (Just about everything, it seemed, required authorization; the school was paranoid about being sued and had an army of lawyers at the ready and armed with hand grenades in case the whole operation went to hell. At least that was the scuttlebutt.) An oath must be taken by his or her dorm mates not to entice the starving student with even a cracker; they must promise not to slip them anything more than perhaps a juice box. After two weeks, starvation students are taken to the infirmary, though all course work must be completed before expiration in order to be eligible for graduation. (Can't be lying around doing nothing, I suppose.)

10. Suicide by cop is forbidden. So is parasuicidal behavior, such as a "cry for help" (referred to as the Pussy Move by students), unless such behavior, like Lori's, took place before enrollment; then it is considered practice, not performance. Cutting and eating disorders are tolerated only if they are part of a bigger plan. Asking

someone to kill you is a no-no and seeking mental health counseling is prohibited. Suicide attacks are taboo. Committing suicide in the presence of a loved one is an automatic F. Eighty percent of home suicides are cleaned up by a family member, and 75 percent of those cleaners will attempt suicide later in life or at least seriously contemplate it.

11. Self-defenestration (throwing oneself out a window) and jumping from a great height (whether or not a window is involved) accounts for less than 2 percent of reported suicides in the US. In Hong Kong, however, jumping is the most popular method of taking one's life, coming in at a whopping 52 percent.
Feeding oneself to a crocodile or a shark is one of the least used methods in any country (that has access to such creatures) and would present a problem as far as martyrdom goes, because, absent eyewitnesses, the creature would have to be caught and cut open like the shark in *Jaws* to see if there were any undigested body parts. The Martyr School considered the unnecessary slaughter (of animals) a sin.

12. In Famous Suicides I and II (required underclassmen courses), we studied personages such as Johnny Ace (singer, gunshot wound while playing Russian roulette—still counts, though barely—December 25, 1954); Diane Arbus (photographer, pills and slashed wrists, a true twofer, July 26, 1971); Sir Robert Clive (British conqueror of India and Bengal, slit his throat *with a penknife*, a tough choice, our instructors told us, but quite dramatic, November 22, 1774); Kurt Cobain (musician, shotgun, the definitive way out and a tricky one as it usually involves using one's toes to pull the trigger, April 5, 1994); Sigmund Freud (founder of psychoanalysis—mocked at the Martyr School—morphine overdose administered by a doctor at Freud's behest, September 23, 1939, though physician-assisted suicide was generally thought of as cheating); Hermann Göring (Nazi leader, cyanide taken the night before his

scheduled execution, October 15, 1946—pussy); Ernest Hemingway (writer, shotgun, July 2, 1961; a family tradition: Ernest's sister, brother, father, and granddaughter all took their lives into their own hands); Terry Long (football player, drank antifreeze—a *very* ballsy play, June 7, 2005); Lawrence Oates (Arctic explorer, walked out into a blizzard, telling his companions, "I am just going outside and may be some time," March 16, 1912); Sylvia Plath (poet, stuck her head in the oven, February 11, 1963; she was followed by the woman her husband, the poet Ted Hughes, had left her for, Assia Wevill, who drugged her daughter and herself before turning on the oven, March 23, 1969— even the Order of Martyrs believed taking someone out with you was bad form; completing the hypoxic triumvirate, poet Anne Sexton, Plath's Boston University classmate, chose carbon monoxide poisoning in the garage, October 4, 1974); and let's not forget Virginia Woolf (writer, filled her overcoat pockets with stones and walked into the River Ouse, March 28, 1941, an act of guts *and* concentration, we were taught). None of the above were considered martyrs, by the way, just damn good examples, most of them.

13. Irony abounds in martyrdom (a refuted point in The Eschatological Paradox, an elective for upperclassmen, but something I picked up on early). The Apostle Paul wrote, "For to me to live is Christ, and to die is gain." The disciple Stephen was the first Christian to *gain*; he was stoned to death after mouthing off to the Sanhedrin. His execution was witnessed by the Apostle Paul, then called Saul, who at the time was dedicated to persecuting the early disciples of Jesus. At the Martyr School, being put to death in the name of faith was not a martyrdom "devoutly to be wished," the Lottery of Future Saints notwithstanding. Tertullian, an early Christian theologian, wrote in *Apologeticus* that "the blood of martyrs is the seed of the Church," a concept which some academics, like Nicole Kelley, believed led to the "articulation" of the Christian identity: that "to

be a Christian was to suffer," and thus, according to professor Judith Perkins, in the sacrifices of the "noble army of martyrs," early believers "could see vindicated the triumphant worth of suffering." At the Martyr School, this concept was called "mirroring"—the early martyrs accepted their persecution with grace and embraced their execution as sacrifice, suffering for Christ as He had for them. But although the Martyr School venerated such saints as Sebastian and Agnes of Rome, it was not because of their martyrdom. The death of Cato the Younger, statesman and Stoic, who committed suicide rather than live in a world ruled by Julius Caesar, was an example closer to the theology of the Martyr School (even though Cato was a pagan). The founders of the Order believed they lived in a carceral world, where the dolor of living was suffering enough. True martyrdom had to come from one's own hands. Rather than being an offense towards God, the Elders looked upon suicide as the logical response and ultimate sacrifice: giving up as a way of giving yourself up— suffering for Christ, just in a fucked up way.

14. In *The Myth of Sisyphus* by Albert Camus, the author asks whether the realization of the absurd requires suicide. His answer, "No. It requires revolt," is considered by the Martyr School to be, in itself, absurd.

> Note: *The Myth of Sisyphus* was among the books the school referred to as the *Librorum Prohibitorum* (called by us the Nightlight List). They were considered contraband unless they were required texts, and if they were, the books had to be turned in at the end of the semester to be locked away from curious minds, but a dog-eared copy of *Sisyphus* was passed around by a few like-minded people, with each student adding notes in the margin or highlighting phrases. In our junior year, Suzette began calling our informal little group of dissidents, the Reluctants. I said little but thought we should be called the Aware, although it would not

accurately describe all of us. Camus warned against living "not for life itself but for some great idea" that will ultimately "betray it." For him, suicide was "a repudiation," not exactly the kind of thinking taught at the Martyr School. He believed death to be the "most obvious absurdity" and suicide was "acceptance at its extreme." You could see why Camus was considered both dangerous and heretical by the school. He wrote, "It is essential to die unreconciled and not of one's own free will," and he came to the realization that "[r]arely is suicide committed...through reflection." Camus struck a bell for "rebellion against...mortality and its limits," a bell heard (if not always heeded) by the few Reluctants reading by nightlights and flashlights, hearts pounding and synapses firing: "revolt gives life its value."

+

Unlike most of the handbook, this section was addressed directly to us.

From the *Martyr School Handbook*:

The Final Embrace

During your time at the Martyr School, your religious and scholastic training has been preparing you for your concluding act. While we strive to give you the tools to overcome any fears, whether they are those you arrived with or ones that developed during your years at the Martyr School, there is one you must face alone: the fear of the Embrace. Is your soul free enough from sin to enter the Kingdom of Heaven? Have you suffered enough? Have you truly reached the final reel? The answers lie not between the pages of books or betwixt you and your confessor, but between you and your conscience, you and God. While it is our best hope that we do not fail you, often the only stone in your passway is you.

Reconciliation is not just the result of the sacrament of penance. In its truest form, it is the Final Embrace, which is often called the Final Clinch, but a clinch isn't enough—a clinch can be desperate, intense but ephemeral. In the Final Embrace, you are returned from whence you came; you were broken by the world and are restored; you are reconciled to Him. At the Martyr School, we lead you to Mount Mariah, but in your personal Binding, you are both Abraham and Isaac, and the Lord will not stay your hand.

There is no third reel without the Final Embrace.

+

By the first of June, Jerome was back in my bed. Call me weak. (Just don't call me needy.) It was like this: the school year was ending in about two weeks, I didn't seem to be any closer to bringing Lori home (*I still had the summer* was my mantra; *I still have a year*, I told my mother), and if I pleasured myself one more time, I thought the skin on my fingers would become permanently wrinkled. (After Lori and I had begun mending the fence, I fell off the pussy wagon—I'd only had three days chaste.) But the pool of boys at the Martyr School was shallow. I couldn't go after an underclassmen (they looked too young to have sex and far too young to want to die—I didn't want to push anyone over the edge again like Christy), and all the upperclassmen were so obsessed with ending it all, I wondered how they could possibly go through with it, seeing how the planning of the act had become such a passion. Jerome was simultaneously skulking and sulking around campus. It was easy to take him back. (Steal him back.) He looked like he would have done whatever either sister instructed.

Lori's dedication to her exit plans had left Jerome out in the cold, and I scooped him up and gave him warmth almost a week after Lori and I reconciled. (From Suzette Downey, always a font of information, I found out that my sister's new chosen method was a gunshot; a plastic bag over her head was her second choice, and her new safety, despite her acrophobia, was jumping, which told me how far I'd strayed from my original brief.) Lori was more into being a martyr than Jerome was; Jerome was into Frisbee. (I think Jerome's parents hadn't known what to do with the hairy pituitary case that was their son—he told me he'd taken to quietly wacking off while in the confessional just for kicks—and so had shipped him off to die a martyr for Christ, though Jerome claimed his family wasn't very religious. I bet they would have sent him to the Lycanthrope School if the peach fuzz on his upper lip had become more pronounced.) When I approached him in the gazebo at the end of May, I was sure he grew hard as soon I said hello. (He had that look on his face.) I know I was as wet as the grassy common in the morning. So it was a foregone conclusion that we would go to bed—the next day in fact—his time with my sister (for now) nothing more than a failed trial separation as far as I was concerned.

Here was the thing: it didn't affect my relationship with Lori whatsoever. I went out of my way to not mention Jerome unless it was necessary—I couldn't pretend that the boy wasn't back in my life, but I wasn't going to rub it in her face or give voice to my now-assuaged anger. Although Jerome and I snuck around for a bit, we stopped when Lori seemed not to care. Still, we never flaunted it in front of her; there were no public displays of affection. Lori seemed to take a steely-eyed approach to her chosen major and dedicated all of her time to studying proper muzzle angles and learning how to obtain optimal destruction with a variety of firearms. (One had to make sure that when the bullet entered the skull, it exerted the most kinetic energy possible whether or not it exited the head.) She stayed on the Jumpers' Floor though. Despite my weak entreaties (I liked having the room all to myself—and Jerome could stay over if we managed not to piss off the RA), Lori remained with the shaky (and jumpy) would-be-jumpers, a queen, I imagined, among the wingless, mostly male, drones. (Wrist-cutting was my major because it was such a popular method; I thought it would be easy to get lost in the crowd. I wasn't prepared for how excruciating it was to practice during lab class or how quickly the number of wrist-slicers dwindled as the school culled the cutters from our numbers. Cutters were easy to pick out, I thought: the scars on their arms looked like lattice work.)

As Lori became more hardcore about her future martyrdom, I tried to stop being judgmental and just focused on what I was really there to do, but when it came to talking with my sister, I found myself walking a tightrope: I didn't want to scare her off, and I didn't want to nudge her into deciding to apply for an early exit. (While her grades weren't stellar, they were good enough.) Somehow I had to make a case against the cult of the Order and try to counter whatever nonsense they had ingrained in my twin but still make sure she didn't know Mom had sent me to the school on a mission. I told myself when the time came, I had to offer answers and alternatives, not panaceas and nostrums; solid contingencies not twice-boiled contrivances—and it seemed as if that time was coming sooner than expected, as Lori began to decline in a hurry during the first full week of June. But all of my overthinking seemed to leave me in a middle ground, a limbo, where I sounded insouciant whenever I spoke to my sister about any topic close to the still-beating heart of the matter (self-deliverance, not Jerome). Being stuck, as well as intimidated by the task at hand, often had me, a "lowly player," concentrating more on my high-wire act than on Lori's proposed final curtain call.

+

AT RISE:

> LORI'S dormitory room, small with an arched roof. There are two beds across from each other. One is stripped bare, the other a tangle of sheets and clothes.
>
> The room is in disarray with books laid open face down and balls of paper nowhere near the waste basket. Her notebook journals are stacked haphazardly near her bed. Dirty Styrofoam plates and half-burnt candles are everywhere. Holy cards—funeral cards—featuring saints are on the floor, set up like a game of solitaire.
>
> > (As I enter, I send the cards skidding across the floor. Lori doesn't look up.)

ME

Hey, you ready for Mr. Clarke's class?

> > (I sound chipper even though climbing the stairs to the Jumpers' Floor made me queasy. Lori's windows face north like mine, and I peek down at the spiked fence.

When I turn around, I walk into more rows of holy cards. Lori doesn't take notice. I start to retrieve them but stop when I notice that cards are spread out over different parts of the floor or collected in sloppy piles.)

LORI

What does it matter?

(She is sitting on the floor in her pajamas, her nose in a Kierkegaard book, shivering although it is balmy outside. Her skin is oilier than usual, and her hair looks dirty.)

ME

In the larger scheme of things, it doesn't. But to Creepy Clarke... I don't know if he's married—he's not exactly a chick magnet, all those sweater vests—but I imagine him at home, smiling that science teacher smile as he jerks off into a beaker thinking about his young—

LORI

You "imagine" Mr. Clarke masturbating, do you?

(She doesn't look up from her book when she speaks, and there isn't a trace of humor in her question.)

ME

Who doesn't fantasize about riding his mustache?

(Lori shrugs. I look at my watch.)

Let's get you into the shower. Wash away those blues. You'll feel as good as new.

LORI

What does it—?

ME

Matter, yeah? Well, why don't you tell me what's the matter as I usher you into the—

(My sister shushes me with a finger and turns to a dog-eared page in her book. Her finger follows along as she reads to me.)

LORI

"What matters is to find a purpose, to see what it really is that God wills that I shall do; the crucial thing is to find a truth which is truth for me, to find the idea for which I am willing to live and die."

ME

Well...Kierkegaard misses the point a bit, don't you think? The question is: what matters to *you*? Answer that and you'll find your purpose. How's that for cereal box wisdom? And when was the last time you washed your sheets? They're—

(My sister carefully places the book on the floor, then kicks it, sending it skidding across the room and under the unused bed across from hers. According to Suzette, not one of the jumpers wanted to be her roommate.)

LORI

What matters to *me*?

ME

Not laundry.

LORI

Nothing and everything.

(I kneel down next to her.)

ME

Lori, you're depressed. You can't make a rational decision while you're sad. Look, we'll have to make sure we're not tailed, but if I go with you, would you make an appointment with a—

> (She turns her face so that it is inches from mine and speaks to me as if I were a child that doesn't understand.)

LORI

Sadness is the opposite of happiness. Depression is the absence of hope. They're not the same thing, Lisa.

> (I sit on her bed, exasperated, but jump up when I remember her dirty sheets, almost knocking over a stack of notebooks and a bowl of moldy Ramen noodles.)

ME

Right. So, what *do* you hope for?

> (I page through one of Lori's notebook journals, slowly at first, then picking up speed.)

It's on every... You wrote the same thing on the center of every page? Wait, I know this. It's John Donne, right? From...

> (I snap my fingers rapidly. It's on the tip of my tongue.)

LORI

From *Biathanatos*, his defense of suicide.

ME

Right.

> (I read from the notebook.)

"...methinks I have the keys of my own prison in mine own hand, and no remedy presents itself so soon to my heart as mine own sword."

(I turn the page and, for reasons unknown, I read the passage in an English accent, gesturing dramatically.)

"…methinks I have the keys of my own prison in mine own hand, and no remedy presents itself so soon to my heart as mine own sword."

(No reaction. This time I use a French accent.)

"…methinks I have the keys of my own prison…"

(Lori stares blankly at me.)

Not amused?

(I slam the notebook shut.)

Well, neither am I.

LORI

What do *I* hope for, you asked.

(The scorn in her voice is palpable.)

I don't even know what hope is. Can you even hear me? Are you too blind to listen?

(Neither of say anything for a long beat.)

ME

How 'bout that shower? You still have that pink loofah Mom sent you?

(Lori whips a holy card at me.)

LIGHTS FADE.

+

I wore a different set of blinders with Jerome. The issue of Jerome's illicit affair turned legitimate (albeit brief) romance with my twin sister wasn't broached, not at first. The makeup sex was too good, I was too lonely, and the school year was coming to an end. (Jerome had yet to say if his parents would be renting him another sweltering shack for the summer, though it was almost certain they would; Jerome's presence, it seemed, made them uncomfortable.) Sure, I desired closure on the whole mess, but body warmth trumped relationship status discussions every time. I never understood those girls who felt it necessary, at least every couple of months, to start a state of the relationship discussion, which almost always turned out poorly. Boys were never prepared, despite the frequent appearances of these generally one-sided conversations. I've seen a few of them occur in public. "Do you love me?" "Do you *really* love me?" "Then why were you talking to Hallie in chem lab?" "Do you think my thighs are fat?" (Any questions involving weight should send all boys running for the hills, but boobs speak louder than words, and the boys stuck around until the discussions turned into nagging and off they would go in search of a new skirt.) "Would you stay in New Orleans for the summer with me?" "If you're still alive next spring break, would you take me to Paris?" "Would you take me home to meet your family?" "Would you die for me?" That last question was a popular one in intimacy analyses at the Martyr School. It was a classic in that it was unanswerable; everyone at the school (except me) was there to die—and not necessarily for their high school sweetheart. The brightest boys just answered, "Yes, honey" and dove in for a deep kiss, hopefully smothering further discussion and dissection. Me, I've never had one of those kinds of conversations; either it was on or it wasn't; either I knew or I didn't. Heartbreak was part of life, something which most of us will have to deal with at one time or another. (For those at the Martyr School, if they did, so what: the heartache would be over shortly; if they didn't, well, there was going to be a lot of life's little treasures they were going to miss out on. Besides, a touch of heartache could be a good motivator— for whatever.) I didn't turn to drugs or booze or nooses; I masturbated. But despite my cavalier (and sincere) attitude about not rehashing the past, I was increasingly aware that the issue of Jerome's infidelity needed to be addressed soon—but in a way that didn't include Lori's participation. (I wanted to entice my sister home, not potentially drive her further away.)

Maybe allowing myself to be caught up in the distractions that came with being a teenager (in a cult) made me unable, for a long while, to discern whether this story, our story, was a tragedy or a romantic comedy. (There were elements of both, I thought.) Sometimes it was hard to know if the nervous laughter elicited by *Eternal Sunshine of the Spotless Mind* was meant to be nothing more than that or was the director softening you up for a gut-wrenching dénouement. Did the bloodletting of *True Romance* take away from Clarence and Alabama's love affair? Much of what occurred at the Martyr School was so harrowing, the only way for me to survive (long enough to die, the faculty believed) was to accept what was grievous and calamitous as the new normal, and I eventually came to the conclusion that this was one of those dark romantic comedies (think *Wild at Heart* maybe or *Seeking a Friend for the End of the World*). I knew that no matter what type it was, most rom-coms followed the same pattern (even if some, like *Heathers*, perverted the steps), so I knew this was usually the part of a romantic comedy called the Final Clinch, where our lovers, after weathering the Initial Dislike, the First Fight, and the Sleepless Nights; after dancing through the Pop Song Montage and surviving the Contrived Mix-Up and the Angry Breakup; and now hot on the heels of the Individual Realizations and the Big Speech, *finally* wipe the film from their eyes, shed their inhibitions and preconceived judgments, and grasp, eyes now wet, the person they'd been going round and round with or the one who'd been standing in front of them the whole time. (And Lori thought I hadn't been paying attention to her once-cherished romantic comedies!) Usually my memorable relationship moments have been in between the clichés of the genre, and yet here I was having skipped from lily pad to lily pad following along the tried and true formula (albeit in the most fucked up setting possible). So, the Final Clinch was around the corner, right? Not this time; nothing in this story followed a normal path. There was to be no great blowout between Jerome and me that led to a soul baring moment. There would be no final coming together on a beach as the sun was going down or on a Manhattan rooftop in the light of a full moon as Big Apple werewolves howled Gershwin behind it all. This Meet-Cute (if you could call it that) wouldn't end in marriage like in a Shakespearian comedy. It wouldn't end with one partner withering away in a hospital bed as the audience shuffled out in tears and properly disposed of their popcorn buckets. It wouldn't end like an anti-romantic comedy (as in *Before Sunrise*) where the characters part, their love forever ingrained in their souls but, they believe, never again to be held in their arms. There would be no *real* reunion, no correction of the classic romantic comedy mechanism of the missed connection (see *Before Sunset*), and thus no growing old together in a tangle of compromises (see *Before Midnight*)—though of course, at the Martyr School, growing old wasn't part of the curriculum. Being teenagers, we tripped, but not over tropes, on our way to tragedy. I feared that our story, Lori's and mine, Jerome's too, would end in a chaotic storm, redder for some. Students were here for one reason and one reason only, right? We studied all subjects but concentrated on one. This wasn't the Jedi Temple. This was the Martyr School. We were here to die for Jesus, or so we were taught.

+

From the journals of Lori Duke:

Quotes I Like

[It is a profound truth that] dying voluntarily is a choice intrinsic to human existence. It is our ultimate, fatal freedom. That is not how the right-thinking person today sees voluntary death: he believes that no one in his right mind kills himself, that suicide is a mental health problem. Behind that belief lies a transparent evasion…of personal responsibility fatal to freedom.

Dr. Thomas S. Szasz

While rom-coms…continued to flounder, cinematic romance…thrived,…[managing to] still capture the deeply relatable idyllic honeymoon stages of early love; however, they do so in not only a more realistic way, but also in order to eventually push towards [an] even greater truth…. These romances—with their hiccups and outright fallouts—understand that the greatest challenge around love is succeeding in keeping it alive.

Alexander Huls

+

The question remained: when would it be time to confront Jerome about his cheating on me with my sister? The asking flirted with my tongue and lips that Saturday afternoon. Of course there was a larger underlying question: was it even worth the effort? I thought that after all my time at the Martyr School, I would be used to letting things go, but maybe that would be my final lesson. So after too much thought and watching too many of the wrong kind of movies (*Unfaithful* with Diane Lane, Hitchcock's *Dial M for Murder*, Julia and Natalie in *Closer*, even a jaunty one detailing an emotional affair, *You've Got Mail*), I summoned—*asked*—Jerome to my room. He entered, shaking a brand new box of condoms he'd bought in the French Quarter. (I always inspected every rubber bought in the Quarter for pinpricks; there was a constant rumor floating around that local youths poked tiny holes with pins through the condom boxes.) He landed next to me on the bed and began undoing his belt. I stayed his hand.

"On the rag, babe?" he asked, ever so sensitive, as I moved to a chair.

I shook my head, resisting an urge to punch him between the eyes. "No, Jerome," I answered. "We need to talk about Lori."

He sat up, a look of concern knitting his eyebrows. "What happened to Lori?"

"We need to talk about Lori—and you."

Jerome pursed his lips and stared down his long legs. He swept the condom box to the floor, but it was less a sign of an oncoming tantrum than a macho expression of an exasperated capitulation, which I silently applauded: I wanted to get the box of Trojans off my bed and out of the way of the upcoming discussion/blowout; Jerome's mind should be on the subject at hand and not on any other part of his body (or mine).

"I'll kick things off," I said, "by saying I'm not in New Orleans to commit suicide. *Ta-da!* I'm here to make sure Lori doesn't. I'm here to convince her to leave the Martyr School and return to Philadelphia."

Jerome's mouth hung open. Someone could have used it as an ashtray. "But...twins...the school..."

I waved my hand. "Yes, the school was over the moon when they received my application so soon after Lori's. Twins!

What a coup! And if their paths ended at the exact same time—a suicide pact—why, that could be the big spread in the yearbook!"

Jerome looked confused and a little hurt.

"What the school doesn't know," I explained, "won't hurt them and could fill the Superdome."

Jerome leaned back on his elbows.

"You do what you want with that information," I said. "If you're on a path, well, that's your choice, pal, dumb as it may be. I'm not here to stop you. Just Lori."

I turned my chair around and leaned my arms on the back like a detective in a movie.

"But I didn't ask you here to talk about what I'm going to do. No, we're here to discuss what you *did*—what you did with Lori." I rested my chin in the palm of my hand, cupping one side of my face, hoping it would at least partially hide a flush of premature righteous anger. "When did it start?"

"The sex stuff?"

"Sure."

Jerome scratched the fuzzy growth on his chin. He stared at the ceiling. He played with the bottom of his untucked shirt. "Right before you and I did it the first time," he answered, not looking at me.

The woman is wild, a she-cat tamed by the purr of a Jag-u-ar.

Jerome couldn't even manage a blush.

I held onto the chair for fear of falling to the floor and managed to whisper, "Maneater," before Jerome started talking again.

"Lori was a little jealous about me and you."

Somehow he managed to look wounded. Amazing.

"Well, a lot jealous. But you knew that—*Wonder Twin powers activate!*' and all. I didn't know why, not really. I should have though. I mean, it's not every day that someone throws their shoes at you."

Was that pride I heard lurking between his syllables? He coughed as if he were suppressing a small laugh.

"Remember when she—"

Jerome cut his reminiscence short. I had water in my eyes and murder on my mind, and I think he caught a whiff of the latter, as he tried to ignore the former.

"After the Kateri Dance, after you and I started dating, I didn't speak much to Lori. Hardly at all that first week. So, one

night, midnight or so, me and Evan snuck off to the swamp to
party with a couple of upperclassmen, which was a big deal, 'cause
we were only sophomores then. I was pretty loaded when the Scum
raided our little party. Somehow I made it out of the swamp, but I
was having a hard time running, and I could hear the guards getting
closer. I was ready to give up when I turned a corner and two arms
grabbed me out of the dark and a hand covered my mouth. It was
Lori. I didn't even know I was close to the girls' dorms. She'd come
out through the south emergency door. You know, the one where
when you hit the exit bar, it doesn't trigger an alarm. Said she'd
been awake and wanted to see what all the fuss was about."

The details disturbed me: I remembered Jerome and Evan,
between classes, sharing their story about how they evaded the
Scum. (I believed the bonding experience led them to becoming
roomies.) In fact, I heard the tale often enough on drunken nights
in the East Lot or in the Quarter, that I used to amuse myself by
trying to guess which version they'd tell—the story grew legs over
time—but not a single version involved Lori.

"Lori said there were always empty rooms there, just like in
the boys' dorms 'cause—well, just 'cause. As she smuggled me to
one, I could hear the Scum's Florsheims pounding the stairs.
Outside, one of the upperclassmen yelled, as the Scum took him
down. Lori worked fast. She closed the door but didn't lock it. She
told me to turn on a desk lamp and crouch behind a hamper.
Because no one bunked there, the mattresses were stripped, but
Lori found a blanket in a closet and jumped into one of the beds,
covering herself up. If the Scum did a room check, this one would
look at least partially occupied. But they never did, and after a
while, Lori motioned for me to come over and sit on the bed. I
kept whispering, 'I'm sorry' over and over."

I pinched my leg—hard.

"Lori told me to stop apologizing. She talked about how
Mr. Horner told her class that in every fire, there was a burn. You
just needed to change your perspective—were you watching it,
setting it, or, with your angels by your side, in it? Lori said that
this—our being holed up, hiding from the SKM—was an
opportunity to cause some destruction." He blew some air out of
his mouth. "Self-destruction. She was a virgin—at least that's what
she said and what everyone believed—so she thought if she made it
with her sister's new boyfriend *before* her sister did, then she would

not just be hurting herself (she claimed she had no *real* feelings for me—at the time anyway), but she would also be secretly hurting you, which in turn would hurt her even more because she loved you and looked up to you so much. Lori said she was mad you came with her to the Martyr School. She didn't know why you came—but I don't think anyone did. I didn't until just now. You never seemed like you wanted to be a martyr and no one forced you here or dropped you off. Lori suspected it was a social experiment of some kind. I thought she was a little...off, but she wouldn't let it go. She thought you were mocking the school and her decision to apply and enroll. Then you left the dance with me after I'd come with her. So she was pretty pissed. And, like I said, jealous."

Jerome didn't look happy to be the prize—and I believed him.

Maybe it was just the oddly elevated mood in the dorms, which fairly hummed: quick, thundering footsteps above; doors slamming all around. Music from two rooms met and competed in the hallway.

And I find it kind of funny, I find it kind of sad
The dreams in which I'm dying are the best I've ever had...

It was Donnie Darko versus Lloyd Dobbler from *Say Anything*.

Without a noise, without my pride
I reach out from the inside...

I coughed and made sure not a drop fell from my eyes. God, I thought, if this were only a romantic comedy after all! (A romantic comedy about a school for suicide!) Screw all the introspection, fuck the Order of Martyrs' Final Embrace—where was the seemingly elusive but (according to the movies) usually inevitable Final Clinch? Isn't this the appropriate scene?

"And now?" I asked.

Jerome raised his eyebrows. "I'm with you, babe. As far as Lori still being jealous, I don't really know. Not for sure. But I ran into her on the common a couple of days ago, and she was nice as pie, asked me how it was going with you. And—this was odd—she asked me if I'd miss her."

Thinking of where we were, I knitted my brow. "Why was that odd?"

Jerome sat up and absently rubbed his crotch. (Do all boys do that?) "Well, we're all supposed to be checking out at the same time, right before graduation next year. How would anyone in our class miss anyone else?"

The boy had a point. The hairs on my arms were standing up. "Unless…unless she was talking about going home!"

You can make yourself believe anything if you want it bad enough.

Jerome raised his hands. "Whoa, she didn't say anything about…well, she did say she was tired of the weather in New Orleans. She said Philadelphia *really* had all four seasons, sometimes in extreme: blizzards, scorching summers, the whole bit. She said it was the best way to experience—"

"April showers bring May flowers," I said, giddy and lightheaded. "And what do May flowers bring?"

Jerome shrugged his shoulders.

"Pilgrims!"

Now—here it was, ladies and gentlemen. Hold onto your popcorn and get your tissues ready. The Final Clinch. All apologies made (sort of). All forgiven (kind of). Forge ahead.

I jumped from the chair, knocking it over, and tackled Jerome. We wrestled, then sat up and held each other tight. I was facing the windows, staring over Jerome's shoulder at the bright green leaves and twisted branches of the southern live oaks that populated the campus, the "live" part of its name so at odds with all the talk here of becoming dead. I could see a bald cypress and a southern magnolia too. This was a beautiful place, the Martyr School, and I started thinking that maybe I was lucky to have had my time here. No, that was too much, but still… I didn't know if I could (or if I had the strength) to rescue Jerome too, but the thought was going through my head now. Trying to convince Lori (or extract her if necessary) was going to be difficult enough, but I didn't realize until just then that I had *another* person to rescue, and it wasn't Jerome: it was me. I didn't want to die, but I didn't want to leave this life either. As terrifying as it could be, the Martyr School had become my world.

Everything's ephemeral and I was beginning to realize there was a strong possibility I cared not a whit.

Lori's body fell past my eyes so quickly, it didn't register for another few seconds or so. But some part of my brain recognized the dress—the pretty red one Lori had worn to the Kateri Tekakwitha Dance. My brain registered the long brown hair on one side of her head (that seemed to be falling upward as she fell down) and the thin face, which later I would think looked more like mine than it ever had before. (Did I make all of that up—what could have I really seen in that blip of time—or was the pull of the twin indissoluble?) It took a few heartbeats before the images and their context collided. Just before I heard the first cheer (and was that a boo that followed?) and the first scream (yes, underclassmen could still be counted on for reacting to the school's spectacles for the horror shows they were), my brain slapped itself into action and my body followed. Jerome, almost comically, was left holding air briefly before joining me at the windows, but I left him there to spring down the stairs. The Jumpers' Floor was five stories up, but even if Lori could have survived the fall, the remainder of the fence and the red-rusted iron row of spikes, of spears…

As I ran down the steps, Otis Redding's voice echoed a lie in my head.

Hush, darling, don't you cry
I'm coming home to dry your weeping eyes

The Christy Lesson (in the argot of the jumpers, who saw his impalement as less pure by dint of poor planning) had been lost on my sister (or maybe it was deliberate, but I couldn't believe she would choose such pain and violence—although neither the jumpers nor I took into consideration that Christy could have landed where he landed on purpose, for Christy's second story window jump, done in a fit of romantic anger, had taken his manhood as well as his life). As I pushed my way through the growing crowd (some clapping, others tsk-tsking, for my sister wasn't part of the accelerated program), I saw Lori above their heads, and that was when I knew the Christy Lesson had truly been ignored (or embraced). The reason my sister seemed to float above the crowd, I learned upon reaching her, was that she had fallen directly onto one of the metal fence spikes (the same one, I thought, that had lanced Christy's groin). She was impaled through her chest, face downward, her long brown hair now hanging straight down after its brief reach for the heavens. A dried rose was pinned to her dress. I knew instantly that it was the rose I'd dropped when I'd discovered Lori and Jerome in bed together. I didn't know what it meant. Was I to blame for her death? Had she really been in love with Jerome and not just using him to get back at me? Or was this just the end result of a trajectory begun with the Gerardo Incident?

Otis never let up.

Hush, darling, and don't you be blue

I'm coming home to see about you

Removing Lori's body from the spike took the deacons some time.

There was blood everywhere. Lori would have liked the mess, I thought, and she would have loved the drama.

+

I didn't stay and watch them carry Lori's body away in what I knew would be a silence unnatural even for a school such as ours. I knew I had to call my mom before someone in the administration building did, and so I hurried (without appearing to hurry) to our room in the girls' residence hall. But before I could pick up the phone, I stood in front of the bathroom mirror and slapped my face until little red dots appeared on my cheeks. The wails I expected came later—my mom just thanked me for calling, her voice descending into a quavering whisper before she abruptly hung up, a damning indictment of my failure to save Lori from the school, from herself. I returned to the mirror but before my raised hand could connect with my cheek, I heard the squawk of a walkie-talkie echo from the hallway. I lowered my hand. I didn't need more blood. I needed a plan.

The school had been *thrilled* to ensnare twins. I'd half expected Lori and I to be the first sophomores featured on the cover of the yearbook, some freak show version of Jacob and Esau—and I did not use the reference lightly. When we'd first arrived, we were paraded past the headmaster and the monsignor, the academic dean and the mother superior, and there were a lot of photographs. When the traveling bishop arrived for the Lottery of Future Saints during our first year at the school, we were brought to meet him. He was old and nearly blind and, after he blessed Lori's forehead with oil, the school superiors were so preoccupied with promoting the Duke twins to the bishops' entourage, they didn't notice when Lori remained kneeling, wiped her forehead with her sleeve, and received a second blessing, my blessing, just by saying, "Bishop, I am here too." Was it simply a matter of wanting to feel superior? I didn't know and didn't care. I was willing to play Esau to her Jacob. What did it matter? I had no idea at first *why* Lori and I seemed to be so important to the Order, but it was clear from day one that we were. I came to believe it was just that the school wanted parents to send their entire brood; they wanted to able to say: look at what this family is willing to sacrifice—twins!

I didn't realize I'd been pacing, but when I stopped I heard the shuffling of heavy boots in the hall—the changing of the guards. My guards.

There was no way they were going to let me come out of this breathing. Maybe they wouldn't act immediately, but they *would* act. With only a week left before commencement, what was one more body? Lori may have ended up a Fallen Failure, but she still committed suicide and wasn't that what the cult wanted anyway? They needed me to complete the pair, one way or another, as if we'd been part of some kind of sick public relations campaign. At first I believed it was essential to the Order for me to graduate next year (voluntarily or otherwise) to keep up the façade, so future brochures could crow about the twins and their glorious deaths— felons of themselves to Christ, sweeping Lori's inconvenient early exit under the rug. But I started to think they wouldn't risk waiting until *my* commencement a year from now. Might be easier to stick me on ice (not so metaphorically) until next year; having "self-immolated" (what other method could they choose?), my body would only be recognizable by my teeth, so no need to worry about anyone looking too closely—or they could have my exit be early and public. (An execution by any other name…) Who would know the brochure was a lie besides the administration? All the students in my class would be dead by the time the next printing came out, touting the sacrifice of the twins. The rest of the student body would be dazzled by doublespeak.

I'd always thought that if Lori succeeded in ending her life, I wouldn't cry. It seemed like what she'd wanted since the eighth grade—and as if suicidal ideation and cries for help weren't enough, she'd managed to get a scholarship to a school where, with only one notable exception in recent history (the two gun valedictorian), 0% of graduates were present at commencement, felled by their own hand (after years of instruction) or taken down by the SKM; it was much more than a danse macabre; it was like Jonestown with

202 · *Get Out, You Ghosts: Stories from the Workshops Volume II*

textbooks and labs, and it was all willfully ignored by law enforcement and local government.

I'd learned from writing a research paper that New Orleans had one of the highest murder rates of any city in the country, 41.3 per 100,000, and Louisiana had a suicide rate of 15.26 per 100,000—*without* counting teenage martyrs. Since successful escapes were rare, the Martyr School had a nearly perfect record: of all the children enrolled, almost every one took their final breath on the consecrated campus.

The next day I began packing up Lori's room on the Jumpers' Floor. As she had no roommate, her mess spread from wall to wall, worse than I remembered it. (When we'd shared a dorm room, the other girls used to call us the Odd Couple but enjoying my annoyance at Lori's mess made them blind to the frequently cluttered state of my desk. Lori, however, made mess an art. I always told Jerome she could teach a class on being messy, and one time he responded, "You're tellin' me; you should see my room," yet another little remark I'd let slip by.) Despite Lori's propensity for chaos and dirt, and despite even her duplicity, I thought it was too bad that we hadn't been roommates at the end, for I was certain that in the days following her death, the Scum would make sure I didn't begin dismantling my own room, just my sister's.

All Lori had was a small suitcase and a dirty gym bag that smelled like a place where many pairs of sweat socks had gone to spawn. (There was also her colorful, mostly pink backpack, which didn't, for whatever reason, make the Scum's report when they did a quick inventory of her room; they never even mentioned it; it was only the most obnoxious-looking thing in her dorm, but in that mess, I suppose it was hidden in plain sight …) I knew my mom would want everything that had been my sister's, and I knelt on the dusty floor to collect the holy cards and tried to make some sense of her journals, since none of the entries were dated. This process reinforced the idea that, at least while I breathed, the things in *my* room were part of *me*: to leave behind or to hold close to myself; they were worth fighting for—or maybe I was. While my mom wanted the pieces of Lori collected, she would probably like to have at least one daughter not returning home in a wooden box. But one thing at a time, I told myself, as I placed Lori's dirty clothes in the suitcase next to her clean ones. I left the used condoms in the Ziploc bags where I'd found them. Let someone else try to figure that mess out.

Paging through Lori's journals and books made me jumpy; each passage I heard read in her voice. There were a few seconds when I wanted to make a run for it, right then and there, until I stumbled across an underlined passage in a book by Yuval Noah Harari, odd for someone like my twin who seemingly swallowed the fiction of the Order whole: "...only *Homo sapiens* can speak about things that don't really exist, and believe six impossible things before breakfast. You could never convince a monkey to give you a banana by promising him limitless bananas after death in monkey heaven."

Well, I was neither a follower nor a monkey, but I was in a cage nonetheless, a cage, I decided, that could no longer hold me. I put myself in here; I can take myself out, right? I didn't know the answer; I just knew I was going to try.

The author went on to state that "fiction can be dangerously misleading or distracting." This was not underlined, so I did it for her.

Suzette Downey appeared in Lori's doorway, and she looked afraid. She gestured with her chin towards what I imagined was the world outside our walls and mouthed a question that seemed like a statement of fact, her face easy to read, her complexion like an agitated mood ring: *"This whole time?"* I nodded. So even Suzette knew of my tricky and delicate situation. How she knew that I wasn't here to kill myself, I didn't know, but ever the campus busybody, she could have talked with Jerome, even though I figured he'd be hiding in a hole somewhere. However she came by this knowledge, Suzette surely knew if the Order found out my real reason for being here.... I raised a finger to my lips. Suzette crossed her heart and took off. *Cross my heart and hope to die, stick a needle in my eye.* Suzette could be a good egg. (She must have known that my chances of survival were slim to none.) I didn't know why Suzette was enrolled here; she'd found her calling in gossiping, yes, but her real skill was her ability to gather information, and the Martyr School's dormitories and classrooms couldn't compare to the boardrooms and bedchambers on the outside.

I tried to focus on Lori's room. Schopenhauer's *The World as Will and Representation* and Joseph Campbell's *The Power of Myth*, as well as books by Kierkegaard and Sartre, sat on shelves next to some well-worn Nancy Drew hardback mysteries: *The Secret of the Old Clock*, *The Hidden Staircase*, *The Clue of the Broken Locket*, and more. Some of Lori's books had holy cards as bookmarks. I opened a couple at random and read the underlined matter. It was as if I'd been dropped into a discussion Lori had been having with herself. I would later find many other disparate quotes scratched into her journals.

+

From the journals of Lori Duke:

Quotes I Like

Moral freedom…is to be obtained only by a denial of the will to live.

T. Bailey Saunders

For a movie to be a romantic comedy…there has to be a scene where, after the two have realized they've fallen for each other, something happens that forces them apart.

Amanda Dobbins & Shea Serrano

Every religion is true one way or another…when understood metaphorically. But when it gets stuck to its own metaphors, interpreting them as facts, then you are in trouble.

Joseph Campbell

+

Lori hadn't left a note behind to explain her decision to destroy herself, but the one notebook that was open had a quote which I later discovered was from a Nancy Drew book: "Romance and detective work won't mix tonight!" Such was her suicide note or, rather, her epitaph.

Was Lori's suicidal predilection exacerbated by the Order? Most certainly. Had she been a victim of thought reform, of brainwashing? Absolutely. But I couldn't help but feel as if I'd pushed her by snatching Jerome back. So did I cry for Lori? Oh, yes, but for more than my sister. I sobbed for my mom. Maybe I even squeezed out a tear or two for Jerome (or at least my idea of Jerome), the unlikely boy who'd broken two hearts, although whatever I'd felt for him dropped away when Lori appeared to drop from the sky. And I shed uncountable tears for my role in Lori's demise and my failure to carry out the mission to bring my twin back home. Without blaming either my sister or my mom, I wept too for the passing of my teenage years in a destructive cult. Did I cry for those students about to expire before commencement, completing their capstone projects—and for those who fell before them? Of course, but what tears then remained were spent in worry about how to escape. Before all this, Jerome's roommate Evan had been the only one from our class to leave on two feet. But he'd transferred to the Vampyre School, as part of (we'd discovered) some long-established courtesy that stemmed from a century-old truce between the once-adversarial institutions. The one escape attempt of note came during our sophomore year, and since we never saw the boy again, we thought he'd made it, but during a chapel service two days later, we were told to bow our heads and say a prayer for the boy who was found drowned in the bayou. Too intimidated, there were few other attempts, and all were thwarted. What were my chances, then, I wondered?

A plan...a plan...

I never saw Jerome again. He'd never offered condolences in person or in writing. He was just another character in our story; his was an important role that in all honesty could have been played by anyone. I had a hard time remembering what it was that I'd found so special in him. Just past midnight the day after Lori passed away, a few students and I watched through a western-facing window as the Scum rushed towards the swamps with flashlights and dogs. The barking was what woke us up. But the dogs appeared to want to go in the opposite direction. (We'd heard stories of German shepherds being swallowed whole or at least bitten in half by rapacious and bored alligators; apparently, the dogs had heard the tales as well.) In the morning a rumor floated around that Jerome had been rescued by a team from the Lycanthrope School at his behest (the Martyr School and the Lycanthrope School were not on speaking terms), a poor choice as Jerome did not seem to have the faculties to change—just the excess body hair. If it was true that meant two students in our class had left sans body bag.

The next day, I was back in Lori's room, not so much packing as scheming and lazily following Lori's thoughts from book to book and journal to journal. A Sanguine Knight of the Martyrs knocked on the partially open door, unsnapping his holster. His partner lurked in the hallway.

"Your parents claiming the body?" He took a step into my space.

I nodded and didn't back up. The name on his uniform identified him as Gideon, though I didn't know if that was his first name or last. He took another step towards me. Vertically challenged, his mouth was so close to my nose, I could smell the garlic that had accompanied his lunch.

"They burying it here or flying it back east?"

It.

"The latter, and it's *parent*," I said. "Singular." The correction had no effect on his aspect. Gideon continued to scan Lori's room, which generally looked no different than it had yesterday. He had a cold, and when he coughed (not bothering to cover his mouth), it sounded like a bunch of coffins coming loose from the earth.

I was sure my mom was already making the appropriate phone calls and arrangements, but even if I knew Lori was destined for God's Allotment, I would have lied and nodded anyway.

"Then if you intend to send…" He gestured towards Lori's suitcase and bag and the piles of stuff I'd made around it. "…her belongings with the body, everything needs to be inspected first." He seemed to choke on a stifled cough. "The bags can't leave this room until they're logged, tagged, and secured by us. Any boxes need to be sealed with security tape after they've been gone through." He coughed into his arm, leaving a slimy wet mark on his sleeve. I finally backed up.

What if instead of offing myself or being murdered during an escape attempt, I caught whatever this Scum had and withered away in the infirmary? I'd be irony incarnate.

Cough. Rattle. Cough. "Understand, girl?"

I responded with the slightest movement of my head, and when he left I gave his back the finger, a gesture his partner caught.

Trying hard not to look thrilled, the second guard—younger and eager for action—burst into the room, brandishing his weapon. Though he couldn't look me in the eye, he nevertheless eye-raped me, giving particular attention to my left boob. He might as well have had "misogynist" and "virgin" carved into his rosaceous forehead.

" 'Rule 2.1: all students will defer to the Sanguine Knights and treat them with respect. Failure to do so—' "

Gideon called him back. "Let it go. Remember: it's catch and release, until otherwise advised—and this one is already caught."

The second guard holstered his weapon with reluctance. "I'm going to write you up!" he said to me, his face ablaze. It was quite a performance.

"Stop the nonsense, kid. Go make sure there's enough lime in the shed."

Lime?

"But—"

"Just do it already." *Cough, cough, coffin.* "Missy here ain't goin' nowhere—yet," Gideon said, as he left the room and lit a cigarette. He was obviously the senior Knight here, probably bucking for a promotion; his uniform only had two stripes (and the crimson and bone insignia on the opposite arm). Officers had an exploding star patch.

I picked up a Nancy Drew book and threw it at the back of the guards' closely shaved heads, but my throw went wild, and the book sailed out of an open window. (Neither Knight noticed as they exited.) Another couple of inches to the left, it would have crashed through the adjoining one, which was closed. The window on the right had remained open since…the event. Lori hadn't leapt from the roof, although the student body seemed to believe she had, probably because most jumpers of both genders took off from their respective roofs, the natural go-to launching pads. No, Lori went out the window, this very window, which faced north. Right here was where Lori had stood for her final seconds before flipping that switch and surrendering to gravity. Standing in the same place and imagining, without meaning to, her mindset, led to a wave of nausea, and all in a rush, it was as if I was looking through a black shroud. My extremities went numb, and for a heartbeat I thought:

I'm going to faint—until I reached over and shut the window. The feeling passed.

The Scum verified, either directly or through inference, everything I believed to be true: I wasn't going to be allowed to go home for Lori's funeral (if our mother was coming to New Orleans to claim Lori's shattered body—she wasn't—they would have had to let me go), and the reason they posted at least one guard outside my door was that they didn't want me to quietly start packing my own belongings. (We were taught that flight was a natural reaction when someone you were close to expired before you did.) Lori's room was kept locked, and they had a Scum or two at her door whenever I was let in. The Knights had even deputized a couple of the more zealous Eds to set a watch on the stairs between floors. Disassembling my room like I'd been sort of doing with Lori's was out of the question. I wouldn't have been surprised if my keepers kept count of my tampons. They even searched my makeup bag (in case I had a set of lock picks, I suppose.)

I sat on the floor in Lori's room next to a box I was starting to fill with her books. There was a roll of tamper resistant tape on the windowsill, ready for when the box or any subsequent boxes were filled. (The Scum also had zip ties for her luggage.) Sneaking my stuff up to her dorm room or vice versa was a no go; they searched me every time I left either room. I used to think the joke was on them: I could just walk away (assuming I could get away)— my books, clothes, tchotchkes, beads: just stuff; I had no attachments to anything or anyone at the Martyr School except for my sister (and, at times, Jerome, but his importance was overshadowed by Lori's death, and he rarely came into my head anymore). I could walk away from *stuff*, I believed. But it was *my* stuff, and as I'd been gathering evidence of Lori's existence into a suitcase, a gym bag, and the box I'd found out behind the kitchen, I'd begun to think: fuck the Order. Why would I (try to) leave without *my* stuff? But one thing at a time, I reminded myself.

One thing indeed.

A plan…something…

I paged through a couple of Lori's journals, looking for what, I didn't know. I picked up a Sartre volume, opened to one of Lori's holy card bookmarks, and read the highlighted line: "I have no use for noble souls; what I need is an accomplice."

An accomplice.

Was that what my sister saw in Jerome, an accomplice? It seemed unlikely, and as much as I went along to get along, Lori probably knew that she couldn't count on me, not for assistance or to be part of a sisterly suicide pact.

...what I need is an accomplice.

I felt guilty about throwing the Sartre book out of the window (which I'd opened earlier; it was stuffy up there), but I did it anyway—it was getting to be a habit. As long as it didn't rain, the book only had to survive the humidity and the fog. Students rarely cut through by squeezing between the red-rusted spikes of the fence. The space between the spear-like posts was just wide enough to get through, but since the fence was frequently moist, the color perhaps reminding students of Christy's blood-soaked skewering (and now Lori's), most didn't even try. Besides, there was only an emergency door on the northern side of the girls' residence hall, and the trees and thick brush, combined with this pernicious remainder of a fence, created a dead-end at the northeastern corner. The book would be down there waiting for me.

It would be down there waiting for me...or for someone.

As I was about to take a break, unsure why I was even packing up my sister's books, I remembered her kicking a Kierkegaard paperback under the unused bed, where I found several other books, adorned with dust bunnies, where they may very well have stayed had I not bent down. (Of course, the next occupants could be neat freaks...) I rescued a couple of textbooks plus Jean Améry's *On Suicide: A Discourse on Voluntary Death*, Dante's *Inferno*, Milton's *Paradise Lost*, a Rimbaud collection, and yet another Nancy Drew mystery.

I stared at the cover of *The Sign of the Twisted Candles*: Nancy Drew's wary attention was drawn to an old man with a long white beard. But in the forefront was a tall, lit candle, perhaps used by Nancy to get where she was. Although the candle was straight, the wax had been twisted, so that it looked as if a diagonal staircase was going round the candle. For whatever reason, it reminded me of one of Miss Marguerite's sex toys (minus the flame—probably; all that was missing was the image of a saint or a voodoo symbol, a vevè, to make the Big Easy experience complete). I read the synopsis at the beginning of the book and stared at the start of the last line: "With only the sign of the twisted candles to guide her..."

That was it.

I had a plan…and a twisted candle of sorts.

The first thing I did was to empty Lori's backpack and smuggle it (beneath my own knapsack) downstairs to my room, where I hid it in the bottom of my hamper, under some towels and my I ♥ Geeks t-shirt. If the Scum looked in my hamper but didn't go through it, the colors of Lori's bag blended right in (except I never wore pink).

The next day after morning chapel and between keening phone calls from my mother and attempting to avoid my classmates, their outstretched hands and murmurs of "Good transition," even though they knew Lori was one of the Fallen Failures, I kept the appointment I'd made the day before, shortly after quitting my sister's dorm room, with the Director of Student Life. (Without an accomplice, I needed to cover all bases.) I couldn't figure out if the director's title was meant to be ironic, a wink and a nod from an Order obsessed with suicide and whose members, it seemed, got off on watching teenagers die, the more twisted the method, the better—or if the job title was devoid of irony altogether, a much more frightening prospect: we were in the hands of a group of fanatics who'd become oblivious to the implications of their calling; forms were filled out, term papers graded, bodies piled up—just another fun-filled and fulfilling semester!

The Scum kept me on a short leash with Gideon in the lead and his partner as the caboose. They even accompanied me to the administration building for my appointment with Mrs. Bruno, the Director of Student Life, whose face had so many wrinkles, she looked like she was perpetually sucking on a lemon. Her demeanor matched her appearance: Mrs. Bruno dealt with me as if I was something distasteful; I imagined her burning the chair I would have sat upon once I left. But I didn't sit—I stood and placed my hands, my fists, on her desk (ooh, maybe she'd burn the desk!) and asked for and was given what the surprisingly soft-spoken woman said she'd never once allowed during her long tenure: bereavement leave. (It was hard to take my eyes off her neck folds and the watch that strained against a wrist as thick, it seemed, as both of mine combined and then some.) Mrs. Bruno signed the form and dropped the pen in the trash can.

I was hustled to the office of the Director of Campus Ministry and Security, Gideon again in the lead, his subordinate behind, where I imagined him drooling while he rubbed the butt of his gun. (It was to be their default accompaniment configuration.). I smiled on the way: I knew it wasn't Mrs. Bruno's decision to grant me bereavement leave, no matter how brief. This had been discussed at the highest levels—twins and all. It was meant to appease me, to keep me from running, I was sure. The news that not one but two Sanguine Knights would accompany me home was not unexpected. I only hoped it wasn't Gideon, a born bully, and his horny radish of a partner. I didn't think I would be able to handle those two for even another day. It was intimated that my mother would have to put up the Scum, which I knew would make her cross and maybe even more depressed, for we didn't have a guest room. The only available room would be Lori's. As much as putting them in there would hurt my mom, I knew she wouldn't want them camping out on the sofa and love seat, not with the steady stream of visitors—relatives, friends, neighbors—that had been coming since my sister's death. My mother blamed herself for letting Lori go to the Martyr School and having the Scum bunk in her lost daughter's room might break what spirit she had left. But if all went right (every detail), neither my mom nor I would have to be concerned with the Knights whatsoever when I returned home and would probably, hopefully, never have to again.

Lori's belongings aside, I would be allowed to take one bag of my own besides my backpack (after they were inspected once more and fastened with cable ties, I was informed). The bereavement leave was for three days, including travel time. Any finals I missed would be administered immediately upon my return, according to Mrs. Bruno.

I bowed my head as the Director of Ministry and Security, who oversaw the Scum, barked out what I already knew regarding my deportment. I had to play the part expected of me—the surviving twin wracked by disappointment and sorrow that was tempered by my faith and the belief that the adjective "surviving" was temporary.

There was a hiccup in my plan, I learned a little while later: my plane was to leave the next afternoon (a day sooner than I'd originally been told). As I was to travel with my sister's body, it didn't leave me much time (but I'd set the plan in motion already; now there was no room for error). I believe the Order would have had me on that plane—in my own box—but because I'd been part of a twin act, they were probably hoping for a more dramatic and fulfilling (i.e., self-terminating) finish, one better than any they could fake, to herald in their public relations materials, such as they were. I did wonder why they would show the hen the way out of the coop when there was a possibility that the hen wasn't even aware there was a door. They even told my mom that they'd send me home after I requested leave (never expecting me to have the balls to do so, I suppose). Mostly they told her what they did to keep her quiet, though they appeared to conclude that they didn't have to worry about her being litigious since they also seemed to believe they still had a hold on me. I assumed they'd been listening in on my phone conversations, during which I promised my mom I'd come home for the funeral if I could but stressing that I had to be back to finish my finals. My insolent behavior with the Scum notwithstanding, it must have seemed to the Order like I'd wanted to be here more than I wanted to be home, especially after I had a fight with my poor mom, which included a tearful defense of the school. Mom had no idea it was a performance. (The fight wasn't part of the plan, but my mother started talking about why she'd sent me there in the first place, and I had to shut her down.) The administration rolled the dice. Despite my school spirit, I'd made it clear I couldn't just leave my mom to handle everything by herself. I made sure to add some obvious reluctance to leave New Orleans; I needed to seem like a good little lamb, one who dutifully returns to the slaughterhouse after burying the remains of one of its own. If I laid it on a tad heavy, it was only because I was the slightest bit worried that the Order would see through my playacting and would snuff me out *after* Lori's plane took off, just to be perverse (if I actually was on the plane, which was most definitely not part of the plan). A minion from the Director of Campus Ministry and Security (who had bandages wrapped around a stump where his left hand had been) told me that the bill for the round trip would be sent to my mother. (I wondered why my mom didn't just pay for my ticket up front, but then I realized that the school most likely intended to bill her for my escorts' seats too.)

The next morning, after my sister's belongings were picked up, inspected (somewhat), and secured (still no one mentioned the absence of her backpack), I received the official word: Lori had flunked out of the Martyr School, and a letter to that effect would be sent to my mother, which I initially thought just added insult to injury, but in the wake of a wasted life, the letter seemed…appropriate, in that they were going to treat my mom the same way they treated us: with disrespect—we were malleable and disposable. (The hard truth was that whether we were beatified or ended up one of the Fallen Failures like Lori didn't really matter; the Order was only interested in the ending; the rest was window dressing.) They thumbed their collective (and apparently untouchable) noses at my mom just because they could, for there was no reason to further upset a mother who had lost a child, except perhaps that her imagined wails further enhanced whatever jollies the Order got from encouraging teenagers to kill themselves (after providing detailed instructions). But always eager to tout the benefits of their beliefs, the letter would imply (I was sure) that instead of squandering our teenage years and twisting ourselves up with teenage concerns, we were taught how to end them and in doing so, glorifying God. That part of the letter would assume my mother bought into their particular brand of bullshit. The letter that was delivered by hand to me was unnecessary and designed to be manipulative: you can do better than your sister if you just stay on the path. With lots of pushback from the Scum, I marched towards the academic dean's office in the admin building, actual tears this time soaking my cheeks. (Since Lori's death, when dealing with the powers-that-be, I usually just contorted my face, covered my eyes, and the tears were assumed.) My Scum guards, the diminutive engine and the satyric caboose, frowned all the way there, whispering into walkie-talkies. Gideon, struggling with a rattling cough, didn't like deviations from the schedule, and he and his flushed-faced partner were certainly less than pleased (and taken aback) when I ignored the dean's secretary and her administrative assistant (their mouths great big Os) and barged into the dean's office. Taking advantage of my escorts' momentary confusion, I moved to the side of the dean's desk (which appeared to spook her a bit) and asked if I could bring the letter home to my mother, if they hadn't already sent it. My notification said they were *going to* send a letter home; I assumed it would be going out the same day I received mine. (I knew that the mail hadn't been picked up yet— Nestor's cologne had a way of hanging around and my nose hadn't been assaulted when we entered the administration building—so even if it had left the academic dean's office, it would be "just" a matter of retrieving it from the mail bin in the front hall—but I knew Gideon would never let me near it.) The dean, a matchstick compared to Mrs. Bruno, was known to be stern and unyielding, isolating herself from the student body, which might explain why she had the letter handed over to me without much of a fight or feigned hysterics at my bursting in unannounced; her staff was more reluctant but dared not defy the matchstick woman. I had to hide a grin from my Scum guards, who were probably too busy scowling at their walkie-talkies to have noticed anyway.

This whole rigmarole ate into the morning, and the clock was ticking. The guards still didn't allow me to close my dorm room door all the way (but it was just enough); they wanted to make sure I didn't start taking my room apart at the last minute. Besides clothes and school books, I was only to take the essentials, which I did. I was just going home for two nights, right? The previous day the Scum had searched my travel bag for contraband. They also wanted to verify that I had not somehow compressed my entire wardrobe in there—and because men are often intimidated by women's sexuality (when not being intimidating themselves because they thought it was their right and us their prey), I'd included my Mary Magdalene glow-in-the-dark strap-on for shock value. The Scum didn't question its inclusion, though it did startle them; they seemed to not know what it was at first, but Gideon must have figured it out for he dropped it like a hot cake. They confiscated the little recorder I used for taping lectures; I had to give them something to write me up about, but nothing that would hinder my schedule. I was told to bring my travel bag, along with my book-laden backpack, to the only final I would take before I left, as I was to go directly to the airport after the exam.

Since I was allowed to close the bathroom door, I excused myself, running the shower as I sat on the toilet lid. I needed a few moments before I proceeded with my plan to outrun the maelstrom that Lori's exit had created. The Martyr School had been here years before us and would in all likelihood continue long after we were gone. Lori's act forced me to bow, but I'd never bend, no matter how strong the ill wind, no matter what.

I loved my sister. I really did. But living in a Lori-centric world was not an easy lot for me. Even the Scum guards outside my door were there because of what Lori did. As sanctimonious as I could be—above it all—I had to admit that I was the slightest bit irked by everything that had happened. Of course, I was emotionally crushed, and yes, Jerome had faded from my mind, almost as if he'd never been there other than as something two sisters fought over, a doll, a toy. I wasn't jealous of Lori or the attention paid to her death, and I believed everything regarding the evils of the Order, but the fact was that, once again, something Lori did upended and interrupted my life. She had done it by coming to the Martyr School and then by leaving it. Maybe these thoughts were just the result of days of constant scheming, without a true second to contemplate the sheer absence of my twin. Even at night, by the time my mind quieted down, it was too late: I was out like an exhausted candle.

Because we were only required to wear our uniforms during regular school hours and Sunday Mass or at certain school functions, I'd accumulated quite a bit of clothes in my two years at the Martyr School (I was a thrift store devotee), so back in my room, the door still somewhere between closed and open, I readied myself for my exam, to be administered in the late morning, by unearthing Lori's backpack from the bottom of my hamper (without being noticed) and stuffing it with as much of my clothes as I could without going overboard or making it bulky. Besides a couple of souvenirs, I didn't want to take anything from this hellhole that wasn't mine. I'd moved the Mary Magdalene glow-in-the-dark strap-on to Lori's backpack the evening before; seeing its ghostly luminescence as the sun set, I had a feeling it might have an important part to play in my lunge for freedom. Again Miss Marguerite's voice echoed in my head: "The cock glows in the dark, so you can always find your way home.") On top of the clothes I had a plastic bag with certain items, such as my triquetra pendant, that were to be used later for dramatic effect. When I was finished, I stashed my sister's backpack under what had been her bed. (The SKM had already searched the room this morning; I doubted they would do it again, not with our departure looming.) My travel bag, which had an earthy tone, had no more clothes in it than if I were actually just going home for Lori's funeral and planned to wear nothing else but a black dress and the clothes on my back while I was there. The bag also had some blank notebooks my sister had undoubtedly intended to use for future journals, which made it look fuller. (Her actual journals I kept for myself, stuffed in her backpack.) In lieu of the strap-on I included extra underwear and bras on top (mine as well as some of Lori's that I'd smuggled down by wearing them), hoping that might keep the Scum from digging further during the final inspection and noticing how little apparel had actually been packed or how my travel bag contained no toiletries. I figured if Mary Magdalene had temporarily thrown them off their game earlier, a teenage girl's undergarments would at least distract them somewhat. Regardless, they were anxious to clear my luggage before my exam. But every time they started to go through my travel bag, I told them I wasn't quite finished packing. But the truth was that I wasn't done pacing in the small bathroom. I knew I was wearing on their patience not to mention running out of time; morning was draining away and the plan didn't leave much room for error, although I kept looking for some until the Scum finally banged on the bathroom door. I pushed my way past them, and while they bitched and pointed at their watches, I added a lace teddy that I never knew Lori owned to my bag. Just to annoy my guards, I also rummaged around the dorm until I found an old pair of her sneakers, which I also added. But when it came time for my final baggage inspection, the Scum barely blinked at the contents of the travel bag before they zip-tied it, apparently unmoved by the sheer amount of undergarments (although the younger one caressed select pieces until Gideon smacked one out of his hand). They peeked into my backpack and expropriated a small plastic pencil sharpener, which seemed to please the younger one, who held it above his head, as if he'd found a switchblade.

I'd contemplated showing them different backpacks each time they came in—my Army green bag or Lori's more colorful one—to muddy the waters just in case my plan went sideways. I recalled what Miss Marguerite had said: "…girl, you have to remember what you need to do, even if what you need to do changes, no?" But in the end, I saw no upside to muddy water and wondered if I was misinterpreting Miss Marguerite, for if my guards (Gideon and the radish) weren't so thickheaded, their vigilance veering into boredom (even for the eager beaver junior Knight), they would have discovered what had been buried in the hamper and was now beneath Lori's bed. Checks were every fifteen minutes, during which they would poke around and dutifully mark their clipboards. This led me to believe they hadn't installed a camera in my room—a camera would have stopped my escape attempt cold. I knew that I really only had one move and I made it: when the Scum were out of the room, I cleared my throat rather dramatically, as I retrieved my sister's backpack from under the bed and dropped it out of the window. I didn't know exactly where it fell—I couldn't risk looking (and I thought it best to shut the window)—but since I didn't throw it, I was pretty sure her pack landed roughly in the area where the books had fallen: between the girls' residence hall and the spiked fence that had, eagerly perhaps, accepted Lori's and Christy's foolish sacrifices; there it would be somewhat shielded from view, and my unlikely co-conspirator would probably only need to partially squeeze through the spikes to snatch it up.

When the time came to leave for my exam, the Scum entered without knocking, and I bitched until the angry young one's face was more vermilion than usual; they weren't used to being talked to in that manner, and it thrilled me to bruise this particular rufescent Knight's ego—he was an easy target. Gideon, despite his bully syndrome, seemed to care less, which I found disturbing; the immovable ones tended to treat us like meat for the grinder, particularly the girls. But Gideon's constant coughing and sneezing—he was still not covering his mouth—humanized him, at least enough to make his presence a tad more tolerable than most other Knights, even if his hygiene was nothing less than deplorable; still, his tough guy shtick was difficult to take, especially since he was at least an inch shorter than me. Neither guard mentioned the travel bag (not mine) that stuck out a little from under my desk. Lori had left it behind when she moved to the Jumpers' Floor—just something to slow them down a little when the *shite* hit the blades, 'cause I was sure my room would be one of the first places they'd check when I went missing, even though, logically, it would be the last place I'd be. (The Scum could be somewhat predictable.) I'd found Lori's travel bag in her closet and its color was close to mine, which was why the Scum never confiscated it. I had a hunch they wouldn't notice it when we left, so intent were they on playing prison guards and getting me to my exam in a hurry (plus Gideon was hacking his brains out, which I'd been counting on). It was another risky move (its mere presence signaled my intention to run), but it turned out that those were the only kind of moves I had today. Still, the heightened tension worked in my favor: I was aware, mindful. I helpfully held my backpack while they zip-tied it.

By the time I made it to my exam, Suzette Downey had come through and picked up Lori's backpack. (I had a late slip, so there were no worries about corporal punishment; I knew if someone hit me, all bets would be off, to my detriment.) We sat across from each other, and I could see it on the floor, covered by her pasty white legs, with her own backpack planted on her saddle shoes. I could even see the dirt and some red rust flakes on her garb from where she had to squeeze through the fence to grab the bag, and I pretended to brush away the swamp gnats that were unavoidable that time of year. Suzette caught on and did the same, until the evidence was off her sleeves and jumper. We had to wear our school uniforms to take our finals. (A new rule.) Instead of being annoyed, I realized it might camouflage me during an upcoming part of the plan.

I was so caught up in the possibilities of what was to come, it took me a couple of minutes to focus. This was Miss Kremer's class. (Miss Lonely Heart we called her, because she always appeared to have just finished a good cry.) The largest part of the exam was an essay question on *Wuthering Heights*: How are Catherine and Heathcliff's bodies like prisons, and do the characters see them as such? I needed more than one blue book. I knew all about bodies being prisons. The concept was ingrained in every student here: suicide just kills the vessel; what was left—your soul—was offered to God, who no longer took much interest in temporal matters. That was what they would tell me if I got caught, shortly before staging my suicide: "You've let God down."

Well, God would just have to live with my living, I thought.

+

From the *Martyr School Handbook*:

God created us to suffer in His name. That is the only reason for our existence: a test on a grand scale. It is easy to praise the Lord when one is flush or wanting. It is quite another thing to praise Him as the figurative flames scorch you and the literal ones consume you, for He expects pupils to martyr themselves and finish what the harsh world has begun before the rot that infects the students turns to poison. Escape from the world is not retreat, and suicide is not surrender.

Remember, you cannot escape God's Eyes. Wherever you go, He is there, waiting and not always patiently.

+

After the bell rang, Suzette scurried out with Lori's knapsack. (She'd emptied her bag, leaving the books on the floor under her chair, then stuffed Lori's backpack into hers somehow, all without bringing attention to herself.) This was the best course of action. Suzette was in no danger: bulging book bags and backpacks were normal this time of year. Students were anxious to sell back what textbooks they could to the school bookstore as soon as that subject's exam was over. I couldn't risk making a covert switch in the classroom, even though Miss Lonely Heart had her nose in Kate Chopin's *The Awakening* and appeared to be too transported to notice. But I'd already decided beforehand there were too many ways to fuck up a schoolroom transfer. It was the wrong environment; too close, plus the sudden appearance of a bulge on my back might be tantamount to putting a target on it. No, the plan was in motion, and while the switch *would* take place in plain sight, it would happen on my terms.

When we were little, playing hide'n'seek, Lori would always cry to our mother when her frustration at not being able to find me reached a fever pitch. Mom would cool her forehead, give her a sip of pink lemonade and ask her, "Where's the best place to hide?" Every time, Lori would appear stumped—I could usually hear every word—until, with more promptings from Mom, she would exclaim, as if it was the first time she'd ever done so: "In plain sight!" and she'd narrow her vision and notice, say, that the sofa cushions were a bit lumpier than usual (because I'd squeezed my small body under them) or that the cabinet door beneath the sink stuck out a little (because I'd been sitting in there, barely fitting between the various cleansers and scrub brushes and the black bucket that was always beneath the drain trap because of a leak). That was the idea here: hide in plain sight (briefly). Lori couldn't or didn't want to get out and leave the Martyr School, but me: I was ready to go, go, go.

I knew we'd cut through the cafeteria on the way to the car pool; I was counting on it big time. It was the most direct route, and I knew the Knights would be hungry—they were always hungry. (Disturbingly, Gideon tossed the car keys to his choleric partner, but I had more important things to worry about and hardly any time to spend on worry. Besides, if I got in their car, I could kiss my ass goodbye.) In the cafeteria, I pulled off one of the trickier parts of the plan. After woofing down a protein bar, I asked the Scum if I could use the bathroom, and one of them cleared it out and stayed outside by the front door. (That would be the diminutive and phlegmy Gideon—the Knight I was hoping for: the point man not the caboose.) I was too stressed to pee—seconds counted. I closed my eyes and started to count to ten, reached seven, and as the lavatory smells assaulted my nostrils, I opened my eyes—*here goes*—and quietly as possible removed the lid of the metal trash can. I shoved my travel bag down into the sea of dirty paper towels, wishing all the while that I'd brought gloves. Once the bag touched bottom, I arranged the trash, then replaced the lid. I worried that a janitor would come around before I was in the wind. The student body was small, but I'd never seen an overflowing trash receptacle during my time here. And what if Gideon swept the bathroom before we returned to the cafeteria? I couldn't even just make a break for it then, no. *Breathe, Lisa, breathe.* I tried to count to ten again, reached four, and thought: *fuck it.* When I walked out of the lavatory; Gideon grunted and barely looked at me. True to form, he led me back to the noisy and crowded cafeteria. Being in the lead, he couldn't see that my backpack was no longer strapped to my back but dangling from my hand, its Army green close enough to the earthy color of my travel bag to pass. I just needed for Gideon and his florid fellow Knight (who was still eating) to not notice that I only had a single bag for a couple of minutes, if that. It felt like I was performing a Seussian sleight of hand: *two bags, one bag, nothing to see here folks.* Just another risky ploy from my extremely slim playbook.

Gideon's partner's face was just about lowered into his lunch, but he left his food as soon as he saw us. It was too crowded for him to position himself directly behind me though. When I didn't see my accomplice—this was her cue—I dropped to one knee and stuck a few fingers (which was all I could manage) into the side opening of my zip-tied backpack. I needed to stall. "Hold on please." The Scum stopped. *I am looking for what: tissues, Chapstick, a breath mint?* I looked up and the Knights were staring at my bag. *Not good.* "Okay, I'm cool," I said. "I just wanted to make sure I had extra tampons." Nothing shuts down guys like the word "tampon." My guards turned around and headed for one of the exits at a pace that almost left me behind. Time dripped like blackstrap molasses off a sugar cookie. No accomplice in sight; panic clutched at my throat; my fingers and toes went numb. Swiveling my head, I thought that if I could make it around the serving counter and the lunch ladies (most of whom bore a tattoo of the crimson and bone insignia of *Schola Martyris* on their right wrist), I could scramble to the doors by the loading dock and head into the bayou, but I counted my breaths and by the time I was back behind my guards, who'd stopped to chat with the Scum on cafeteria duty, my heartbeat had slowed back to normal somewhat. *All in good time.* I watched a janitor cross the cafeteria going who knows where. When my travel bag was discovered in the lavatory trash receptacle, it would most likely be treated as a potential bomb, and the appropriate authorities would be called—which might make it easier to get out or even more difficult, especially if they placed the campus on lockdown; it was hard to say. I thought of the mice in the back of Mrs. Goldfarb's classroom, clambering around toilet tissue cores and torn newspaper in an old aquarium, awaiting their turn to be experimented upon (usually while they were alive) or attempting to escape. Switching backpacks was one thing; ditching my Scum escorts would be a little more difficult. Though I had no intention of waiting around, like Mrs. Goldfarb's mice, to see what happened next, I couldn't do it alone.

I knew, before this day, that like Sartre, I needed an accomplice.

Suzette Downey had talked to Jerome, that much I knew from the few girls who'd felt brave enough to visit me and (quietly) offer their condolences (Suzette's always open mouth made her life largely an open book), but it wasn't until last night's study group that I found out what she knew or guessed and how tightly her mouth could be shut. No one expected me to attend a study group—I never had before—but one goes to extremes when looking for a co-conspirator. There were informal study groups at the Martyr School held in dorm rooms or common rooms. But the most intense exam study groups were held in classrooms and were led or moderated or overseen by a member of the Order (a priest, brother, or nun, even a lay person). My Scum guards were taken aback when the night before my exam and departure I said I wanted to go to a particular study group, which I announced as I walked past them with my books (I should have been in mourning,

I suppose), and when I entered the classroom, everyone in the group stopped talking—except Suzette of the Reluctants. I took that as a good sign.

The study group that usually met on the second floor common room of the girls' residence hall had been relocated to the castle. The classroom was set up so students sat around three long tables with wooden tops (engraved by bored students past), the kind whose legs fold up, like the ones we used in the residence hall for game night. The tables were arranged to form sort of a U. As I made my way towards Suzette, who was at one end of a side table, she shooed away the girl seated next to her. (The girl looked ready to take flight anyway the closer I got.) Other than a greeting, Suzette and I didn't speak. Ignoring the substratum of whispers and the bored gaze of the moderator, I wrote in my notebook and slid it next to Suzette—not a big deal; this was a study group, and students partnered up or formed trios and quartets to share information and books, so Suzette and I didn't have to pass notes back and forth the traditional way (secretly). Even though the moderator was half asleep, the Scum were just outside the (open) door, and whether they could help it or not, almost all of the students' eyes were on me, most flitting fitfully throughout the session, others blatantly staring.

Suzette and I corresponded in my spiral notebook, which was where I learned that Jerome, after my sister's suicide, told Suzette about why I was *really* here. I don't know what her reaction had been at the time, but now she seemed neither shocked nor concerned. It turned out that because of her friendship with Lori (which I thought I'd have to exploit to get this done), the biggest gossip of the school managed to keep what Jerome had said to herself. She may have even known about my ex and the Lycanthrope School, but I didn't inquire (and didn't care). I needed Suzette to do two things for me, things that would be seen as aiding and abetting a subversive, an appellation I was sure would surface just for trying to enact this part of my plan. Every subversive, we were taught, had eventually committed suicide, repudiating their past behaviors. Since *every* was a big word to swallow (they obviously weren't counting the very few who'd managed to escape), I understood this to mean that the Scum had eventually silenced those who broke or dared criticize their belief system. So for Suzette, this was a serious risk; if my notebook was confiscated before I had time to destroy our study group correspondence, Miss Downey would surely swing next to me. But Suzette signaled her openness when she scribbled, "Twins," in the notebook; she knew my margin of error was razor thin. "Maybe summer," she wrote and I shook my head. (It was now or never.) Suzette understood. She wrote, "Then you'll be safe if the Scum takes you home for the service because they won't try faking your exit at home—no publicity." What she meant was no public spectacle for their followers not to mention potential students and their parents for whom curiosity about the prep school had grown dangerously close to intent. (She wasn't taking into consideration that the SKM could plow me down in Philly and smuggle my body back to school for the big reveal.) These lines she wrote in pencil, but "Twins" had been written in red ink. It was as if the slashing red echoed through my skull: *they're not going to let me live—not unless I think on my feet.* Suzette had been friends with my sister before Lori had ascended to the Jumpers' Floor; her usually sweet face betrayed the growing trench of indignation just beneath it. "Only two things?" she wrote, but that was it, that was all I needed Suzette to do, just two tasks. The first was retrieving Lori's backpack and delivering it to me. The second task would require a bit of skill. Since I knew I would need more than luck to pull off my cafeteria disappearing act, I had a part for Suzette to play.

I had no way of knowing if they would do me in beyond the state lines. Being safe in Philadelphia wasn't exactly a given, and if I attempted to elude my Scum escorts during my bereavement leave, I figured my guards would do just about anything to bring me back or it would be their asses. But if for some reason my plan failed, and I entered my hometown with a pair of Knights, the school, I (mostly) believed, would never try anything once I was there, because the Director of Campus Ministry and Security had told me that they would *entertain* a classmate while I was gone, in case I didn't return: a life for a life, I guess, was the implication. What was to stop them from slaughtering their hostage if I managed to break away now, escape? I didn't know, but I couldn't allow this threat to hang over my head; all the students planned on dying before they graduated anyway. If I was found in New Orleans (or probably anywhere in Louisiana for that matter), I'd never see the next day. But what made me (fairly) certain they wouldn't hunt me all the way back east (or whatever direction I fled)? Nothing except they wouldn't know who I contacted before or after my escape besides possibly my mother—the Philadelphia police, a cult watch group, the Feds. (The hostage gambit only worked as a deterrent if I was still within reach, otherwise why kill a potentially good suicidal candidate if I ran when self-destruction was how the Order got its rocks off?) But I was getting ahead of myself: first I had to actually break free of the Scum and make it far enough away locally so that my theory could be tested a bit, and I had to do it as quickly as possible so that I had a ghost of a chance rather than the chance of becoming a ghost. If I managed to get off campus, I had a safe house in the Quarter, a way station of sorts run by an ally who would see me on my way back east. She'd made herself known to me long before Lori met her end. I'd called my ally when I knew it was time to go, when I'd found an accomplice from amongst the student body. The details, she said, would become known to her, and I didn't doubt it.

ME (on phone): Uh, *Mom*, I'm going to—
ALLY: You know I can't do a pickup that far out, yes?
ME: I understand. I just need—
ALLY: I will be awaiting delivery.

If I made it as far as Philadelphia, I could just hide for a while. Maybe the Scum would just give the obvious places in the city a cursory glance, write me off, and retreat back behind their seemingly politically protected walls, perhaps figuring that if they let me be, I'd forget the whole experience. (Wishful thinking.) However it played out, I decided I had a better chance of getting out of this alive when I reached the City of Brotherly Love (alone) rather than play cat and mouse here in the Big Easy, running hither and thither. But most would-be escapees made a break for it willy-nilly, children at a chess board for the first time. The way I thought about it, the Order wouldn't expect me to make the first move on their turf, their sacred campus, their blest killing grounds. So that was exactly what I did.

The next day (the date of my scheduled departure), on the way to the cafeteria after Miss Kremer's exam, I saw Nestor's mail truck near the administration building. I knew I had about five minutes, maybe a little more if the mailman had to hoof it a bit before he exited the school and continued on his route. (I hadn't been timing his comings and goings like I'd wanted to—my extra-curricular activities having been severely curtailed—but I'd been living on campus long enough to have a good idea of Nestor's movements.)

We'd only stopped at the cafeteria because my guards were hungry, which I'd counted on, but I would have asked to go even if they had other plans. The cafeteria was my staging ground, and even though her entrance was a tad late, Suzette played her part perfectly, reaching for me as we passed each other, saying in a loud, clear voice, "Good transition," and, as I expected, because it was Suzette (who despite being a gossip was considered a shoe-in for class president next school year) and because Lori had been revered, especially after moving to the Jumpers' Floor, a bunch of girls did the same (including the obligatory touching) until I was surrounded, as often happened in these situations (and why I wanted to avoid them prior to reading Sartre and Nancy Drew). Gideon and his young, inflamed partner were engaged in animated conversation with the cafeteria guards, who'd commandeered a table and were digging into a large pizza, eating standing up (to keep an eye on their charges).My escorts both wielded a slice, which was about as preoccupied as I was going to ever get them. (I was sure this would cost Gideon a promotion—making him feel even shorter—but being sickly didn't make him a sympathetic figure, just a pathetic one, another eager cog in the Order's wheel.) I didn't know what my accomplice had told the other girls (any one of whom could have turned us in, but Suzette told me she'd handle it if it happened). The girls remained in a circle, their arms outstretched, reciting prayers aloud, as I dropped to my knees. (I saw Gideon look over at the tableau of girls and shake his head, as he shoved pizza into his maw.) Lori's backpack sat between Suzette's saddle shoes, and I switched it out for mine, gave one of her calves a squeeze, and scurried on my hands and knees to the northern set of doors, pausing to crawl beneath a rare empty table. None of the students looked at me twice. I don't know how long Suzette and company would keep it up, but I didn't need much time to get out of the building. When my guards realized I'd given them the slip, they'd sound the proverbial alarm (God, I hoped it was proverbial; I think an actual alarm might scuttle my plans), but I hoped beyond hope they wouldn't send a team to the administration building, which was where I was headed. I figured first they'd search the swamplands, the parts of the woods closest to the campus, the bayou, the dorms. When they finally went through girls' lavatory trash receptacle, they'd find my travel bag, filled with an excessive amount of underwear and the like covering enough clothes for one day and a few blank notebooks, as well as most of my non-apparel belongings, things like the crystal earrings I'd bought with my first paycheck and the little block of wood painted with Robert Johnson's image that I picked up in the Quarter—but it was just stuff, I'd had to remind myself, and the strong-willed, I believed, could abandon (some) stuff, as long as it was of their own volition. Besides, leaving things behind might even make them believe I was calling it a day, especially since I'd tagged most items in my room with someone's name—Suzette, Avery, Delaney, et cetera. (I couldn't bring myself to write a suicide note; just thinking about it left me unsettled and qualmish.) On my hands and knees beneath the cafeteria table, I could feel every second, the throb in my temple keeping time, as the girls continued to create a teepee with their uplifted arms. As sweat outlined my brow and dampened my palms, I managed to take the plastic bag out of Lori's backpack. People about to commit suicide often give away prized possessions before breathing their last. So how about the girl who abandoned things one would think would mean the most to her (photographs, the triquetra pendant, Lori's journal with the John Donne quote written on every page)? These I left underneath a cafeteria table just to sow a little confusion, right before I snuck out of the doors. The fresh air rushing past me as I ran towards the admin building did nothing to dry my sweat, for I was far from free, being still trapped on the campus, and freedom, I knew, came with a cost, one I believed I was prepared to pay with my hide, with my very derrière.

+

From the journals of Lori Duke:

Quotes I Like

I have just now come from a party where I was its life and soul; witticisms streamed from my lips, everyone laughed and admired me, but I went away—yes, the dash should be as long as the radius of the earth's orbit————————and wanted to shoot myself.

Søren Kierkegaard

[C]ould it be that there is a kind of dual response—straightforward reverence for a small number of rom-com greats and a kind of guilty-pleasure celebration for the stratum of standard-issue rom-com product below that, which maybe isn't all that great but nonetheless foregrounds women's experiences in the way no other genre does?

Peter Bradshaw

Wanting to die is not the same as wanting to go home.

Blythe Baird

+

When Nestor emerged from the administration building, I waited, my heart hammering to beat the band, with one leg up on the rear bumper of his mail truck, which was parked off to the side. He jumped a little when he saw me but was soon back on his game. (I figured he wasn't privy to the goings-on at the school, not in any concrete way.) While in the middle of his come-on, such as it was, I pulled up my skirt, revealing enough teenage thigh for him to shut up. It was then as our friendly neighborhood mailman drooled over my flesh that I asked him to go somewhere with me. He blanched and backed off, looking this way and that (as was I, but in a much more subtle way). His behavior and reactions were as I'd anticipated; I had no reason to think he'd act otherwise, for I was sure he was (mostly) all talk, but as long as there were no members of the religious order around, no laity, I knew I could pull this off—although I couldn't believe Lori had left me with no other options. As his protestations continued, even cycling down to whispers, I opened Lori's backpack, revealing the Mary Magdalene glow-in-the-dark strap-on—my twisted candle. Nestor's transformation was immediate (and somewhat expected; I didn't think he could resist double penetrating me.

"When?"

"Now. I'll get in the back of your truck and show you…"

"That's against—show me what?"

"…where to go."

"Where? No, no, it's full. The truck."

"I'll fit." Pause. "We'll make me fit," which I was sure he heard as, "We'll make *it* fit".

He never asked me if I was seventeen, which was the age of consent in Louisiana. (I was.) It would have been disturbing had my plan been less dire. I wondered what would be worse: having his thingie in my vagina and the saint in my rear (which is how I imagined it would work), or the other way around? Did it matter, really? Being double penetrated was just a step on the path to freedom (hopefully). I was glad I'd stuck a condom in Lori's bag.

My head, my body, kept swiveling, checking in every direction for Scum. Left and right, behind me. The eastern gate was diagonally across from the front of the administration building. A wide stretch of lawn separated admin from the road that led to the gate. Left and right and back again, my head on a pivot. One thing in my favor though: I believed I'd hear the pounding of their boots before I saw them; the Scum were anything but furtive in their approach to…anything. Besides, some of them would be grilling Suzette and company right about now. Miss Downey just had to hold up for these hopefully few precious minutes. Suzette had assured me the others would know nothing. The Knights that weren't putting my fellow students through the mill were surely already on their way to search the most obvious places on campus. But not Gideon and his partner, not for long; dollars to doughnuts, they would be detained for questioning by the Director of Campus Ministry and Security. Do Knights disappear like some students did? I supposed their fate depended upon whether I was found or not.

I dangled Mary Magdalene in front of the mailman again.

"Where exactly?" he asked. His breath came in clips.

I figured I had about ten minutes, fifteen tops—well, twenty including travel time. Any longer and the mail truck's continued presence on campus would more than likely arouse suspicion. But that was all the time I needed; I didn't think the mailman could hold out very long; in fact, I was counting on it. As I moved towards the truck, Nestor's feet remained planted. I sighed and jumped in, throwing Lori's colorful knapsack in the back. (Standing out in the open would catch somebody's attention soon enough.) There wasn't a passenger seat—the driver sat on the right—so I just crouched down. If the Scum saw me, I'd have to run (which would be ridiculous) or surrender (which would never happen). I knew if the Scum caught up to me, the only funeral I'd be attending, if you want to call it that, would be my own, sooner than expected.

Nestor kicked a small stone and appeared flustered.

"The woods," I told the suddenly reticent mailman. "The cemeteries." I could feel the seconds whoosh by and expire. "Look," I told him, and as he peered into the truck, I undid two buttons on my blouse and lifted my skirt high enough for him to see my underwear, but only for a second. I didn't want Nestor getting cold penis on me; I wanted to make sure he was up for this. (Jesus God, I hoped he was like Christy and Jerome and the thing just popped up! I couldn't imagine having to handle a flaccid mailman.)

When he got in the truck, I told him the way to go through the woods so that he'd pick up Quartz Road, which led to the cemeteries, and he started the engine.

"Wait," I told him, my hand almost touching his arm but not quite. We jerked to a halt.

Shit. What if the truck got stuck on the way? The woods were rather thick in the northern part of the campus. What if the truck was seen going into or coming out of the woods or driving around the back of the administration building? It would be stopped and searched for sure. While I still thought that was a remote possibility, all of a sudden it wasn't remote enough.

I made Nestor turn off the engine, and I could tell by his face, the way it fell, the sweat on his brow, that even though he was scared (probably for the same reasons I was), he was more scared that this assignation wasn't going to happen. To reassure him, I placed my hand on his damp forearm. Indeed, there were small sweat stains blooming all over his short sleeve blue USPS shirt.

I knew I was cutting it close time-wise. In my head I could hear the Scum beating the bushes, scouring the campus. My plan hinged on a hope that the administration building and the surrounding area wouldn't be a priority in their search. Who knows how they'd do me in if they found me (let alone what they'd do to the horny mailman); I didn't want to die in a freak mail truck accident. I was surprised the SKM didn't have more men on the eastern gate already; the guard tower appeared to be unoccupied (or I would have been spotted already), and there was just one guard in a little enclosure manning the boom barrier, as the big black iron gate was open during the day. I just hoped that if the guard had looked our way before I jumped into the truck, that we would've been just a blip, so familiar was the sight of the mailman accosting female students, but I figured if I had been recognized, we'd be surrounded by now.

"Think you can run?" I asked Nestor; he just swallowed hard and nodded. "Good, but first we have a couple of things to do—and to do quickly."

To begin with I suggested turning the truck around so that it faced the eastern gate. Being pointed in the right direction would be a big help. Next I told him to go to the back of his truck and pile up a few Priority boxes on the ground while I waited in the cab. All mail for the administration, faculty, and ordained and non-ordained members of the Order were delivered to the admin building—including students' mail, the envelopes steamed open or so the rumors went. The administration had their own flunky who delivered our mail to the little dull silver mailboxes built into the walls of the dorm lobbies—no need to have an outsider like Nestor traveling around the campus and interacting with the doomed student body any more than could be helped. There were two exceptions: the monsignor's mail, which was delivered directly to his apartment adjacent the rectory and the headmaster's, delivered to his office in a small structure between admin and the castle. I thought it unlikely, but if for some reason the Scum came looking for me at the administration building before they finished combing the usual spots, they'd discover the mail truck still here, the back shut. The few Priority boxes stacked on the ground would make it seem as if the mailman had left the packages out inadvertently. If they sought Nestor in the admin building, they'd come up empty, and maybe (hopefully) they'd just assume that he was delivering mail to the two heads of the Martyr School. If he'd driven to their respective addresses, he'd have to drive a circuitous route, then turn around in the full faculty and Order member parking lot. It was easier for him to hoof it across the wide expanse of lawn between admin and the rectory, which I'd witnessed him doing before. (We thought he really did it because he'd have more of a chance to run into female students.)

Nestor turned the truck around, but when he got out, he remained in place, his feet planted, even after I explained the plan a second time.

Nothing. *Tick-tock, tick tock.*

I reached into Lori's backpack. *Here goes,* I thought and stuck the yet-to-be-used Mary Magdalene glow-in-the-dark dildo in my mouth. That was enough for Nestor. I watched from the cab as he opened the back door and took out several Priority Mail boxes. If asked, he'd been in a hurry, "please don't report me to my supervisor," but most likely no one would look twice at boxes piled up outside a mail truck—not if Nestor and I were quick about it— and who at the Martyr School would dare steal from the United States Postal Service?

When he was done, he asked it (without looking me in the eye). I'd been expecting it, but I didn't think it would take him this long to ask—and good thing he did, because although I was ready to be voluntarily violated, I'd been too worked up to actually strike the deal.

"Why?"

"I need a ride...out of here."

He stepped back.

"I need you to be a smuggler," I added, appealing to his inner Han Solo. (Most guys have one, in my admittedly limited experience.)

He looked trapped, but nodded, and I jumped out, put on Lori's backpack (which wouldn't exactly blend in), and led the huffing and puffing mailman to the woods. (*Please nobody see us, please.*) I'd done my homework and knew to follow the stream until I picked up the fire trail, which would fork off with Quartz Road on the right leading to the cemeteries. The woods on the northern side of the campus ran wild for a good fifty acres or so. The underbrush started alongside the road from the eastern gate and merged into a copse before joining the rest of the woods. I crossed my fingers and hoped that no one walked out of the admin building just as we ran across the road. (If we went around the back of the building, there could be many sets of eyes: service people, priests heading to their posts, students hustling their way to their next exam.) I dove into the underbrush. (The guard at the gate was in his enclosure facing away from us.) After a sprint to the copse, it was slow going; the undergrowth was thick, but once I reached the woods proper, I hit the ground running, and all I could hear was air passing by my ears as I headed west. If Nestor got cold feet and turned around, I wouldn't know; I wasn't going to risk losing a second by checking. I needed for us to clear the admin building and get into a deeper part of the woods where we could locate the stream. Once we did—and there was Nestor almost falling into it and splashing a little too much—finding the fire trail wasn't difficult, and I kept my eyes open for the fork and Quartz Road, which ran northwesterly; every other path, even the fire trail, led to the swamplands, notorious for raucous parties and a favorite hiding place for hopeless runaways. If you partied hard and snorted God knows what, if you wanted to have a threesome with everyone watching, then the swamplands were where you went. If you wanted to enjoy a beer or two and smoke some weed, or if you needed a place to make out and possibly run the bases, then the cemeteries were for you (the East Lot anyway)—and they were *probably* going to be one of the last places the Scum searched on campus (I kept telling myself), if not *the* last before they went deeper into the woods. Just because they didn't dispatch a team to the cemeteries at first didn't mean they wouldn't eventually. I tripped for the third time and wondered if Nestor would still be attracted to me with bloody knees and dirt on my uniform, my shoes and socks drenched; the thought dissipated with a nervous laugh: who was I kidding? I could roll around in dog excrement, and dirty ol' Nestor would still be harder than Chinese algebra (as Jerome had been fond of saying).

The mailman wasn't exactly in shape, so to make sure he was still behind me now that we weren't running like the devil was on our tails, I listened for his strenuous breathing and kept moving until we reached Quartz Road. In a quarter of a mile, I made an abrupt right turn. Cutting through the woods wasn't the quickest way to reach the cemeteries, but I felt it best to stay off the prescribed path. When we got close, we hid behind a thicket of cypress trees to make sure the caretaker wasn't fiddling about, but there was no sign of him or his ramshackle truck. There also wasn't any auditory evidence of having been followed. (The Scum were not celebrated for their subtlety.) I gave one of Nestor's hands a good squeeze before we made our made our way to our destination. I was pretty sure he'd object to doing it in one of the cemeteries, but he hadn't said a word about it this whole time—I think he was in too deep (or about to be, wink, wink) to voice an objection.

My brain would not stop weighing the variables.

I thought that if the Scum did check the cemeteries during their initial search, they'd just stick to the East Lot, a known spot for imbibing and/or screwing relatively undisturbed. Cemetery or not, compared with the other parcels like God's Allotment, partying by the tombs of the Elders never bothered us. Even those kids that bought into the Order's mysticism didn't have a lot of respect for their keepers. (Teenagers will be teenagers, right?) If the Scum wanted to check the East Lot off their list, it would probably be a drive-by down the glittery road to ruin. Maybe one of them would poke his head in a mausoleum or two, but I doubted it. We may have used the East Lot as a place to be bad (or our version of bad), but not one of us was ever brave enough to crack open a mausoleum. For sure, the SKM would never give God's Allotment, which is where we were headed, more than the briefest of looks, if they even bothered. For one, except for a couple of ancient and large Spanish moss-covered southern live oaks, God's Allotment was flat and featureless, consisting mostly of copse graves that *everybody* was afraid of walking on. I told Nestor to be careful when we entered the cemetery, but I doubted he heard me over his strenuous breathing. I tip-toed so as to not disturb the awful, final resting places of the Fallen Failures.

+

From the journals of Lori Duke:

A Quote I Like

"I promise to be as careful as a pussycat walking up a slippery road," Nancy [Drew] assured the housekeeper with a grin....

Carolyn Keene

+

It was behind one of those southern live oaks in God's Allotment where I removed my jumper and just about everything else and began figuring out how to properly get the mailman into the double-leg harness once he'd let his regulation shorts fall to the ground. When he removed his Scooby-Doo underwear, I found myself face-to-face, as it were, with an ass that had so many pimples, it looked like a connect-the-dots puzzle. (He didn't seem to be in much of a hurry, stalling even, but my ears were filled with the sound of a ticking timepiece, like Captain Hook forever hearing the swallowed clock inside the crocodile that had taken his hand.) It was only then that I realized I'd run all this way with a sex toy in my hand. The area was heavily shaded, but the dildo still glowed, and in that glow, which I believed was a sign that I was heading home, Mary Magdalene looked suspiciously like Our Lady of Guadalupe, whose velvet paintings and plastic figurines Miss Marguerite sold in her shop right next to ones depicting the voodoo Lord of Death, Baron Samedi, and the Creole voodoo queen, Marie Laveau. I felt sorry for Mary Magdalene, mislabeled a whore by Pope Gregory I in the sixth century and now, with her bare feet pointed towards the mailman's pubic region, the image of her head was about to be buried inside my anal cavity. But as I adjusted the strap-on (the dildo above his phallus), Nestor looked at me and shook his head. (Other than briefly running the back of his hand against one of my thighs when we were hiding behind the cypress trees, Nestor had never touched me.) I didn't understand. I stood in front of him wearing only my saddle shoes and socks (in case I had to run—I'd advised him to do the same). The saintly dildo had been a shot in the dark. (I pushed down a clawing panic as the words SEVEN INCHES flashed behind my eyes; did all seven inches go inside me?) I thought this was what he wanted—a female (teen) ready and willing to be double penetrated but the horny postman never stared at my boobs or anything; he hadn't looked me in the eye since I'd undressed. He leaned over and respectfully helped me back into my underwear, his head turned away. (It seemed like he barely touched my skin.) He undid the straps and stepped out of the harness, letting Mary Magdalene fall to his shoes. I'd avoided looking at his penis until now: he wasn't hard; he didn't even have a chubby. A pretty (or relatively pretty, for I must have looked a fright), newly naked teenager stood before him (in a cemetery, but still), and his penis never stirred.

But after Nestor helped me into the harness (which I donned without thinking) and as he began attaching the straps, I got it—partially. Nestor was impotent. Instantly, I felt bad including him in my scheme, manipulating him. I reached for his penis; the least I could do was play with it even if it never became tumescent. But he stayed my hand and dropped to his knees behind me; I could feel his breath on my bottom. But instead of performing anilingus, which I expected to be part of the deal, he merely kissed each cheek, and after a momentary hesitation, pressed his nose between them for a few seconds then jumped up, his dingus not even at half mast. That was when I understood everything. I didn't waste any time. (And to think: this wasn't even the most difficult part of my plan.) I dug around in Lori's backpack for the small bottle of Mother JuJu's Anytime Anal Lubricant, which I told him to apply liberally to himself. He put his hands against the southern live oak and pushed his butt out. (I expected to catch some awful whiffs, but the cigarette smell masked any other odor.) Although my initial attempts at penetrating his anus with the strap-on dildo were awkward and uncomfortable, the mailman was surprisingly tender, reaching back to cover one of my hands with his to lead me in, but he couldn't find the opening at first, and then both of us were struggling for insertion. It was obvious he'd never done this before (neither had I!), so from the moment Mary Magdalene entered his ass, my thrusts were slow and measured and the whole act took about two and half minutes, which, quite honestly, was about two minutes and fifteen seconds too long. (I imagined the saint's glow had faded.) Abruptly he stood straight up and Mary slipped out and it was over. If he hadn't been impotent, I figured he wouldn't have been able to hold out long with a teen banging his tail, but he'd kept both hands on the tree and never even bothered to try diddling with his ding-dong. I did think it odd that someone so obsessed with teenage girls' behinds wanted to be anally penetrated himself, until I realized that my offer was as close as he was going to get to having anal sex—with anyone of any age. He was just more of a decent fellow then I'd taken him for; he couldn't bring himself to penetrate (or double penetrate!) me, so he took it himself. But I don't think position, age, or even fading phosphorescence (which he couldn't feel but maybe the *idea* enhanced the experience) had anything to do with his relative briefness. No, I think despite all his perverted talk (which had dried up when I pulled him into my plan), he struck me as being embarrassed by sex. Whether his erectile dysfunction had anything to do with it, I don't know, but something told me it had always been this way for him. His face was beet red and it wasn't from exertion. As I donned my jumper (he looked away while I dressed), I told him he could keep the strap-on which I'd left upon the grass.

He seemed surprised at its existence, and after he gathered himself (I had to tell him to pick up the pace), he left Mary Magdalene on the ground. Since everything seemed symbolic somehow, in one surge of adrenaline, I ripped off the insignia patch from my uniform and tossed it on top of a small pile of leaves. That ought to confuse the Knights when they stumbled upon these "clues."

Nestor whispered, "We just made love."

"That's one way of looking at this," I whispered back.

"You fucked me." Again in hushed tones (as was appropriate.)

It hit me harder than I would have thought: Nestor had been a virgin—and more than, an innocent of sorts. His ass-oriented harassment of Martyr School girls was a front, the words and gestures undoubtedly learned from the Internet.

We shut up as we heard the bustle of a group of Scum making their way west on the fire trail, heading most likely to the swamplands. They passed the fork and seemed to have no interest in Quartz Road or the cemeteries. Still, they were so close…too close. The divergence was narrow here. I gestured to Nestor to be still, but I needn't have bothered; his eyes were as wide as I imagined mine were and his face was no longer red. We were frozen in place, as if we were playing freeze-tag on a summer night in Philly. I wondered if Nestor's ass throbbed—even though I'd tried to be gentle, Mary Magdalene was significantly bigger than any penis I'd ever seen live. Waiting for the Scum to pass, I stared at the insignia patch I'd just torn off, in particular the spear the Lamb had apparently fallen upon on purpose, but for the first time I focused on its one visible eye (for he was in profile), which had not a look of religious ecstasy but rather a combination of resignation and desperation. It was just an artist's rendering, I told myself, but, as quietly as possible, I bent down and placed the Martyr School insignia patch under the business end of the strap-on. It wasn't an impotent ephebophile who'd truly fucked me, and I wanted whoever found this to know it. (Okay, I was the top, but it was my metaphor.)

To my surprise, even after having been in Nestor's darkest regions, Mary Magdalene still held on to a little bit of her glow. Miss Marguerite had been right after all about the sacrilegious strap-on with the phosphorescent saint dildo: its light *was* going to help me get home. As the Scum moved out of earshot, I thought:

the dildo has gotten me this far. I just needed the apparently spent mailman (metaphorically-speaking) to take me to safety (quite literally). After that, it would be on me (with some support) to get the rest of the way, to get out of their reach, to get home.

Specifically what I needed Nestor to do right now was make it out of the woods and return back to his truck (with me). We'd lost precious minutes waiting for the Scum detail to pass. (I didn't have to look at my watch to know that we were way past my twenty minute estimate.) Soon enough, the guards would start to look into areas previously ignored—if they hadn't started already. I nodded to a moist Nestor, and we started back.

When I poked my head out of the woods, there was no traffic on the steps of the admin building, and other than the one manning the gate (or, rather, the boom barrier), there were still no other guards on the ground. The immediate area was preternaturally quiet. I supposed the eastern gate was considered to be a low risk area given its proximity to administration headquarters. I booked through some tall grass and made for the copse. The huffing and puffing whey-faced mailman crouched next to me behind some thick underbrush; his shirt had come untucked and was lifted up on one side revealing his belly, pallid and sweaty, matching the complexion of his face; it was like looking at the underside of some bug found beneath a rock, a bug that smelled of pharmacy cologne and Winstons. I was careful to be out of what I figured were the normal sightlines from the guard tower, but it still appeared to be empty. I wondered when the plane carrying Lori's body would take off. I didn't think the Order could stop a commercial flight, but I would feel better knowing it was in the air. I thought I heard the scuffing of boots, but then it stopped, and I still only saw only the one guard at the gate. I hoped that if Nestor was spotted emerging from the copse, the sole guard's surprise and confusion would slow down his reaction time long enough for Nestor to make it to his truck. Yes, the barrier was down, but the mailman could possibly smash his way through it. (It worked in the movies.) The guard wouldn't have time to close the big black gate, and the school wouldn't dare stop Nestor off campus, I thought and hoped. Of course, the Order could call the police, maybe have an Amber Alert issued if I made it to the truck or if they assumed I was on it even if I wasn't, but I didn't know how quickly that would go into effect (or if they would even broadcast the alert since I was no longer a minor). There was a chance that even if they did see Nestor hustling out of the copse, they wouldn't necessarily see me. (I was more careful and not as clumsy.) It was a good thing Nestor appeared to comprehend the inherent danger in his decision to help me. I needed another accomplice not dead weight.

The local and state governments, for reasons unknown, looked the other way when it came to the Martyr School, it was said and believed, but returning a kid who clearly didn't want to go back and was obviously frightened of the prospect—I figured that would be too much to ignore. But perhaps not: wishful thinking shouldn't be confused with wish fulfillment. Maybe the Scum *would* hunt me across state lines; it was a possibility, as much as I believed it wasn't. As far as Nestor was concerned, I was pretty sure the mailman would disappear along with his truck if he was caught with me on campus. It was then I thought it was best to wait a bit before tearing out of the underbrush in case they were on to me and poised to swarm the truck. The once-horny mailman understood.

I didn't know how he'd get out of it, but I hoped Nestor knew that he couldn't (and shouldn't) go back to the school—ever, even if no one saw him running towards his vehicle (which, in the end, no one did) and especially if we managed to pass through the gate.

Go!

Nestor tossed the Priority boxes back in the truck and inched it towards the boom barrier. The one guard posted was busy lazily pacing and smoking. The few seconds it took seemed like some very *long* seconds. Hunched over, I skirted around the truck, and dove behind some Penny Mac hydrangeas. Before the guard turned back around and caught sight of Nestor in his truck, I jumped in the slowly moving vehicle, scrambled over Nestor's lap ("Faster, faster," said the mailman), and squeezed in between the mail tubs and packages in the back, clinging to Lori's backpack. Seconds later, the truck came to a stop. The guard exchanged a few words with Nestor, never mentioning the general alarm or asking him to open his truck.

"Running behind schedule, huh?"

"I know but try to get someone to sign for a package at the monsignor's office if Mrs. Dunlop is *indisposed*."

Nestor asked if he could bum a cigarette, and the guard was more than happy to share and even proffered his lighter. I wanted

Nestor to get the hell off campus, but I knew what he was doing. If asked, the guard would say that there had been nothing unusual about the mail truck or the postman. He might not even mention it in his report, it was such a routine sight. I had a decent (albeit obstructed) view of both of them. It was good to keep in mind that this chummy guard was also a Knight, a Scum. I could see Nestor's right hand, and it shook as he tried to light the cigarette, but the guard had turned away to respond to some crackling words on his walkie-talkie. I marveled at my hands—they were absolutely still. Nestor was a jittery mess (because of his aiding and abetting or because he had just, a short time ago, had Mary Magdalene up his bottom, I didn't know), but the guard seemed distracted, then annoyed.

"I swear they want the skin off my back. But whatdaya gonna do?" he asked Nestor as he replaced the walkie-talkie. I heard the squeak of the boom barrier being raised up. He waved Nestor on. I wondered if the mailman realized the question was rhetorical, but he played it cooler than I expected.

"Looks like rain. Smells like it too. See you tomorrow?"

"Wouldn't miss it for the world," the guard replied. "I don't think I'll ever get off gate duty."

One, two, three—and we were on the street. I resisted an urge to pee. I'd already told Nestor where he needed to take me. Traffic was light, and Miss Marguerite stood in the doorway in her gypsy garb, two of her men behind her. I never thought I'd be so happy to see a stuffed armadillo.

+

As soon my feet hit the pavement, Nestor sped off. As I clung to Lori's backpack, I hoped he could keep out of the Scum's reach, and I also hoped he would swear off making lewd comments to high school girls (if he was ever around some again). Nestor had rambled in a tremulous voice all the way to Marie Laveau's Voodoo House and Magick Adult Emporium. He seemed to believe that he would be in trouble for going off his route and running so late, but I hoped his behavior would lead to his route being changed so that it no longer included the Martyr School, which, besides probably saving his hide, would remove him from guaranteed temptation, though his experience with me in God's Allotment may have scared him straight, so to speak. Before hopping out of the postal truck, I thanked him, and he blushed, stared straight ahead, and mumbled a thank you back, then took off.

Miss Marguerite made me a strong cup of tea and added a generous amount of whiskey. When I finished it, she led me to a cot in the backroom, and I was out like a light. When I started to wake up, it hit me in a way that it hadn't while I was at the Martyr School: my twin, my other half, had ended up, by her own machinations, skewered on a spike, and I'd failed to save her. I shook and sweated, and as I sat up, something else reverberated in my brain: I wouldn't be here if it weren't for Lori. At least I was able to save myself, and maybe that was the best I could have ever hoped for—maybe it's the only thing, for if you can't save yourself, what was the point of even thinking about rescuing somebody else.

+

From the journals of Lori Duke:

A Quote I Like

When life is so burdensome, death has become for man a sought-after refuge.

Herodotus

+

My twin was lost to me. One half of me was gone, gone, gone.

It was still night when I woke again and realized I was moaning. The only light came from a candle beside Miss Marguerite, who sat next to the cot eating an onion like an apple. "When you went there, you were to save two people," she said, sounding more than ever like Marie Ouspenskaya, who played the gypsy woman in *The Wolf Man*. I closed my eyes and stopped moaning. *Say what the gypsy woman said as the Wolf Man was dying, say it for—*

" 'The way you walked was thorny, through no fault of your own. But as the rain enters the soil, the river enters the sea, so tears run to a predestined end.' "

Miss Marguerite blew out the candle. The room smelled strongly of her onion and the garlic braids which hung above the windows.

Finish it. The last line. Finish the—

" 'Now you will find peace for eternity.' "

Amen.

My remaining time in the French Quarter was enshrouded in a liquor-and-tea fog. ("To keep you from, you know, losing your marbles before what may come, the great escape or the last stand. So you won't be too sharp until then, yes? You'll talk to your mom when you are back in your city. Do not use a phone.") There were no worries there: even though I wanted to call...*someone*, my mom at least, I couldn't: all the phones had been removed but the one up front next to the register, and my cell phone was long gone. I never stepped outside, not a toe, and I spent the rest of my time in New Orleans at Marie Laveau's. I stayed there for three days—just till Miss Marguerite's men were fairly confident that the Scum weren't casing the place. I thought for sure they'd find me, but Miss Marguerite told me, "The Knights are notoriously lazy during the hot season." She spoke in Creole to one of her black-shirted men, then switched to English for my benefit. "I want two out front and the same number out back. Not enough to rouse suspicion but enough to discourage an attack. Have them posted strategically— yes?—so as not to stand out *too* much but just enough. They're looking for us to have everyone out but that would be like flashing a big sign—no?—that says their little lost lamb is here." After he left, she winked at me. "My men, they are not only on the outlook for vampyres, the scourge of the city; they also regularly challenge the tricksters of Kalfu, a loa not as easily appeased as Papa Legba. Kalfu controls the crossroads. This city is nothing if not an intersection between the quick and the dead (although it is hard often to tell the difference)." The old woman seemed to grow in height, blocking all light except for whatever gave her a fierce fiery outline. "The blood of a wild pig sacrificed to Erzulie Dantó, the mother of the Petro loa, has stained my skin." She rent the front of her dress, one that had seen many washings, and indeed, from the bottom of her throat and plunging down into the dark recesses of the small part of the dress that remained intact was an almost pulsating line of bright red. "For I am strong in Dantó and her fierce reckoning shivers through my ancient frame. My men have withstood those far more powerful than the scarecrows that 'guard' your former school. For more than three centuries, our kind has been fighting for this city, and we will continue down this path until the last of those who serve what lies in the dark expires or the last of us does." The light diminished until Miss Marguerite was once more an old woman with staple wounds on her fingers. "The Order may have power in this world, but in the next they are nothing more than dust beneath the feet of the loa that have them."

Voodoo. In some ways it seemed more comforting than whatever one would call the religion taught at the Martyr School. (It wasn't Catholic despite their insistence.) The Order may have their Elders, but I bet they avoid the crossroads, even if they weren't smart enough to avoid those who tread through them regularly.

"My men, they are familiar with the Sanguine Knights of the Martyrs. They've done battle with them and emerged scarred but victorious. The enemy's tenaciousness is not softened by herding teenagers, no. The Sanguine Knights—the SKM, the Scum you call them—they believe they cannot die but by their own hand or by dying at ours, which to them is just another form of martyrdom. That comes from a very powerful mind fucking. And you pupils—you are not enough; they come looking for homeless and destitute teenagers. Nobody knows why, but my men and those of others like me fight them regularly."

Others like you? My mind pondered the possibilities as Miss Marguerite prepared absinthe for me. I moved to a chair and stared at the sugar cube until it dissolved.

"Drink" and she lifted the glass of green liquid to my lips. I winced before gulping it down.

"Compared to them, the werewolves, bad witches, and vampyres are bothersome flies. Silver, *gris-gris*, stakes—these have been the tools for ages before ours. It is easier to prevent the flies from *becoming* than to fight those who cannot wait to die—yes?— because we have something they don't, child."

A few words slid from my mouth, and I hoped they sounded like, "And what's that then?" because that was what I meant to say.

"We want to live."

"Oh." I checked the glass to make sure there wasn't any absinthe left.

"We want to live well and long and we're not bat shit crazy."

"That explains it," I said. Coming from deep inside my addled brain, as I slipped off my chair: "I can't fight."

Miss Marguerite laughed, as sound so unfamiliar, I crawled beneath the table—a reasonable response given all the talk of Knights and bad witches and the like—and found myself eyeball-to-eyeball with a gassy Jubes. As I stared into his milky white eyes, I understood all of his pain, felt all of his losses. As I attempted to address his feline issues, the vision impaired cat tried to scratch me but connected with a table leg instead, a musical table leg. " *'Come sail away, come sail away, come sail away with me,'* " sang the table leg in a tremulous tenor. It took a tremendous amount of will power not to sing along.

What potion had she put in my drink?

"You can't fight?" Miss Marguerite said. "But you've been fighting all along. You're fighting now."

She helped me up and patted my knee. Jubes hissed. "We're just keeping you on ice for a couple of days. Trust me, yes? I know how to dispel *these* spirits too. You'll be sharp as a tack when the time comes."

"Tackle," I murmured.

"You not a lure," Miss Marguerite said. "I promise."

"Not alluring," I slurred, as I headed towards the floor again. "I'm the pretty one."

Miss Marguerite shook her head and cupped my chin. "You're the only one, child."

I cried until I passed out. When I awoke (a day later), Miss Marguerite had worked her magic, for my head felt as clear as the day I'd first arrived in Louisiana. I looked around at the shelves of backstock—voodoo dolls and sex toys and plastic religious statuettes—and felt closer to home than I'd felt in ages. Someone had carried me to the cot when I was in my cups, and when I swung my feet over, they hit Lori's backpack, and I knew I was ready.

Nobody puts Baby in a corner.

+

From the journals of Lori Duke:

A Quote I Like

"I know myself," he cried, "but that is all."

F. Scott Fitzgerald

+

Miss Marguerite gave me a new pair of sneakers and a duffel bag filled with new clothes, along with a train ticket. She said that she knew my trip wasn't going to require a lot of different outfits, but just in case, for any reason, I had to disembark before the train reached Pennsylvania (or if I had to stay on until it reached New York City), I'd be prepared. When I asked if I should dye my hair before I left, Miss Marguerite shook her head and said that the protection spells she would cast for me, though not foolproof, made such drastic cosmetic measures unnecessary.

"Just put your hair up," Miss Marguerite said. "That and a costume change once on board should be enough to confuse to any nosy Knight who hadn't picked you out already. I'm told the bathrooms on the train are generally quite clean."

Although the table leg was no longer musical, I imagined it was, only this time it was Leonard Cohen it sang instead of Styx.

Everybody knows that the boat is leaking
Everybody knows the captain lied
Everybody's got this broken feeling
Like their father or their dog just died...

Miss Marguerite told me that her men have been watching the Scum, as they staked out the bus and train stations. "I'd give you a car," she said, "but now that the Sanguine Knights' watch has decreased somewhat—they still check the depots sporadically, but my men can see them coming a mile away; your Scum are not exactly inconspicuous—I think by train is best. A bus might be even better; patterns could change based on traffic, but a train is faster. A car would leave you all alone. No good. I doubt they will pursue you past the borders, but we take no chances. One of my men will ride the train with you, but you will not know who it is. When you reach your city, he will let me know, and I will have a call placed to your mother, and she'll be told when to expect you. The school confiscated your cell phone, yes?"

I nodded. The wounded nuns took it during orientation, the day they broke my hymen and gave me the official school jumper. The older kids told me never to expect it back. They said that the Order exported your contacts and messages, then destroyed the phone.

"Good," Miss Marguerite said. "Less temptation. There is money in your wallet—no thanks needed. Use it to take a cab home from the train station. Until you arrive home, stay away from phones of any kind, understand? Just to be safe. But I'm going to make an offering for your protection."

She closed her eyes and began singing a song in a voice that sounded older than she was—ancient, even. Candles were lit, and she drew a symbol, a vevè, on the floor in chalk, then made an offering of something that appeared to be covered in blood. What it was and whose blood, I didn't know and dared not ask.

When the ceremony was finished, Miss Marguerite said, "So you may travel through your crossroad.

"And I don't know whose blood that was either. I always have some on hand. It keeps for about two months if you know the right spells, use the right powder, and have a decent refrigerator."

She dipped a finger in a little bit that had spilled.

"Tastes like cat." She turned to one of her men. "Was this our cat?"

As if on cue, Jubes waddled into the room carrying a not quite dead mouse.

"Living proof," the old woman said, "that some of us are granted more than nine lives."

While Miss Marguerite investigated the possible felicide, I tried to tamp down my anxiety by paging through the old magazines that were collected in piles in a corner of the room. The table leg kept me company, or so I imagined.

And everybody knows that the plague is coming
Everybody knows that it's moving fast
Everybody knows that the naked man and woman
Are just a shining artifact of the past...

Reading a review in an old *Entertainment Weekly* for a movie I'd never heard of, I was struck by a laughing fit that I was sure would bring Miss Marguerite back, but I couldn't stop, and I reread part of the review over and over:

"Most romantic comedies have a half dozen situations at best: Meet Cute, Infatuation, Pop Song Montage, Contrived Mix-Up, Angry Breakup, and Final Clinch. [This film] is about the many unclassifiable moments in between."

The reviewer couldn't have been a graduate of the Martyr School, which left the question: had the Order cribbed from a movie review (one that wasn't—*gasp*—written in Latin) to update their handbook? It was almost too absurd to consider, and it made the deaths of Lori, Christy, Piper, and the others—whether they ended up beatified or counted among the Fallen Failures—part of the sickest joke of all. I could only hope that, if nothing else, the school was eventually sued for plagiarism.

The table leg's song faded out...

That's how it goes

Everybody knows

When it was time, Miss Marguerite gave me a "brownie most magical" and told me to eat it in front of her. The old woman also gave me a journal, bound in old black leather, since I was without one of my own. She was accompanied by two taciturn guys, both sinewy and unassuming-looking, both Creole—my escorts to the train station. "They can kill with their fingers," Miss Marguerite said, "but they also carry very big guns." I wasn't sure what scared me more: the Scum or men who could kill with their fingers. Miss Marguerite stroked my head before I left. "Worry not, for we are stronger than all of them, as are you." By "them" did she mean the Order or the other kids at the school? Miss Marguerite took a negative view of suicide. "No offense, child." Did it even matter anymore? What Lori had done was past; I just wanted to no longer be part of Lori's past. "Don't ever come back to our city," Miss Marguerite said. "Not when you're grown up, not when you're old and leathery like me. The Order has a long memory. Unless they have connections in Philadelphia that I am not aware of—and I have the gift of what you would call 'remote viewing'—they will never go after you once you are home, I think. The Order is nefarious; they survive by having believers in high places, but generally that just means in New Orleans, maybe in other parts of Louisiana, but no further, as far as I can see. So do not come back. Do not call the shop. You may write but do so sparingly. Even caution your children, when you have them, from entering our city. The spell I cast should last past my expiration date, which is not as near as you would think. The spell will pass to your twins." I looked on in horror, my eyes a pair of O's. Miss Marguerite laughed in a gentle manner, holding my hands in her hard, wrinkled little paws. I didn't know I was crying until I opened my eyes and saw that her small brown hands were wet. " 'The way you walked was thorny,' " she said. "Now go—go find peace for all your days yet to come."

By now I was pleasantly stoned. The men who escorted me from Marie Laveau's Voodoo House and Magick Adult Emporium spoke Creole to each other. When we neared the Union Passenger Terminal, one of them got out of the car, "to case the place," the other told me in broken English, making his fingers into a gun, "for Knights, you understand me?" I nodded, and when the other man came back, he indicated that all was clear. His face was impassive, his manner aloof, and I bet his heart rate never changed when he hunted for Scum or vampyres or werewolves. The man who'd spoken to me, Andre, said that they had men watching from the rooftops (he tapped his ear piece), and there were no signs of any Scum in the immediate area, but he thought they might come to the terminal shortly before the train arrived. "We have enough to hold them back, I think, but we go now to your train, you and I and Armand, okay?" I wanted to run back to the safety of Marie Laveau's; I just imagined some epic battle between two of New Orleans' hidden forces, but I let myself out of the car, clutching my ticket, Lori's brightly colored backpack slung over my shoulder. Armand carried the duffel bag Miss Marguerite had given me. They waited on the platform with me, their charge, until it was time. Before they left, Andre took off an amulet that hung around his neck and placed it around mine.

"For strength?" I asked.

Andre shook his head. "No, it is so you will not..." He murmured in Creole until his face brightened. "It is so you will not give a fuck."

It must have worked or Miss Marguerite's brownie was stronger than I'd first thought, for I truly, at the moment of my departure, did not give a fuck. My train left the station without incident. (As it pulled out, Andre and Armand stood on the platform in their black t-shirts, their arms crossed. I gave them a little wave, and Andre broke character and waved back; even Armand smiled.) The train crossed into Mississippi without a surprise appearance by the Scum. I wondered which of my fellow passengers worked for Miss Marguerite, but I was too caught up in myself to really study everyone. Truth was, I wasn't even aware we'd left New Orleans at first. It wasn't that I didn't have faith in Miss Marguerite, her spell, or her men, but it had already seemed as if Lori's story couldn't end until I joined her in Philadelphia, come what may. She'd pushed me away while she was alive, but the second I saw her body fall it was as if I could feel her hand on my ankle, trying to pull me down. It was all about her. It was time I disengaged and made it all about me. I uncorked the bottle of cabernet sauvignon Miss Marguerite had packed for me, and I tried to start losing the past, my past, Lori's past.

+

From the journals of Lori Duke:

Quotes I Like

They tell us that suicide is the greatest act of cowardice…that suicide is wrong; when it is quite obvious that there is nothing in the world to which every man has a more unassailable title than to his own life and person.

Arthur Schopenhauer

Among the most fundamental obligations of romantic comedy is that there must be an obstacle to nuptial bliss for the budding couple to overcome. But society has spent decades busily uprooting any impediment…. Love is increasingly presumed…to transcend class, profession, faith, age, race, gender, and (on occasion) marital status.

Christopher Orr

+

The trip was to take roughly twenty-eight hours, but I was tired of sleeping; I was tired of pretending. I admit to being worried about reconnecting with the ghost girl I saw in the window's reflection and used to see whenever I closed my eyes at night. But after a while I realized that I wanted nothing to do with a ghost girl, and I never saw her behind my eyelids again or anywhere else. I left her behind somewhere in Mississippi, and before the train crossed into Alabama, I took my clothes and such out of Lori's backpack and stuffed them in the extra bag Miss Marguerite had given me. I walked towards the next car, and when I opened the door, I dropped Lori's backpack on the tracks. I didn't even watch it get caught up by a wheel. It would have only taken a second, if that, but that would have meant another second was given over to someone else's story. I returned to my seat and wondered what *my* story would look like.

"May I?"

It was someone my age. He looked like he was sick, he was so pale. He was all bundled up and wore sunglasses and a black fedora, as well as a scarf around the lower part of his face, which he let down to talk. Not exactly summer-in-the-south garb.

I nodded, and he sat down next to me.

"I got on in New Orleans, but soon I was surrounded by little old ladies who knew each other and spoke a Slavic language. Plus the sun's just pouring in on that side, murderously hot. I saw you sitting by yourself and—"

"And you needed to escape. You can stay, but I'm afraid I'm not in the mood for company or small talk."

If he was so hot, why didn't he ditch his scarf and hat, not to mention his overcoat?

He smiled. I couldn't help but smile back. "It's just you and your reflection, huh? At least you have that," he said. "But I understand. I won't bother you."

I hadn't meant to be rude. I offered him a swig from my bottle of wine. He smiled again and said, "I've been waiting forever to say this: 'I never drink...wine.'"

"*Dracula*, 1931."

"Very good," he said, still smiling.

I turned back to my reflection and found that it was smiling too.

+

From the <u>*Martyr School Handbook*</u>:

Suicide is not so much a choice as a lifestyle, and suicidal ideation is not so much a lifestyle as a way to live. To die for Christ, whether it be by a student's own hand or another's, is a glorious opportunity and privilege. Students must live the lifestyle, accepting the effrontery and contempt of heathens and atheists without becoming inured to the pain inflicted by the outside world. They must bear these insults and slights and injuries, obloquies of the ignorant, knowing that at a predetermined time, with clear minds, clean bodies, and prepared souls, they will enter the Kingdom of Heaven having fallen on their swords in Christ's name. Matthew 16:24-25: "Then said Jesus unto his disciples, If any man will come after me, let him deny himself, and take up his cross, and follow me. For whomsoever will save his life shall lose it: and whomsoever will lose his life for my sake shall find it." For what else frightens outsiders and inflames the infidels as much as belief in the risen Lord? What scares the agnostics and rattles the cafeteria Catholics as much as true faith that shows the former to be prisoners of a paradox and the latter to be nothing but selfish beings, willfully ignorant of (or bewildered by) the articles of our faith? John 15:20: "If they have persecuted me, they will also persecute you…" What separates eating fish on Fridays or giving up sweets for Lent from being willing to place a knife at the throat of a son or daughter at God's behest or putting the muzzle to one's own temple in order to offer their body to Him that rewards the persecuted? It is a chasm whose width is indeterminable, for any but what Kierkegaard called a Knight of Faith, "the only happy man, the heir to the finite" who is able to find "joy by virtue of the absurd" and is not overly concerned with "the sword hanging over the beloved's head" or his own. The ignorant are spiritually incomplete, thus incapable of comprehending how Abraham could even consider sacrificing his son, let alone understand the matter of martyrdom other than from what they read on the back of funeral prayer cards. How could they fathom the holy path of self-deliverance? The cynics and skeptics are blind because they are unaware that they cannot see. Belief and faith make the outside world shake and tremble, for they thrive on the idea that God is dead or at best bored or asleep, or else they believe He speaks through a televangelist's greedy, frothing mouth. At the Martyr School, students who have heretofore had to live with the degradations and defilements of abusers and bullies will learn to brave the arrows and stones of the ignorant, receive a wide-ranging and liberal education, and expire upon graduation with full knowledge that the outside world will never conquer true faith.

+

During the time of my escape, the seniors at the Martyr School began dropping like flies. 'Tis the (graduation) season. The Scum who weren't assigned to finding me (if I was still a concern) would have started recovering the students' bodies, taking them to the school's morgue. (The authorities willfully ignored the alternative schools' need to maintain their own morgues; to suddenly impinge upon the institutions' autonomy would only shine a light on, in some cases, years and years of pretending that they didn't exist, despite the high body count involved with each.)

I hoped I didn't blow Nestor's mind too much, but I bet a very different mailman woke up in the middle of the night shivering. You didn't have a teenage girl insert Mary Magdalene into your bottom, so you would help her escape, and walk away with your psyche unscathed. Nobody spent time at the Martyr School without being scarred.

I did hope Nestor was assigned a new route, far from the city's nightmare schools; he'd gotten a good look at himself up close and didn't need to be frightened more. I also hoped he would never make another lewd comment or gesture to a female teenager (or any woman) again, but something told me the poison was out of his system: he now knew what he was and what he was capable of—not a pretty sight.

Two nights before Lori killed herself, I broke curfew. (Although the school didn't concern itself too much with what time we upperclassmen returned from our excursions (watched as we were by the SKM), if you were on campus by a certain hour, you were not allowed to leave.) Looking back—it seemed to be years not days ago—it was as if I wanted to breathe in the odd mixture of Cajun, Creole, and French cooking; of po' boys devoured at midnight; of alcohol fumes so strong that you barely notice your own dragon breath; of the French Quarter so crowded, body heat and the smell of sweat (almost) overpowered the ammonia bouquet of the urine-scented streets. Rather than slog through the swamplands, I climbed the wall by the northern gate when I discovered the guard deep in conversation with an obviously intoxicated glittery girl who tottered on her heels and played with her belly button. The guard had let her in (a big no-no), and he now had one arm on the gate (which he hadn't locked), backing the shimmering and now shaking girl into a corner. The guard tower was lit up, but I didn't see any more Scum up there, just a very still shadow on a wall that may or may not have been carrying a rifle; even the ever-searching floodlights were still, each focused on one spot. Once I was over the wall (using another stray gargoyle to reach the top and a doormat to blunt the glass, a trick I'd learned from Jerome), I crossed the street and found a rock the size of my fist and threw it at the guard station, shattering the glass, before hustling down an alley; that ought to keep the glittery girl safe from being sexually plundered, I thought. Six blocks later, I merged with the revelers in the French Quarter. I had a feeling of failure deep in my gut, despite Jerome, despite having the entire coming summer to convince Lori to return home; I was filled with imagined defeat, but for the moment, I was free. When a boy of about twelve said he could tell me where I got my sneakers, I laughed and gave him a ten spot. I was out of my cage and amongst my own kind. Still, it took all of fifteen minutes for a Scum to pick up my scent, but for whatever reason, he hung back. They would later try to pin the rock throwing incident on me—until Lori fell or, rather, jumped. But no matter what happened, I thought then, nothing can take away the one night when I stood back and let the French Quarter enter me rather than me tumble into it. It was here, I thought, where I was most alive, at Bourbon and Toulouse Streets, at Preservation Hall, at Blues End or Pirates Cove, on Royal Street or Jackson Square, amid costumes and ghosts of funeral parades past, drowning in music that never ended. I would have tried to escape then and there, but there'd been two Scum tailing me since I'd left the Napoleon House. Why I wasn't busted for breaking curfew, I didn't know? They were giving me a long leash.

As the train attempted to lull me to sleep, and the pale bundled up boy next to me talked softly (but distinctly), telling me tales I didn't yet believe, whispers of life and death and a place in between, I stared out of the window and watched my past speed by. Lori and I were both heading home, except that my twin was bringing her broken past with her, as fixed as she had been on the fence spike, arrested. She'd made the most of her time at school. While I could barely comprehend my journey to rescue my obviously damaged and ultimately doomed sister, Lori had taken a single-minded approach to her odyssey: it was a quest for a quietus as loud as thunder, deafening enough to do more than drown out her pain, for at the end of her quest was an end to her mental anguish. Lori's commitment to her suffering made her putty in the Order's hands. They were able to establish a foothold in her mind, which they could never do with me, not because I was immune to thought reform or even heartache, but simply because I did not care enough to surrender, thus the Order could find not even a toehold.

Lori and I had different ideas of heaven: mine involved a shuddering guitar, hers began shuddering on a fence spike (or so I imagined her death throes). Whichever way I looked at it, it didn't feel fair the way the Order played on Lori's suicidal ideation—then again, New Orleans celebrated losing yourself, and it only made sense that fairness went out the window with the superego. I mourned not so much for my sister as for the city, whose undercurrent, swifter than the Big Muddy and significantly deeper, was death itself: the unconscious reveler, the costumed ferryman, the *nothing* blessed and sold as *something*—and, God, did I love it so.

+

From the *Martyr School Handbook*:

Tuition for the final semester is due before expiration and commencement. The bishop will not beatify any student whose tuition is not paid in full. Bodies of students with an unpaid balance will not be released to their families nor will graduation tickets be honored until accounts are settled.

+

I plopped in Dad's big chair in our living room. The duffel bag Miss Marguerite had given to me was slumped in a corner by the front door, where it had been since I returned home. The problem traveling by train was that it ensured I would just miss Lori's funeral service. I borrowed my new friend's cell phone and called my mom to tell her how sorry I was—about everything, but all she cared about was that I'd escaped (I spared her the details) and was coming home. The train then lurched to life, and the connection was broken. I could have maybe made it to the interment if I took a cab from 30ᵗʰ Street Station, but I decided to skip it and hopped on the El. I knew there wouldn't be a headstone yet, but nonetheless I pictured one with the words IT'S ALL YOUR FAULT engraved on it with a screaming diamond wheel. IT'S ALL YOUR FAULT, YOU LET ME DIE, YOU DIDN'T SAVE ME. It was horse hockey, I knew, but at the time I believed it anyway. My mom went to the cemetery every day, and one afternoon, with more hurt in her voice than usual, she asked me why I never went with her to visit my sister and my dad. Through tears I'd forgotten I'd stored up, I told my mom I'd had my fill of death, and she nodded and held me and kissed me until I couldn't tell whose tears were whose. A few managed to hit my lips, and my tongue wiped them away. Our sorrow and loss and regret tasted the same—but the salt in our tears felt nothing like the salt we'd each rubbed into our own wounds, nothing at all. The latter made you scream, but tears were just what you had left when you could (at least for the moment) scream no more. I wished more of mother's tears had fallen on my lips. I wanted to be inundated with sorrow; I wanted to take my mom's grief. My heart was becoming numb when I thought of Lori. I'd been afraid I would be haunted by the image of her body falling or worse, but instead, when I thought of my twin sister, I saw her glowing face and wild smile after she'd thrown first at Piper's stoning, and then I would feel the horror of inaction. "…thus the native hue of resolution / Is sicklied o'er with the pale cast of thought…" Hamlet was dead on the money.

I could come up with seemingly valid excuses. Of course, my mom didn't know the whole story (and she never would): that my sister committed suicide right after I learned that she'd been sleeping with my boyfriend and had started doing so before I did. While it was true that I didn't save her, there was a moment there (right before she did it for me) that I wanted to kill her, but it was passing. (All of this happened in such a squished period of time, minutes, if that, it seemed.) I had forgiven, for reasons passing understanding, the boy whose face I can't even conjure up in my mind. It was during the Final Clinch (I just didn't know how *final* it was), which I assumed would be followed by a good old-fashioned pounding in the hay, that I realized getting laid seemed more important than Lori's betrayal, than Jerome's. While my sister was immersed in the study of dying, I'd been getting on with living in a place where just about every student ended up in a box before commencement. It wasn't easy to carve out a life amid so much preparation for death.

I'd found, in the days since arriving home (with nary a Scum in sight) that I was of two minds about Lori's suicide. The one that I'd never dare share with Mom revolved around the thought that Lori always tried to make everything about her and now everything was. On the other hand, with my twin gone, it was like a bit of the oxygen had been sucked out of wherever I was. Sometimes I struggled for a breath, an effort that was becoming so frequent, I'd forget I'd been breathing since birth—and in that endeavor, loneliness was just a word. How could I miss someone who wouldn't go away? Two minds.

But no blame came my way. My face alone told the story (albeit abridged). My neck told a different one, but my mother was too inside her grief to take more than a passing notice of my sudden partiality for turtlenecks even though it was summertime in Philadelphia. Laurence was the name of the boy I met on the train, and he was a junior at the Vampyre School. He was on his way to the Big Apple for the summer; in August he'd return to the Big Easy, a place I longed for even though I'd just left. My escape was necessary, imperative even, but it took all the will I had to leave New Orleans, I loved it so: the murky air; the sleazy, creepy, fun French Quarter; the muddy Mississippi; the gypsies; the street musicians; the barflies; even all the vampyres (the Quarter was full of the undead), though I had found them an irritant, like mosquitoes, during most of my two years at the Martyr School. Pretend Béla Lugosis and Christopher Lees. But that was until I met Laurence on the train. I was already a little tipsy by the time he asked if I minded if he sat next to me, and once I realized he was a bloodsucker, emboldened by Miss Marguerite's wine, I insulted him by calling him Frank Langella. But I needed warmth and apparently so did he. (The fact that vampyres weren't warm wasn't lost on me, but the kind of warmth I needed didn't require a particular temperature, just a persistent tumescence.) While I imbibed to make it easier to face my mother (and seduce a creature of the night), my bundled up companion steeled himself with copious amounts of suntan lotion and furtive sips from the bags of blood he kept in a refrigerated cooler. He had intended to take a couple of summer classes so he could stay in New Orleans, but one of his fangs had broken during a (nighttime) rugby match, and he'd been sent home and told not to return until he had the proper equipment. But one fang was enough to puncture my neck. (He didn't need my blood; it just made him very hard.) And, God, getting bit felt so good. I told him to do it again and again; he moved too fast for anyone on the train to notice. I told him to bite me in the same place. I didn't want to look like a whore who'd returned from break, a ring of hickies surrounding my neck, nor did I want to be a vampyre (the capes alone annoyed the hell out of me), but Laurence said he was neither skilled enough nor equipped enough (with only one fang) to turn me. This boy made me realize I would be going back to New Orleans (but not to the Martyr School). I thought I'd never be able to return. I imagined the Scum passing out "missing" fliers with my face on them, stapling them to utility poles on the off chance I came back. But Laurence told me that my larger-than-usual puncture marks alone (made from multiple bites) would keep the Order at bay—part of the century-old treaty. I could return when he did; I would be under his protection. My plan was to attend a public academy; I wasn't about to trade one scary religious school for another. New Orleans was where I belonged, among the freaks and artists and drunken tourists and street hustlers. I was hooked. While I didn't want to howl at the moon or sleep in a coffin, truth was I didn't know whether I was going to actually hit the books, become a grifter, puke in the streets, or pole dance even. Furthermore, other than avoiding the darker side of scholastics, I didn't care. I had no idea how I was going to tell my mom; I was sure it would break what little of her heart remained—but when you find a place to call your own, you just thank your deity of choice when you get there and unpack your bags.

"Do you want cookies, dear?" my mother asked. (Baking was her answer to all of life's challenges and tragedies; Lori had been both.) Her voice was hoarse, and the dark crescents beneath her eyes made her face look like it was melting; I imagined what it would look like when I told her I was returning to Louisiana, and I had to hold back my tears, for every time a relative or a friend stopped by with a casserole, their waterworks opened my mom's floodgates, and her crying would continue, in varying degrees of intensity, the rest of the day.

"You have to eat, Lisa. And take that scarf off. It's ninety degrees out. You'll make yourself heat sick."

I should have worn a turtleneck.

"Is that like waiting an hour after you eat before jumping in the pool?" I asked, trying on a smile I knew didn't fit. It was difficult to meet her eyes, but I tried my best.

My mother almost smiled back. (I was quite sure hers wouldn't have fit either.) "Something like that, smarty-pants," she said as she walked away, almost in slow motion or like she was swimming upstream. She struck me as a copy of my mother, an old painting of a woman that recently had some of its paint violently scraped off.

I stared at the black leather journal in my lap. It wasn't like I wanted to pick up where Lori had left off, but now I had my *own* story to tell.

I pulled the recliner handle on Dad's old chair and sighed my best sigh. (It was easier than smiling.) "I'm home for good," I lied, adjusting my scarf to hide the hickey of all hickies. "What's for dinner?"

+

From the journal of Lisa Alessandra Duke:

Quotes I Like

The absurd man will not commit suicide; he wants to live, without relinquishing any of his certainty, without a future, without hope, without illusions...and without resignation either. He stares at death with passionate attention and this fascination liberates him. He experiences the "divine responsibility" of the condemned man.

Jean-Paul Sartre

Romantic comedy is the only genre committed to letting relatively ordinary people...figure out how to deal meaningfully with another human being.... They take our primal hunger to connect with another and give it a story. And at their best, they do much more: they make you believe in the power of communion.

Wesley Morris

-end-

Shotgun Sonata

Do not go to my grave.
Mary knows, I am not there.
Look for me in between pages
and on people's lips.

Kamad Kojouri

They were gathered at the cottage on Fawn Lake in Lackawaxen Township because the reporter was writing a book. No one wanted him to get any details wrong about their role in Augustus' life. Palmer's sister, Gretchen, was already taking notes. His ex-wife was holding court. It was the type of situation Palmer had spent the past ten months trying to avoid, staying away from the city, away from the county, nestled in the womb of the old family vacation cottage on the lake. The fact that it was the same type of cottage where Augustus' shot heard 'round the world occurred was not lost on Palmer. (The family owned two such cottages: the one on Fawn Lake and the one in Mondauk County.) It was, Dr. Gene Houseman had said, part of his therapy. A radical approach, the doctor contended, was sometimes the best approach. The psychiatrist said the same thing about submitting to a group interview, which the reporter thought would be "a more dynamic approach." He supposed that Dr. Houseman also wanted to write a book about his semi-famous patient's case someday, and Palmer was too weak to not give him permission (getting sober hadn't made him resolute, just more amenable), but he knew the doctor would at least have the decency to change some names to protect the innocent, the guilty, and the dead—or at least he hoped. Not so the reporter, whose springboard into their lives (Palmer's in particular) had been a well-received article in the *Mondauk Common* that was really nothing more than a recitation of well-worn, dusted off facts. But when the reporter had arrived at the cottage, he told Palmer he wanted to "go deeper" for the book and "find the you inside you." That was when Palmer suspected it might turn out to be a trashy tell-all. The psychiatrist, if he ever penned his tome, would tread carefully if only to avoid lawsuits and scaring away future quasi-celebrity clients.

Ah, so many books, Palmer thought, so little time.

"Allegro, I said," Palmer's ex-wife explained to Dr. Houseman and Mia and Diane and the reporter. (She never acknowledged Palmer's brother and sister, and they gave her a wide berth.) "During the Classical period, it meant not only a tempo, but a kind of development, a degree of working out the theme."

"Octavia teaches Baroque and Classical at the Conservatory *and* the University," an obviously impressed Dr. Houseman told the reporter, flashing a piece of knowledge he most likely gained during his sessions with Palmer.

"The Romantic period too," Octavia sniffed. She took a long cigarette from a gold case and placed it between her surgically enhanced lips without bothering to ask Palmer if it was okay if she smoked. The doctor lit it for her. "There was more formal structure during the Romantic period, even if students appreciate it less and less."

"Thrilling," Dr. Houseman said quite sincerely.

"Her real name is Miriam," Palmer said somewhat under his breath (but loud enough that Diane lowered her head and Mia, clinging to the edge of an ottoman, turned hers this way and that with the confused look he'd once found so adorable but which now repelled and appalled him). "Miriam Weintraub," he added. That she still traded on his surname annoyed him more than he let on, but it was nothing compared to the silent fury that had raged deep inside him when Miriam announced that she'd changed her first name. While it was up for debate whether or not his father, Augustus, was named after the first Roman emperor, it was a fact that Augustus Caesar had a sister and a half-sister both named Octavia. Because the half-sister was older, the emperor's full sister was often called Octavia Minor, which was Palmer's preferred sobriquet for his then-wife, but despite his ire, it was an epithet he'd never spoken aloud, not even after their divorce. He knew a thing or two about changing names.

"Miriam Weintraub," he repeated but felt no better for it.

Octavia ignored Palmer and said nothing for a few awkward seconds before reaching past the psychiatrist and picking up a decorative bowl from an end table. While the doctor stared at her cleavage, she told him, "The name change was necessary because of my book deal." She placed the bowl on the glass coffee table and proceeded to use it as an ashtray. "Random House wants my take on the history of the sonata."

So, so many books, Palmer thought.

Octavia's absurd lie was the final word on the subject of her *praenomen*, though Palmer figured that everyone in the room (except the doctor) knew that Octavia had changed her first name shortly after marrying Palmer, long before any book deal (if she even had one). But Octavia had a way of encouraging Palmer (or anyone) to try to refute, embarrass, or one-up her, confident that such a move would rarely occur. And if one did, it usually just glanced off her Botoxed armor, frustrating her challenger, and there would be no follow-up (Palmer had shot his load when he spoke her real name), for women feared her alien femininity (or so he'd been told) and men would become beguiled by the wafts of perfume emanating from between her fake breasts. (The implants had followed hard upon the name change and cost a great deal more.)

It wasn't that Octavia was beautiful—she had been before years of cocktails and cigarettes and a tempestuous marriage gave her beauty a sunburned haggardness—but she exuded the *idea* of sex, particularly the idea that, with her, one could have a taste of forbidden, if slightly turned, fruit. The Dr. Houseman of Palmer's sessions, so formal, so tightly wound (despite his shallow attempts at casualness, evident mainly in his excessive use of corduroy), had disappeared. The psychiatrist now looked like a horny (salt-and-pepper-bearded) schoolboy about to slice his first piece. Palmer wasn't all that surprised. He remembered feeling the same way even when she was just Miriam Weintraub, a fellow grad student, seemingly as insouciant and innocent as a budding schoolgirl; she was one of the few people who didn't mention his father—at first. Octavia came at her male marks in whatever guise made them hard. His ex-wife collected men; during their marriage, she'd had a litany of sloppy affairs that he chose to ignore when he realized he didn't care. He once saw his wife put a box of condoms in her purse; Palmer thought she should carry antibiotics instead.

Dr. Houseman had insisted (in a passive-aggressive way) on being present—Palmer had even signed a letter of consent or something of the like—although the psychiatrist repeatedly stated that he was not here to be interviewed; he was only here for emotional support. He did, however, twice make sure the reporter spelled his name correctly.

Palmer's sister, Gretchen, after answering a few superficial questions (the reporter had spoken to her first), hung on the periphery, while her twin brother, Milo (who'd only stared mutely at the reporter), appeared to be trying to merge with the shadows in a corner of the room. Neither spoke to Palmer. They hadn't for years. The only time Palmer remembered his father mentioning them was when he said, "They're unnaturally close, those two, even for twins." Harsh words—having Augustus for a paterfamilias was no picnic—but they were true. "Your mother should have given them separate rooms."

"Whatever I said goes for Milo," Gretchen declared, as if reading Palmer's mind. Milo's nod of assent was barely perceptible, but the reporter's attention had already turned back to Octavia who played with a button on her blouse, as if she was deciding whether or not to undo it.

"Would anyone like some coffee or tea, yeah?" Diane asked, her nervous tics and flying hands belying a strong but soft center. "Okay-dokey, Doggie Daddy," she said when no one responded, her eyes glistening and landing every few seconds on Palmer. "Why don't I get the water boiling just in case?"

Mia got up from the ottoman and knocked over some picture frames on a little wooden end table. "I can help." Diane shook her head, and Mia plopped back down with the same grace with which she had stood. "It's no bother," Diane said from the dining room before disappearing through the saloon doors into the kitchen.

Mia was nervous. Mia was nervous about her first meeting with Palmer's mother, who was due within an hour or so. She was nervous about the reporter. She was nervous about being around Palmer's psychiatrist, whose attendance she felt was some sort of invasion of her boyfriend's privacy. She was certainly nervous about being in Octavia's intimidating presence. But Palmer knew that Mia was also nervous about the mailman, the weather, the recent choice of a new Pope (she was a hazily lapsed Jesuit), supermarket coupon expiration dates, expiration dates in general, and oral sex. Whereas Octavia oozed sexuality and looked almost ravishing even in the late afternoon light (if one ignored her bad boob job and cigarette skin), Mia's hair was frazzled, her sweater ragged, her skin sallow. Looking at her now as she stared up at a print of Matisse's *Woman in a Hat* (one hung in all of the family abodes) made Palmer's stomach turn, even though he would climb next to her tonight in bed and most likely climb on top of her too, if she wasn't too pooped by the day's festivities. But who Mia didn't appear nervous about was Diane, which was a good thing, all in all, Palmer thought, but a mistake on Mia's part.

When Diane returned from the kitchen, she began straightening knickknacks above the fireplace, her fluttering hands putting each piece in jeopardy. Mia was transfixed. Palmer looked away.

Diane was an art history professor and dressed like a man at times. She was partial to vests and men's hats, fedoras and bowlers especially. (Palmer first took her for a sharply dressed lesbian.) But she was quick witted, and her beauty grew on Palmer during his ten months' convalescence at the cottage. She was his neighbor, and during those first howling weekends (the howling was all his), Diane had taken care of him, although they'd never met before; his howls had sent her running over. She nursed him, helped him get past the shakes and the sweats, and cleaned up after he vomited. She bought him a journal to write in. (It mocked him from its home in a nightstand drawer—there was only one writer in the family. He hadn't been able to keep up with Augustus' drug regimen; how could he dare pick up a pen when he'd failed at the needle?) He and Diane took long walks around the lake once the withdrawal symptoms had subsided. They even held hands once when it was icy; he was pleasantly surprised to find that her palm was as sweaty as his. And one night, as the pasta sauce simmered, they made love on her divan as Brahms' third played in the background (on vinyl) and wood crackled and sparked in the fireplace. Neither of them had spoken of it since, although Diane had purchased him a used recording of Brahms' third at a flea market. He hadn't been able to bring himself to listen to it.

Diane rushed backed into the kitchen, as if she'd heard the kettle whistle—Palmer hadn't—but when she returned, the tea she served was iced. Curious, he thought.

"Well," the reporter said, letting out a long breath, "shall we get started then?" Gretchen snorted; she and Milo had been nothing more than the opening act, and Palmer saw this brief moment of self-awareness bloom on his sister's face. It was not pretty. He'd never experienced what Augustus had called Second Fiddle Syndrome. Palmer was the baby and with parents like his, he should have been the emotionally abandoned one, the child most likely to develop a borderline personality disorder. But while he was being either smothered or bullied, the twins, though older, were ignored; he never knew why. He watched Gretchen's normally rigid posture slump for a moment, as if she'd just taken stock of her (and Milo's) worth in the room, but she maintained her vigilance, placing her body between the shrinking Milo and the reporter's back. Palmer cringed when his sister, without turning around, reached behind her into the shadows and hooked a finger around one of Milo's belt loops.

Augustus, when he bothered introducing Palmer at all, used to refer to him as his only child. How Palmer wished that were true right now!

The reporter was young, eager, and so plain in appearance that Palmer knew he wouldn't remember what the writer looked like after he left. "There's a lot of ground to cover," the reporter said. "I'd like to conduct extensive individual interviews after today, as I've mentioned, but this is the ideal launching pad. Wouldn't you agree, Octavia?" Great, Palmer thought, Dr. Houseman wasn't only the only visitor taken with Octavia. Should be a hell of a book. "And, I'm sorry," the writer said to Mia, "you'll have to excuse me. There was quite a bit of activity when I arrived. You're the neighbor, right?" The reporter glanced down at his notes.

Mia looked to Palmer for help, and after a few seconds, he reluctantly opened his mouth. "She's my girlfriend." A pot banged in the kitchen. "The woman making the tea, Diane, she's my neighbor. Lives just across there," Palmer said, pointing out the windows, but the reporter was staring at the four vintage cameras arranged on a shelf.

"Is that a Hasselblad?"

Palmer blinked. "Yes." Diane had bought the cameras at auction and put up the shelf. He didn't know if it was the fleeting familiarity suggested by Diane's gift of old cameras that no longer worked or just the fact that he wanted to divorce himself from art of any kind, but he avoided looking at them.

"Do you have a darkroom here, Palmer?"

Octavia snorted, and Mia came to life. "Yes he does," she said even though he didn't; Mia was easily confused. "I've seen his work. Palmer's a wonderful photographer. He has a wonderful eye. Great composition. I don't know, maybe a book someday or…"

"He's just taking shots," Octavia said dismissively, blowing smoke through her nostrils. "Shots of the lake, shots of his *girl*friend, nature shots. A bird is a bird is a bird, right, Palmer?" She looked around the room. "Am I right?" The reporter and Dr. Houseman nodded.

Diane was behind him. Palmer could smell her woody perfume. "She's a handful, alright," she whispered. Palmer bowed his head, and Diane slipped away to lean against the wall a few feet away from him.

It was difficult to watch Dr. Houseman slaver like a groupie. Bitch of it was, Octavia seemed to be flirting back. (She'd finally undone that button.) Yes, she was flirting with the reporter to be sure, flashing some leg, leaning over so the newsman could get an eyeful of her expensive bosom, but her banter with him was just that: banter. Palmer knew the difference. There'd been a long conversation earlier about the sonata-rondo form, and Octavia's heavily lipsticked mouth lingered on certain words and phrases when she faced the doctor: *dominant* key and *exposition* (a stretch even for her); and she made known her disregard for a particular use of the form as being generally, "too discursive, too reluctant— can't have that now, darling, can we?" Palmer understood the play: giving the reporter something to look at might encourage him to write her as a sympathetic character, but ensnaring Dr. Houseman—well, he was Palmer's secret keeper, darling, wasn't he?

"Diane—it is Diane, right?—you live by the lake year round, you're the nursing neighbor?" the reporter asked, and Palmer glared at Octavia.

"Hmm, I'm just here, yeah, to observe and make tea," Diane said, releasing a breathy laugh. "I don't, ah, stake claim to any alliterated titles, yeah."

The reporter looked down at his notes, ignoring Diane's cleverness. Palmer half-expected Octavia to retort (inaccurately) with "meddling mistress," but she was suddenly too busy inspecting her manicure to be bothered with alliteration.

"Dr. Houseman, how long have you been treating Palmer?" the reporter asked.

Dr. Houseman looked up at his patient who nodded back, a needless gesture, but Houseman loved dramatics. "I was just asked here to be a…buttress, if you will," the psychiatrist explained, as Palmer looked elsewhere (for hearing the doctor lie made his stomach clench, but watching him was worse). "However I would be happy to give you insight—albeit limited insight." Dr. Houseman looked around the room, setting up the punch line with a bouncing head and an oversized smile. "Can't go breaking the confessional seal, now, can I, without so much as a by-your-leave?

"Yes, I've been treating Palmer going on four years now, ever since his first…well, we're all friends here…his first *attempt*." The doctor shook his head with almost genuine bewilderment. "It's never far from his mind, I'm afraid." Octavia patted Houseman's knee, as if to indicate how sorry she was that the doctor had to listen to Palmer's history of self-harm and suicidal ideation. The psychiatrist went on, "The second, more recent attempt, ten months ago…well, *that* was a surprise." Octavia sighed; she was clearly over the topic. "But," the doctor added, straightening his posture, "he did go off his meds against my advice."

"Now," the reporter said after writing in his notebook and checking the digital recorder he'd placed on the coffee table, "if you can go into detail: what kind of psychotropic drugs are we talking about?"

The front door burst opened, slamming against the wall.

"Someone say something about psychotropics?" Palmer's mother flung her coat to the man standing behind her. Had she been listening at the door? "My first husband—that was Charlie—he was on all sorts of drugs. Didn't do a damn thing for him. Hey, what's a lady have to do to get a drink around here?"

Palmer went to the sideboard and made his mother a highball. Out of the corner of his eye, he could see Mia tighten up and attempt to shrink. He mixed his girlfriend a White Russian to calm her nerves. Diane gave his mother a little wave and a tight smile which she ignored. The reporter and the doctor jumped to their feet to greet the late author's wife. "Mrs.—"

"Sit, sit," she said in her cigarette-ravished voice. "Call me Elaine." Her blouse was white and glittery, and she had an oversized blue cashmere scarf wrapped loosely around her neck. Her hair had been freshly coifed and frosted. She wore too much makeup (more than Octavia even); it looked haphazard or perhaps it was just the result of being applied by the unsteady hand of a boozed-up senior citizen. Her perfume was stifling. "This is Art," Elaine said, jerking a thumb at her companion who didn't seem to know if he should take off his sport coat or not. "Art, this is everyone and their brother." Palmer handed her the highball. "What's with all the ice? No, never mind, never mind. I'll drink it."

Art was a senior citizen too, his face lumpy, but his chest and arms were evidence that he most likely did push-ups every morning. "Hello everyone and their brother," Art said in a gravelly, avuncular voice. After Diane took their coats, Elaine sat on the love seat facing the doctor and Octavia, and she pointed Art to the far end. (Palmer knew his mother would want to sit close to the reporter.) Elaine perched on the edge of her seat, so Art had to maneuver his way between her legs and the coffee table. She never moved, and Art bumped the table hard enough to send crimson potpourri flying from what looked like a small garden urn.

"I have to say it's decent weather you're having up here for the fall," Art noted as he plopped next to Elaine. "Hardly needed them jackets. Must be a nice place to vacation, Pete."

Pete. His mother winked at him. Palmer decided that correcting Art wasn't worth the scene his mother would stage.

"He's not vacationing," Elaine said.

When he was twelve, his father, who'd never paid him much mind up till then, told him he was old enough to choose his own name (since Palmer wasn't crazy about the one he'd been given), and he chose Peter simply because he liked it. All that summer, he'd insisted everyone call him Peter. When he went back to school, his mother wrote Peter on all his copybooks and even on his backpack. Worst of all, she sent him to school with a letter for each of his teachers informing them of his new name, and one teacher read it aloud to the class. The other children mocked him, which led to Palmer hiding out in the boys' lavatory one afternoon. A member of the faculty eventually found him, and his location was mistakenly broadcast over the school's PA, which led to accusations by his classmates that he'd been busy playing with "Pete's dragon." He'd been a fan of the Disney film of the same name, but since then, just hearing Helen Reddy made him break out in stress-related hives. It didn't help that his mother took to calling him "the peter," but it was his father who ordered the nanny into the study and told her to get on her knees and kiss his son's peter until it spit, for a soused, pants-less audience of one. His father's onanistic exertions only paused when he struck his son for trying to leave the room before the nanny finished her job.

Art approached Milo with an outstretched hand, but Palmer's brother just about turned to face the corner, and Gretchen stepped between the two men.

"*Pshaw*," Elaine said. "*That* son doesn't like touching. Probably wears gloves when he takes matters into his own—"

"Elaine." Palmer stared at the reporter's digital recorder. "Mother." The word sounded distant and hollow, but it stopped her. Milo began weeping.

"I thought we was gonna—" Art began, as he returned to Elaine's side.

Elaine raised her arms in mock surrender, unsettling her bracelets. "I didn't say anything." Unlike his ex-wife who strived for an impenetrable defense, Elaine preferred all offense, all the time; for her, the best defense was decimation. If she raised the white flag, it was merely a stalling tactic until she could stain the cloth red. She played possum only to kill the actual possum. If a salvo missed the mark, no worries: there was always plenty of ammunition; she collected dirt. Not even Augustus could withstand her endless barbs and precipitous surges of fury and gleeful vitriol; in a marriage of narcissists, Elaine took the cake because her name had actually once been in lights. "Easily broken bulbs," Augustus wrote in his first novel, a portrait of the artist as a middle-aged woman, mistaking fragility for dull silence. Despite the lights being long dark, the former brilliance of the marquee augmented the burned-in spotlight behind Elaine's eyelids, and she protected her afterimages with a vehemence of a lioness protecting her cubs. The irony, Palmer thought, was lost on his mother and his long-discomforted siblings.

"I don't even know why they're here," Elaine said. "Augustus left more to charity than he did those two, and my husband was not a charitable man."

Art still had his hand extended. Elaine stood up and smacked it.

"Read the room," she said, as she made a glittery return to the love seat. "Christ."

Art stared at his hand as if he just discovered it was there, then quickly hid it in his pocket before taking his seat.

Gretchen scribbled in her pad—Palmer could hear the pen digging into the paper—before grabbing Milo's arm. "We're going."

"Ta-ta," Elaine said, waving one bejeweled, liver spotted hand as they left.

Palmer stared at the slammed door, sure that he should have said or done something, but Gretchen and Milo were strangers to him, and their prescience here was unnecessary; they no more knew Augustus than he them (something the reporter seemed to sense almost as soon as Palmer's sister opened her mouth). Given his mother's reputation as a jezebel (which matched nicely with Augustus' notoriety as a philanderer), there was more than a decent chance that Gretchen and Milo were his half-siblings. (The reporter was either planning on glossing over the affairs, or else he had information which he hoped Elaine would substantiate; the latter, Palmer knew, would be a foolish move and would show just how unprepared the journalist was.)

Palmer's mother had barely looked at Octavia, but his ex-wife stared at her former mother-in-law until Elaine suddenly turned her head and focused on her. "What?" Elaine asked Octavia, fingering her earrings. "See something else you want to get your greedy hands on?"

Octavia's face reddened. "I was Palmer's wife, so I got *half* of everything," she hissed, as if she'd been legally due a moiety of their marital assets. "You can get an *army* of lawyers. Nothing's going to change that."

"Not everything, bitch," Elaine said under her breath. "You didn't get half of *everything*."

Octavia squinted. Palmer knew she hadn't heard his mother clearly and thank God.

"Okay, now, now," Art said. He wore a short sleeve, orangey dress shirt even though it was deep into autumn. There were sweat stains under his arms. "How 'bout a drink? Everyone? Elaine, you need to be topped off? I'll take a vodka if you're pouring," he said to no one in particular. Diane brought him over a drink. Art grabbed her by the wrist. "What a filly you got here, Pete. If I had this fine a catch, I wouldn't think about suicide for a second."

Silence.

Beat.

Beat.

Beat.

"How about some music?" Diane asked, wiggling away from Art, and she put on a record. Brahms' third, of course. Diane gave Palmer the briefest of looks that said…what? He didn't know and turned his head away. His mother winked at him. She didn't miss much.

"I really like this music," Mia said, sipping her White Russian, a little milk moustache gracing her upper lip. "What is it?" She was oblivious to Diane once again being referred to as Palmer's girlfriend.

"It's a secret," Diane answered, being uncharacteristically sarcastic. "Apparently."

"Actually," Octavia added, "Brahms was a master of the counterpoint and—"

Elaine clapped her hands together and her many bracelets jangled. "We're not here to talk dead composers. We're here to talk about a dead author, pardon my frankness. The first authorized biography."

"Talk about always looking for the penny," Octavia said.

"Well, if it's heads up, darling," Art said, "then what's wrong with that, I say. We could all use a little luck."

The reporter cleared his throat. The guy was in over his head, but Palmer thought he did a good job of not letting it show. What a terrible way to start a book, interviewing everyone at once. But, Palmer thought, what did he know? The reporter was working it, while Palmer whined away the hours in the family cottage on Fawn Lake.

"I'd like to start with Palmer," the reporter said, "and get away from a chronological approach. We'll just let things fall as they may."

Elaine waved her hand. "*Pshaw.*"

"Palmer, do you write? Have you tried your hand at writing?" the reporter asked. Elaine nodded and snorted simultaneously. "Do you think your photography tries to address the same issues as your father's work?"

Palmer looked out of the windows, glanced at Dr. Houseman, then looked the reporter in the eye. "You mean, are my suicide attempts a way of imitating my father, or is the mental illness inherited, something passed down from father to son?"

"I wasn't suggesting…"

"Palmer, an artist?" Elaine laughed. "Right. And elephants fly."

Even Octavia bristled a little. Mia seemed distracted by her White Russian; Mia rarely drank.

"Oh, he's an intellectual and all," Elaine said, producing a cigarette. Art lit it for her and looked around for an ashtray. Diane brought one and took away the decorative bowl. "He's educated. Finest education money can buy. But he's got no talent! Me, I walked the boards for years, honing my craft, before films came calling. I had my time. It's passed, I know, but goddammit, I was good. I was talented. I was nominated, for Christ's sake, lest anyone forget. And Augustus—finest writer of his generation. No one could touch him. They were all pretenders. Even his writer friends—they were all jealous. Augustus had talent in spades. But this one," she said, gesturing towards Palmer, "this one: after his father died, they all told him, these greedy publishers, take a shot, go 'head, take a shot, pick up the pen, knowing full well that even if he did, which he didn't and won't, it wouldn't have much of a bang, but they were just looking to make a quick buck. Oh, Palmer's got feelings aplenty. Lots of ideas, lots of things to express, but no talent with which to express them—not even in photography. It's a huge tragedy—worse than Augustus' really. All those ideas and no way to let them out." She shrugged. "But he got the lion's share of the money. That's something." She squinted her eyes and blew Palmer a kiss. "Takes care of his mother right." She winked at Octavia who scowled back.

Diane asked the reporter if she could refill his iced tea or get him something stronger.

"And who are you again?" he asked and everyone laughed.

"I'm the neighbor," Diane said, one hand fluttering near her neck. "Remember, yeah? *Just* the neighbor."

"*Just* the neighbor," Mia concurred.

Elaine looked around Diane at Dr. Houseman. "And who is this distinguished-looking gentleman?"

The doctor straightened his posture again and tried to suck in his stomach as he introduced himself. Octavia looked ready to throw up.

"He's Palmer's psych…he's Palmer's doctor," Diane said.

"Palmer's *doctor,*" Mia echoed.

"*Pshaw*," Elaine said, rattling the cubes in her drained glass. Diane made her a fresh highball. "This one, the one dressed like a man, this neighbor, *she's* the one who took care of him the last ten months when he was screaming his damn fool head off."

"Took care of him," Mia agreed, sounding like a tipsy parrot.

"You're one good-looking fellow, Doc," Elaine said, "but let's call a spade a spade."

"Elaine," Art said.

She brushed her escort off. "No, I'm not kidding." She pointed at the reporter. "You better get this down, sonny. This one—Diane, is it?—the art teacher, she nursed him, fed him, bathed him, made sure he got some exercise and fresh air."

"Bathed him," Mia said, nodding her head up and down. She'd finished her White Russian.

"Wouldn't be surprised if she took care of something else too."

"Something else," Mia said, looking around with helplessness painted on her pale face. She too rattled her ice, but Palmer shook his head no to Diane, and Mia returned to staring into her old-fashioned glass. He'd been with Mia a little too long, Palmer thought, long enough to realize that she didn't know him any better before his breakdown than now, and yet he had her down cold.

"Elaine," Art said, clearly embarrassed, "what Pete does is Pete's business."

More *Petes*. Two in one sentence.

"*Who* Palmer does, you mean. And this is the girlfriend?" Elaine asked, swiveling to point to Mia. "This skinny, anemic wisp? Well, I hope you're on top, darling. Palmer might crush you missionary style."

"Missionary style," Mia repeated, clearly confused.

"Well, what a fine coterie you have here, Palmer," his mother said. "Your father would be proud. Three women in the room besides your mother and you banged all three. Gotta hand it to you. You can pick 'em."

"Elaine," Art said, but Palmer saw that the man knew he was out of his depth.

"All three?" Mia asked, staring at the thermostat. (Everyone turned to briefly look at it too.) Palmer shushed her. The Brahms skipped.

Silence. (Except for the record.)

Beat.

Skip.

Beat.

"Well, shots all around, I say!" Elaine cried, slapping Art on the knee. "You, bath girl, set 'em up. Irish whiskey, everyone? Tullamore Dew?"

"Just like…" the reporter began.

Elaine leaned over and touched the writer's leg, nodding furiously. "Just what Augustus drank. Pulitzer Prize-winning Augustus. Finest writer of his kind…of his time, I mean. Finest drinker too." She made a show of brushing away the ash she'd left on the reporter's trousers. "Hell, Faulkner, he was a fall down drunk, and he won the Nobel Prize! I mean, who was on that committee: Jack Daniels, John Jameson, and Johnny Walker?" She turned her head from side to side in anticipation of laughs that never came.

Diane caught Palmer's eye, but he looked away. She brushed past him as she headed to the kitchen, emerging with a serving tray. At the sideboard, she poured shots of Irish whiskey. No alcohol for him though, he thought as he watched Diane serve the drinks. Not anymore. Not for ten months now.

"Thank you, honey," Elaine said. "A little thick around the thighs and a little thin in the arms. Those must have been some baths!"

"Elaine," Art said, "I don't think the kids want to talk about—"

"Nonsense," Elaine said, spitting. "It's *all* they *ever* talk about. And *talk*. They do more talking than screwing!"

"Elaine," Art said again, but it was obvious to Palmer that this was just a reflex; Art had no more power to stop Elaine than anyone else in the room.

"I don't think I should drink this," Mia stage-whispered.

"I don't think so either," Palmer said, glaring at Diane who pointedly appeared not to notice. Diane's back must have been facing him when she'd given Mia the whiskey. The whole situation was, like most situations, clearly out of his hands.

Mia did her shot and grimaced.

Elaine ignored her, raised her shot glass, and half closed her eyes, lowering her head, a recalcitrant saint in repose. "May neighbors respect you, trouble neglect you, the angels protect you, and heaven accept you."

Everyone else did their shots except Diane. She placed hers on the sideboard.

"Now why's the doc here?" Elaine asked.

"If you don't mind me saying so," Dr. Houseman said, "I was a big fan of yours when I was a young man, a student. I went to see all your pictures."

"Tossed off one or two to me, did you?" Elaine asked, angling her head just so. "So do I still float your boat or are you just a middle-aged accident watcher?" She cackled. Palmer wasn't surprised that the familiar undertone of her voice—sinister and condescending—sent blood rushing to his fists. He often had to force himself to unclench whenever he was around his mother. Augustus used to call her Madame Minacious.

"The way you've been staring at Octavia's tits, doc, it's more like you're a newborn and hungry as hell. No, no. Don't stop on this broad's account. Those tits cost my son a pretty penny. Take a gander. Get an eyeful. Maybe you can wank off to those tonight, doc."

The psychiatrist, who'd been watching Elaine as if she were in a play or a film, suddenly didn't know where to look but just as quickly returned his attention to a glaring Octavia.

The Brahms skipped again. Palmer didn't remember her copy skipping when he and Diane were naked, vulnerable.

"I wanted to get one or two questions out of the way, just to—" the reporter started.

"So now we all know why we're here," Elaine interrupted. "Doc here wants to get off and leer at the survivors. Ex-wifey, why, she's here to protect her image and to make sure not a penny is spoken of that her lawyers haven't accounted for. Art—Art's here to do the bump with me and to drive; my eyes aren't what they used to be, honey. I'm here to make sure the story's told right finally. Augustus would have wanted it that way. My son is here because he can't help himself. Neighbor lady, well, she wants to stake her claim on Palmer. She's boyish but not *too* dykey. Hell, she grabbed him by the balls and took what she wanted, didn't she? But why can't neighbor lady hold on to my golden boy? Well…maybe Palmer just wanted some strange during bath hour and doesn't really like the part time Gertrude Stein-type, not to play house with anyway. Either that or she's a lousy lay—but I bet he's worse."

Elaine leaned towards Mia and squinted. "And you, Mousy-Mouse. You don't know why you're here, do you, and Palmer doesn't either. You may be only hours away from being jettisoned for Annie Hall over there."

"Mother…"

"Hell." Elaine leaned back and shooed Mia with her hand. "Give her another shot, and she'll walk out into the woods of her own accord. Maybe a hunter will throw her over his shoulder or truss her up with the other dead bunnies."

Mia fell back onto the ottoman as if Elaine's shooing hand had hit her.

"Elaine," Art said. "Bunnies, mice…"

"No, Art, no. Let me be," Palmer's mother said. "Why don't we talk about what we're all here to talk about? It ain't about who's diddling who or who wants to get some diddling done or even who wants to screw who over. Sorry, *whom*. No, we're here to talk about Augustus blowing his damn head off. Isn't that right, Palmer? We're here to talk about this *great* man of letters and how his suicide note consisted of…"

The reporter leaned forward. The suicide note was a great subject of conjecture in the literary world and beyond.

"…nothing. He didn't leave one. Unless, like tea leaves, you want to read something into the blood and pieces of skull and brain left on the wall. Give me another drink, *boy* toy…screw it, give me the bottle."

Diane handed Elaine the bottle of whiskey without looking at her.

"Now, the money," Elaine went on, "the money's another thing altogether. Turned out my name was on nothing, and the old white-haired bastard left most of his estate to his youngest son. him literary executor too, which makes Palmer here able to stop anything unseen from being published posthumously, which, in turn, keeps money out of everyone's coffers. Mine, his (though obviously he doesn't care), even frozen funbags over there."

"I earned what I got," Octavia said, her back up. Earned how, Palmer wondered: by being married to him? He supposed that being at Augustus' beck and call didn't make him all that great a husband.

"Don't believe a word she says—Octavia *Minor*," Elaine said. "With her, it's all image, image, image. Had fat sucked out of her ass, did you know that? Write that down. More interesting than her take on classical music, I can tell you. Pure academic. Doesn't *feel* a goddamn thing."

There had been many pejoratives used to describe his mother, Palmer knew, but at the moment she struck him as being fearless—which made her all the more dangerous. But his mother missed the one similarity she had with Octavia (and Augustus): their self-mythologizing was exhausting. If Octavia was the slightest bit wounded, it didn't show.

Hi mother slugged from the bottle.

"How 'bout a glass, Elaine?" Art asked with a low, scratchy laugh, looking around for encouragement and finding none. "I mean, we're not riding the El here."

Diane leaned against the sideboard with her arms folded. Palmer tried to catch her eye, but she wouldn't let him; it was his turn to get shut out. Mia's fingers played along her chapped lips as she stared open-mouthed at Elaine. Dr. Houseman stared at Palmer's ex-wife's chest. Octavia tapped her nails against her cigarette case. Art inspected his shoes.

Tap, tap, tap, tap, tap…

"So how was it," Elaine began anew, "that the initial police investigation said that the location of the body and the location of the splash of unwritten words and cranium matter made for an inconsistent angle?"

"What does that signify?" The reporter looked as confused as almost everyone else in the room did. "An angle inconsistent with—"

"What if the powder burns on Augustus' hands came from hunting in Limerick earlier in the day?"

Tap, tap, tap, tap, tap…

"Is that true?" the reporter asked, clearly taken aback and excited.

"Maybe," Elaine flirted, "maybe not. But one thing's for sure…" Another long drink from the bottle. "…if that police report *did* exist, it doesn't anymore. In this life, honey, it *is* who you know and it *certainly* is who you blow."

"Are you suggesting…?

"Elaine," Art said, reaching for the bottle, "I think you've had enough."

Elaine clunked the bottle gently against Art's head, and Art went back to picking at his shoes.

"That's all off the record, Jimmy Olsen."

"You need to say 'off the record' before—"

"I knew the police chief in that backwards county pretty damn well. Straight arrow but loves his whiskey." She moved the digital recorder closer to her. "Augustus had been going there for years to write his books. There and this place. But it was winter, and I guess these here Poconos became too cold and desolate even for a depressive like Augustus, and I was staying at our house in New Orleans, so there was no way he was flying down there."

Tap, tap, tap—

Elaine snatched the cigarette case out of Octavia's hand. "My husband got to Anchor Hop in Mondauk County, went to the cottage on the river, and then…" She slammed down the gold case on the coffee table. "…*kaplooey.*"

The reporter, the doctor, and Mia started. It was so quiet in the aftermath that Palmer wished for another round of tapping…anything.

Elaine took the pregnant pause to term, adjusting her scarf, lighting a cigarette, and picking lint off of Art's pants, all the while wearing a mask of distress. She scratched her overly-hairsprayed head, and Palmer imagined an amber from her cigarette lighting her head on fire. " 'Course in those days, Augustus was usually stinkin' drunk before noon, so there's no way in hell he could have even gotten to Mondauk from here unless he had his usual driver. And do you know who that was?"

"No," the reporter answered, clearly dazzled: an old movie star was telling tales out of school about her deceased husband, the literary legend.

The woman pointed to Palmer. "Caesar's son over there."

Beat.

"And I bet dollars to doughnuts he was as drunk as his father; he was just better at driving soused."

Dr. Houseman got up and excused himself as he reached around Diane to make a fresh drink, which he downed in one gulp before returning to his perch.

The reporter turned to Palmer. "Is that true? You were there   when...?"

"*There?*" Elaine cried. "Why, Palmer—"

"I want to make love to you," Dr. Houseman blurted out, his hands on Octavia's knees.

"Jesus Christ in a bucket," Elaine said.

Diane covered her face with her hands.

Mia scrunched up her nose. "Who's making love?"

Elaine jerked a thumb towards the doctor. "Where'd ya find this one? In the Yellow Pages under 'lascivious'?"

Palmer didn't respond. Dr. Houseman had always seemed so...normal, so together. Sure, some of his methods, some of the things he did in the name of psychiatry were nontraditional—such as his insistence on coming today—and Palmer had always ignored the doctor's hints of his overactive social calendar (sometimes people liked to show off once they found out who Palmer was), but there had been nothing to suggest behavior such as this. The psychiatrist was obviously a lightweight. Diane had been right: all Palmer really needed was this cottage, some distance from it all, and the sympathetic ear of someone who cared deeply for him, someone to whom he didn't hand a check.

Elaine leaned back. "Everyone fails you, don't they, Palmer? After a while you have to start thinking it's you—which led you to Doc Valmont over there, I'm sure."

Diane launched herself from the sideboard. Palmer thought she would have pounced on his mother if Mia, floundering on the ottoman, wasn't so distracting.

"Do you know...?" Diane sputtered. "You do, I know. Augustus was your husband, yeah, but how you deal with it and how Palmer deals with it... Do you know how hard it's been for Palmer to live with...to live with his father's suicide? His *famous* father's suicide? Do you have any idea how many nights we've spent—"

Elaine dismissed her with her hand, and Diane deflated a little. Lying wasn't her strong suit.

"We don't need to hear about your tawdry nights with my son. It's bad enough Miriam Weintraub is here, ready to spin tales to the ink slinger about Palmer's problems in the sack." The cackle was back. "Like father, like son."

Diane looked ready to rally. Palmer didn't have the slightest idea why she'd bother.

But it didn't matter: Elaine waved Diane off again. "Shoo-shoo, Jodi Foster. To listen to details about Palmer half-mast with your WASPy box…ugh, just imagining your leg pimples and ass dimples…"

Diane returned to the sideboard, and Palmer knew that not only would they never make love again (if that had even been in the cards), but that they would never be friends again, not true friends. His mother had done it again.

"I don't have to listen to this," Octavia said as she stood up, but no one paid any attention (except the doctor), and she sat back down. Dr. Houseman had stood when she stood and sat when she sat. When he'd stood up, Palmer could see that the doctor was physically aroused.

"Wait!" Mia yelled and everyone stopped talking. The record finished playing and the needle's arm lifted and returned to its rest position. "Wait, wait, wait." Mia rubbed at her eyes. "Doctor Gene, he wants to sleep with Octavia. And Octavia was married to my Palmer. Obviously. And Art…Art is…with Palmer's mother. I don't know who the reporter wants to…screw or who he has screwed here or even if he's straight or not. But Diane…you gave my Palmer a *bath*? You saw my Palmer with no clothes on? Were you in the bath *with* him? Did you wash…? Wait, wait, wait."

Elaine released a dramatic sigh.

"I remember that sigh, I do," the doctor said, as Octavia frowned. "It was from that picture you did with…" He snapped his fingers rapidly.

Mia pinched her cheeks and poked her forehead. "You're in love with Palmer…?" she asked Diane. Diane looked away. "You are! Look! You're flushed. You are!"

"Bingo!" Elaine cried. "Glad you can join us."

"Palmer," Mia asked, "did you know? I hope you didn't lead this woman on. I hope you didn't…"

Elaine laughed a phlegmy laugh and lit a cigarette. "Oh, he did, honey, don't you worry. But according to plastic girl over there, he's no great shakes in the sack, isn't that right? Her body language tells me that she hasn't had an orgasm since she started 'experimenting' in college. And you," Elaine said, leaning over and cupping Mia's chin in her hand, "you wouldn't know if he was any good or not. I'm guessing my son broke your hymen—unless a relative got to you first or there was some horse riding incident."

"Cut it out," Diane growled. "Leave her alone."

Mia pointed a finger at Diane. "You…you made love…you made love to my Palmer."

Diane reddened again but chose not to respond to Mia, a good choice, Palmer thought, considering the way the afternoon was proceeding.

Elaine blew some smoke rings. "Cut the drama. In this room, Palmer's peter is well known, almost better known than me, if that's possible. Why just this morning—Art, tell them—just this morning, at the shops on the way up here, I signed three autographs, and I didn't even have my face on."

Diane shook her head. "You…look, why doesn't everyone leave?" She looked at Elaine. "Why don't you leave?"

Elaine puffed out her glittery chest. "I'm his *mother*, darling, not some recuperative fling."

"But you're not helping!" Diane cried, clearly exasperated. "Palmer agreed to participate in this, this *book*, this group interview, because his doctor thought it would be therapeutic. Mia's here, sure, uh-huh. But then his ex-wife arrives. The goddamn *doctor* shows up too, yeah. And you—you're just here to soak up what's left of your moment in the sun, but let me be the first to tell you: it's been dark on your side of the block for quite some time. Art…I guess you needed a witness, an audience for encore performances. I don't know. I'm sorry, Art."

"No, no worries," Art said, leaning forward and pulling on his sharply creased pants. "If I could get a little club soda …" Elaine filled his glass with whiskey. "Well, I don't usually drink this much firewater before—"

"You'll drink it," Elaine said.

"According to Dr. Houseman, this was supposed to be the beginning of Palmer exorcising some demons, getting closer to the truth," Diane said. "And you've made it a circus. A goddamn circus, yeah."

"Palmer knows the truth, honey," Elaine barked.

"You made love with Palmer," Mia said to Diane, who looked away again. "You saw my Palmer naked."

"I meant what I said earlier," the doctor whispered loudly to Octavia, who was publicly having none of it, but Palmer knew she would sleep with Houseman just to see what information she could get out of the psychiatrist. "If you just gave me a shot… Octavia, I could you make you very happy."

"For two minutes," Elaine scoffed. "Not worth taking your clothes off for. I know the type, believe me. All brains, no bang—and that applies to either of them."

Diane turned to Palmer. "Here," she said, gesturing around the crowded room, "here's your truth." She started towards the front door, but Palmer caught her arm and pulled her back. For a moment he held her, Diane's back to his front, then let her go. She returned to leaning against the wall, her eyes never leaving his face until he turned away. Mia followed this dance with interest but seemed to lose the context quickly.

Elaine stubbed out her cigarette and asked Diane, "You think I'm that dour bitch with the loud getup in *Woman with a Hat*, bitter and maybe a little dotty?" She gave Palmer a sly wink and he winced. The print of the Matisse hanging in the Mondauk cottage had been splattered with his father's brain matter. Augustus always said he would rather have been a painter than a writer, and Palmer's mother frequently made the comment, somewhat derisively, that when he wasn't writing, his head was inside some painting or other, usually a Matisse, his favorite artist. ("Better to be a *Fauve* than a liar," his father said when comparing Henri's art to his own.) When Palmer's mother first saw the stained print, she said to her son that his father's head was finally so far up Matisse's ass, he'd left parts of it behind. None of the critics, journalists, or scholars that poured over the great writer's life made anything of his exiting in front of a print that depicted the great painter's wife, Amélie (who was not old, dour, or bitter at the time of the work's creation, according to Matisse's biographers, although she was attentive to the point of being suspicious). There was also a bit of irony that even those who mentioned the Matisse print missed. The story goes that the painter's colleagues kept asking him what colors did he use for the dress and hat that exploded in such loud brilliance on the canvas, and, according to one of his pupils, "Matisse, exasperated, answered, 'Black, obviously.'" As Baudelaire wrote (and Augustus was fond of quoting), "We are all celebrating some funeral or other."

"You want to talk about the truth, missy?" Elaine hissed at Diane. "Well, let me tell you: no quack, drug-slinging headshrinker knows the truth. Palmer's not that evolved. The hussy over here, with her fake ta-tas and liposuctioned ass, she knows diddley. Mousy on the ottoman? Forget about it."

Elaine stood up, and Palmer could almost glimpse the former B-list movie actress beneath the sparkles and the scarf, the garish makeup and the cloud of alcohol fumes mixed with heavy perfume. The deep lines that accentuated the features of her face told the tale of a lifetime spent chasing the limelight—no matter how dim.

"You don't know jack about the truth, sister," Elaine said. She looked down at the reporter, muttered under her breath, "What the hell," and cleared her throat. It sounded like a death rattle.

"You tell tomboy, Petey?" Elaine asked. "While she was giving you those sponge baths, those full release massages? Did Palmer tell you his *secret*, Willa Cather? Oooo."

Octavia sat straight up. Palmer knew how his ex-wife's mind worked. She'd been waiting for a deep, dark secret to rise from the muck. Whatever was coming next: could it change her financial standing, maybe even reveal hidden assets? The forensic accountant she'd hired when she left him (shortly after his father's will was probated) had come up empty-handed, but Octavia was always convinced there was more. She'd made out like a bandit in their divorce settlement (he hadn't wanted to go twelve rounds even though she was the adulteress), but *some* was never enough for Octavia, even when *some* was *half*. For someone so obsessed with living a life of gold cloches and Aubusson rugs, her grasp of the situation at hand was laughable. She was wealthy because he'd commingled a large amount of what he'd inherited from his father with marital assets—that was it. He didn't quite know how the so-called slayer rule worked in this type of situation, but the possibility that it wouldn't work in Octavia's favor if he was in prison made him smile inwardly.

"Oh, he can't take a picture," Elaine said, "but he took a shot, didn't you, Petey? (That's what Augustus called him when the old bastard was half a bottle down: Petey.) So you took your shot. You took one hell of a shot. And Mommy took care of it."

She drank from the bottle again. "Where's the Brahms now, missy, huh? Get to the point, yeah, yeah. After the drink got Augustus, after the drink got its claws in him, right in his brain, my husband couldn't *stand* Palmer, even though my son did everything for him. But there wasn't enough machismo there for the author of *The Fury and the Phallus* and *Hedda's Pistols*. See, Augustus, he knew this one had a head full of ideas but a handful of limp dick. So he smacked Palmer around. Smacked him good. Not that I approved, but what's between a father and a son… One time…"

"Mother, no."

"…Augustus put him in the hospital."

"Mother, no."

"Fell down the stairs. Right. The old standby. Poor excuse, I know, especially when the person at the bottom of the imaginary stairs was in his early twenties and his father's personal assistant. But it turns heads in more ways than one, fame; turns some blind before they even think to put out their hands or stick them in your wallet. They just like being next to you. 'An autograph? Sure! Don't mind the bloody kid though.' "

"Mother, please."

"That was the first of many falls down a flight of stairs. And it got worse after Augustus couldn't write anymore. Oh, he could still *write*, but he couldn't *finish* anything. If he managed even the smallest piece, part of a short story or a chapter, it was trash. Couldn't string two sentences together. None worth a damn anyway. His publishers protected him, shielded him, because of the Pulitzer. He was good for their image, but they couldn't very well release his discursive scraps. The less he wrote, the more he drank. The more he drank, the less he succeeded in screwing one of his ready-made whores and the more Palmer fell down the stairs. Hell, we started taking him to different hospitals, you know, just in case, but we needn't have bothered. The spotlight can be blinding. One doctor suggested that Palmer had a vestibular problem, like Jimmy Stewart in *Vertigo*—and both of my son's arms were broken and his face looked like a poorly drawn Rorschach test! Weintraub, his wife? She didn't care. Palmer was a grown man. Young, but no longer a boy. Man enough to get married and hump the hussy back when she was a B-cup at best. Still, he drove for Augustus, acted as his valet, took care of his papers, and, on occasion, fell down the stairs. Price of being close to fame, I guess."

The reporter had stopped writing, but the digital recorder's red light was still on, and his mother acted as if it was only for her, just another stage light.

"Did I tell you how Augustus and I met?" Elaine asked the reporter as she lowered herself back on the love seat. "It wasn't the story the publicist fed to the rags. It wasn't a 'meet-cute,' as they say in the movie biz. Nope. Set up by the studio. They thought—"

"What...I'm sorry?" The reporter raised his hand as if he were in school. "You said, 'You took your shot.' What shot were you referring to? Something to do with Palmer's photography or a failed attempt at writing...or something else?"

"Oh, honey," Elaine said, "you're slow on the uptake, but you come around, scribbler, don't you? A grower not a show-er."

In the awkward lull that followed, there was a gentle snoring. Mia had passed out on the ottoman.

"Mother, please," Palmer said. "Elaine..."

Diane put her face in her hands again.

"Oh, I think the bath queen knows or at least has a clue—that pause in her earlier outburst. So telling. Come up during morning calisthenics, did it? The doc is in the dark for sure. But a mother always knows. Well, stringer, it goes like this." Elaine tightened the scarf around her neck and swung one end over her shoulder for dramatic effect. Palmer knew it would be one of her greatest performances. In that moment he also knew he'd shot the wrong parent.

Palmer stared at the little red light on the digital recorder.

Yes, neither parent respected boundaries (more likely they didn't even see them), and, yes, his father was a letch and a frequently abusive dipsomaniac, but his mother didn't need alcohol to be pernicious; she took a special glee in being insidious. She'd been eating away at him from the moment she spat him out and complained to the doctor that he wasn't crying enough.

"By the time in question, Augustus was in his cups every day, all day. Real, real gone. Been that way for about three weeks. Palmer's all bruised. Stitches. The works. The Mondauk County police have been to the cottage several times. Me, I stayed in the city. I didn't even sleep in the same room with the man anymore even when he was around (which wasn't often), because when I did, I'd wake up and there'd be vomit in the bed. Probably crabs too. I'd already cut him off long ago and outsourced that chore. No great loss—both pens were broken or just about! So this one day— the *big day*, scrivener—Augustus, who like I said had been out of his gourd for weeks, takes a baseball bat—a Rawlings, wasn't it, hon?—and starts swinging for the fences. He takes out the typewriter. He takes out the lamp, the windows, his chair, part of a bookcase."

Elaine paused to light another cigarette. There was nothing Palmer could do to stop her from finishing the story. There was no fight left in him; he was spent. He reached for Diane, but Diane kept her face lowered into her hands. Dr. Houseman gripped the arms of his chair, staring at Elaine as if he were watching a movie. Mia continued snoring lightly.

"Then he went for Palmer. According to the police report—the *real* one anyway, not the official claptrap—he swung three times at his son's overstuffed head. Plenty of thoughts, lots of ideas, but zero talent, you know? So, strike one. Strike two. Strike three, and Palmer took his shot. The shotgun was in the cottage. Everyone knew Augustus liked guns. He wrote about them enough. So Palmer took his shot. *Whammo!* End of a legend and the start of a new one."

She winked at Palmer; he hated it when she winked. It was like a mindless reflex; to what, he didn't know—to everything, it seemed. When she winked, it was as if one half of her face collapsed. She held her winks too long; she was an eye patch and a parrot away from saying, "Aye, matey."

Instead she repeated, "A mother knows."

"Or was told?" asked the reporter.

"What's the difference?"

The reporter looked from Palmer to his mother and back again. Art was now staring at the ceiling, having, apparently, exhausted all the entertainment value from his shoes. Octavia looked vindicated. (For having the good sense to leave him? He didn't know.) She didn't comprehend the potential ramifications of his mother's on-the-record reveal. Palmer wondered if Octavia would go up a cup size if she somehow got to keep all that she walked away with in the wake of their divorce. He knew it didn't occur to her that since their split happened after Augustus' demise, there was a chance the slayer rule, which prohibits someone like him from acquiring any property or receiving any benefits from the victim's estate, could be applied retroactively if the death was no longer deemed a suicide, thus possibly affecting the state of her coffers. Seeing her face flush with superiority, not realizing there could be a dead rat beneath the gold cloche, pleased him.

He didn't care a whit about the money; it was never about the money.

For now, Octavia wanted to gloat and he didn't object. In fact, he decided to follow Art's original preoccupation and study his footwear, seeing how they appeared to be glued to the floor, which was just as well: wherever he ran, he could never escape the parental shadows, even after one had seemingly become a stain.

Diane's hands left her face. The evening he'd spent in bed with Diane had been the most wonderful night of intimacy he'd ever experienced. He thought she was attractive, though her body was oddly shaped. Still, they had seemed the perfect fit. Even though sobriety hadn't improved his performance issues much, they'd made love all night or tried to, stopping only to turn the Brahms over (and over and over) and once to eat ice cream out of the container with two spoons. He'd told Diane things that night (and in the early morning) that he'd never told Dr. Houseman (he hadn't known how far doctor-patient confidentiality stretched in cases such as his) or even Mia, who was, in all honesty, a bookmark. Gentle, unassuming, and honest, if a little daft, Mia, he assumed, would float out of his life the same way she'd floated in. But by telling Diane everything, he'd taken his neighbor, caregiver, and new lover out of the running—*he* did that, he realized, not his mother. Though Diane instantly forgave his sin, he would never forgive her for that forgiveness which he most clearly did not deserve.

But there was no underestimating Diane. When she raised her head, Palmer flinched. Her usually fluttering hands were still. She appeared ready to cut the spotlight on the minor celluloid sex kitten of the past. "Right, right, yeah, hmm," Diane said, "so you used what you had left to use. You scrambled 'cause a police investigation, all the negative press of an abused son, no matter his age, defending himself from his famous father, could have blemished your reputation and obscured the star you so desperately clutch. Fade to black—that's what you fear. Uh-huh. 'Cause your husband will be remembered for ages and you won't."

Diane snapped her fingers. "Wait, wait, no: you scrambled 'cause you didn't think ahead. Uh-huh. The shotgun. Palmer hates guns and it wasn't one of Augustus', was it, yeah? That was probably in the original police report too, right, right? Even casual readers of Augustus' work know he disliked shotguns, rifles. He was a .44 Magnum man. Collected them, right? Uh-huh. What did he write in *Isaac Rises*? 'Shotguns are too blunt to be anything but the opposite of poetic. I wouldn't kill my best friend with a shotgun.' Yeah."

Elaine shook and seethed and seemed to be shrinking, but for once, she couldn't get a word out. Palmer wondered if Diane had prepared this speech ahead of time like an Oscar nominee would—only nobody was going to play his neighbor off.

"You, you gave the shotgun to Palmer or told him where you hid it—and waited. Uh-huh. You gave the gun to your son who had already been physically battered and psychologically tortured for years—*years*—while you embarrassed yourself and floundered around in films with diminishing returns. Disaster movies, yeah. All-star comedies. *Television*."

Elaine's head whipped back as if slapped.

"You probably helped him stage it. The least poetic end for the man who made you a punch line. But it backfired on all fronts, didn't it, yeah? Your star didn't brighten any—it just became a tabloid ember, and Palmer, after it all, was named literary executor, uh-huh, but left a man of ash, and all you do, all of you, me, is huff and puff."

Diane turned her head to glare at Dr. Houseman for a moment (to underscore, Palmer guessed, just how feckless she believed his efforts to be; the patient supposed she hadn't prepared a diatribe for the doctor, so a withering look would have to do). Palmer watched the whole scene as if it were in a movie; he felt far removed and wished Diane had made some popcorn. He blinked, and for the next few frames, Elaine was an overly made-up old lady who spoke from the shadows.

"I only did television because my agent—"

"Shut up," Diane said. "The reporter's gone, yeah. You don't have to perform now."

The reporter was indeed gone. Palmer noted that the writer hadn't bothered to close the front door behind him. He wondered what reporter worth his salt would leave in the middle of this—unless, of course, he was going for the headline in the evening edition, the book be damned.

Without an audience, those that spoke did so with the volume way done, even his mother, who managed to wrench the dimming spotlight back.

"But you'll be performing later, won't you? Maybe you can turn Miss Mousy-Mouse, dance the Shepherd's Crook, and release your inner Eleanor Roosevelt."

Mia came to and rubbed her eyes, gawking at everyone in the room. Dr. Houseman was standing, pressing his business card into Octavia's hand. Sometime during the proceedings, Octavia had managed to undo another button on her blouse. She remained seated while the doctor fawned, giving him the best possible view. Their audience of one gone, Palmer grabbed everyone's coats. Art stood up, stretched, and shook Palmer's hand, thanked him for the drink. Palmer watched his head turn this way and that looking for a coaster or an appropriate place to leave his glass—the cottage was crammed with antique furniture—before finally stuffing it in his sport coat. He asked Palmer to point the way to the head but never went, choosing instead to wait patiently for Elaine to gather herself. The erstwhile star of silver screen, stage, and, yes, the boob tube, seemed to be taking her good old time composing her regal self before rising. She kissed Palmer on both cheeks after Art helped her into her coat.

"You used to be so much fun when you drank," she said to Palmer before she left. His mother didn't bother to close the door either. Diane was gone too. Out through the back door perhaps, or maybe she'd slipped through the front when Palmer hadn't been paying attention. He knew she wouldn't be coming back. She was probably already packing a bag and would soon hop in her little car and head for the city to wait out Palmer's departure. He was only a visitor at the lake; Diane lived here. Palmer knew then he would never see her again, never mind becoming mere acquaintances, just as he knew he would never return to either of his family's cottages.

"Who were all those people?" Mia asked, rubbing her temples. "Were they important?"

Palmer shrugged and walked across the room and closed the door.

-end-

The thoughts that come often unsought, and, as it were, drop into the mind, are commonly the most valuable of any we have, and therefore should be secured, because they seldom return again.
— John Locke in a letter to
Mr. Sam'l Bold, May 16, 1699

Thank You

Thank you now and forever, Beth Meier.
You've made me a better writer, my friend

Thank you Steve Brandsdorfer & Dominique Messihi
of Pepper Lillie for another wonderful cover design

Thank you, my Readers— without you, I would be
just screaming into the void

Thank you, Mom for being my Ma. I love you
Thank you, Kath—you define greatness

Thank you:
Coleen Hynoski—for your return
Margaux Kent—for your artwork guidance
Kayla Montgomery—for your inspiration & bravery
Sam Pineda—for your photograph

and
my family,
Ed, Kelly, Brian, Caitlin, Matthew,
Allie, Tommy, Joanie, & Aunt Pat

plus
Everyone who helped with The 50 in 52 Project fundraiser
for RAINN (2018-19) or who sponsored me

Pamela Tusiani—your suffering did not go unheard

Acknowledgements

My writing mentors:
Rose Horch, academic dean, Holy Ghost Preparatory School
Vince Houseman, Holy Ghost Preparatory School
Dr. Claude Koch, LaSalle University

About the Author

I consider it a challenge before the whole human race…
— Queen

<u>One of the following five statements is false:</u>
- Michael-Patrick lives in the borough of Ambler, PA.
- Michael-Patrick has been a vegetarian since 1987.
- Michael-Patrick loves to paint sunflowers.
- Michael-Patrick's late grandmother, Ro-Ro, once ran a football book.
- Michael-Patrick graduated from prep school in 1985, started college the same year, and graduated in 2012.

<u>One of the follow five statements is true:</u>
- The author loves the smell of ham in the morning.
- The author's favorite poem is "somewhere i have never traveled,gladly beyond" by E. E. Cummings.
- The author believes a Lab's ears are made of rayon.
- The author once went on a date with Winona Ryder and took her to a football game.
- The author loves the About the Author page.

E-mail answers to:
michael@michaelpatrickharrington.com

www.michaelpatrickharrington.com

Michael-Patrick Harrington supports the following charity organizations:

- o National Multiple Sclerosis Society: nationalmssociety.org

- o Brookline Labrador Retriever Rescue: brooklinelabrescue.org

- o RAINN (Rape, Abuse, & Incest National Network): RAINN.org

- o National Education Alliance for Borderline Personality Disorder: borderlinepersonalitydisorder.com

- o Borderline Personality Disorder Resource Center: **nyp.org/bpdresourcecenter**

www.ingramcontent.com/pod-product-compliance
Lightning Source LLC
Chambersburg PA
CBHW060851250626
47159CB00008B/2690